Five Golden Rings

Five Golden Rings

A Christmas Collection

SOPHIE BARNES
KAREN ERICKSON
RENA GREGORY
SANDRA JONES
VIVIENNE LORRET

AVONIMPULSE
An Imprint of HarperCollinsPublishers

Excerpt from *Nights of Steel* copyright © 2012 by Nico Rosso.

Excerpt from *Alice's Wonderland* copyright © 2012 by Allison Dobell.

Excerpt from *One Fine Fireman* copyright © 2012 by Jennifer Bernard.

Excerpt from *There's Something About Lady Mary* copyright © 2012 by Sophie Barnes.

Excerpt from *The Secret Life of Lady Lucinda* copyright © 2012 by Sophie Barnes.

"Mistletoe Magic" copyright © 2012 by Sophie Barnes.

"His Perfect Gift" copyright © 2012 by Karen Erickson.

"War of the Magi" copyright © 2012 by Rena Gregory.

"Her Christmas Knight" copyright © 2012 by Sandra Jones.

"Tempting Mr. Weatherstone" copyright © 2012 by Vivienne Lorret.

EPub Edition DECEMBER 2012 ISBN: 9780062264992

Print Edition ISBN: 9780062265005

10 9 8 7 6 5 4 3 2

Mistletoe Magic

SOPHIE BARNES

Chapter One

Hallidan
December 1, 1810

A LOUD RAP at the door announced the arrival of yet another afternoon caller at Rosedale Park. Having said good-bye to her previous guest no more than five minutes earlier, Leonora Campton was standing precisely halfway between the parlor door and the taupe silk sofa when the heavy knocker that her father had installed right before his departure for the East Indies sent a shudder through the old brick walls of the house. Whoever it was seemed quite determined to be heard. One thing was for certain, Leonora decided as she swiftly perched herself on the nearest seat, arranged her skirts, and cast a quick glance at the tea tray: a maid would soon materialize without her ringing the bellpull, for the sound must surely have carried throughout the house, to the attic and all the way to the kitchen below.

Not knowing whom to expect, Leonora neatly folded her hands in her lap and regarded the parlor door with the perfect poise that her mother had put such effort into teaching her. Chin up and shoulders back, she made a conscious effort to smile just enough to look polite—a delicate balance that had taken hours in front of her looking glass to master, for in her own estimation, she always felt she looked like a grinning idiot whenever she was forced to play the part of the ever-hospitable lady of breeding.

Whatever concerns she might have had, however, quickly fled with the arrival of a graceful woman dressed in a lovely pink gown topped with a fuchsia-colored velvet spencer. "Duchess," Leonora said, rising to her feet as the lady in question swept past Simpson, the butler, who'd barely managed to open the parlor door, much less announce the Duchess of Arbergail's arrival before the woman had managed to cut across the floor to his mistress. "What a pleasure it is to see you again."

"How very kind of you to say so, my dear," the duchess replied, pausing for a moment to give Leonora a complete, head-to-toe inspection. "Though I must say that it is high time you exchanged your mourning gowns for something more lively. You are still young, after all, and one must not forget that it was your mother herself who always said that life is not for the dead but for the living."

"It seems wrong somehow," Leonora began, her mother's all-too-early death still a fresh wound in her heart. "I cannot help but feel as though I'd be betraying her by moving on so soon."

"My dear girl." The duchess's voice was filled with genuine concern as she took Leonora's hand in hers and pulled her down onto the sofa that stood nearest the fire for what seemed to be rapidly developing into one of the duchess's typical tête-à-têtes. "Your mother and I were the closest of friends—so much so that we might as well have been sisters. I have mourned her passing every moment of every day, and I shall continue to do so until I draw my very last breath, but rest assured when I tell you that this . . ." She made an elaborate gesticulation with both of her hands to indicate that Leonora's ensemble did not pass muster as far as she was concerned, no matter the circumstances. ". . . is not what she would have wanted for you. She was a spirited woman, your mother, and I can assure you that it would grieve her to know that her otherwise vibrant daughter had withered away the moment she departed this earth, as you so clearly appear to have done."

"I lost my mother," Leonora felt compelled to point out. They had been close, the two of them, for she was an only child. What she didn't care to discuss was that she'd practically lost her father too, for he'd sought a means of escape from all the heartache and grief by setting sail as soon as the first opportunity had arisen. He'd returned a week ago, only to set out again two days later, and while Leonora could easily understand his reasoning (for she knew she would have done the same had she been in his shoes), she still wished he would have stayed a little longer, for her sake—after all, he *was* her father, and the truth of it was that she rather missed him.

A soft knock at the door sounded, and they were momentarily interrupted as a maid, just as Leonora had predicted, arrived with a fresh pot of tea on a tray that also carried cups and a plateful of biscuits.

"She has been gone for over a year now, Nora," the duchess told her with a kind sense of familiarity that immediately filled Leonora with warmth. It was true what she'd said earlier—the duchess and her mother had been like sisters, and the duchess had always been like an aunt to Leonora—more so than her real aunts had been, for she'd had very little contact with her blood relations growing up. "It is high time that you got on with living your own life—it is what she would have wanted for you."

Leonora hesitated. She knew that the duchess was right—if for no other reason than her mother had made her promise on her deathbed that she would mourn for no more than a year at most, after which she must move on, venture back out into society, and make a heartfelt attempt at finding a husband. This had been her mother's utmost desire—that her daughter would find both love and happiness with a houseful of boisterous children. In light of the fact that she'd still been in mourning during the summer season, Leonora had hoped to shirk this particular duty for a while yet. Still, Christmas spent in complete solitude did sound a bit too depressing. "Perhaps you are right," she heard herself say, though she realized that her voice sounded anything but certain.

The Duchess of Arbergail apparently didn't notice, or if she did, she chose to ignore it, for her face brightened as she clapped her hands together saying, "Wonderful!" She then poured each of them a cup of tea, eyeing Leonora with a conspiratorial twinkle to her eyes over the brim of her teacup as she took a healthy sip. Setting her cup on the table, she then confessed, "In truth, I must admit to having an ulterior motive for wishing you return to society right now."

Leonora paused momentarily, with the brim of her teacup resting against her lips. She then took a tentative sip.

What on earth can the duchess be up to now?

She didn't have to wait long before the duchess reached for her reticule, opened it, and promptly pulled out an object that had been carefully wrapped in a burgundy piece of velvet. "This is for you," she said as she offered Leonora the small bundle. "It is time for you to resume your mother's work."

Leonora raised her eyes to meet the duchess's gaze, but found no answers there—just a reassuring smile and a small nod. Leonora was finding it difficult to imagine what her mother and the duchess had been up to. Eager for answers, she quickly began unfolding the velvet until a small, leather-bound book was revealed. Again she paused, sensing that opening it might reveal a secret she'd rather not know.

"It's quite all right," the duchess said. "Your mother wanted you to have this."

Taking a deep breath as she pushed her misgivings aside, Leonora slowly opened the book to the first page, upon which was written her mother's name in her own hand. Swallowing hard, she forced back the threatening tears and the tightness in her throat as she turned the page to reveal a newspaper cutout—a wedding announcement from the twenty-second of May, 1803, asking one and all to rejoice in the most happy occasion of Miss Brookston's union with the Earl of Margate.

"I don't understand," Leonora muttered, feeling more puzzled than ever, or so she thought until she continued to flip through the pages only to discover many more similar clippings—all of them wedding announcements from the past seven years.

"This is your mother's book of achievements," the Duchess of Arbergail pronounced, as if this explained everything.

Leonora stared back at her, completely confused, until it suddenly came to her. "Oh dear Lord, Mama was a matchmaker."

The duchess chuckled as she shook her head with obvious amusement.

Apparently she'd decided to take her time with her explanation, for rather than say anything further, she simply reached for a biscuit and proceeded to peck away at it. Leonora took a deep breath.

Dratted woman—if only she would get to the point.

"In a way, I suppose you are correct," the duchess finally ventured. "But she was so much more than that." Eyeing the four corners of the room as if she half expected an eavesdropper to be lurking behind the silk curtains, she lowered her voice to an almost inaudible whisper. "She was a guardian—one of only six ladies comprising The Ring of Protectors."

"I beg your pardon?" Really, what else was there to say

in response to such an outrageous statement—and about her own mother no less?

Surely the duchess must have a few bats loose in the belfry.

"We are a very private club with the sole purpose of promoting the marriageability of wallflowers, bluestockings, and such—women who would make excellent wives if someone would only take them under their wing and offer them a bit of proper guidance. After all, when everything is said and done, a man would love to have an intelligent and kindhearted woman by his side, but first, he must be made aware of her existence. That's where The Ring of Protectors steps in."

Leonora gaped at the duchess. "My mother was a part of this, you say? In earnest?"

"Oh yes," the duchess said, taking another sip of her tea. "Your mother was quite successful—very discreet and with fourteen successful marriages to speak of."

"I had no idea," Leonora muttered as she slumped back against the sofa. In truth, she was filled with a multitude of emotions all at once—pride in her mother's accomplishments, disappointment that she'd never shared this part of her life with her, sadness that she never would, and an unwilling jealousy toward the many women who had. It was all very confusing.

"Well," the duchess said with a note of apology. "The important thing is that you're finding out about it now—especially since we would all be thrilled for you to take your mother's seat in the ring. After all, she inherited hers from your grandmother, so it only seems—"

"My *grandmother* was a part of this?"

"Oh yes, my dear, our little club is not as new as you might think." She took Leonora's hand in hers and offered her a warm smile. "Please tell me you'll at least consider it. I believe it would not only give you a purpose but allow you to gently ease back into society without feeling too stranded. And the Christmas season here in Hallidan won't be nearly as overwhelming as what will await you in London next year."

"I'm not sure I—"

"You will make a perfect guardian, of that I assure you. Do you not recall your debut? Everyone was fawning all over you—your poise, your grace, your charm, your looks . . . you would have been a grand success if . . . well . . ." The duchess tactfully stopped herself from continuing that sentence. "What matters is that we get you back out there."

"How does it even work? I mean, how do you select your charges?" Leonora asked, warming to the idea of a project that would, as the duchess correctly put it, give her the excuse she needed to attend all of the season's events as well as focus her energy on something other than her grief.

"Well," the duchess said—her tone increasingly enthusiastic. "We have compiled a list of suitable young ladies. There is one at the back of your mother's book there, but since it was a little out-of-date, I have taken the liberty of updating it." She nodded toward the small notebook that Leonora still held in her hands. "At the beginning of each season, we decide on who should focus on whom—generally we each have two young ladies to watch over each year, but since this is your first time, we've only given you one for now."

Leonora could scarcely believe how organized all of it seemed. She had tons of questions, of course, but for now, she asked only the one that she felt mattered the most. "Who is she?"

The duchess's smile widened to a victorious grin. "I can only tell you that if you agree to join our cause."

Feeling as though she was leaving her past behind and leaping toward an uncertain future, Leonora nodded. "I do."

Chapter Two

"FRANKLY, PENNINGHAM, I'D be most obliged if you could point me in the right direction. This dratted business with Baron Wolfston is beginning to wear me down," Connor Talbot, the seventh Earl of Redfirn said as he sank back against one the comfortable high-backed chairs that stood in his library at Redfirn Manor, and reached for his brandy.

Across from him, his friend studied him with a pensive frown before saying, "Really, Redfirn, I still don't quite comprehend how you managed to end up in this mess to begin with."

Connor winced. He should have known the man would be unable to stop himself from stirring up the past and just offer a simple solution to the problem at hand—Penningham's nature was far too inquisitive. However, in this instance, it did appear as though Penningham had suffered a lapse in memory. "Perhaps because you were foxed at the time," Connor offered. It was the only explanation really since Penningham had been very much present at the card table that fateful evening three weeks earlier. However, his mind, it seemed, had not.

Penningham appeared to consider this, for his frown deepened as he gazed off at some point in the distance. Clearly, Connor would have to jog his memory, for his friend did not appear as though he were even remotely close to recalling what it was that had taken place—in his own home, of all places. "It was at one of those blasted liquor and cigar parties of yours. As you can imagine, I had my fair share of brandy—bloody stuff must have clouded my judgment. At any rate, I ended up losing to Wolfston, and now I must do the gentlemanly thing and pay my debt to the man . . . loath though I am to do so. But you know how it is out here by Hallidan. There are no fewer than seven large estates within as little as five miles of the town—eight if I include yours. We're all rubbing elbows with each other. Avoiding the man will be close to impossible, not to mention that he threatened bringing the matter to my mother's attention!"

An annoying grin suddenly appeared on Penningham's face. "Ah yes—the fog is beginning to clear." And then he actually had the audacity to laugh. "I bet you wish the stakes had only been a sum of money."

It had certainly been one of Connor's many regrets. That, and the fact that he'd had a glass too many that evening. His head had certainly suffered the consequences, and now, it seemed, so must his pride. Of all the damnable favors, why in the name of all that was holy had the old man insisted that if he lost, he'd play matchmaker for the old man's son?

It was beyond pitiful—not only for Connor, but for Grenly too, he'd imagine. The lad might be a little young and awkward, but surely, this went beyond anything that any man might wish for. It was . . . it was . . . oh, bloody hell, it was deplorable. Utterly and completely shameful. Which was probably why Wolfston had insisted that his son was to know nothing about their arrangement. *Christ!*

The old blighter knew that Connor was one of the most popular men about town. There really wasn't much point in denying a fact that was obvious for all to see. And Wolfston had cunningly taken advantage of his inebriated state. It hadn't been until the following morning that the reality, and severity of the situation, had begun to sink in. He would not only have to befriend Grenly in a manner that did not suggest he'd been coaxed into doing so but find him a wife to boot—a suitable one with good connections. It was enough of a muddle to warrant another glass of brandy. Downing the last few drops from his tumbler, Connor reached for the decanter. "No need to sound so pleased about it," he muttered.

Penningham at least had the decency to appear as though he were making a stoic attempt not to broaden his smile. He failed miserably. "Forgive me, but for one whose life has always been so charmed, I cannot help but feel a faint twinge of satisfaction in knowing that you're just as susceptible to a stroke of bad luck as the rest of us."

Connor groaned. It was true that Penningham almost

always lost when he gambled, but he didn't have to look so damn pleased about Connor's sudden misfortune. "You're diabolical," he said. "And here I was, thinking that the two of us were friends."

"Oh, but we are, Redfirn—the very best of friends." His eyes sparkled with something that suggested he might be about to prove it. Connor stared back at him with growing anticipation. "In fact, it just so happens that I have the perfect lady in mind for your little scheme."

"There's no need to make it sound so sordid."

Penningham arched an eyebrow. "Isn't it?"

Connor heaved a sigh. Of course it was, but all he said was, "Just tell me who the chit is, so I can get the matter settled as swiftly as possible." Connor had never socialized much during his stays in the country. Whenever he removed himself to Redfirn Manor, it was to seek an escape from all the functions he felt obligated to suffer each Season, not to endure the whole thing again on a smaller scale. Besides, he really had no idea who would be present over the holidays for the simple reason that he hadn't cared enough to bother to find out. Penningham would know, however—he always did for some absurd reason.

Whatever his luck at the gaming tables, Penningham made up for it by keeping a mental tab on each and every aristocratic family at all times of the year. Naturally, this included all of the marriageable young ladies in them— their finer qualities as well as their flaws would be listed. In truth, Penningham was a veritable fountain of information for any gentleman who wished to seek a wife.

Penningham arched his fingers beneath his chin and suddenly looked quite serious. "She is The Lady Amy Dalton." He paused, allowing Connor a moment to consider the name and, more to the point, if he'd ever heard of the woman before. Connor was certain he had not, and shook his head to indicate as much. "She's the daughter of the Earl of Loughton—visiting her mother's side of the family for a few weeks or so. Not a diamond of the first water by any means—in fact, her last three seasons will attest to that, but then again, I don't believe your charge is in any position to be all that picky. From what I've seen of the fellow, he's a little . . . ahem . . . unpolished."

Connor groaned. He really didn't need reminding that Grenly was greatly lacking when it came to looks, charm, and grace. He was too tall, too skinny, and without the necessary confidence to make those first two attributes inconsequential. He did have one thing in his favor however—his father was wealthy beyond compare. Apparently, it wasn't just taking advantage of drunk earls that he was good at. From what Connor knew of the man, he was fierce when it came to investments, and it had paid off in staggering amounts of money—money that would one day go to Grenly.

"I doubt I'll have much success at convincing Mr. Grenly to set his cap for an unattractive lady."

"Did I say that she is unattractive, Redfirn?" Penningham asked with marked irritation. "There's more than one way to catch the interest of a potential mate, you know. You don't have to be so damn shallow all the time."

"Oh stuff it, Penningham. Everyone knows that the first thing to draw two people together is their looks."

"That may be true," his friend agreed, looking suddenly wise beyond his years. "But it's hardly enough to keep them enamored with each other for fifty years to come. Looks fade, and you'd be a fool not to remember that."

Connor sighed. Again. Of course, his friend was right though he knew he'd hardly be one to convert to his way of thinking. He had a very clear picture in his head of what his future bride would look like if he ever found himself inclined to marry. She would be tall, slim, blond, and have a pair of blue eyes to take his breath away. Naturally, she would also be good-natured and easy to get along with—a woman who would keep to herself for the most part, busy with whatever projects or charities she might enjoy, while he would be free to pursue his own interests. A proper, uncomplicated match. Perfect.

"As it happens," Penningham was now saying, "Lady Amy has other qualities that I believe ought to be considered. For one thing, she and her family have remained completely untouched by any scandal—a feat in itself, considering the world we live in. Furthermore, she's very fond of books and has a sharp mind for—"

"She's a bluestocking," Connor stated, cutting off his friend.

"She's highly educated, Redfirn. Your man Grenly won't be bored with her, I can guarantee that."

"Can you now?" Connor asked languidly as he folded his arms across his chest. "Then answer me this, Penningham. If she's such a fine catch, how come she hasn't been snatched up already, hmmm?"

Penningham rolled his eyes before leaning across the table between them and saying in a hushed voice, "Not all young ladies possess the skill of making themselves noticed. Indeed, there are those who prefer not to draw attention at all. I believe Lady Amy falls directly into this category. Trust me in this—Grenly could do a lot worse."

Well, it wasn't as if Connor had anyone else in mind anyway, and besides, the faster he resolved the situation, the faster he'd be able to move on and enjoy the holidays in peace.

Chapter Three

"AMY, I MUST say that you look quite splendid in that gown," Leonora commented, hoping that her compliment would offer the impossibly shy woman enough confidence to at least act the part of an aristocrat instead of looking like she'd much rather be cowering in a corner. It had been quite a task to "accidentally" make her acquaintance, not to mention befriend her to the point where the woman wouldn't question the motive behind Leonora's sudden interest in her. After all, she wasn't dealing with an idiot. As it turned out, Amy was more intelligent than most, and Leonora had feared that she would see right through her from the very beginning. But Amy's desire for friendship had apparently made her ignore any suspicions that she might have had in that regard.

The trace of a smile touched Amy's lips. "Thank you for saying so." She clutched her reticule against her chest as they moved forward in the receiving line to greet their hosts. "I wasn't certain about the pale blue since I've always thought one needed blond hair and pale skin in order to make that work, but I have to admit that I'm quite pleased with the result. Thank you, Leonora, for taking the time to help me select it."

A warm feeling of pleasure settled in Leonora's chest. It felt good—wonderful in fact—to have done something meaningful that would hopefully help Amy blossom into the lovely lady that Leonora herself had discovered to be residing beneath Amy's placid demeanor, plain garments, dull coiffures, and serious expressions.

During their ten days' acquaintance with one another, Leonora had managed to mold her new friend into a young lady who now stood a far better chance of turning heads. It was true that she was a bit tall, but she had a very fashionable figure that was sure to make more than one woman present envious. In fact, Leonora had on more than one occasion wished that she might be as slim as Amy, but Mother Nature had decided otherwise and offered her rounded curves instead—not that she was plump by any means. Oh no. Not at all. Leonora was simply endowed with an ample bosom and some rather shapely thighs.

Thanking Lord and Lady Oakland for inviting them this evening, Leonora and Amy continued on through to the ballroom. "Raise your chin and straighten your back," Leonora murmured as she placed her gloved hand against Amy's arm, slowing her pace to a near standstill. "And take your time as you make your entrance. We want to be seen, and we want *them* to know that we don't find them the least bit intimidating."

Amy's eyes widened, but before she had a chance to offer a response, they were automatically ushered forward. "Perhaps a refreshment would —"

"Not yet," Leonora said, noting the tone of alarm in Amy's voice. Taking her by the arm, she guided her forward. "The refreshment table is a wonderful tool for us to use as an excuse—a means of escape from unpleasant company, so to speak. If we already have a glass of punch or lemonade in our hands, we'll hardly be able to claim a sudden need for something to drink."

"I hadn't considered that," Amy muttered. "How fortunate I am to have your guidance."

"Think nothing of it," Leonora told her with the same degree of happiness one might feel at taking in a stray kitten. "Oh look—there's Lady Miranda and Lady Charlotte, two very good friends of mine whose acquaintance I'm sure you'll enjoy. Let's go and say hello to them." She didn't mention that her real reason for steering Amy in that direction was because it would force them to cross paths with Lord Bartram, who was currently having what appeared to be a rather serious discussion with Lord Urnton. Both gentlemen were very eligible, not to mention rather dashing, and even though it might be unlikely for Amy to strike a match with either one of them, she would certainly be noticed by others if Bartram or Urnton invited her to dance.

"SHE'S HERE," PENNINGHAM muttered close to Connor's ear as he came to stand next to him. Grenly, who was standing on the other side of Connor, seemed much too absorbed by a piece of lint on his jacket to have noticed that Penningham had even made an appearance.

They'd positioned themselves off to one side, close to the terrace doors, where the frosty night air added a bit of freshness to the otherwise stifling heat inside the ballroom. For just about the millionth time, Connor cursed Wolfston to the best of his abilities. He hated attending these sorts of events. As if formal clothing wasn't uncomfortable enough, one had to be forced to wear it in a room holding well over two hundred people and offering barely any circulation at all. Even the tropics would be more comfortable by comparison.

"Right over there," Penningham was now saying, tilting his head a bit toward the entrance. "The tall woman in the light blue silk."

Connor spotted her instantly. How could he not? The woman was practically a giant—or so it seemed when compared to the much shorter brunette standing next to her, not to mention most of the other people in the room. Casting a sidelong glance in Grenly's direction, he made a mental shrug. Perhaps the two would be perfect for one another after all—two beanstalks in a field of sunflowers. "Thank you, Penningham," he drawled in a low tone that was almost swallowed up by the loud chatter of voices presently competing with the orchestra. "You've been immensely helpful. I'll let you know how it all turns out."

"Please do." Turning to Grenly, Penningham then

said, "Best of luck with it." Having no idea of what Penningham might be talking, Grenly merely nodded a little daftly.

Connor took a deep breath as he watched Penningham disappear into the crowd. He then turned to Grenly. "When did you last dance with a lady?"

"I . . . urm . . . that is—" Not the eloquent response one might expect from a well-turned-out gentleman.

"Well then," Connor remarked, forging ahead in spite of the chasm he sensed might be waiting for him to fall into. "There's no better time than the present. We are at a ball, after all, and one can hardly attend one without dancing. It simply isn't done."

"It's not?" Grenly asked, looking visibly shocked. "But I always thought that—"

"Forget what anyone might have told you. We are gentlemen, Grenly, and as such it is our duty to dance with at least one lady this evening. Now then—how about that lady over there? The one in the light blue gown?"

"I don't know . . ." Grenly shuffled his feet a bit as he stuffed his hands in his pockets. It was all Connor could do not to lose his patience with the man. And then the young viscount said the most damning of things. "She's a bit tall, don't you think?"

Well, if the kettle had ever called the pot black. Was the man not aware of his own height? Surely, he must know that a shorter woman would never work for him. After all, there were the laws of physics to consider, and some things simply weren't possible. "Not at all," Connor managed. "I suggest you ask her to pair with you for the next set. If you enjoy her company, you can always ask her to join you in a waltz later." Seeing the immediate panic on Grenly's face, Connor let out a deep sigh. He had a debt to pay, he reminded himself, and he would do so with style and, he added, without hitting anyone. "Just do as we discussed, and you'll be fine."

But Grenly didn't budge. Not for a full minute at least, and Connor was almost ready to push the young viscount out into the crowd himself, when Grenly apparently took courage and stepped forward on his own—much to Connor's relief. The way he moved though . . . Connor stifled a groan. It was like watching a reed being whipped by the wind, and even that would probably appear more coordinated than Grenly did at present. Still, Connor forced himself to watch as the viscount made his way toward his quarry, turning his head from side to side as he went and muttering what could only be an apology to each and every person he passed. Well, at least he was polite.

It wasn't until Grenly was standing right beside Lady Amy and had caught the lady's attention that Connor managed to breathe a sigh of relief. Everything would be fine. The two of them would dance, then Connor would proceed to instruct Grenly on how to . . . *What the devil?* It was difficult for him to discern precisely what it was that was going on, for he could only see Grenly's and Lady Amy's heads above the throng of people surrounding them, but they were both looking down as if talking to . . . *Oh bloody hell!* It was the brunette. Connor should have bloody known that Lady Amy's companion would toss a cog in the wheel and complicate matters—women always did. Well, there was nothing for it. Grenly and Lady Amy were going to dance, and that was that.

Balling his hands into tight fists, Connor straightened his back and took a very deep breath before diving into the noisy crowd.

"THANK YOU so much for your kind offer, but we really are in quite a hurry as you can see," Leonora said, her head tilted as far back as it could possibly go in order to stare up at the man before her. She'd known who he was the instant he'd stepped in front of them, or at least she knew *of* him, and from everything she'd heard, it was her impression that the man was a bit of an idiot, not to mention clumsy and . . . she caught herself immediately. Really, she didn't know him at all, and she was not the sort to be mean or unkind to others. If anything, she felt a bit sorry for how embarrassed he was now looking, but it really wouldn't do to let Amy dance with him. Heavens above, she was trying to turn the equivalent of Grenly's female counterpart into a swan—associating with him would put an end to all her plans for Amy before she even began. She gave Amy's arm a firm tug.

"Aren't we being terribly rude?" Amy whispered, her posture a little askew as she tried to bend toward Leonora's ear.

"Not at all," Leonora replied in an equally low tone. Offering Grenly an apologetic smile, she raised her voice, and said, "Unfortunately, we have a prior engagement that we really must keep."

"We do?" Amy asked.

"Certainly." Leonora added a firm nod that she hoped would look convincing given the fact that Amy had clearly decided *not* to follow her lead. "Have you forgotten that when we happened upon Bartram and Urnton in the park the other day, both gentlemen claimed to be quite eager to dance with you this evening? And once we add their names to your dance card, I'm afraid it will be quite full."

Amy gaped at her. Clearly, she was not entirely pleased about the fib Leonora had just told. Didn't she understand that she had her best interests at heart, and that if she was to make a successful marriage, they would have to avoid men like Grenly? The lie wasn't mean-spirited. On the contrary, Leonora meant to spare his feelings, but with Amy staring accusingly at her and Grenly looking as if he'd unexpectedly found himself knee deep in mud, her conscience was beginning to make her feel more than a little rotten . . . not to mention shallow.

Drawing her shoulders back, she strengthened her resolve and, giving Amy a harder tug than before, she offered Grenly what she hoped would look like a polite nod of dismissal before turning away from him and . . . umpf. Somebody bumped into her, nudging her sideways until she feared she might lose her balance. She quickly recovered, however, and, turning toward the clumsy fool, immediately caught her breath.

Before her stood a man like none she'd ever seen before—either that or her time spent in mourning had made her forget it was possible for one singular human being to look like this. She doubted it, though. In fact, she was quite confident that there had never before existed a man quite as handsome as this one. His hair was jet-black, his jaw chiseled as if Michelangelo had sculpted it himself, and his eyes . . . she couldn't quite discern their color at this distance though they did appear rather dark. That wasn't what had her momentarily struggling for air, though. His eyes were sharp and assessing, yet vibrant at the same time, as if he was judging each of her attributes, categorizing and rating them until he came up with a final score—a number that would determine whether or not he found her worthy of his company. It was most unsettling.

And then he spoke. "I do beg your pardon, Miss . . ." He raised an eyebrow, then paused while he waited for her to fill in the blank.

Leonora swallowed hard, for his gaze was so penetrating it almost seemed as though he were presently observing the inner workings of her mind—that he knew exactly what she was thinking.

Heaven forbid.

"Lady Leonora," she eventually managed as she gave herself a mental kick in the backside for acting like a girl just out of the schoolroom. She might not have vast amounts of experience with men, but she was certainly popular enough, confident enough, and well-read enough not to find herself struggling with her own tongue. Apparently, the man before her was having a rather alarming effect on her wits.

"Yes, of course you are." The gentleman bowed ever so

slightly, but from the mischievous twist of his lips and the bland expression upon his face, Leonora was quite confident that he had no idea of who she might be. "Would you care to dance?"

"With you?" she gasped, horrified by her unexpected question—a question she'd had no intention of voicing aloud.

He grinned back at her as if she might be a juggler or a clown or some other person there for his entertainment. He might be handsome, but Leonora was quickly determining that he was also most annoying. Besides, she had a job to do. "As I've just explained to Mr. Grenly here, Lady Amy and I are otherwise engaged with Lords Bartram and Urnton. Our dance cards have been filled, and besides, we have not been formally introduced. It would be highly unseemly to —"

"Forgive me, my lady." He reached for her hand and lifted it toward his lips, placing a gentle kiss upon her knuckles. "Lord Redfirn at your service."

Chapter Four

Oh, she'd heard of him all right, but Lord Redfirn never ventured out into public when he visited Hallidan. He'd been abroad doing heaven knew what when she'd had her debut, then her mother had died, and she'd removed herself from society as well for . . . well, until now. And the things she'd heard. From what she understood, the man spelled ruin. His popularity was notorious—he was every gentleman's friend and every woman's ideal match. There were probably many diaries scattered all over England—their authors claiming to have fallen irrevocably in love with Lord Redfirn.

Leonora made her decision then and there. She would *not* follow the herd.

Schooling her features in the hope of looking as bland as he'd done earlier, she said, "Indeed?" She offered him a polite smile. "Well, I do hope that you enjoy the rest of your evening, Lord Redfirn—you too, Mr. Grenly. Perhaps we'll meet again in the not-so-distant future." And then, spotting an opening, she gave Amy's arm a hard yank and stepped forward, only to find herself held back by she knew not what, but whatever it was, she felt exceedingly frustrated.

Turning in the hope of discovering the hindrance, she grimaced when she saw that a portly gentleman had stepped back in order to offer space for another couple, and that in doing so, had planted the heel of his shoe directly on the hem of her gown.

Lord help me.

Lord Redfirn's smile widened until she found him grinning at her with marked amusement—his perfectly white teeth gleaming as though his valet might have buffed those too after finishing with his lordship's shoes. Meanwhile, Amy had gone completely still, indicating that she wished to shrink into obscurity, while Grenly turned his head away, quite keen to ignore the brewing altercation entirely.

Eager to be on her way, or more to the point, remove herself from Lord Redfirn's vicinity, Leonora angled around until she was able to give the man who'd caused all this trouble for her a gentle tap on the shoulder. "Excuse me, but would you kindly step forward a bit?" She dropped her gaze toward her trapped hemline. "I'd much appreciate it."

The man gushed a string of apologies, for which Leonora thanked him kindly before returning her attention to . . . *What on earth?* Where was Amy? She'd released her arm in order to draw the other gentleman's attention, and now she was gone. It took her all but a split second to register that Grenly had vanished too, and who stood before her now but Lord Redfirn, smiling with a devilish sort of satisfaction that had the odd effect of both vexing her and making her stomach feel all jittery inside. Really, she had to get away from him—if for no other reason than to save Amy, and perhaps herself too, if she thought long enough about it.

"Now then," Redfirn said, moving a bit closer to her and taking her by the arm. "I do believe you promised to dance with me."

"I did no such thing," she gasped. "And you're not on my dance card, so you can't—"

"Let me see that." And before Leonora had a chance to react, he'd snatched the card from her hand, examined it, and scrawled his name right next to one of the waltzes.

Leonora was mortified. Not so much because of his rudeness but because after claiming how full her dance card was, Lord Redfirn now knew that it was entirely empty. At least he had the decency not to comment as he handed it back to her. "Shall we?" he asked instead, offering her his arm. "You look as though you might enjoy a glass of lemonade before our dance. We can walk past Bartram and Urnton on the way if you like."

Oh dear Lord. He might not have called her bluff directly, but he'd certainly alluded to it in a most forthright fashion. "That won't be necessary, my lord," she told him, gritting her teeth beneath a most benign smile. Somewhere along the line, Lord Redfirn had managed to tuck her arm into the crook of his own. There was no immediate escape in sight—the man was clearly determined. "In fact, I suddenly find myself quite parched." And with that final statement, she allowed him to guide her forward, all the while ignoring the heat that was flowing from his body and into hers.

Considering all of the womanly advice that her mother had given her before her much-too-early departure from the earth, Leonora quickly began reciting the Lord's Prayer inside her head, hoping that it might have the same effect as a bucket of ice water.

Regrettably, it did not.

CONNOR WAS FEELING immensely satisfied with himself. He'd achieved his goal even though he had looked failure in the eye for the briefest of moments. But then the fates had stepped in and helped him in his cause, distracting the very stubborn and determined Lady Leonora just enough to allow Grenly and Lady Amy to make their escape. He could practically hear the wedding bells ringing already. Success was close at hand.

Casting a discreet glance toward Lady Leonora as they made their way toward the refreshment table, Connor forced back the laughter that threatened to burst past his lips. She looked furious and, he decided, somewhat perplexed—as though she was desperately trying to find a way to escape his company. Well, she was welcome to try, but now that he had her safely by his side, she would have to put up one hell of a fight to accomplish it, and judging from her elegant demeanor, he was quite confident that she wouldn't wish to draw that sort of attention to herself.

She was a funny little thing really—not at all the sort of woman he would normally consider attractive. In fact, physically, she was quite the opposite in every way. Her hair was warm chestnut instead of blond, her eyes brown instead of blue, and her figure, as far as he could tell, was more curvaceous than what he was used to. This last attribute however, did not put him off in the least—on the contrary, it made her appear more womanly in some peculiar sort of way. Her bosom for instance . . . high and plump and . . . he forced his tarnished imaginings away from Lady Leonora's body and tried to focus on his objective. He wasn't there to seduce a young woman but to settle his debt by getting Grenly married.

"My lady," he said, as they arrived at the refreshment table and he offered her a glass of lemonade.

She stared at it for a moment, her nose wrinkling a little while her mouth worked its way into a scrunch. Meeting his gaze, she finally surprised him by saying, "Frankly, my lord, I'm really not all that fond of lemonade. If you don't mind, I'd much rather have a glass of Champagne."

Connor thought he might explode from laughter, but he managed to hold it back and simply incline his head. "Certainly," he said, offering a smile that he hoped would look agreeable.

She accepted the glass he offered her with grace, but her stiff posture coupled with her shifting eyes told him that she was still eager to run off in search of Lady Amy.

"I'm sure your friend is quite all right," he said as he raised his own glass to his lips and took a lengthy sip.

"How can you possibly say that?" she asked, her eyes growing wide with indignation. "Mr. Grenly is hardly . . . well, he's not . . ."

"The man you had in mind for her?"

Lady Leonora immediately clamped her mouth shut, her eyes narrowed, and it seemed as though she tightened the grip on her glass. *Hopefully, it won't shatter,* Connor thought as he eyed the delicate crystal with some concern. His companion was obviously struggling to keep her temper in check. "Mr. Grenly's not so bad," he finally told her, not because he believed it to be true but because he was starting to feel a little bit guilty about ruining Lady Leonora's plans.

"Oh really?" she asked, immediately lowering her voice to a whisper and stepping a little bit closer. She must have realized that this was not the sort of conversation she cared to have others listen to. All the same, Connor decided that he could have done without the proximity, for he was now forced to inhale the most sweet and intoxicating scent of jasmines. "Do you know him well enough to make such a claim?"

"I barely know him at all," Connor immediately told her. He doubted it would help his cause if she knew that he'd deliberately helped Grenly further his acquaintance with Lady Amy, much less that he planned for the two to embark on a hasty courtship followed by marriage. Judging from everything Lady Leonora had said so far, he hardly thought she'd approve.

"Neither do I, save for my recent conversation with him." She turned her head a little to indicate the spot where she, Grenly, and Lady Amy had been standing a short while earlier when Connor had interrupted them. "But it is my understanding that he's *not* the sort of man I wish for my friend to associate with."

Feeling suddenly mischievous, Connor said, "How's that?"

Lady Leonora's eyes widened, and her teeth bit into her lower lip with such aggression that Connor immediately wondered if it might not be wise to placate her a little before she caused herself permanent damage. Besides, her lips were rather full, he'd noticed. In fact, they looked delicious. It really wouldn't do for her to tarnish them in a bout of anger. But before he managed to find the necessary words, she said, "He's not handsome, or gallant. He can barely string two words together and he constantly looks out of place and . . . and . . ."

Connor leaned closer.

"Gangly."

Oh dear. Connor stifled yet another grin. "Well, it's certainly quite apparent that you do not like the man."

"I never—"

"It's quite all right," Connor told her as he gently removed the glass from her hand and set it on the table beside his own. "I'm not one to judge."

"We have to save her!"

We? Interesting.

"There will be plenty of time for that later, my lady, but right now, I do believe it's time for our waltz." And then he took her firmly by the arm and steered her in the direction of the dance floor.

IF THERE WAS one thing that Leonora was certain of, it was that she'd never felt more confused in her life. On the one hand, she was terribly angry with Lord Redfirn for keeping her away from Amy. When she'd met with the Ring of Protectors shortly after the Duchess of Arbergail's visit roughly one month earlier, she'd assured them all that they could trust her to make a brilliant match for Amy. She cringed to think how disappointed they'd all be with her at their next meeting. Dancing with Grenly would hardly facilitate marriage to a handsome and dashing young duke, marquess, or earl. On the other hand, her traitorous body had decided that it rather enjoyed being touched by Lord Redfirn's warm hands as he rested his fingers against her elbow and guided her forward. She'd danced with quite a few men before though there was no denying that it had been a while, but none had caused such an uproar in her stomach or made her skin prickle and her heart beat faster. There really wasn't any point in denying that whatever her duty toward Amy, and no matter how vexing she'd found Lord Redfirn's company thus far, she wanted to know what it felt like to be held in his arms as he guided her around the dance floor.

"Has it been a while?"

His words jolted her out of her reverie, and she realized that they were now standing across from one another as they waited for the orchestra to get fully under way.

"You look a bit nervous," he added. "I thought per-haps—"

"Yes," she muttered as she looked up at him, her eyes locking onto his. She was determined not to be intimidated by his splendor, no matter how plain she felt right now in his company. "I've been socially absent for some time."

He must have deduced the cause for such an absence, for he did not press the matter any further and, to his credit, looked suddenly repentant. "Forgive me, my lady—that was badly done of me."

And there went her heart.

The music started, Lord Redfirn bowed while Leonora curtsied, then he reached for her hand and pulled her toward him until his hand was resting against her lower back. It took every ounce of willpower she possessed not to sag against him in a delirious state of heavenly bliss. Never before had she been held with such combined assurance and grace. His body was solidly built, and yet he moved with undeniable elegance.

Casting a hesitant glance toward his face, she saw that his eyes were indeed dark brown though perhaps with a hint of green, and while he might appear serious at a distance, she was close enough to spot a distinct tilt to the corner of his lips, as though he was purposefully suppressing a smile. "You dance remarkably well," she said, feeling a sudden desire to hear his voice again.

His eyes met hers. "A simple enough task when one has

the right partner," he murmured, as his gaze abandoned hers in favor of a spot just a little bit lower . . . *Heavens! Is he staring at my lips?* It certainly seemed so—and with a sudden neediness if she hadn't completely misread him. But then he looked back up, his eyes drifting past her shoulder as if to study something off in the distance, and Leonora immediately realized that her brain must have gone on holiday—the man couldn't possibly look more bored. "You dance very well too, I might add."

Leonora looked back up, surprised to find him watching her with that lopsided smile of his. "Thank you, my lord—it's very kind of you to say so."

"I was wondering—If I call on you tomorrow . . . will you receive me?" He must have seen the appalled look upon her face, for he quickly added. "Unbelievable as it may seem, I find myself enjoying your company and was hoping to further my acquaintance with you. However, I have no desire to wait in line along with a dozen other men, so if you'd rather I stay away, then I'd be much obliged if you'd say so now."

Well, as far as forthright went, Lord Redfirn was certainly the very definition of the word. Perhaps he wasn't as bored as she'd imagined. Warming to the easy tone of his voice, she couldn't help but say, "A dozen? Will that really be all? Frankly, Lord Redfirn, I rather suspect they'll be lined up all the way to Hallidan."

He raised an eyebrow. "Not if your . . ." He coughed and let the words he might have spoken fade into oblivion.

"Not if my what?"

"Hmmm?"

"You were saying, not if your . . ." She gave him a pointed stare.

He frowned as if unsure of whether or not it would be wise to tell her what he'd been about to say. Eventually, he shrugged, lowered his head a little toward hers, and whispered, "Not if your dance card is any indication."

Aha! So he wanted to play *that* game, did he? Very well then. Without as much as a moment's hesitation, Leonora misstepped just enough to place one foot on top of his.

She was rewarded by a very loud wince along with a grimace. "You did that on purpose, you little minx."

"Not at all," she countered. "If you recall, I'm quite out of practice—my apologies."

"Then perhaps it would be wise of me to keep a firmer hold on you." And he pulled her closer—scandalously so.

Leonora had never been one to swoon, but she felt certain that now might be an appropriate time to start. She felt energized and bold, not to mention giddy from the feel of him so close to her, coupled with the scent of sandalwood that floated in the air around him. There was no question about it—he'd ruined dancing for her forever, for no other man would ever measure up.

She wondered if he felt the same, or if she was the only one affected, but when she looked at him, he seemed once again distracted by something else. *Oh bother.* He'd said he'd call on her, but it was becoming abundantly clear that it would only be a courtesy call—not one that indicated any further interest on his part. It was torture, acknowledging how easily he'd swept her off her feet, but at least there was some comfort to be had in knowing that she didn't own a diary and that her thoughts about Lord Redfirn would not be committed to posterity, as those of so many other ladies undoubtedly had been.

Chapter Five

LORD REDFIRN DID not make an appearance in Leonora's drawing room the following day as he'd said he would. Nor did he make one the day after that though he did send her a box of chocolates along with a note of apology. And while she couldn't help but admit that she was more than a little disappointed by his absence, Leonora was afforded little time to dwell on his lordship given that she still faced the task of finding Amy a suitable husband.

"Why are you so opposed to Mr. Grenly?" Amy had asked the previous day, when Leonora had visited her for tea. "I quite enjoyed his company last night—he's really quite amusing."

Regardless of her own assessment of Grenly, Leonora knew she ought to consider Amy's opinion on the matter, but with a desperate desire to prove herself to the duchess and the other members of The Ring of Protectors, Leonora found herself saying, "You mustn't misunderstand me, Amy—I'm sure he's a lovely young man, but he's not your only option."

They had then gone on to examine a list of other eligible gentlemen that Leonora had compiled earlier in the day. "So you see," Leonora had finally concluded after Amy had agreed that Lord Winnfield and Lord Fulton were very handsome indeed. "It's important to consider every potential candidate wisely. There's no rush, and certainly no need for you to attach yourself to the first gentleman who asks you to dance."

"But Mr. Grenly—"

"He has been most polite in his attentions toward you, for which one can only commend him. However, I would advise you not to encourage him any further until you're quite certain that he's the man you wish to marry. And don't forget, once we attend the Yarlton Ball on Saturday, there will be other gentlemen vying for your attention—of that you may be certain. As agreeable as Grenly may be, I think you should give the other young gentlemen a chance as well. After all, you must consider that whomever you choose to marry, your decision will be permanent."

Leonora had left her friend's company feeling much relieved. She felt certain that she'd managed to make Amy realize that she should not focus on Grenly alone and would hopefully soon be able to tell the Ring of Protectors that Lady Amy would be marrying a most eligible gentleman. To celebrate her accomplishment thus far, she decided to take a stroll through Hallidan's town center and visit the milliner's.

So preoccupied was she with this fabulous turn of events that she failed to watch where she was going and almost got herself trampled by a couple of bays as they came trotting along Main Street, pulling a curricle that naturally, as luck would have it, belonged to none other than Lord Redfirn.

"LADY LEONORA! ARE you quite all right?" He'd reined his horses to an immediate halt as soon as he'd realized that the woman about to cross the street had no intention of checking to see if she might be about to step in front of a moving vehicle.

"I . . . erm . . . yes, thank you," she grumbled, looking rather put out by their encounter with one another. She dropped a hasty curtsy and made as if to hurry on her way. "Forgive me, but I have an appointment that I must keep—good day, my lord."

Connor caught her by the arm before she managed to step away from him. "I would be more than happy to offer you a ride." He saw no point in telling her that he'd actually been on his way to her estate—not when she was staring at him as if he had an ulterior motive in mind, which, of course, he did.

"That is most kind of you," she said. "But quite unnecessary."

Once again, she moved as if she planned to escape him, but for some peculiar reason, Connor refused to let her go. Instead, he tightened his hold on her arm and pulled her back. Her eyes widened with apparent outrage.

"Unhand me!" Whatever temper she'd kept at bay the other evening was rapidly rising to the surface.

"Lady Leonora," he said in his most soothing tone, "I cannot as a gentleman ignore your safety, and considering that you were very nearly run down by a curricle, I should feel far more comfortable if you would please ride with me instead. Besides, it's terribly cold today." He nodded toward the seat of the carriage. "There's a thick blanket up there."

"I . . . I . . ." He could see her struggling to find an appropriate comeback. "It was *your* curricle!"

"All the same." And then, before she could say or do anything further, he placed his hands upon her waist in one swift movement and lifted her up into the carriage.

"You . . . I . . . Urgh!"

Connor simply grinned. He'd missed sparring with her, he realized, but he'd been busy during the last couple of days and hadn't managed to call on her as soon as he'd hoped.

First, there had been Grenly to attend to. Connor had helped him select a meaningful present for Lady Amy—an antique collection of Plato's work in five beautifully bound leather volumes. They had cost a small fortune, but when Grenly had mentioned Lady Amy's interest in philosophy, Connor had immediately known that this was the sort of thing she would appreciate.

Then there had been Wolfston to deal with. The old earl had appeared unexpectedly on Connor's doorstep the day after, just as Connor was getting ready to head out with the sole purpose of paying a visit to Lady Leonora. Wolfston had demanded a detailed report of his son's progress, and by the time he had left again, it had been too late in the day for Connor to make a social call without appearing either rude or desperate.

So here he was now.

"This is highly irregular," Lady Leonora told him firmly, as he climbed up beside her and placed half the blanket across her lap. "Not to mention unacceptable in any number of ways. People will see us—without a chaperone. My lord, I insist that you hand me down this instant, or I shall be forced to take matters into my own hands and jump."

He wasn't entirely sure that she wouldn't follow through with her threat, so he said the only thing he imagined might stop her. "And risk breaking an ankle? Where will Lady Amy be if you're unable to remain by her side throughout all of the holiday celebrations?"

He saw her wince and knew what she was thinking without having to ask: either unmarried, or worse—married to Grenly. Allowing himself to smile just a little with the satisfaction of having gotten his way, he whipped the horses into motion.

Continuing down Main Street, Connor turned to Lady Leonora after a moment's silence. "Where am I to take you, my lady?"

She must have been woolgathering, for she turned to him quite suddenly as if he'd startled her. "I . . . that is . . . I um—"

Connor grinned. "You have no prior engagements, do you, my lady?" He could practically hear her grinding her teeth together in irritation. "Whyever would you wish to be rid of my company? I can be quite charming, you know." And just to annoy her a bit more, he waggled his eyebrows.

"Really? Because after seeing you last, I was left with the distinct impression that you intended to call on me, yet I've seen not as much as your shadow since then. Indeed, I daresay that if I hadn't happened upon you just now by chance, you would have carried on avoiding me indefinitely." She turned a pair of flashing brown eyes on him. "You, sir, have made your intentions *quite* clear indeed."

An uneasy twinge of something most unsettling filled Connor's chest at that moment. Until then, he'd had no thoughts of intentions at all, and yet she gave him no choice but to examine them now. She was clearly vexed, but he'd somehow come to expect that from her—after all, he'd known her rather briefly, and in that short time he'd purposefully "tripped her up" on more than one occasion. She was right to feel miffed.

Be that as it may, it hadn't occurred to him that she might be offended by his lack of attention toward her—he'd rather imagined she would have been relieved when he failed to appear at her front door. Clearly, this was not the case, which could only indicate that she'd been thinking of him far more than she was ever likely to admit. The most terrifying thing of all was that Connor had been thinking of her too. Repeatedly.

"I did send you chocolates," he said, feeling some absurd need to defend himself. The woman had painted a most unsavory picture of him, and considering how busy he'd been and that he wasn't her beau, he rather thought she was being a bit harsh. He'd even had to ask Penningham who she was and where she lived. How humiliating to discover that she was *the* Lady Leonora—of Rosedale Park. He ought to have at least suspected as much—especially given the fact that she'd told him she'd been absent from society for some time. Her facial expression had indicated that she'd probably suffered a loss, and he hadn't even bothered to offer his condolences. Yes, he'd apologized, but in light of the fact that the woman had lost her *mother*, he still felt like a complete ass. He'd have to make it up to her somehow.

She let out a deep breath beside him. "Yes. Thank you. They were delicious."

Turning the horses toward the park, Connor suddenly said, "I love strawberry tarts." He'd no idea why he'd said it, and for a moment he felt a bit daft, but then he just shrugged and turned his head toward her with a grin. "Do you like sweets, Lady Leonora?"

At first, she just sat there with the same stony expression she'd managed to paste on her face the minute she'd seen him coming toward her. But then something startling happened—she began to transform. Little by little, a light pink flush rose to her cheeks, while her lips curled upward with a bit of mischief. "I adore them, my lord." Her gaze swept sideways for a moment before returning to his. "Mama always insisted that I'm only allowed one per week. She was very firm about it—so much so that even after her passing, Cook still adheres to this rule though I do sometimes send my maid to fetch me a little something extra from one of the tea shops."

"Surely your father must be able to convince your cook to prepare more sweets for you." He immediately regretted his words, for the look of anguish that filled Lady Leonora's eyes was so raw and honest that he was suddenly overcome with a need to protect her.

"My father embarked for the East Indies shortly after Mama passed. He was eager to get away from everything that might remind him of her."

Including you.

She didn't say it, but Connor could see it in her eyes. "I'm so terribly sorry," he said, finally seizing the chance to say the right thing. "It must be very difficult for you."

"Yes," she whispered, turning her head with the pretense of looking at some of the shops they were passing.

Once again, he found himself thinking of something to say in order to steer the conversation back to a lighter mood. As it happened, he was saved from the task by the lady herself. "I've no idea what to do about Lady Amy, my lord. Perhaps you might offer some advice?"

"Lady Amy?" he asked, feigning ignorance. Whatever would Lady Leonora think if she knew that he'd deliberately set out to distract her while Grenly furthered his relationship with her friend? She'd probably be livid.

"You recall the tall, blond-haired woman I was with the other evening? The one whom *Mr. Grenly* has decided to set his sights on?"

"I vaguely remember . . ."

"Well however pudding-headed Mr. Grenly might be,

he's certainly mastered the art of courting. Lady Amy has not only received the exact same books she's been fawning over at the bookshop, but this morning the most thoughtful poem arrived."

Connor tried not to smile too much. It had taken him less than half an hour to write that poem for Grenly. "Perhaps you've underestimated him," he suggested, as they trotted past the entrance to Hallidan's park. "The man might not be as bad as you think." He didn't need to look at her to know that she was probably frowning.

"If you ask me, he must be getting some sort of assistance or guidance from somebody. I only wish I could figure out from whom, so I could confront the individual. It's false advertising and highly immoral." She sighed. "You must think me a complete highbrow, for which I cannot blame you. I know I'm being particularly critical of Mr. Grenly, but Lady Amy is my friend—it's very important to me that she make the right decision." There was a note of desperation to her voice that Connor could not dismiss. He groaned inwardly. Was that guilt rearing its ugly head? Surely not.

"All I want is for her to be happy," Lady Leonora continued. "And while Mr. Grenly may be attentive and thoughtful, he lacks both charm and elegance, not to mention that he seems a bit too eager for my liking. I mean, one book should have sufficed, but he sent her five—*five!*"

"I erm . . ." Connor knew that buying five books had been a bit over the top, but he'd wanted to make certain that Lady Amy would be thoroughly impressed. "From what I understand, Lady Amy is quite well-read. If you ask me, Mr. Grenly's gesture seems rather considerate."

Lady Leonora turned to him, wide-eyed and open-mouthed. "Are you defending him?"

"No!" That came out a bit more forceful than he'd intended. Connor took a deep breath. "Not in the least. I merely think it wise, not to mention polite, to give everyone a fair chance."

"You think me judgmental and rude," she muttered—her gaze seemingly fixed on some distant point upon the horizon.

Would it ever be possible to say the correct thing to this woman, Connor wondered. With no intention of chastising her, he'd certainly done a good job. It was yet another moment in desperate need for a change of topic. "I think I know precisely where to take you," he said as he guided the curricle down another street. He shot her a cheeky grin. "With a penchant for sweets, I'm certain a visit to Mrs. Potter's will be just the thing to make your encounter with me a little less regrettable."

Judging from the warmth that seeped into her eyes and the dimples that suddenly dotted each cheek, he'd been absolutely correct. It wasn't a moment he was likely ever to forget, for the happiness that radiated from her at his suggestion not only made him realize that she was quite possibly the most beautiful woman he'd ever seen (even if she wasn't blond with blue eyes). It very nearly took his breath away.

Chapter Six

"My dear Leonora—It seems like an age since I last saw you," the Duchess of Arbergail exclaimed as she came hurrying toward Leonora and Amy, who had just begun their ascent toward the theatre's balcony to locate their seats.

"Duchess," Leonora murmured, half managing a curtsy as she stood there partly turned with each foot on a different step. Amy fared no better, it seemed, and for one horrifying moment it appeared as though she might take a tumble. Thankfully, she found her balance. Leonora breathed a sigh of relief. "I didn't realize you planned to remain in Hallidan for the holidays—you usually journey to Brenton, isn't that so?"

"Not this year, my dear," the duchess said with some regret to her voice. "Unfortunately, my dear brother wasn't feeling quite up to a houseful of guests this year, so my husband has invited his sister and her children to spend Christmas with us instead."

"Oh, I'm so sorry to hear it," Leonora said. "I hope he'll be all right—your brother that is."

"Oh, it's nothing too serious—a rather persistent case of influenza." The duchess looked sideways only briefly before returning her gaze to Leonora. "Unfortunately, we have all ventured out this evening, so there is no more space in our box, or I would invite both of you to join us. I'm so sorry."

"That's quite all right," Leonora said. She then offered the duchess a secretive smile. "I believe we're well seated in the very middle of the first balcony."

The duchess nodded with complete understanding. This was a tactical maneuver on Leonora's part with the express intention of getting noticed by one and all.

"Then I shall wish you a very enjoyable evening indeed, ladies." The Duchess of Arbergail nodded politely toward each of them in turn before taking her leave and vanishing into the crowd.

Continuing upward, Leonora and Amy were just arriving at the top of the stairs when another voice could be heard, calling Leonora's name. Contrary to the duchess's, however, this one was deep and masculine, having the immediate effect of sending shivers across Leonora's skin. Her stomach tightened as she turned her head, only to find herself catching her breath. She'd forgotten how elegant Lord Redfirn looked in his black evening attire, for although he'd paid her several visits over the course of the past few weeks, she hadn't seen him at a formal event since the evening when they'd first met.

"What a pleasant surprise," his lordship was now saying as he turned his attention on Amy first and, much to Leonora's pleasant surprise, reached for her hand and placed a gentle kiss upon her knuckles. There was no denying the blush that rose to Amy's cheeks. Straightening, Redfirn then turned his gaze on Leonora, and said, "Please tell me you'll join me in my private box."

This wasn't at all what Leonora had been planning, but it was also an offer that was very hard to refuse. As it was, she was growing increasingly certain that if she didn't sit down soon, her legs, which had long since been turned to jelly, would in all likelihood give out beneath her and send her tumbling. Besides, she reasoned, it might work in Amy's favor if they were seen socializing with Lord Redfirn rather than with Grenly. "Thank you, my lord. That is indeed most generous of you," she said. "We would be happy to accept."

"Splendid!" Redfirn smiled at both of them, and if Leonora wasn't completely wrong, it did seem as though he added an extra bit of warmth to the smile he offered her.

How had she managed to fall in love with such speedy efficiency? Dear Lord, she'd never been so besotted in her life. Accepting one of the arms he now offered to each of them, Leonora sent up a silent prayer that he wouldn't guess what was in her heart. If he so much as suspected . . . In light of their relationship thus far, he could only think her a silly little nitwit.

"Here we are," Redfirn stated as soon as they'd entered his private box. Taking Amy by the arm, he led her forward to a centrally located seat with a perfect view of the stage. Leonora couldn't help but be impressed. He'd clearly realized the purpose behind taking Amy to the theatre this evening and had decided to help Leonora showcase her friend to the best of his abilities. Favoring him with a pleasant smile, she silently mouthed the words, "Thank you," as he turned back to face her.

With a slight nod, he acknowledged her appreciation and returned to her side, saying, "If you would please take the seat next to her, Lady Leonora, then I shall —"

"Forgive me for intruding, Lord Redfirn, but I saw you from across the way and was wondering if I might perhaps be allowed a brief word with Lady Amy?" It was Grenly who'd made an unexpected appearance.

What an unfortunate turn of events.

Leonora turned to Redfirn, who looked as though he was struggling to find an expression that would suit this new situation the best. The result was a bit of a grimace. "Mr. Grenly, was it?" Grenly managed a curt nod while his eyes remained on Lady Amy, who had turned an equally longing gaze on him. Leonora opened her mouth to say something—anything at all—that would serve to send the eager viscount on his merry way, but Redfirn beat her to it, saying, "Well, we've certainly plenty of room. Won't you join us?"

And then the one man that Leonora had been trying to keep away from her friend, marched across to a vacant seat that stood to Amy's left and promptly folded himself into it. It was a disaster. Out of options, Leonora served Redfirn one seething glance before marching across to the chair he'd initially designated for her. She didn't glance in his direction when he came to sit beside her though she was painfully aware of his presence—she would have had to be dead not to notice the way his shoulder and thigh brushed against her, and consequently, her fan was swiftly put to good use.

The music started with the notes of the overture rising through the air, the curtain was slowly raised, and Leonora was momentarily distracted by the soprano who stepped out onto the stage—right until she felt Lord Redfirn's warm breath against her neck. "My apologies, my lady," he murmured with a cadence that sent shivers racing down her spine and straight toward . . . *Heavens*. The sensations that were presently scurrying through her body were really quite indecent. She shifted a little uncomfortably in her seat while Redfirn leaned closer still and lowered his voice even further. "There was little I could do to avoid his presence without being purposefully rude."

"I know," she replied in a hushed tone meant only for his ears. She didn't turn her head in his direction as she spoke, however, fearful of the monocular-watching dragons and other gossipmongers who were only looking for the tiniest excuse to spin a juicy tale.

Silence followed for several moments after as the soprano embraced her aria with a voice that Leonora feared would only encourage most of the mamas present to become more persistent in regard to their daughters' music lessons. But no matter how lovely the performance taking place on the stage was, Leonora was finding it practically impossible to focus. On the one hand, there was Amy for her to worry about. Being seated next to Grenly would not encourage the suitors whom Leonora had in mind for her. On the other hand, she couldn't ignore Lord Redfirn's company. He might have decided to pay more attention to the opera than to her, but she was nonetheless acutely aware of his rather masculine presence.

Another torturous forty-five minutes, and the first act finally drew to an end. With a deep sigh of relief, Leonora rose from her seat. "Would any of you like to join me for a refreshment? I find that I am verily parched." She then looked directly at Amy, hoping that her friend would understand her meaning.

As luck would have it, Lord Redfirn was the first to answer with, "What a wonderful idea. What say you, Lady Amy? Care for something to drink?"

"Thank you for asking, my lord, but I'm really quite content." She must have seen Leonora's helpless expression, for she hastily went on to say, "Don't let that keep you, though—we'll be quite all right until you return."

"But . . . but . . ." Leonora found herself stammering. "You cannot—nay you must not—be alone with him, Amy. Think of your reputation."

And then the unfathomable happened. Amy, who had otherwise seemed so quiet and docile, speared Leonora with a very sharp stare. "We are in full view of at least one hundred people. I daresay that nobody will bat as much as an eyelid." And then she smiled and waved her hand, effectively dismissing Leonora completely. "Go on—Lord Redfirn will keep you company."

Leonora felt as though she'd just bit into a very sour lemon, but what was she to do? She couldn't throw Grenly out of Redfirn's box without causing a scandal. Redfirn . . . that was it. Surely he would help her if she turned to him. Refusing to give up on Amy's future— even though Amy herself appeared shockingly disinterested in making a proper match for herself—she placed her hand on the arm Redfirn offered her and allowed him to steer her out into the vestibule.

"WE HAVE TO do something," Lady Leonora said as soon as they were out of earshot.

"Hm?"

"About Lady Amy and Mr. Grenly," she explained. "I don't believe they're right for each other, and what's worse, it's become impossible for poor Amy to meet other eligible young gentlemen when Mr. Grenly is always *there*." She made an elaborate gesture with her hands that all but indicated that Grenly was somehow omnipresent.

Redfirn suppressed a smile. "From what I've seen, Lady Amy seems quite taken with Grenly."

Lady Leonora rolled her eyes. "What is she to think when she doesn't know any better? Lady Amy has no experience with being courted—it's only natural for her to be charmed by the first attentive gentleman who comes along."

Redfirn stopped walking, effectively halting Lady Leonora too. She turned a questioning gaze on him. Whatever her motive for putting a stop to Lady Amy and Grenly's acquaintance, she was clearly incapable of seeing the truth of it all—that Lady Amy and Grenly were not only perfectly suited for one another, but that they both *desired* to be together. Why Lady Leonora was so opposed to their union was beyond him. It was time to steer the conversation in a different direction altogether. "And what of you, Lady Leonora?" he asked, giving in to his roguish streak. "Do you know better?"

Her lips drew together in that delightful little pout she always managed whenever she was miffed. The deep blush that had rapidly begun to rise in her cheeks, however, could hardly be ignored. "This is not an appropriate topic of conversation," she said, lowering her voice to a soft whisper.

"I feel inclined to point out, that you, my lady, were the one to bring it up." This earned a gasp. Emboldened by her discomfort, which to his way of thinking could only suggest that he must be having quite an effect on her, he said, "Be that as it may, I certainly have no issue with telling you that I *do* know better. My experience with women is hardly what one would call limited, and . . . Please don't look away." In spite of the fact that she appeared to be in the process of planning her escape, she did comply, turning her lovely brown eyes toward him. He smiled—not because he was trying to manipulate her in any way but simply because he couldn't help it. "What I wished to say is that you are, without a shadow of a doubt, the loveliest woman I have ever seen."

Her expression was worth every word. He'd spoken the truth, but not without some measure of uncertainty and fear. After all, one hardly made such claims unless one intended to further one's relationship. It was a topic he'd pondered for some time already, but in light of the fact that he'd thoroughly enjoyed Lady Leonora's company for the past few weeks and looked forward to seeing her with great anticipation, this seemed like the next logical step. Naturally, there was also a more elementary reason. Indeed, he really wasn't sleeping well at all lately, what with all his imaginings about kissing her and undressing her and what she might look like, feel like, taste like . . . It was a torture unlike any he'd ever known before.

It was probably a full minute since he'd made his declaration, and still she did not speak, but simply stood there staring back at him, so he leaned a little closer, and whispered, "Would it offend you if I called you Nora?"

She shivered a little in response and finally shook her head. "Not at all," she breathed. And then she smiled—a smile meant only for him—and it made him feel as though he were ten feet tall.

"In that case, you may call me Connor, if you like. Or Redfirn—that's fine too." She nodded as if in a daze. Reaching the refreshment table, he wasted little time in procuring two glasses of Champagne for them. "And if you will permit, I shall call upon you tomorrow afternoon to officially commence our courtship with an outing to Hallidan's Picture Gallery. My mother will be happy to chaperone."

"That would be lovely," she said as she took a careful sip of her Champagne.

Regarding her with the admiration and fondness he'd developed for her during the course of their blossoming friendship, his smile broadened into a helpless grin. Things were looking up for him—he would soon be rid of Wolfston, and with a lovely bride to make the entire ordeal worth every minute. *A splendid outcome indeed!*

Chapter Seven

"I MUST SAY, Nora, that when we first made you a part of The Ring of Protectors and put Lady Amy in your care, we never imagined that it would turn out quite like this."

Leonora cringed. The duchess and her friends had good reason to be disappointed with her. She'd assured them all that she would find a most eligible young gentleman for her charge, and instead she'd ended up with Grenly. How it had gone so terribly wrong, she wasn't quite sure. With no idea of what to say, she reached for her teacup and took a tentative sip.

"In less than a month," the Duchess of Arbergail continued, "Lady Amy has been seen with Mr. Grenly repeatedly, and from what you tell me, it does indeed appear as though a proposal is forthcoming."

"Yes," Leonora nodded glumly. "It seems so."

"Well, you really must be commended for your efforts, Nora. None of us expected such a speedy outcome."

Leonora froze, her hand reaching for one of the biscuits on the table before her. Abandoning the treat, she leaned back in her seat instead and turned what she was sure must have been a most confused expression on the duchess. "I beg your pardon?"

The Duchess of Arbergail smiled. "When we handed Lady Amy over to your care, it was intended as a test. Not that there's anything wrong with her, mind you, but her height and her shyness don't work well in her favor. Gentlemen tend to prefer women who are shorter than they are—I believe it helps to reassure their sense of masculinity."

"So you approve of Mr. Grenly then?"

"Oh absolutely." The duchess's expression turned to something that could only be considered wise. "He's taken a genuine liking to her, and she too seems quite smitten. Additionally, he shall be able to provide for her rather well, not to mention that whatever he might lack in regard to grace, he certainly seems to make up for in kindness. Indeed, it is my assessment that the two are rather perfect for one another—I'm surprised none of us noticed it sooner."

"I just . . ." Leonora bit her bottom lip. "I had hoped that Lady Amy might marry an earl at the very least."

The Duchess of Arbergail chuckled. "My dear, you mustn't lose sight of what The Ring of Protectors is about. It's not about *you* proving yourself by marrying your charge off to the man with the best title. It's about facilitating a match that both parties will not only be happy with, but that they are both likely to benefit from. It's about Lady Amy's future, Nora, and if Mr. Grenly is the man she wants for herself, then it would be wrong of you to try to prevent it. She's the one marrying him after all—not you."

Oh dear.

Leonora felt like a complete snob. She'd believed all along that she was acting with Amy's best interests at heart—except deep down she knew she hadn't been. Instead, she'd treated poor Grenly most rudely. There was nothing for it; she would simply have to apologize to the man and perhaps try to make up for her meddling nature by helping Amy select a stunning wedding gown as soon as Grenly asked for her hand—which he would. There was no doubt about that.

"And while we're on the subject of paramours and such," the duchess said with a wry twist to her lips. "I couldn't help but notice that Lord Redfirn seems to be showing quite an interest in you."

Leonora felt herself blush all the way to the roots of her hair. "He made his intentions known to me the other evening at the theatre and has, with my permission, begun courting me. Unfortunately, with Papa being away, there was nobody for him to turn to, so I was rather hoping that you and the duke might oblige in that regard— should it come to that."

"Most assuredly. I shall anticipate the moment with great enthusiasm. Oh, Nora, your mother would be so happy for you." The Duchess of Arbergail's mouth broadened into a wry smile. "He must be quite fond of you indeed. Only a man completely smitten would buy such a costly gift for a lady he's not yet betrothed to."

"I'm sorry?"

"I didn't want you to think I was keeping an eye on you, my dear, so I refrained from saying anything, but when Lady Edgewater told me that her husband had seen Lord Redfirn at Hardy's Bookshop, I quickly put two and two together. Apparently, he made quite a fuss about having the books he'd picked out wrapped in a manner that would please a certain lady that he was buying them for." Leonora could do nothing but stare back at the duchess in horror. "Frankly, I couldn't be more pleased—he's such a fine-looking gentleman."

"Did Lady Edgewater happen to know which books he picked?" Leonora asked, though her heart had already dropped to her toes. Lord Redfirn, it seemed, had used her most efficiently to his advantage. She'd been right. There *had* been someone else behind Grenly's sudden success, and she'd been so bloody enamored of him that she'd been made blind. *Damn Lord Redfirn and his dashing good looks.* She kept a steady eye trained on the duchess. There was still hope—she could mention Shakespeare, or even someone as controversial as that Wollstonecraft woman. Just not Plato. Anything but Plato.

"I believe she mentioned philosophy." Leonora found herself holding her breath while the duchess took another sip of her tea. "Ah yes, I remember now—it was a collection of Plato."

And just like that, Leonora felt her heart break, taking whatever hope she'd had along with it.

Chapter Eight

The Hedgewick Christmas Ball
Two weeks later

CONNOR GLANCED AROUND the ballroom. It had been beautifully decorated with fir garlands hanging along the length of every wall—the rich, green accented by the occasional red bow. Bordering on the scandalous, a bunch of holly and mistletoe, tied neatly with golden ribbons, hung directly above each doorway. Connor wasn't surprised. Lady Hedgewick was famous for causing mischief. He wondered if she would mind that he'd taken one of the mistletoes and tucked it away in his pocket, should he happen to need it later, deciding after a moment's speculation that it was unlikely she would.

Feeling restless, he shifted between his feet. After repeatedly being turned away unceremoniously by Lady Leonora's butler, he'd grown increasingly agitated. The fact that he couldn't get her out of his mind did not help. What the devil had gone wrong? They'd been getting along famously, and he'd been confident that whatever attraction he felt toward her had been reciprocated.

Could he have been mistaken? He frowned a little as he considered the prospect—then shook his head. No, he didn't think so.

There was only one explanation that came to mind—Lady Leonora must have gotten wind of his interference regarding Grenly and Lady Amy. He wasn't sure how it might have happened, but he ought to have been wise enough to know that it eventually would. It required supreme stealth to get by the gossipmongers unnoticed. For some unfathomable reason, news of an event always seemed to precede the actual event itself.

Stepping aside to allow a couple of debutantes past, he responded to their shy smiles and fluttering eyelashes with a scowl, which had the immediate effect of sending them scurrying—much to his great satisfaction. He took a heartfelt sip of his Champagne and cast another glance toward the door. Where the devil was she? He'd been told she'd be in attendance this evening, and if he was going to stand any chance in hell of becoming mentally sound once more, he simply had to see her again. He had to explain himself and apologize and . . . and tell her how he felt about her.

"You needn't guard the entrance so doggedly, Redfirn." It was Penningham, of course—sharply dressed as always though with a rather annoying smile upon his lips. "She'll be here."

Connor attempted a careless shrug. "An entrance may also be used as an exit—I was merely staying close to it in case I happened to spot a mama towing her daughter in my general direction."

"Is that so? Then why not position yourself closer to the terrace doors instead? Surely, that would be far more convenient?"

"And have said mama convince her young daughter to follow me outside as I attempt my escape? No thank you. We all know how many young and unsuspecting gentlemen have been carted off to the altar in precisely that manner. I shan't be one of them."

Penningham at least had the good grace to laugh rather than roll his eyes as the situation might have demanded. Connor took another sip of his drink. He was well aware that Penningham knew precisely what he was about, but it didn't hurt to try to maintain one's dignity, for heaven's sake. Turning his head in the direction of the dance floor, he spotted Lady Amy and Grenly, who were presently in the middle of a rather rambunctious reel and appeared to be having a marvelously good time, no matter their missteps. Everything aside, the two were indeed quite perfect for one another.

Grenly had visited him directly following his proposal, which had, as Connor expected it would, resulted in an immediate "yes" from Lady Amy. They were presently in the process of planning a March wedding from what Connor had been able to gather. And, of course, the topping on the whole sweet affair had been that Connor had finally been able to shake hands with Wolfston and bid him good riddance although the old earl had definitely been in one of his cheerier moods—indeed, he'd appeared quite transformed from his blunt old self. The prospect of numerous grandbabies undoubtedly had something to do with that. Long live the line of succession!

"Isn't that her?" Penningham's voice brought Connor's head swiveling around on his neck. "Heaven help me—I believe *I'm* in love."

It took a moment for Connor to spot Lady Leonora, but once he did, he could well imagine every man present that evening falling on their knees for her. She looked ravishing—like a fine strawberry tart or some other sweet confection. He hastily elbowed Penningham in the ribs. "Best forget about it, old chap. She's mine." He then strode forward with the determination of a man who'd just crossed the desert and spotted a watering hole.

LEONORA'S STOMACH WAS a cacophony of jittery nerves. She was certain Lord Redfirn would be there this evening, and no matter how many times she'd considered feigning a headache and staying at home, she knew that she had to venture back out in public sooner or later. It simply couldn't be helped. But if she was going to put in an appearance, then she'd certainly do so with style. It had taken no less than five wardrobe changes and three different attempts at her hair to achieve the desired effect. She had to admit that she was rather pleased with the end result. The gold lace with the creamy silk beneath it had quite a lovely effect. There was only one problem in fact—she'd realized on her way over in the carriage that she'd picked the gown with only Lord Redfirn in mind. It was most infuriating.

So here she was, with two gentlemen already added to her dance card. All she had to do now was avoid the one man who had laid siege to her thoughts. If she could only locate him, then at least she'd know which direction to head toward. She turned her head a little as she made her way forward with the intention of reconvening with Amy once she and Grenly finished their dance.

But then she spotted him, and it was as if a thousand things began to happen all at once. Her heart started hammering, her skin began to prickle, she grew unacceptably hot, and yet she still managed a shiver. Worst of all was that Lord Redfirn had clearly noticed that she had spotted him, for his pace all of a sudden seemed to pick up dramatically—as if he sensed that she might make a run for it. And then, much to her own surprise (for it was certainly not what she'd had in mind when she'd imagined meeting him again—a nonchalant demeanor had been more like it), she did precisely that. Not that she could really run, given the number of people around her, but she did start off toward the side of the room, where some wide-open double doors beckoned her.

After a bit of maneuvering and more apologies than she'd ever spoken before in such a short period of time, Leonora finally stepped out into a long corridor, which, in stark contrast to the ballroom, was almost completely devoid of people. Pausing momentarily, she turned her head and looked up. *Good heavens.* Was that mistletoe? Surely not.

There was no time to linger—not if she still wished to avoid Lord Redfirn. Which she did. Didn't she? She no longer knew what she wanted, only that she'd been hurt by his dishonesty, and while a simple apology on his part might have helped, she'd barricaded herself in her home, not giving him the chance. She now found herself in one of those situations where everything had escalated to such a level that it was near impossible for her to turn back and look the man in the eye without feeling like a silly young girl in leading strings.

Hurrying toward the nearest door, she quickly opened it, stepped inside, and locked it. A moment later, she heard somebody try the door handle. Redfirn. She half expected him to call out her name and insist she open the door, but no—nothing like that. After a couple of tries, the footsteps receded, and Leonora sank back against the door, feeling not at all relieved but rather shockingly disappointed. Was that really all she was worth? A half-hearted effort?

Lowering her head, she let out a miserable sigh and sank quietly to the floor. Returning to the ball would have to wait—she was no longer in any mood to be sociable. Instead, she let out a heavy sigh at the same exact moment that she spotted a pair of men's black shoes, no more than five feet away from her. She froze. And then her gaze drifted up . . . and up and up and . . . still up—all the way past the black trousers, the tailcoat, the shirt buttons, and the cravat—until they settled upon the face. *Oh dear heaven above.* There stood Lord Redfirn, looking not only mighty pleased with himself but also rather miffed. How on earth had he gotten in?

"There's another door," he said, answering her unspoken question a bit too smugly for her liking.

Of course there is. Why hadn't she considered such a possibility? A number of reasons came to mind though there was no sense in considering them now when it obviously made no difference to her current dilemma—namely that she looked as though she'd collapsed on the library floor and that the man she'd been trying to avoid was now towering over her with not so much as a footman present to add some measure of propriety. They were alone—completely and utterly alone—and with both doors shut.

It was most unseemly. No, it was scandalous and would spell either ruin or marriage should anyone happen to find them out. The thrill of excitement that curled inside her stomach as she wondered if Redfirn had planned it that way could not be denied. And yet, for whatever stupid womanly sense of misconstrued pride, Leonora found it impossible to let her annoyed façade fall away, saying simply (and a notch too coolly), "I see. And it didn't occur to you to knock?"

His brows knit together, and he studied her for a moment. "No," he said, defiantly crossing his arms and clearly deciding to stand his ground.

She wasn't getting away without a confrontation, she realized. Well, if he was so determined, then there was little point in waiting. Rising to her feet with deliberate slowness so as not to ruin her gown, Leonora straightened, raised her chin, and looked Lord Redfirn squarely in the eye. "You deceived me."

Momentary shock registered upon his face. He was either surprised by her straightforwardness or felt unjustly accused. As it turned out, it wasn't the latter, for he responded, surprising her in equal measure by saying, "Yes. I did."

Leonora felt her throat tighten. "Why?" Not as forcefully spoken as before but closer to a whisper.

"Because I had a debt to settle with Mr. Grenly's father, Lord Wolfston." He sighed, ran his fingers through his hair, then strode off toward the side table and began pouring a glass of brandy for himself. He then poured a second one and handed it to Leonora. "Would you please be so kind as to sit with me for a while? I'd like to offer you an explanation if I may."

Leonora stared down at the drink she was now holding in her hand. She hadn't asked for it, but curiously enough, she rather felt as if the situation called for something to ease her aching heart. Taking a hesitant sip, she flinched a little as the strong stuff bit at her insides. Eyes trained once again on Lord Redfirn, she gave a curt nod and seated herself on the sofa opposite him. "Please do."

The next ten minutes were a tumultuous wave of emotions. Leonora felt her heart mend and break at least three times, so that by the time Lord Redfirn was finally through, she felt so depleted that she really had no desire for anything other than to go home. She eyed her glass, which was still half-full. Perhaps a drunken stupor would be just the thing to numb her mind and help her forget about the ever-charming earl who sat before her.

Oh, he hadn't meant to hurt her (he claimed), he'd

been indebted to Lord Wolfston, and surely she must be able to see that as a gentleman it was his duty to pay his due (balderdash), he hadn't expected to find any resistance from one of Lady Amy's friends (was the man delusional?), he definitely hadn't expected to actually *like* one of Lady Amy's friends (how flattering), and he'd rather thought she would forgive him in light of how well it had all turned out (annoying man—he was probably right).

"So you must admit that," he was now saying, leaning slightly forward in his seat, "all things taken into account, you're overreacting a little."

"Overreacting!" She hastily took a large gulp of her brandy to stop herself from resorting to the alternative, which was to scream in frustration.

Men.

"Yes," he continued adamantly, apparently rather fond of the large hole he was digging for himself. "I . . . Oh, damn it all to hell!"

Leonora felt her eyes widen in response to that remark, especially since it was followed by a swift burst of movement as Lord Redfirn shot to his feet, strode around the table between them, and planted himself directly beside her on the sofa. Her lips parted, for she planned to speak—to say something that might illustrate what a bad idea his rash decision had been. But the words wouldn't come, and instead she found herself staring at the man quite stupidly, not to mention painfully aware that her heart was beating twice as fast as usual and that her whole body had begun to hum with anticipation.

His gaze didn't meet hers for the longest time. Instead,

he kept his eyes trained on her hands, eventually reaching out and gently taking one of them in his own. The contact was electric—soft and sharp at the same time. Leonora's stomach tightened, her breath caught, and when he finally raised his gaze to meet hers, she felt herself wanting something so foreign and so powerful that it took every ounce of willpower not to leap away from him. And then, bringing her hand reverently to his lips, he simply said, "I'm sorry, Nora."

"You . . . you what?" she squeaked, mortified by how easy it must be for him to read her thoughts from her intonation alone.

"When I began this business regarding Mr. Grenly and Lady Amy, I had no idea that I would end up risking my own heart in the process." Leonora blinked. "When I suggested a courtship, it wasn't with any ulterior motive in mind—indeed, my intentions were most noble, and still are."

She swallowed hard, scarcely allowing herself to believe in the possibility of what he was saying. "But the dance when we first met, and the night at the theatre—"

He placed a silencing finger against her lips. "Deliberate attempts to offer Mr. Grenly and Lady Amy a chance to further their acquaintance, I admit. But during the course of it, I got to know you, and I have to say . . ."

He fell silent, and Leonora found herself holding her breath as she waited for him to continue. But he didn't. Instead, he simply reached inside his jacket pocket and pulled out a sprig of mistletoe. The corner of his mouth edged upward to form a most mischievous smile, and before she had a chance to consider what was up and what was down, she was being pulled toward him with strong, deliberate hands, until there was nothing more between them—just the feel of his lips gently brushing against hers. It was indescribable. Remarkable. Wonderful. It was a moment that she wished would last forever, and yet somehow, it wasn't enough.

Leonora wasn't sure what came over her, but her arms were suddenly around Lord Redfirn's neck, her fingers raking through his hair as she scooted a little closer to where he sat. Was that a low growl she'd just heard? Whatever it was, it sent a wave of ticklish warm pleasure cascading through her.

Chapter Nine

CONNOR WAS IN heaven. He knew he'd wanted Lady Leonora (or Nora as he liked to think of her) for quite some time, but he hadn't realized just how much until this very moment. Damn, but he could hardly keep himself under any measure of control. He wanted to touch her, kiss her, lick her . . . Her hands abandoned his hair and drifted down his back instead. She had a soft touch, perhaps a bit hesitant. He liked it, though, for it confirmed what he'd known already—that she had no experience with any other men—and something very elemental and masculine inside of him started cheering.

A soft murmur of pleasure escaped her lips, and he caught the moment, seizing the opportunity to deepen their kiss while his restless fingers traveled over her shoulders, down her sides and up again, until one hand came to rest against the side of her breast. She pressed herself closer, and there was no mistaking what she wanted of him, but he did not oblige her just yet. Instead, he pushed his tongue forward, running it along her lower lip until she opened her mouth to him completely.

Moist heat welcomed him, and as she began to respond with her own tongue mimicking his, he allowed his thumb to brush lazily against the side of her breast. He knew the slowness of his progress was undoubtedly a torturous ordeal for her, but he also knew that it would lead to far greater pleasure later. Still, he did feel his resolve momentarily waver when he directed his attention to kissing her neck, and she started squirming beneath him like a restless cat in heat. "Easy does it, Nora—lovemaking is like sampling fine chocolates. One must savor every nibble." He eased back a little—just enough to hook a finger in the neckline of her gown and pull it down a bit.

Lord have mercy on my soul.

The thoughts that entered his head at the sight of her creamy white breasts, peaked by two erect, rosy tips, were not in the least bit honorable. His tongue came forward in one slow, sweeping, motion to lick at the hardened bud, and as it did, he felt Nora tremble . . . he heard her murmur his name . . . and he felt himself tighten into an unbearable hardness.

"Tell me you want this." His voice sounded raspy to his own ears. She pulled him tightly against her chest, and he complied with her silent plea, taking one breast completely in his mouth and suckling on it until she groaned. He pulled away just enough to catch his breath. "Please, for the love of God, please tell me you want this,

Nora. Tell me now if you wish for this to end, or I assure you it will be too late."

"Connor." His heart soared at the sound of his name upon her lips. "I need . . . Please don't stop."

Like a hound at the races, he was ready to go, but he had to make certain—had to be completely sure that he was doing what was right not only for him, but for her. He raised his head enough to offer her a level stare. "Marry me, Nora."

Her lips trumpeted a little while her eyes seemed to focus. It was almost as if some fog that had otherwise been obscuring her reality had finally subsided, and she was seeing the world for the very first time. She smiled—a wide and glorious smile meant only for him. It was a wonderful moment—one that not only assured him of how she truly felt about him but that she finally knew how deeply he felt about her. "Yes," she said. And then to confirm it, "Yes, I'll marry you."

Still, it had to be said—he had to voice his emotions— she deserved at least that much. It wouldn't do to take the cowardly approach now, so, bending his head, he leaned closer to her ear, and whispered, "I love you, Nora. With all my heart, I love you."

Wrapping her arms about his neck, her voice quivered as she responded with the words he longed to hear. "I love you too, Connor."

His lips were on hers again immediately, then they were trailing along the length of her neck, along her collarbone, and toward her breast, where once against his efforts were rewarded with a sigh of pleasure. Her growing

desperation with his lack of haste sent his fingers traveling up her leg and toward her thigh quicker than he'd intended. But really, whom was he trying to fool? The truth
of the matter was that he was unlikely to see this through
to the end unless he started hurrying things along.

So he did.

He pushed her skirts all the way to her hips, leaned
her back so she was reclining with her head against the
sofa's armrest, and gently urged her legs apart. She was
hesitant about this, of course, but his kisses coupled with
his playful touch soon had her relaxing anew, and when
he felt the tension abandon her completely, he allowed
his fingers to brush along her inner thighs until they met
with her core.

"Connor." His name was but a sigh as her hips rose
against his touch.

She'd closed her eyes, but the need she felt—the raw
and undeniable desire—was etched in every part of her
expression. Watching her thus, he gently rubbed her, eliciting a groan from somewhere deep inside her.

"Please," she murmured, her eyes opening ever so
slightly as she made her plea. He'd never been more eager
to comply with someone's wishes and hastily leaned back
to make quick work of the buttons on his breeches.

Their coupling was passionate and fast, with Connor
barely managing to bring Leonora to her own ecstatic
bliss before he too went tumbling over the edge—
collapsing on top of her as his breathing gradually slowed.
They remained like that for a few minutes until he felt her
stir beneath him. "Forgive me," he muttered as he raised

himself back up so he was resting on his arms and looking down at her. "Is this more comfortable?"

She nodded, hesitated for a moment, then said, "There's something I have to tell you."

He felt himself frown. "Ought I be worried?"

"I don't think so, but I don't want us to enter into marriage with any secrets between us." That sounded reasonable enough. Connor pulled himself completely off her and helped her sit back up, taking a moment to adjust his clothing while she did the same. When she was done straightening her gown, she gave him a somewhat assessing look. She'd told him not to worry, but considering how long it was taking her to say whatever it was she meant to tell him, he couldn't help but feel a sense of growing trepidation.

"I recently became a member of The Ring of Protectors," she suddenly blurted. "Shortly before I met you, as it happens."

Connor wracked his brain for a moment, but eventually shook his head. He'd never heard of such an organization. "What does that mean, exactly?"

For the next ten minutes, Leonora told him everything—or at least he supposed it had to be everything since he could hardly imagine there being anything else left to say once she was done talking. Suddenly, however, everything regarding Leonora began making a lot more sense. "Lady Amy was your first . . . ahem . . . project, I take it?"

Leonora nodded. "Though I didn't think of her as such for long. In truth, I genuinely like her and think of her now as a true friend, but I . . . well, there are some high-ranking ladies involved, and I suppose I wanted to . . ." She bit down on her lower lip and paused.

"You wanted to prove yourself to them by making a splendid match for Lady Amy. Am I right?"

She stared back at him with deep, fathomless eyes—eyes that Connor knew he could easily lose himself in forever. "Yes," she whispered, averting her gaze. "I know now that I was wrong, but I cannot help but worry that it might lower your opinion of me—I treated Mr. Grenly very poorly."

"We both did," Connor admitted, surprising even himself by his statement. "You for underestimating his value as a match for Lady Amy, and I for thinking of him as a nuisance—a man I couldn't wait to be rid of. We were both at fault. The best we can do is learn from our mistakes." He smiled then, recalling how much he and Leonora had argued when they'd first met and knowing now the real reason behind it. "Look on the bright side. It brought us together—eventually."

And the smile she offered him in return told him that although she might not be blond or have blue eyes as he'd always imagined his wife having, there was no other woman in the world who was as right for him as Lady Leonora . . . Nora . . . Soon to be Lady Redfirn.

About Sophie Barnes

Born in Denmark, SOPHIE BARNES has spent her youth traveling with her parents to wonderful places all around the world. She's lived in five different countries, on three different continents, and speaks Danish, English, French, Spanish, and Romanian. She has studied design in Paris and New York and has a bachelor's degree from Parson's The New School For Design, but most impressive of all— she's been married to the same man three times, in three different countries and in three different dresses.

While living in Africa, Sophie turned to her lifelong passion—writing. When she's not busy dreaming up her next romance novel, Sophie enjoys spending time with her family, swimming, cooking, gardening, watching romantic comedies and, of course, reading. She currently lives on the East Coast.

Visit Sophie Barnes's Web site at www.sophiebarnes. com. You can also find her on Facebook and follow her on Twitter at @BarnesSophie.

His Perfect Gift

KAREN ERICKSON

Chapter One

SHE WORE A ribbon around her neck.

Lady Eleanor Fitzsimmons, eldest daughter of the poorest earl in all of England, had not a jewel on her person this evening. Nor was she in possession of any sort of precious gems any evening. Just a single thin ribbon wound about her elegant throat, usually matching the color of her gown.

Her three-seasons-old, faded, and well-mended gown, it should be added. Everyone knew she hadn't donned anything fashionable since her debut.

Not that her lack of fashion detracted from her beauty, oh no. The gentlemen still swarmed. The ladies still gossiped. And the younger debutantes still wished Lady Eleanor to find a husband posthaste, so she could be eliminated once and for all from the marriageable ladies' list. They mocked her family's well-known poverty, both behind her back and directly to her face. Her father's

gambling habits were legendary—as his losses were spectacularly grand.

Throughout it all, she wore a polite smile. Nothing
fazed her.

Ever.

His gaze went unerringly to the elegant length of her
neck, not a stray dark brown tendril daring to mar such
creamy perfection. The damned ribbon drew him in,
brought all his attention to that singular spot, the strand
of peach-colored silk resting just above where her pulse
fluttered. He'd paid plenty of attention to her throughout the years. Sometimes it was slow and even, with the
gentle beat of life that no doubt flowed within her like a
lazy, meandering river on a summer's day.

But other times her pulse beat madly, as if she were
agitated. Or achingly aware—for more than once she'd
caught him staring though she never acknowledged it.
Nay, Lady Eleanor never confronted him, for it would
be unseemly. Above all else, she practiced a decorum he
supposed he should admire.

He didn't. How he wished he could see Lady Eleanor
Fitzsimmons at her rawest, in those most intimate moments when her every flaw, her every vulnerability was
revealed. Where she couldn't hide behind the fan she
kept clutched in her hand or the serene expression she
wore like a mask on her pretty face.

Only that delicate pulse at the base of her neck gave
her true emotions away.

Ashton leaned against the wall, one hand in his
pocket, rubbing his thumb and index finger against the

gold ring he carried with him. The simple band had been in his family for generations, his mother had worn it last. She'd given it to him recently, begging him to find his future duchess.

He'd made his choice once. Long, long ago, when he'd been a different man, living a much different life. And she rejected him.

He watched her now. Yearned for her.

Funny thing, that. How much he still wanted her, yet she didn't want him. How she turned down his proposal her first season, hoping for a better prospect, he supposed. After all, he'd been the mere second son of a duke when he'd made that most eager marriage offer. Utterly besotted with her too, which made it all the more humiliating when she rejected him so smartly, all of nineteen, letting down a man well into his twenties in a gentle sort of way that belied her young age.

He'd made a fool of himself over her and vowed then and there he would never do so again. Held up that vow too, with his notorious reputation as an elusive bachelor amongst the *ton*. His father had died soon after the humiliating rejection, leaving his elder brother to take over the dukedom, at which he'd been an absolute failure.

Henry had then become a rabid topic of gossip when his foolish drunken duke of a brother had died just over a year ago. Falling off his horse in the slums of London after deftly escaping from a particular house of ill repute, avoiding the gentleman who'd come to collect the funds Robert so foolishly owed him from a gambling debt.

His brother had lost his life all over a few pounds.

Money he had, a debt he could've paid easily. Ashton wondered if it was the thrill of getting away with something that had driven Robert to do such a stupid thing.

Something he contemplated quite often during those long nights when he couldn't fall asleep.

So he was the Duke of Ashton. He, plain old Lord Henry William Stuart for the majority of his nine-and-twenty years, had become the ninth duke and was expected to carry out all the duties he'd never been groomed for. If he was doing a poor job of it—which he was, he knew this for an absolute fact—then how could it be his fault?

You must marry and soon. Find a young chit, wed her, and bed her. Gain that heir you so desperately need, the duchess had told him one evening not a fortnight ago, pressing the cold, thin ring into his hand. Her voice quivering in that way it did when she was trying her best to be firm, convincing.

Yet no ladies interested him. Oh, he'd had his share of women, many of them widowed, a few of them older, wiser, not interested in anything beyond a dalliance, a brief affair. Truthfully, he hadn't indulged since his brother's death. Becoming the duke had turned him celibate.

The pressure, the duty that came with the title, took everything out of him. So much blessed work and so little time to accomplish it all. Not to mention the eager mamas who besieged him at every social event he attended, pushing their fresh-faced debutante daughters upon him like a gift. Gifts he didn't want, for there wasn't a single lady amongst all of London society he to marry.

Well. Save one particular Lady Eleanor. And she despised the very ground he walked on.

A young man approached her, slobbering over her hand, all moony-eyed and tripping over his feet like a gangly puppy. She greeted him politely, inclining her head, offering Ashton a most fascinating view of the back of her neck, how her spine bent with the movement. A short, curling bit of hair fell from her coiffure, tickling her delicate skin, and how he wished he could go to her, tuck that errant hair back where it belonged, bury his nose in those fragrant tresses, and inhale deep.

He hadn't forgotten her intoxicating scent. Or the silky feel of her hair. The memories were burned indelibly on his brain.

Her slim shoulders stiffened, and she lifted her head, her nose in the air as if she scented something amiss. Turning her head slowly, she looked to her left. The movement was subtle, no one would detect it except for him. He couldn't *not* notice. She merely had to enter a room, and she became its universe when he was near.

It was both that simple, and that complicated.

She glanced over her shoulder, her lids lifting, revealing those dark brown eyes that haunted his thoughts, his dreams. Her gaze met and held his for a long, aching moment. He stopped breathing, stopped thinking, focused solely on her, then she did something so unbelievable he was sure his eyes were playing tricks on him.

Lady Eleanor inclined her head and gave it a little jerk, indicating . . . what? That she wanted him to approach? That she wanted him to follow her? So they could go somewhere private and illicit, where he could finally put his hands all over her delectable body again?

Either suggestion was laughable not but a second ago. Hell, they were still laughable.

She indicated with a quick flick of her fingers, a little wave that said he should come to her, and without thought, he went like a well-trained dog, his feet moving of their own accord.

Finally, he'd broken through that impenetrable shield she'd erected around herself. Sweet triumph surged through him when he stopped to stand beside her, his arm brushing against her shoulder. The brief contact sent a jolt through him, and he inhaled sharply, desperate for control.

It wouldn't do to make a complete ass of himself in front of the *ton* again. Once was more than enough.

"Your Grace." Her sweet, throaty voice brought to mind images of tangled limbs, damp skin, and swollen lips. "Might I ask you a question?"

"Absolutely, my lady. Anything you wish to know, I shall tell you." Well, perhaps not *anything* she wished to know. A man had his secrets, after all.

She turned to face him, those velvety brown eyes seeming to see right through him. "If you wish to make a mockery of me in front of all of society, then I beg of you, please get it over with and quick. I've grown rather tired, knowing you're always lurking about. Plotting and planning my social demise as if I'm blissfully unaware of your presence."

His jaw dropped, the denial lodged in his throat. So

she had noticed him. He had truly believed her blissfully unaware of his presence.

That tiny admission caused hope to flicker to life deep within him.

"Don't look so shocked," she chastised, pointing her finger in his face. "As if I wouldn't notice you. You've watched me for what feels like an age, ever since you inherited your poor brother's title, God rest his weary soul. I know you're still angry with me for rejecting your suit."

Ah. Now it was becoming clearer. She wasn't too far off though his plans never included humiliating her amongst society. Making her his though, most definitely.

"And don't try to deny it either," she said when he opened his mouth. "I'm sure you've already had quite a laugh over it all. You suffered through my rejection only to become a duke. At this very moment, I could've been your duchess, probably have given you at least your precious heir and been plump with the second. Looking forward to another holiday season with our growing family surrounding us and all that pleasant nonsense."

Ashton clamped his lips shut, his mind awhirl. She spoke as if she'd thought about this quite often. As if she regretted turning him down. But was it only because he was a bloody duke? Or could it be something more?

He was more determined than ever to find out.

Chapter Two

"LADY ELEANOR." He bowed before her, magnificent in his black evening clothes. His dark brown hair pushed away from his forehead though it curled appealingly about his nape. His face was clean-shaven, his cheeks and jaw smooth, revealing every vividly stunning feature. He was so terribly handsome it was hard not to stare.

She refused to, chose instead to focus on a point just above his left shoulder. She should hate this man for how he followed her about. How he made her feel, so full of wanting and wishing and regret she grew near overwhelmed with it all.

Yet she couldn't hate him, no matter how much she tried.

"I must say, I'm rather shocked by your accusations." He paused, letting his words sink in as he watched her with those intense blue-green eyes. "You truly believe I wish to have my revenge on you?"

"Of course," she offered stiffly, holding her breath when he moved closer to her. Inappropriately close. She breathed in his familiar scent, let it wash over her, and she turned her head. Watching instead the dancing couples who swirled by as she desperately tried to calm her wildly beating heart.

"Then you must think incredibly little of me to believe I would do such a thing."

She had no answer for him. This man she'd once known and cared for. This man she'd believed for a very short time she would marry . . .

He studied her as if he wished to take her apart, she could feel his heated gaze upon her. Not that she could blame him. What she'd done three years ago had been cruel. Foolish. Dreadfully naïve. Her ultimate mistake? She'd listened to her father, who'd convinced her someone better would come along. A titled gent with plenty of wealth who'd take care of her family—and her father's notorious gambling habits—for the rest of their days.

She'd believed him. Silly, considering that the Earl of Cochrane was a known liar. Even to his eldest daughter. His falsehoods knew no bounds. The man would lie about the weather, what he ate for luncheon, whom he was with the evening prior . . .

Lady Eleanor frowned. Well, her father had reason to lie about whom he spent his evenings with. He certainly never spent them at home with his wife and daughters.

"You're especially beautiful tonight." He murmured the words close to her ear, shocking her from her thoughts, and she purposely kept her head averted.

"Thank you." She dragged her formality to the surface, using it as a sort of shield, desperate not to reveal how much he affected her.

Despite the so-called intimate party at which they were both in attendance this evening, there were still well over one hundred members of London society within the cavernous ballroom. Most of them converged on the dance floor though quite a few milled about. Some of them stared pointedly at her and Ashton.

The gossips would discuss their conversation gleefully, of this Lady Eleanor was sure. Everyone knew that after she rejected him, they'd avoided each other.

"Your accusations." His deep, slightly rough voice invaded her mind, invaded her very soul, and she jerked her head up to meet his gaze. "They startled me, Lady Eleanor. That you would think so low of me . . ."

"I'm assuming the feeling is mutual." She sniffed, straightened her shoulders. She sounded like an insolent brat, but the man seemed to bring out the worst in her.

"I'll confess I wasn't pleased with the turn of events three years ago." He took a step closer, so close he brushed against her side, sending a current of tingles washing over her skin. "But I could never hate you, my lady. On the contrary, I find myself rather fascinated by you."

She stepped away from him, his nearness far too distracting. He smelled of leather and sandalwood, a dash of tobacco. And he was so blessedly warm. Hot, even. All that scented heat drew her in. Made her want things she should never, ever consider again.

Like him.

"Fascinated as in wishing to see my societal demise?" She took a deep, fortifying breath. "I can assure you, that moment is most likely drawing near."

He frowned, which didn't detract from his masculine beauty whatsoever. More like emphasized his impossibly good looks. That firm jaw, his full lips, the patrician nose . . . no one could deny that Ashton was a handsome man.

"I'm referring to the fact that everyone will see us conversing," she explained when he didn't reply.

"And why should they care?"

Irritation flashed through her. Was the man dense? "We are enemies," she whispered.

"We are?" A single eyebrow rose at this particular remark. His voice full of amused doubt, he looked ready to laugh. At her.

She stood straighter, her spine painfully stiff. "Of course we are. We haven't spoken since that . . . that dreadful night."

"When you so soundly rejected me?" His voice boomed; surely someone heard that pointed remark.

He smiled, and she had to look away. There were many within the ballroom who watched them with unabashed curiosity. "People are staring."

"Let them stare." He touched her, sending a jolt of pure sensation throughout her entire body. He drew his finger down the side of her neck, toying with the slender thread of peach silk she'd tied there earlier. "What is this?"

"I own no jewels. I thought to adorn myself with a bit of ribbon that matched the color of my gown." Her throat ached with a whimper that wanted to escape as his finger followed the curve of silk to her nape. "You do realize you're touching me in a rather improperly intimate manner."

"I have touched you in far more intimate manners, Lady Eleanor. Or have you forgotten?" Gooseflesh spread all over her skin at his murmured reminder. She'd avoided him all this time so she would forget. Not that she truly could.

The memories of her brief time with Lord Henry Stuart, now the Duke of Ashton, were burned upon her mind.

He rubbed the ribbon's bow between his thumb and index finger. "If you were mine, I would give you all the jewels you could ever want."

"I don't want anything from you, and I especially don't want to be yours." *Liar.* As if she could forget the time they had spent together. The devastation that had overtaken her when her father had told her she couldn't marry him. Henry had been her first choice, her only choice, and she'd been forced to turn him away.

All to do what was best for her family. For her father.

She nearly choked on the bitterness that wound through her.

"You have nothing to say?" He chuckled, and his finger fell away from her neck. "My incessant pursuit of you isn't working, then?"

"No." She kept her gaze trained on the dance floor. "You are wasting your time, Your Grace."

It was best. He was a duke. Above her station and though her heart wished he was serious, her mind warned that he merely toyed with her. His unusual behavior was all part of some long-overdue revenge he wished to seek upon her.

"I wish you would call me Henry. As you did once before."

She turned to look at him, saw all the heat and passion and want for her in the depths of his gaze. She refused to believe it. "We can never go back to how we were before. I've changed. You've changed."

His expression sobered. "What will it take to convince you that I still want you? What will it take to make you mine?"

Icy shock coursed through her veins at his bold proclamation. He still wanted her? He wanted to know what it would take to make her his? She glanced about, wishing they were anywhere but in the middle of a crowded ballroom. "Keep your voice down."

They stood silent, staring at each other, and how she wished she could give in. But she couldn't. She'd humiliated him once. Everyone knew how her callous treatment of his proposal had angered him. After not speaking to her for years, he expected her to gladly accept him back into her life? Thrilled at the chance to be courted by him once more?

"Perhaps this isn't the proper place for such an intimate discussion." His use of the word "intimate" made her think of stolen, wicked moments they'd once shared.

The feel of his strong arms around her, his chest pressed to hers, their mouths locked. The shock she'd felt when he first thrust his tongue between her lips. The delights he'd showed her with that tongue . . .

"My lady?" His inquisitive voice drew her from her thoughts, and she glanced up at him, saw that he studied her with seeming concern.

"Where else shall we discuss this matter then?" The question came out shrill, and oh how she hated that.

He smiled, looking as if he'd won a grand prize. "I was thinking it might be best if I came to your home tomorrow afternoon. Say at two o'clock?"

His innocent suggestion rendered her silent only for a moment. The absolute nerve of the man was astounding. "Are you serious?"

He smiled, the sight of it blinding her. Dazzling her. "As serious as I've ever been in my life."

"I—I don't think it's wise." She could hardly speak with him near, let alone think properly.

"What's not wise? My coming to call at your home in the middle of the afternoon?" He looked shocked, the scoundrel.

"We've already done this once," she said, wanting to choose her words carefully. The last thing she wanted was to offend him—again. "And it didn't work out for us."

"Circumstances were different then. You were younger. I was poorer. I had no title." His forthrightness shocked her.

"I didn't reject you because you didn't have a title." Lies. And he knew it too, if his expression meant anything. "It happened because—" Because her father wanted a husband for her who would have an endless supply of funds.

"There's no need to lie, my lady," he drawled, his voice deep and so very dark. "We both know the truth."

Her heart beat wildly, her breath lodged in her chest. He knew why, yet he still wanted her. Was this some sort of trick? Did he want to lure her back into his arms and ruin her once and for all?

"I see that you've no more protests," he said. "I will make my appearance at your house tomorrow afternoon."

"B—but, I don't—"

"There's no need to argue, darling." He pressed his gloved finger to her mouth, rendering her silent. Her lips tingled at his touch, at the murmured endearment. Desolation filled her when his hand dropped away. "I will keep pursuing you until I finally wear you down."

The man was truly mad. And she despised how easily he aroused her. "Wearing a lady down isn't the way you should pursue her," she tossed over her shoulder as she turned away from him, eager to escape so she could be alone with her feelings and dissect them.

"Really?" he drawled. "Then please inform me exactly how I should convince a certain female that I want her as my duchess?"

She stilled, slowly turned around to face him. He didn't mean it. He couldn't. "You jest."

"Never again will I make light of your feelings. I hope you can offer me the same promise." He touched the ribbon round her neck again, light as gossamer wings. His finger curled about the end of the bow and tugged, causing the narrow bit of silk to unravel. Pulling it from her neck slowly, the rasp of soft fabric slid across her skin like a caress. She shivered, watched helplessly as he tucked the bit of ribbon in his coat pocket. "A keepsake. To remember the color of your gown the night I declared my renewed intentions for you."

"Henry." Her heart stilled, and she pressed her hand to her chest. "Don't say such things, especially if you don't mean . . ."

His fingers clasped around her upper arm, and he tugged her close. "I still want you, Eleanor. You wish for me to be honest, do you not?"

Her eyes slid closed, and his index finger drew across the bared flesh of her shoulder. "Yes," she said shakily.

"We are meant to be together as husband and wife. I will prove it to you, Lady Eleanor. Watch me."

He released her, walked away without another word. She watched him leave, admired the line of his broad shoulders, his long legs. He was a beautiful man, a duke who had just declared his intentions for her, who claimed he wanted her as his duchess.

She turned on her heeled slipper and fled in the opposite direction, pushing her way through the crowd, desperate for a familiar face. She saw her younger sister Olivia standing by a table laden with desserts, looking miserable, as a young gentleman with terrible skin tried to talk to her.

Determination filling her steps, Eleanor headed to her sister's side. It was best to worry and fret over others. She had family to take care of, a mother who grew weaker in spirit every day, a father who was a wastrel, and two younger sisters who desperately needed her guidance. How she wished she could ensure their futures as bright and happy with wonderful gentlemen who would know how to take care of them.

But she couldn't. She could merely help them navigate through the cruel, confusing world of the *ton*, hoping against all hope they would find their true loves. All while she settled for remaining in the background while Olivia and Penelope had their moments in the sun.

The promise in Henry's voice, that same promise matched the emotion in his gaze. She wanted to believe him, really she did, but it was so hard. After three long years, she finally acknowledged him, and he, in turn, declared that he still wanted her? It made absolutely no sense.

Chapter Three

LADY ELEANOR FITZSIMMONS answered the door when
Ashton knocked the next afternoon, breathless and
lovely in a day gown the color of fresh spring grass, a spot
of bright color on an otherwise dreary early-winter day.
The color complemented her creamy skin, made her hair
and eyes appear even darker, and for a moment, he felt a
little dizzy.

Such lush loveliness was almost too much to bear.

Removing his hat, he offered an informal bow. "Good
afternoon, Lady Eleanor. Quite a surprise to see you per-
forming the butler's duties, I must say."

She blushed prettily and curtsied in return. "Hello,
Your Grace. Unfortunately, our butler has taken ill this
afternoon." She offered a benign smile and opened the
door wider. "Won't you come in, please?"

He followed her inside the once-grand town house,
glancing about as she shut the door. The stairwell to his

left appeared unswept, the threadbare rug beneath his feet dusty and faded. Large squares of brighter-colored wallpaper where portraits once hung were everywhere. Indicating they'd sold each and every one of those old family paintings, most likely to pay for Cochrane's debts.

She lived in a virtual poorhouse, his pretty little sprite. The urge to whisk her away at this very moment and set her up in his Mayfair mansion was near overwhelming.

He slipped his hand into his trouser pocket, brushing the gold ring nestled within with his thumb. A talisman, giving him the strength to do what needed to be done.

Convince this woman to marry him once and for all.

"Is anyone else in residence?" The house was deathly quiet.

She shrugged impossibly slim shoulders as he followed her into the front parlor room. It featured more missing portraits, another faded, thin rug, and rickety chairs with spindly legs that looked as if they might snap were he to settle upon any of them. "My mother is upstairs. She's recently . . . taken ill."

"And your father?" His inquiry was both polite and with motive. He didn't want to deal with Cochrane today. The man would latch onto him and never let go. Funny, how a mere pittance of his fortune could wipe Cochrane's debts clean.

She turned to face him, her expression unreadable. "He's out." She offered nothing more, and he decided not to push.

A maid hovered in the corner of the room, her drab gray gown allowing her to blend. She came forward, indicated a tea service that sat on the low table in front of the settee. "Care for somethin' to drink, sir?"

"Molly, our guest is a duke. Please address him accordingly," Eleanor corrected, her voice kind.

"Oh, I'm so sorry, sir. I mean, Yer Grace." The maid bent in an awkward curtsy. "Are ye thirsty?"

Lady Eleanor briefly closed her eyes, shaking her head at the young woman's coarse accent and manners. Chuckling, he said, "I'm quite thirsty, as a matter of fact."

"Then let me pour you some tea." The maid beamed, and he settled himself in a fragile chair, swore it swayed and groaned beneath his weight. Molly handed him his cup and saucer, and he noted the thin crack near the cup's rim, how the saucer's pattern didn't match the cup's.

Lady Eleanor sat across from him, her green skirts spread out across the faded blue velvet settee, her expression sweetly demure. Her whispered thank you when the maid gave her the cup and saucer sent a rush of hot sensation through him, settling in his loins.

He wanted her. Desperately. Could only imagine her heated whispers in his ear while lying beneath him, urging him to go faster, deeper, harder . . .

Breaking out in a cold sweat, he clutched the cup and saucer in one hand, unable to tear his gaze from her. She sat as regal as a queen in the midst of the shabby parlor room, wearing her out-of-fashion gown and clutching a cracked teacup.

Utterly captivating. She didn't realize it yet, but she was made to be his duchess. She was made for *him,* and he'd known it from the first moment they met.

"You have a rather odd look about you," she said rather abruptly, sounding as rude as the maid she'd only just chastised. "Quite possessive, really."

"Indeed?" He sipped from his cup, the fragrant tea near scalding hot, burning his tongue. So she could read his moods well. That would both be an advantage to her in the future and a disadvantage to him in the present.

"You stalked into the house as if you owned it. Quite different from the last time you made an appearance." She drank serenely, her posture stiff perfection. As always, not a hair was out of place, and he wondered how long it took her maid to create such an elaborate coif.

Wondered more what Lady Eleanor might look like with all that dark hair unbound. He knew it to be thick with a slight wave, but he'd never seen it truly down. Did it hang to her waist or perhaps the middle of her back? And what might it look like, spread across his pillow in the early-morning light? Her body draped in nothing but a sheet, her skin would glow from the rising sun, wearing a lazy smile and nothing else as he approached her, ready to take her yet again.

"I suppose you were a different sort of man then," she continued, oblivious to his wayward thoughts, thank Christ. "Now that you're a duke, you must command every room you enter."

"Why, do you believe I command a room, my lady?" He liked the sound of that. Was arrogant enough to hope for her steadfast worship one day, for he would most certainly return the sentiment tenfold.

She studied him, her gaze narrowed, sharp. Seeming to see right through him, and the smallest drop of fear took hold in his gut, spreading outward. That hint of vulnerability she'd shown last evening had given him hope. At her home, in her element, she was able to don and wear her usual mask with quiet confidence.

He wanted to see her unnerved again.

"You're definitely more confident." She bent and set her cup and saucer on the table between them, her position offering a delectable view of her breasts. Round and ripe, he pondered what color her nipples might be. He'd felt them, once. Slipped his hand down the front of her bodice in a fit of mad kissing, brushed his thumb against the distended little piece of flesh until she moaned into his mouth.

Focus!

"With such a position settled upon me, I've had no choice but to embrace it," he explained drolly. "People depend on me, you see. I have to portray myself in a certain manner."

"One that was never expected of you before, I'm sure," she murmured, full of sympathy.

Which he absolutely did not want. "We do what we must and carry on." He met her gaze direct. "I've learned much since I inherited the dukedom."

"I'm sure." The sympathetic gaze she offered irritated, the drum of the rain beating against the windows setting him on edge.

A chill stole over him, and he glanced at the fireplace, saw that the fire burning within looked relatively new, hardly an ember in sight. It remained cold, the warmth from the fire having not permeated the room yet, and he wondered at that.

Wondered if the fire had been lit specifically for his visit.

He decided to get to the root of the matter. "What are your family's plans for the holiday?"

She startled at the question, clutched her slim, pale hands together in her lap. "We have no formal plans."

"No visit to the old Cochrane estate?" Ashton knew for a fact the old Cochrane estate was a drafty, crumbling ruin in the Yorkshire moors.

"I'm afraid not this holiday season." Her gaze met his for the briefest moment before she looked away. The little liar. They probably hadn't been to the estate in years.

He tsked. "A pity. I rather enjoy spending time with family during the holiday, away from the London minutiae. It's rather cozy in the country, especially when it snows."

She jerked her head in agreement. "Absolutely."

Her discomfort was palpable, a living, breathing thing settling in the room with them. He glanced about the parlor, noted that no pine boughs lined the mantel, no clusters of holly filled the empty, dusty vases. His mother had already come over and added a few touches to his home despite Christmas being a month away. "No decorations?"

"What?" Her voice was weak, and when he looked in her direction, her head was bent, studying those clutched hands of hers.

She was upset, and he was prodding her. Why, he

wasn't quite sure. Perhaps he wasn't as over her rejection as he'd originally thought. Perhaps he wanted confirmation her family was in dire need of financial assistance and quick. He could help her in so many ways, could make her life so much easier . . .

"In a house full of ladies, I would assume the entire place would be adorned with Christmas cheer." His mother and sister loved to decorate for the holidays, scouring the countryside for holly berries and bundles of mistletoe.

Lady Eleanor shrugged. "It is hard to find such adornments when one doesn't make many visits to the country. Besides, isn't it a bit early to be decorating?"

It was, though not necessarily for his family. "Such items are available for purchase," he suggested softly. He was searching for the truth, both wishing and dreading to hear her confession.

"For a premium." She sounded bitter as she glared at him. "I believe you've prodded enough, Your Grace. I do hope you've discovered what you wished to find."

He leaned back, the fragile chair creaking with the movement. Ah, now where was her impenetrable mask she was so skilled at wearing? Odd how when they were together, she didn't mince words, seemed quickly to grow weary of playing the game. For the second time in as many days, she'd called him out on his behavior.

He found he quite liked it, enjoyed the bit of banter that volleyed between them. Had a feeling all that fiery ferociousness would make her rather passionate in his bed. Memories of their past few shared embraces confirmed that possibility.

Hmm, a most delectable thought.

"Whatever do you mean, my lady?" He feigned surprise. Toying with her now when he should stop. He was being most unkind, and to the woman he wanted as his duchess. Why couldn't he stop?

He enjoyed the heated banter, the fire in her gaze, the emotion fairly vibrating from her body. Lady Eleanor was a pretty little thing when riled.

She rolled her eyes. "Don't play your silly little game with me, Your Grace. Would you like to hear how poor we are? I can offer you an endless list with all the lurid details. We could be here for hours while I offer you my tales of woe."

Being with her for hours didn't sound much like a hardship. "I have all afternoon."

"You're insufferable." She frowned.

"I've been told that once or twice." He tipped his head. Point one for Lady Eleanor.

"That you come into my home and taunt and tease me about our family's misfortunes is most cruel." Her lips pursed, she looked away, staring at the windows, the slashing rain beating a steady rhythm. "I believe your revenge has been accomplished, Your Grace. Perhaps it's time for you to leave."

She dismissed him. Even in her ragged state, her ragged home, and her ragged mood, she dismissed him like the regal queen that she inherently was. It made him want her even more.

Whereas he'd found her pretty and sweet before, with lips ripe for kissing, now she'd grown into full womanhood. She was a most apt opponent, an equal match. Intriguing and beautiful, ferocious and determined, he knew without a doubt she truly was the perfect duchess for him.

"I wanted to make a request before I go."

Lady Eleanor eyed him warily. "What sort of request?"

"An invitation to my home to celebrate the holiday." He smiled. "At my country estate."

"That is rather . . . impudent of you, don't you think?" She shook her head. "Why in the world would you invite me, the woman who rejected your proposal, for a family holiday?"

She did enjoy reminding him of her rejection. "Consider it a peace offering."

"I find that hard to believe." An unladylike snort punctuated her statement.

He ignored her sarcasm. "If I can forgive you for such a sound rejection, surely you can do me the honor and forgive me for any—rude comments I might've made toward you?" He smiled though deep within, nerves jangled wildly. He was a fool. Why would he allow himself to be rejected again? Was he a glutton for such torment?

No. Because he was still half in love with her. Complete and utter madness, but he couldn't deny it.

"I will consider your invitation." Her gaze met his direct. "If you invite my mother and sisters as well."

Her mother *and* her sisters? Well, he'd believed the mother would figure in. He couldn't have an unaccompanied young lady gallivanting about his estate. She'd be forever ruined.

But her two sisters as well? They were younger, the both of them on the cusp of debuting, and to have his approval would no doubt increase their social stature.

Hmm. He should've thought of this sooner.

Standing, he bowed, contained the smile that wanted to escape as he watched her reluctantly draw herself from the settee. "I will have a formal invitation delivered posthaste so that you and your family may make your plans."

"That will be fine." She lifted her chin. "Thank you for the invitation, Your Grace."

"Oh, it will be my pleasure, my lady," he drawled. Her cheeks turned a lovely shade of pink, and the sight caused his mouth to curve into a wicked smile, sent a dart of dark pleasure through him.

It would be his pleasure indeed.

Chapter Four

"An invitation. To the Duke of Ashton's country estate." The Countess of Cochrane set the elegant ecru-colored invitation on the table with a thump. "This is thrilling news!"

Eleanor winced. She knew her mother would be beyond excited at receiving any sort of missive from the duke. She'd half hoped he would disappoint her yet again and forget to send the invitation altogether.

But she'd had no such luck. It appeared with the other missives late this morning, accompanied by a bundle of letters from creditors. She'd spotted the elegant envelope immediately, the Ashton seal seeming to mock her as she studied it.

The thought of spending days on end at the mercy of Ashton in his home during the holiday season sounded like absolute torture.

And absolute bliss.

"What does this mean?" Eleanor's younger sister, Penelope, had such an expectant look on her face, Eleanor almost felt sorry for her. At the mere age of eighteen, the world was wide open, and she watched it all unfold with eager eyes.

"It means that a duke is giving you girls an endorsement!" their mother crowed. "I say, the Fitzsimmons sisters shall soon rule the *ton!*"

"Mother." Eleanor rested her hand over the countess's. She kept her voice calm, even. "I'm not sure if it's a good idea—"

"Nonsense," her mother interrupted, jerking her hand from beneath Eleanor's so she could wave it about, dismissing her eldest daughter's protests with a flick of her fingers. "It's a splendid idea. What else shall we do over the holiday? Freeze? Poor Hamilton is dreadfully ill because we can't keep the house well heated." She referred to their very old, very sickly butler. "All of London will be completely abandoned by the first of December. Many of them have already left. It's silly to remain, especially when we have a most coveted invitation from a *duke*."

"A duke who was once a mere second son, a man whose proposal I did not accept because Father told me not to." Eleanor paused, letting her words sink in. Did her mother forget the circumstances? Or was she so blinded by the title, it didn't matter who the man was. "I'm afraid the duke's motives aren't necessarily kind."

Lady Cochrane's eyebrows shot up nearly to her hairline. "Whatever do you mean?"

Her mother could be so daft sometimes.

Sighing, Eleanor shook her head, her gaze cutting to her sisters across the table, who watched the entire conversation with rapt attention. "You don't remember? Mr. Henry Stuart inherited the title when his older brother died. He is now the Duke of Ashton."

The grin that broke out on her mother's face could've brightened all of gloomy, rainy London. "Why, that's marvelous! Fantastic, encouraging news. We can give him what he always wanted." She paused, a titter escaping in the silence before she finally burst out with one damning word. "*You*."

Dread plummeted into Eleanor's already churning stomach. "He doesn't want me," she said weakly.

"I find that hard to believe. He's pined for you since the rejection. So, so foolish of me," she muttered. "How could I forget? We have much planning now, my dear. A tremendous amount of planning must occur. We need to make you presentable to the duke."

"But what about us?" Penelope pouted, while her elder-by-two-years sister, Olivia, gave her a withering stare. As the baby of the family, Penelope believed all eyes and attention should always be on her. "If the duke is supposedly so enamored of Eleanor, which doesn't make a bit of sense since she's practically a spinster, then what are we supposed to do while at his estate?"

"Oh, I don't know, perhaps endear yourself to the duke so you can receive an endorsement from him upon the next season?" Their mother shook her head. "Sometimes, you can be a rather disappointing creature, Penelope. One must look at a duke as an advantage to one's station. It does not matter if he's interested in you in a romantic manner or not. If he wishes to invite us into his household, we must be on our very best behavior."

"But I want to be a duchess. It's not fair that Ellie might be one." Penelope scowled.

"Stop acting the spoiled brat for once, will you?" Olivia whispered underneath her breath.

"Both of you stop," Eleanor said wearily. "I doubt the duke has designs on me. I truly believe it's some sort of revenge plot. For all I know, he plans on offering for one of you just to get back at me for rejecting him so cruelly." The thought of it, the mere idea of Henry's marrying one of her sisters, sent her stomach pitching and roiling like the most turbulent sea.

"Oh. So there's a chance, then." Pure delight lit Penelope's pretty blue gaze. She was the most attractive of the sisters, with golden brown hair and skin the color of alabaster, features as fine and delicate as a porcelain doll. Her devious mind and childish ways needed some improving, as did her rather selfish behavior.

She'd been indulged her entire life, even during the last few years of extreme hardship. Everyone did their best to protect Lady Penelope. Eleanor knew that Olivia held some resentment about it but otherwise remained quiet. She was the bookish sister, the one most didn't notice. Such a terrible shame. Olivia was quite the intelligent conversationalist.

And Eleanor was the responsible one. The calm, unruffled, eldest sister who tried her best to keep the entire household together, even her parents.

Especially her parents.

"Don't get your hopes up," Olivia muttered, crossing her arms in front of her chest. "He probably won't notice you."

Eleanor shot a chastising look toward Olivia. At twenty, she still hadn't been given a proper season and was looking a bit long in the tooth for it as well, especially since Penelope's debut was coming up soon.

They would have to share, their mother had declared but a fortnight ago. They could come out at the same time, during the same season. Not that their parents could afford to hold a ball in their honor. Nor could they provide them with new wardrobes, though both girls had each been lucky enough to gain a new gown.

"Let's not turn this into a competition." Eleanor smiled at her sisters. "If we really are going to the duke's estate for the holiday, then let's follow his lead. After all, we'll be in his home, spending time with his family. It's only proper to do as he wishes."

"That's a good idea, Ellie," Olivia said, nodding once. "You're always so practical."

"Indeed she is." The countess smiled. "Such practicality in a young lady, my dear Ellie. Why, you'd probably make a better wife for an estate manager or merchant, wouldn't you? Not that any daughter of mine is going to marry someone with working-class roots, oh, no. That would be the last thing I would wish upon my daughters . . ."

Eleanor ignored her mother's tirade, focusing instead on the fact that in a fortnight's time, they would be at

Ashton's estate. Isolated, in the middle of the country-side, with nowhere to go and no chance to escape. Would he continue his pursuit of her? Or was he drawing her and her family there to flaunt another woman in front of her and make her look stupid?

Or worse, would he flaunt his flirtation with one of her sisters before her? Olivia wouldn't purposely do such a thing, she was a far more sensitive sort, but the duke was quite charming. On the other hand, Penelope would love rubbing in her eldest sister's face that she snatched the duke and Eleanor didn't.

It was a strange predicament, one she never believed she'd find herself in. Regret had kicked her swiftly for years, especially after he'd become the duke. She'd been younger and foolish, still starry-eyed in the midst of her debut year, believing plenty of possibilities lay before her. Worse, believing every lie her father told her.

Mister Henry Stuart had been quite kind, quite af-fable, and rather handsome. Dark and mysterious and charming and a tad roguish, all that intense masculinity had scared her. Thrilled her. Those few cherished stolen moments she'd experienced in his arms, his hands moving swiftly all over her body, his mouth pressed to hers . . .

A shuddering sigh escaped her, and she shook her head.

Despite her worry, she wanted to experience such moments with him again. Desperately.

Chapter Five

Two weeks later

ELEANOR RESORTED TO lying.

It was the only way to remove herself from the terror, the ferocious storm that was her mother and sisters. The constant bickering, the glib remarks from Penelope, the not-so-gentle chastising from their mother, she couldn't take it any longer.

So she'd feigned a headache and begged off yet another boring afternoon of playing cards or writing letters with her family and other female guests in residence, including the duke's lovely sister, Lady Serena, who was the same age as Penelope.

And far more tolerable though Eleanor was loath to admit it. She didn't wish to think ill of her family, but . . .

Supposedly returning to the guest bedchamber for a nap, she'd slipped down an unknown corridor, deciding to do a bit of exploring. The Ashton country manor was unlike any she'd ever seen in her life. A cavernous mansion with endless wings and long hallways, all with a dizzying number of closed doors, she'd been dazzled from the first moment they arrived. Only a few short days ago, they'd come, the countess sure one of her daughters was going to walk away from this holiday party a future duchess.

Eleanor didn't know how to break it to her mother that the duke didn't appear the least bit interested. Not in her, not in her sisters, not in . . . anyone. Their hostess was the duchess, a rather forceful woman who led every bit of entertainment within the household with a stern hand and knowing stare. Why, she'd told Penelope last night after supper, "Do be quiet, won't you? Must you always run your mouth?"

That had sent her sister into a sulk that was still evident this afternoon.

Sighing, Eleanor caught sight of an open door and increased her steps, eager to peek inside. She had no idea where the duke was. He'd made himself scarce, offering a pleasant, polite greeting to them upon their arrival but otherwise staying out of the thick of it. He spent most of his time participating in manly sports out in the drizzling, freezing rain with his younger brother, Lord Tristan.

And if the duke wasn't with Lord Tristan, then Olivia was. Quite an interesting situation, that.

As she drew closer, she noticed that a light glowed from within, casting a beam of gold across the otherwise darkening corridor. Outside, the clouds were near black, bloated and hanging low, a storm imminent, full with the promise of snow. Already, a hard, stinging rain fell, the drops hitting the windows with precise, pinging force.

That shaft of light beckoned, promising a cozy warmth she was suddenly desperate to experience.

She stepped through the open doorway, all the air seeming to leave her in an exhilarated gust. The quiet hush of the room enveloped Eleanor as she stepped farther inside, as if she had entered something quite majestic. She looked around, awed by the subtle display of excess.

The walls were constructed of a rich, warm, wood paneling, and paintings featuring dour-faced ancestors who watched her with skeptical eyes as she passed by. The Oriental rug beneath her feet was plush and thick, the color a vibrant red with an intricate, woven pattern of gold and varying shades of green. A vast array of books lined the many built-in shelves, all meticulously lined up by size and color. A gently flickering fire burned within the fireplace, there was an impressive picture window that looked out upon the wintry gardens, and a grand mahogany desk was situated in the corner.

She went to the desk, her gaze drinking in the items placed neatly on top. Nothing out of place, not a speck of dust appeared, and she wondered how many servants it took to keep this mausoleum in such an utter state of perfection. The study was immaculate, all for a man who was rarely in attendance. She wondered how often the duke frequented his country estate.

Feeling brave, she rounded the desk and eyed the chair for a quick moment before she decided to settle in. She rested her hands on the edge of the desk, contemplating the view around her. Who could ever get much work done, what with the beautiful outdoors calling from beyond the sparkling-clean window? Staring at the fireplace, watching the fire crackle and spark within would certainly prove a distraction. But, of course, her mother always told her she was too much of a dreamer. All the books—so many of them would sorely tempt her to pick one up and indulge in a few hours of enjoyable reading.

It didn't sound like such a bad thing, losing herself in a fictional world, where the characters were happy and at peace with their station in life.

Sighing, she traced the edge of the desk with her index finger. What would it be like, to have such a fortune? To have every fanciful whim met with but a mere request? The Duke of Ashton was one of the most powerful dukes in all of England. With such vast wealth, he could have everything his heart desired.

Except for a wife, she thought idly. He truly was all the talk amongst the gossips. Who would marry Henry—she'd heard that question asked more than once since he'd inherited the title. Everyone wanted to know. Every lady wanted a chance too.

She'd had her chance—and turned him down.

Frowning, she tapped her finger on the edge of a thick journal. It was too ridiculous to even try and comprehend. Despite his inviting her here, despite all the heated promise she'd detected from that personal invitation the afternoon he'd called at her house, he didn't spend time with her now. When it mattered, when he should be flirting and wooing and convincing her that maybe they did belong together after all.

It was frightfully embarrassing, how little she might need convincing.

She picked up a silver letter opener and checked her reflection in the flat side of the heavy blade. No, she wasn't a grotesque beast. But she tended to get flustered in the company of a man, and, well, perhaps he didn't find her particularly interesting when she acted the fool.

Sighing, she set the letter opener back in its silver cup and rested her elbow on the desk. Propped her chin on her fist and stared at the open door. No one passed by, and it was blessedly, deliciously quiet. She'd craved silence, being around her sisters and mother day in and day out. Glancing toward the window, she watched in mute fascination as the first gentle snowflakes began to fall. White bits of fluff drifting through the air, dotting the barren ground, easing the sting of all that angry rain.

"Are you in hiding?"

Eleanor glanced up to find Ashton standing in the doorway, as if her mind had conjured him, contemplating her with an amused glint in his eyes. Clad in buckskin breeches that clung to his muscular legs and shirtsleeves and a dark blue waistcoat that emphasized his broad shoulders and chest, he was, in a word, magnificent.

Her cheeks heated with embarrassment, she removed herself from the chair behind the desk. His observation was correct. His observations of her were almost always correct.

A rather unnerving trick of his.

"Perhaps," she answered vaguely, trailing her fingers along the edge of the desk as she came around it. She sent a glance his way, noticed that his gaze was locked upon her wandering fingers, and she snatched her hand away, clutching the both of them in front of her.

"And if I may ask, what or whom are you hiding from?" He entered the room, stopping just before her. His arms went behind his back, and he stood there, legs slightly spread, expectant expression on his face.

Well, this was embarrassing. How awful would she look, running away from her family? "I didn't answer properly as to if I was hiding in the first place, Your Grace."

"I assume you are if you're lurking about in here." He nodded toward the chair behind the desk. "Did you find it comfortable?"

She glanced behind her. "Find what comfortable?"

"The chair." She turned back to look at him in question. "You were sitting in my chair when I entered the room."

"Yes, about that." She clutched her fingers tight, uncomfortable with his observations. "I don't know what possessed me. I'm assuming this is your study?" At her question, he nodded, and she continued on. "And I'm sure you're appalled at how I've lurked about in your private sanctuary, sitting behind your desk as if I belong here."

His gaze smoldered as he studied her. "I wouldn't consider myself appalled at finding you all alone in my study," he drawled, settling into one of the armchairs that faced the desk. "Though you might be appalled at the thoughts presently running through my mind at finding you."

The man was an utter devil. If her cheeks grew any

hotter, they would surely burst into flame. "I would probably be horrified." She shook her head and decided to sit next to him in the matching armchair. It felt good, to be back in his presence, silly as that was. She'd missed seeing him, talking to him, arguing with him.

Eleanor frowned. She should leave. Pick up her skirts and flee from this room and this man who tempted her. Scared her. Made her want so much.

Too much.

Ashton inclined his head toward her. "May I ask you a question?"

Wariness curled through her. "You may."

"Do you find me a stuffy old gent?"

"What? Absolutely not," Eleanor said, surprised at the question. "Whyever would you ask?"

He shrugged those impossibly broad shoulders. "My brother complained to me earlier. Said I'd changed. I told him I had no choice in the matter. I had to change."

"Of course you did," she agreed with a nod.

"But I don't particularly care being called a stuffy gent, as you may understand." His gaze met hers, his lips curled in the faintest smile. "I was rather carefree in my younger years."

"Too carefree, I'm assuming?" She plucked at a loose thread in her dark blue gown, her skin warm. This was a most intimate conversation they were having.

"For my current position, yes."

"Mayhap your brother merely misses the old you and wishes to recapture those fond memories of the two of you spending time together," she suggested, understanding unfurling within her. She wondered if her sisters felt the same way about her, wished they were younger, and she didn't have such pressing responsibility upon her all the time.

"Perhaps your observation is correct." He studied her. "My apologies for not spending much time with you and your family since you arrived. I've been rather busy entertaining my brother."

"Brothers should come first."

"A brother I see as often as I want. Lovely guests such as the Countess of Cochrane and her beautiful daughters deserve my undivided attention." His smile grew, and she sucked in a breath, coughing after such quick inhalation.

He shouldn't shock her so with such a staggering smile. It wasn't seemly. "Your flattery knows no bounds," she finally gasped out.

"I speak the truth."

"Have you spent time with my mother and sisters? You might be singing a different tune after a few days in their constant company."

He chuckled, the sound warming her insides. Pleasure unfurled deep within her, cascading languidly through her veins, and she couldn't help the slow smile that spread across her face. "It's true, you know."

"I've observed a few—tense moments."

"'Tense' is a kind way to phrase it. Uncomfortable, more like." She shook her head, slowly realizing just how risky this moment was. Together alone, without a chaperone in sight. If they were caught, surely she would be compromised. And surely Ashton would do the right thing.

Marry her rather than risk sullying her good name.

"You have a rather calming nature, Lady Eleanor." His low murmur caused her to turn toward him, their gazes meeting. "I'm surprised you don't use it to its full effect when in the presence of your arguing sisters and mother."

"When they're arguing, they don't listen to me." She chewed on her lower lip. "You think I've a calming influence?"

He slowly nodded, his gaze never leaving hers. "There are many things I think about you."

Her lips slowly parted. "Really?" The word came out a rusty gasp, and she cleared her throat. "You think of me?"

"All the time."

Those three simple words rendered her utterly still. The Duke of Ashton thought of her? That he would make such an admission so easily was staggering—and hard to believe. "Still plotting my revenge, I take it?"

"That accusation has grown rather tired, don't you think?"

He spoke so quietly, she had to lean closer to hear him. "I don't quite understand what you mean, Your Grace."

"I'm trying to tell you that I find you unforgettable."

"Oh." She released a shuddering breath, dropped her gaze to her lap, and squeezed her hands together tightly. She didn't know what to say. "You do?"

"I do." The low rumble of his voice sent tingles scattering across her skin.

Her throat dry, she swallowed hard, trying her best to find words. "I—I appreciate the compliment, Your Grace, but it isn't necessary," she finally said, her gaze lifting once more to find him watching her, his gaze lingering on her chest. Her skin warmed under his blatant perusal.

"A lady should never refuse a compliment, no matter how ill given," he said softly when his gaze met hers.

They sat together in a silence fraught with sensual tension. It was so quiet, the snow falling heavier outside the window now, the only sound within the room their gentle breathing. His scent reached her, sandalwood and spice and pure man.

It unnerved her, made her yearn for things she shouldn't want. Why could she not believe the things he told her? She still felt he'd rather seek his revenge upon her.

It was easier to believe he had ill intentions, what she expected. That he still wanted her, had no issue in letting her have such knowledge, nearly unraveled her.

"Come here," he quietly urged, reaching a bare hand out toward her.

She took it without thinking and stood, allowed him to pull her toward him so she stood before his chair. He tilted his head back, threading his fingers through hers as he studied her. Even through the fine fabric of her gloves, his touch burned. "Has anyone ever told you how beautiful you are?"

Slowly, she shook her head, captivated by the gleam in his eyes, the sound of his voice. Her breath left her in shuddering spurts, her body was flushed and hot, and her knees threatened to buckle. "Only you, Your Grace," she murmured.

He muttered a curse and tugged, causing her to tumble

into his lap. She gasped at first contact, her bottom nestled on his muscular thighs, her hands settling upon his broad, hard chest. Even through the layers of clothing, she could feel the sizzling heat of his skin. Wished that she could unbutton his waistcoat, remove his carelessly knotted cravat, and spread open the collar of his shirt. Press her lips to the center of his chest . . .

"You undo me," he murmured, cupping her face with one large, bare hand, forcing her to meet his stark gaze. His fingertips were rough, his touch gentle. "I cannot think with you so near."

"You're the one who brought me near," she pointed out, whimpering when he drew her head to his.

Chuckling, he brushed his mouth against hers, a teasing touch of damp lips and warm breath. "That you amuse me even during such a passionate moment confirms my suspicions."

"And wh—" She swallowed hard, closed her eyes when he pressed his mouth to her cheek again. And again. "What are your suspicions?"

"Why, you were made for me, Eleanor, and no one else."

Before she could reply, he kissed her, those full, seductive lips nipping at her mouth, gently coercing her to open for him. She did so willingly, her body remembering his and responding with unrestrained eagerness.

With an agonized groan, he took the kiss deeper, his tongue sweeping inside her mouth, his hand still clutching her cheek. She curled her hands into the fabric of his waistcoat, ran her fingers along the row of buttons. Not daring enough to do what she truly wished.

Undress him and expose his beautiful, masculine body to her greedy eyes.

"You still want me," he whispered against her mouth when he broke the kiss. "Admit it."

"I shouldn't." She tilted her head back as he blazed a hot trail with his damp mouth. As his member stiffened beneath her bottom, she knew that he was greatly aroused, and the realization both thrilled and scared her.

If she gave in to him, would he still want her afterward? Or was he merely using her so he could trick her and leave her the fool?

Wrenching her mouth from his, she braced her hands against his chest, giving them some much-needed space. He blinked at her, his brows furrowed in confusion. "What? Why did you stop me?"

"I—I don't know if I can do this." She nibbled her lower lip.

"You want to." He reached toward her, and she pressed him back with her hands. "Isn't that enough?"

Eleanor shook her head. "I want to believe your intentions are good . . ."

He frowned. "But you don't."

"I can't," she whispered. "Don't you see how I must feel? Three years after my refusal, and you suddenly reappear rather forcefully in my life? Saying that you still want me and are most determined to make me your wife?"

"I have always been in your life. You just never noticed."

"I always noticed." She did. No matter where she was, an intimate musicale, a grand ball, a night out at the opera, there he would be. Watching. Waiting, always in the background, always nearby. "Y—you frighten me, if you must know."

"How?" He touched her, and she allowed it, reveled in it despite her worry. Spreading his hand wide, he drew his fingers down the side of her face, along the length of her neck, before curling his hand into a loose fist and rubbed his knuckles gently against her throat. "You must trust me. I want nothing but the best for you. And I believe I can be the one to give it to you."

"But why now? After all these years?" She closed her eyes, her every nerve ending focused on where he touched her. He drew his curled fist down her front, across her chest, brushing his knuckles against her breasts.

"I finally gave in to the need to admit my feelings." She opened her eyes, saw all the stark need shining in the depths of his gaze. "What sort of man would I be if I cannot confess to the lady I want to make my wife how I feel?"

"And how do you feel? Do you—do you love me?" She wanted to snatch the words back the moment they fell from her lips but it was too late. She'd said them.

Such a silly, foolish girl.

For once upon a time, not so long ago, she'd believed herself in love with Lord Henry Stuart. And she knew it wouldn't take much for her to fall in love with him all over again.

"Ah, Eleanor." He smiled, looking rather boyish. She could only imagine him a young, mischievous child, full of life, giving his mama and nanny much trouble. How sweetly naughty he must've been. And oh, how he'd grown into a dark, deliciously wicked man. "You ask for so much."

"I simply ask for the truth." Pressing her lips together, she tried to escape from his lap, but he tightened his arm about her waist, keeping her in place. "Let me go."

"I want to be honest with you." He gave her a little shake. "Look at me."

She met his gaze at his roughly spoken command, a forbidden thrill sparkling through her at the sensation of his fingers pressed into her hip. Her body throbbed with his hands upon her. "What?"

"Love is a very confusing thing. I know I like you." Leaning in, he pressed a sweet kiss to her temple. "I know I desire you." Another longer, lingering kiss to her cheek. "I enjoy being in your company and can think of nothing else but bedding you." This time he kissed her mouth, his tongue tracing the outline of her lower lip.

She gasped and pulled away. "Wanting to bed me and loving me are two different things."

"Do you love me, my lady?"

"I . . ." The words died in her throat. She couldn't say them. Couldn't know if they were true. "I don't know," she said morosely.

"Then we are both in agreement." He pressed his cheek to hers, inhaling deep. "Meet me later tonight. After supper."

She shouldn't. She was only asking for trouble. "Where?" she asked breathlessly. Could she not help herself? Such foolishness only brought trouble.

"Here in my study. Please, Eleanor. Let me prove to you how much you mean to me."

How she wanted to believe him. Everything that was happening was so quick, so confusing, yet it was also her most secret wish coming true. "I don't know."

"Say yes, my darling. Say yes."

Lifting her lids, she met his turbulent gaze. Reaching out, she rested her hand on his smooth cheek, trailed her fingers across his warm skin. "Yes."

Closing his eyes, he turned his head, pressed his hot mouth to her chilled palm. "You won't regret it," he murmured against her flesh.

Eleanor could only hope he spoke the truth.

Chapter Six

ASHTON WAS AS hard as a rock all through supper. To-night of all nights, his mother had seated Eleanor directly across from him, giving him a perfect view of this woman who tempted him beyond reason.

The light of the candles cast a golden glow on her creamy skin. The midnight blue gown she wore had sleeves that fell from her shoulders, revealing smooth, delicate skin he wanted to kiss and nibble. A narrow strip of matching blue ribbon wound around her elegant neck yet again, driving him absolutely mad. Her breasts were pushed up most becomingly within her corset, plumping over the edge of her lacy bodice, and his cock twitched every time she bent over her plate.

He'd give anything to tug the fabric down and bare her breasts for his eyes only. Suck her delectable nipples deep into his mouth until she writhed beneath him, begging for more. Begging for him . . .

"You're in a mood," Tristan muttered. He sat to Ashton's left, Lady Olivia directly across from him, and he sent a scowl toward the lovely young lady that would've sent rabid, crazed wolves running.

Lady Olivia merely flashed him a secretive smile before resuming her conversation with her older sister.

"So are you," Ashton noted, setting his fork and knife across his plate. It was pointless to eat. His stomach had churned with nerves throughout the meal.

What if she refused to meet him? He didn't know what he might do.

"Women." Tristan shook his head, then gulped from his wineglass. "I don't understand them."

"Neither do I, little brother." Ashton shook his head with a soft chuckle. "Neither do I."

Tristan shot him a disbelieving glance. "I find that hard to fathom. You usually have to beat them off with a stick."

"They only want my title and everything that comes with it. A lady who truly loves me for me, well, she's worth all the riches in the land," he drawled.

"You believe so?"

"Absolutely." Ashton nodded, sliding a look toward Lady Eleanor.

She blatantly studied him, her lips pursed, her eyes narrowed. As if she contemplated him to the very depths of his soul and wasn't sure she liked what she found. Unnerving, to say the least.

"What of Lady Eleanor?" When Ashton glared at him, Tristan chortled. "You don't have to speak of her for me to realize you still have feelings for the chit."

"And what is it to you?" Misery coursed through his veins, heavily mixed with irritation. Was he that obvious? He'd prefer not to be. He'd been accused more than once during his younger years of wearing his emotions for all to see.

"I know you're my older brother and the bloody duke and all that nonsense, but I worry about you." Tristan paused, letting his words sink in. "You've carried a *tendre* for Lady Eleanor for years."

"I have, it's true." It was pointless to deny it. He'd embraced honesty, starting earlier with his confession to Eleanor.

"And she turned you down once before."

"Because her father made her. I wasn't the one with the title. And Robert hadn't been interested." His blood boiled at the thought of *any* man interested in Eleanor.

He found her back in his arms, and already he'd laid claim to her.

"And you don't find it odd that she is in your life once more? Now you have the title and the wealth and the money to pay for her father's outrageous debt?" Tristan's brow rose in question.

"I pursued her, Tristan. Let me make that clear. And she could've come after me the moment after Robert died. I've been the duke for well over a year. Not once did she so much as try to speak to me during that entire time."

"Perhaps she didn't believe she had a chance with you. Once you made it known that indeed, she does, now she's in hot pursuit." Tristan shook his head and made a little tsking noise. "You're taking a risk."

"Taking a risk is letting a woman know your feelings for her and not expecting anything in return," Ashton said, his blood running hot. "What do you know of that, hmm?"

"I know nothing," Tristan answered flatly, his gaze unerringly returning to Lady Olivia, albeit briefly. "I don't believe in love."

"I used not to either." Their father had been a cold bastard, their eldest brother much the same. Their mother had learned to endure, and so she wasn't one for showing emotions even in private. Only their little sister Serena was open and guileless.

And that worried Ashton to no end.

"What made you change your mind?" Tristan asked, jarring Ashton from his thoughts.

"The right lady," Ashton answered, his gaze flickering across the table.

Found her watching him yet again, a sweet smile curling her lips, clutching her glass in her hand. *God's teeth, she's beautiful.*

"She wants you?" Tristan sounded incredulous.

"I believe she does."

"Then why are you wasting your time sitting here with me at this bloody boring dinner party?" Tristan sighed. "Go after her, man."

"I cannot pursue her in the middle of supper."

"Mother might become upset," Tristan muttered with disgust.

"I would imagine?" Ashton asked sardonically. He lowered his voice. "After dinner, we are to meet."

"Indeed?" Both of Tristan's eyebrows rose. "Rather risky of you, isn't it?"

Ashton shrugged, idly rubbed the tablecloth with the tips of his fingers. "I'm wooing her."

"Trying your best to seduce her, of that I haven't any doubt."

"Perhaps." A smile tickled the corners of his mouth. "She's receptive. I must take my chances where I can."

"If you're found with her, that's it. It's over for you."

"What do you mean?" Ashton glanced at his brother.

"You'd have to marry her then or risk ruining her. And we know you wouldn't do that."

Why in the world would Tristan believe he wouldn't marry Eleanor? Had he not just made his intentions clear? "It wouldn't be such a bad thing, as I've been trying to tell you." He tore his gaze from Tristan's, watched the youngest Fitzsimmons daughter argue with her mother. Again.

"Are you serious?"

"Of course I'm serious. I'm an honorable man, and I would do right by Lady Eleanor. Besides, it wouldn't be a hardship, marrying her." Ashton paused. "It might be what I'm after if I'm being truthful."

"I see."

Did his brother see? Ashton allowed his thoughts to wander. Marrying Lady Eleanor, making her his duchess, would be the best thing he could ever do with his life. He needed a duchess. He cared for Eleanor, more than any other woman. But did he love her?

One didn't need love in a marriage for it to work.

Look at most of the couples within the *haute ton*. Many of them despised each other, which in turn drove them to another's bed.

But Ashton didn't want to find himself in another's bed. He wanted only Eleanor.

And he was about to prove it to her, too.

Chapter Seven

ELEANOR WANDERED DOWN the hall, glancing to and fro, searching amongst the long shadows. She had no idea where Ashton was. Only knew that he had pulled her aside after dinner, reminding her to meet him in his study in twenty minutes, which was now.

Shivers moved through her as she recalled exactly the way he whispered those illicit words in her ear. Softly, his voice so deep it had reverberated throughout her body. His lips so close to her ear she'd felt them move against her sensitive flesh, the hot gush of his breath. A touch so shockingly intimate and so decadently delicious she still savored it.

Reminding her of that earlier moment in his study, when he'd pulled her into his lap, held her so closely to his body she'd felt his need for her press against her bottom.

She wanted to feel him again. Now. Every night for the rest of her life . . .

Entering the study, she glanced about, but he was no-where to be found. A fire burned in the hearth, its gently flickering light casting shadows that danced upon the walls. He wasn't sitting at his desk or in one of the over-stuffed chairs by the fireplace.

Where could he be?

How he teased. She didn't believe he had it in him. He was so confident, commanding, a polite yet sensual gentleman, and so very smart. Witty. Interesting both to talk to and suddenly so very interested in her once more, which she found delightfully shocking. And worrying, she still couldn't deny it.

Yet when he looked at her, it was as if he saw no one else in the room. When he spoke to her, it was as if his words were for her alone.

She loved that. She believed she could love *him*.

Idiot girl.

Eleanor rested trembling fingers against her lips. How scandalized all of society would be! Her mother would be thrilled. So would her father, if he could rouse himself from his usual drunken stupors to acknowledge the fact that his daughter would become a duchess.

Most would say she was using Ashton for his money. So he could help her destitute family. Some might even say he bought her.

But Eleanor didn't really care about his wealth or what the *ton* thought of them. All she wanted was him.

She swept through the large study, going deeper into the shadows, eager to find him. Outside, it was dark, the thick clouds obliterating the moon and stars. The snow had stopped, but the rain had resumed. A steady beat against the windows that seemed to calm her racing, excited heart.

And then she saw him. Saw him the exact moment he noticed her, and she rushed to where he stood in the doorway. Throwing herself into his arms, he caught her with a chuckle. Shut the door behind them with a quiet click and held her. Against the wood paneling of the door, his body nudged so intimately to hers, they were a perfect fit.

"You're late," he murmured, nuzzling his face alongside hers, his finger tracing the ribbon she'd tied earlier about her throat.

"I'm sorry. It took a while to get away from my mother and the duchess." Her voice hitched, her breathing lodged in her throat when she felt his lips skim her cheek. "They wouldn't stop talking."

Ashton chuckled, his arms tightening around her waist. "I know of what you speak. Their incessant chatter can go on for hours."

"Yes. My sisters are no better." She rested her hands on his chest, her fingers curling into the fine fabric of his waistcoat. He'd changed for dinner, looking more magnificent than ever. "I missed you," she confessed softly, her heart in her throat, her stomach fizzing with nerves. The confession took a great deal, but once the words left her, she felt nothing but relief.

This was all she'd ever wanted. Being with this man, locked tight in Henry's arms. That she was given this second chance was almost too good to be true.

He smiled and bent his head, his mouth close to hers. "I missed you too."

Their lips met, clung, lips parting, tongues searching. He tasted delicious, like the sherry he'd indulged in earlier. He smelled of leather and tobacco, a hint of spice, an edge that was his own masculine scent. She wound her arms around his neck, threaded her fingers through his silky-soft hair, pressing down on his nape so he would deepen the kiss.

He did as she silently bid, curled his tongue around hers, his hands sliding up and down her sides, coming ever closer to her breasts with every pass. She broke the kiss first, her heart racing, her head spinning, and he blatantly cupped her breasts, their gazes meeting as he kneaded her flesh through the confines of her stays.

"Such bounty," he whispered. "Do you remember how I used to . . ."

"Stop." She pressed her fingers to his lips, and he gently bit the tips, causing her to yelp and yank her hand away. "Don't speak of it. Please."

"Ah, don't be shy, my sweet, sweet Eleanor." He slowly drew his thumbs back and forth across the front of her breasts, her nipples beading painfully beneath his teasing touch. "I cannot forget the little sounds you made when I slipped my hand beneath your bodice and circled your nipples with my thumb."

Her body tingled with the memory, her thighs shaking. "Henry," she murmured, unable to articulate what she needed.

Groaning, he swept her into his arms, carried her

to the settee that sat near the large picture window that overlooked the grand gardens. Gently, he laid her down, her head propped on the settee's arm, her skirts spread out around her.

He sat on the opposite end and pulled her feet into his lap, his hands curving around the heel of her slippers. With infinite care, he slipped her shoes off, his fingers curving around her heels, burning her through her stockings. All the while, he watched her, her shoes dropping to the floor with a soft thump as he slid his hands up beneath her skirts, touching her places no man had dared go before.

"Your skin is so soft," he murmured, his expert hands massaging her calves.

She bit her lower lip, desperate to contain the moan that wanted to escape. But it was no use. His magical hands felt too good, and, finally, she tilted her head back and whimpered, licking her lips when his fingers skimmed the back of each knee. His hands went higher, brushing against the ribbons at the tops of her stockings before he touched the bare skin of her thighs.

"Henry." His name came out a rushed exhalation when he stroked the sensitive skin of her inner thighs, pushing between so she had no choice but to spread her legs to his seeking touch.

Glancing up, his gaze met hers, dark and wild, the heat within nearly scorching her. "I'm moving too fast, aren't I, love? Forgive me."

Without warning, he came up over her, his hands pressed on either side of her head, fingers curled around the edge of the settee, his body melding with hers. Her spread legs accommodated him perfectly, and he settled between them, her skirts puffing up around them.

"Christ, you're beautiful," he whispered before he took her mouth in a searing kiss, his tongue thrusting deep.

She could do nothing but take his delicious kiss, smoothing her hands down his back, subtly urging him closer. He trembled beneath her touch, his muscles bunched and hard as rocks, vibrant intensity rolling off him in potent waves. She tried to coax his kiss into gentleness. Drawing away from him before pressing her lips to his once more, she slowed him down, rested her hand against his cheek as she slid her thumb across his jaw.

"See how you calm me?" he asked once he broke the kiss. "I touch you, and all I want to do is take. Take, take, take."

She smiled, traced his lips with the tip of her finger. "There's no need to rush."

"I know." He closed his eyes and hung his head. "God, I know. I've waited for this moment with you for so long. Relived our last intimate encounter over and over again in my mind in the hopes it would happen again."

"After all this time . . ." She swallowed hard, the swell of emotion rising within her threatening to take over. "I cannot believe you still feel this way about me."

"Do you feel for me, Eleanor?" He wrapped his fingers about her wrist, holding her hand in place. "Do you still care?"

"I wronged you," she whispered, her throat raw. "In the worst way imaginable, and I am so, so sorry."

He squeezed her wrist. "You're forgiven, love. Now tell me. Do you want to be with me?"

Slowly, she nodded, squeaked when he leaned in and gave her a brutal kiss. His hands were everywhere, his fingers tugging at the front of her gown, brushing against the tops of her breasts.

She couldn't breathe, couldn't think, could only feel. His heated breath against her bare flesh, his nimble fingers slid beneath her bodice, touching her breasts. She arched beneath him, frightened yet wanting more.

So much more . . .

"Good lud, what is this?" screeched a familiar voice from above.

Icy cold panic filled her, and Eleanor scrambled to push Henry away. He stumbled off the settee, standing before her while she struggled to right her gown. "Lady Cochrane," he said, his voice calm, his breathing anything but. "What a surprise."

"I should say so, you scoundrel." She whacked his shoulder with her fan. "What are you doing with your hands all over my Eleanor?"

"Mother, please." Eleanor stood behind him, rested her hand briefly on his back. She wanted him to know that she wasn't upset. She would stand beside him despite what was going to unfold.

For she knew it was about to become horrific.

Chapter Eight

TRISTAN HAD SET them up. Ashton knew it from the moment he saw Eleanor's mother standing before him, her eyes blazing, her body shaking with righteous anger. He glanced over her shoulder, saw Tristan looming in the doorway, a knowing smile curving his mouth.

Damn his brother. He didn't want it to happen like this. Never like this. He wasn't one to make a public spectacle.

And the last thing he wanted was to humiliate Eleanor.

"What say you about this—this compromising position you've put my daughter in, Your Grace?" She slapped him with her folded fan again, and damn if it didn't sting. "She's a good girl. I will not have you dragging her name through the mud like she's some sort of cheap harlot. Or allow you to treat her as _your_ harlot no matter your position, Your Grace."

"I have no intention of Eleanor's becoming a harlot," he said with a bitter shake of his head.

"Then what is your plan? Whatever are you going to *do*?"

"I . . ." His voice trailed off, and he glanced behind him. Eleanor stood there, looking as if she'd been thoroughly ravished and utterly beautiful with it. Her dark hair loose and falling about her face, cheeks rosy and flushed, her lush lips swollen from his kisses. Her gaze met his, and she patted him on the back, offered him a reassuring smile that sent a zing straight to his heart.

Mine. The word whispered through his brain. She belonged to him. What happened had just ensured it.

"Well?" the countess asked impatiently, stomping her foot.

He turned to face her, his jaw firm, his focus clear. "I want to marry your daughter, my lady."

Both ladies gasped, much to his surprise. Didn't Eleanor understand what tonight's secret meeting was really about? Yes, he'd gotten ahead of himself, but asking for her hand in marriage had been his plan all along.

Now that he had Eleanor back in his life, he wasn't about to let her go.

Slipping his hand into his trouser pocket, he withdrew the gold ring and turned to Eleanor, presented the cherished piece of jewelry to her with trembling fingers. "This ring has been in my family for generations. And I want you to wear it as my wife, Lady Eleanor. Will you do me the honor of agreeing to be my duchess?"

A gasp escaped her, and she bent her head, blinking profusely. Gently, he slipped a single finger beneath her chin, tilting her head up so he could look into her eyes.

Unshed tears formed in their dark depths, a single shining drop slipping down her cheek. He caught it with his thumb, caressing her skin. "Are you sure you want me?" she whispered.

He chuckled. How he adored this woman. That she would need to ask . . . "More sure than I've ever been in my life."

"Oh, Henry." The tears flew freely now, streaking down her face as a sob escaped her. "Yes. Yes, I'll be your duchess."

"Well, my word," the countess muttered, as Ashton embraced the woman who had just agreed to become his wife. "This couldn't have worked more in my favor."

Calculating wench.

He slipped the ring onto the fourth finger on Eleanor's right hand, not wanting to go against tradition and give her the ring on her left hand before they were actually married. "You've made me a very happy man," he whispered.

She nodded, sniffed. Tears streamed down her cheeks freely. "And you, Your Grace, have made me an extremely happy lady."

"I say, what's going on in here?" Tristan asked, strolling into the room without a care, amusement dancing in his eyes.

Ashton glared at his scheming younger brother. "I've just asked Eleanor to marry me," he announced loftily.

"After I caught them in a most scandalous embrace," the countess added with a wink in Tristan's direction.

Lord help him, Ashton knew they were in on it together. The look that had just passed between the two of them more than confirmed it.

"Have you no patience, brother?" Tristan grinned.

"Not when it concerns the lady I want as my wife." He slipped his arm around Eleanor's shoulders, smiling down at her. "Now that I know she's agreeable, I'm rather anxious."

"Do you realize what you've just done, young lady?" Lady Cochrane eyed her daughter. "You're about to become a duchess. You!" She said it as if she were in a state of shock. "I would've believed Penelope or even Olivia snagging a duke, but never . . ."

"Watch how you speak to my future wife, Lady Cochrane," Ashton fairly growled as he tightened his arm around Eleanor's stiff shoulders. "Best you recall that you are speaking out of turn to my duchess?"

Eleanor's mother paled, her mouth gaping open and closing like a dying fish. "M—my apologies, Your Grace. But she is *my* daughter, after all."

"And she shall soon be the Duchess of Ashton, lest you forget, which I am most certain you won't. Once we're married, she'll be above your station, you do realize."

"Of course." The countess nodded, her gray-tinged curls bobbing about her face.

"So it would be best if you not remind my dear, precious Eleanor of what you view are her faults. Because in my eyes,"—he gazed at her, saw that Eleanor looked up at him with wonderment on her face—"she is perfect."

"Oh, Henry," Eleanor murmured, her voice trembling. Unable to resist, he kissed her soft cheek, allowed his lips to linger. Her mother was heartless. Cruel. That she would say such a thing in front of God and everyone . . .

He wouldn't tolerate it.

"I am far from perfect," Eleanor whispered as she leaned into him.

"You are to me," he murmured close to her ear, inhaling her fresh, feminine scent. His entire body stiffened with arousal. "And that is all that matters, is it not?"

Chapter Nine

ELEANOR CREPT DOWN the dark hallway, her slippered feet so light they made not a sound. Candlelight still flickered in the sconces that dotted the corridor, guiding her way to the room she sought.

The Duke of Ashton's bedchamber.

Nerves sent her limbs trembling, her stomach bouncing. She'd paced her very own bedchamber not a half hour ago, fretful over her potential decision. Should she visit him in his bedchamber alone? Or was that most possibly the worst idea she'd ever considered? After all, he'd asked for her hand in marriage. He'd given her a precious family heirloom too, to wear on her finger.

She still couldn't quite believe it. After all this time, he still wanted her. Wanted her to be his duchess, his wife.

His lover.

Her heart lodged in her throat, she settled her hand on the cold metal of the door handle. Fingers trembling, she slowly turned it, going still when the hinges creaked as she pushed open the door.

Warmth greeted her, the flickering light of a fire casting the room with mysterious shadows. Reminding her of her illicit meeting with Ashton in his study only moments ago though this was far more scandalous.

Of course, what did it matter? She was to marry the man and hopefully soon. Why could she not visit with her future husband? Though there wouldn't be much visiting. Plenty of hungry kissing and wandering hands and . . .

Her cheeks heated at the images that filled her mind.

"What the—Eleanor?" Her future husband sounded properly shocked to find her standing in the open doorway of his chamber.

"I—I hope I'm not disturbing you." She shifted on her feet, overwhelmed at what she was about to do.

"Of course not." He rushed toward her, gorgeous in black trousers and an open robe, the silky fabric billowing out behind him as he approached. "Shut the door, love. And hurry."

She turned and did as he bid, trembling fingers turning the lock in its place after she quietly closed the door. Thrilling yet again at the way he called her love. It filled her with hope, silly as that might be. His sweet endearments, his passionate embraces and exciting kisses left her wanting more.

Wishing that he felt more too.

Before she could turn to face him, his strong arms wrapped around her, pressing her against the door. His mouth settled beside her ear, his warm breath caressing her sensitive skin before he spoke. "What do you think you're doing, sneaking into my room at this hour?"

He wasn't angry, was he? Oh, she hoped not. "I wanted to see you," she said hesitantly, silently cursing herself. No need to turn into a ninny.

"Did you now?" His arms tightened around her, his hands splayed across her stomach. "And why did you want to see me, hmm?"

"I missed you." Closing her eyes, she let her forehead thunk against the heavy wood of the door. How could she tell him what she wanted when she herself was so unsure? This was all such a mystery to her. Exhilarating and confusing, she was both frightened and curious.

And achingly aroused.

His possessive touch upon her quaking body only enhanced the swirl of emotions unraveling within her. His large, warm hands smoothed over her, settling upon her waist, so he could slowly turn her to face him. "Dressed for bed?"

Embarrassment washing over her, she kept her eyes tightly closed. "Perhaps."

"Ah." He trailed a finger along first one lapel of her dressing gown, then the other before he teased at the white silk ribbon that hung from her neck. "What is this?"

She opened her eyes to find him studying her, his gaze resting on the spot where each side of her robe met. "If you would move away from me, I will show you."

His lids heavy, his smile lazy, he released his hold on her and stepped back, arms out wide. "By all means, my lady, I await your revelation."

Inhaling sharply, she settled her hands upon the tie of her dressing gown, slowly undoing the knot. He watched her, his entire body still, his bare chest gleaming in the firelight. Dark, curling hair covered his naked flesh, narrowing into a trail that led to his navel and beyond, disappearing beneath the waistband of his trousers.

Dare she even think it, she wanted to follow that intriguing trail with her tongue.

"Go on now," he urged when he surely realized her hesitation. "Don't tease me for too long. I only have so much patience."

The low, seductive timbre of his voice, the urgency of his statement sent her heart flying. Fumbling with the tie, she finally undid it, parting her robe without a sound.

It was his turn to suck in air, his eyes going wide at the sight before him.

She let the dressing gown slip from her shoulders until it settled in a silky puddle on the floor around her feet. Completely nude, she stood before him, her entire body aflame at the heated look in his eyes.

"I come bearing a gift just for you," she said, her voice trembling. "I give you myself, Your Grace. Tonight, I belong to you completely."

He clenched his hands into fists at his sides, his gaze roving over her, lingering upon her most mysterious places. Straightening her spine, she pushed her shoulders back, holding her head high.

Never in her life had she put herself on such blatant display. Not in front of her maid, her mother, her sisters . . . no one. Until this man.

"This . . ." He cleared his throat and approached her once more. "*You* are the most precious gift I have ever been fortunate enough to receive."

He reached out, his fingers curling about the ribbon she'd tied around her neck before she left her room, the gold ring Henry presented to her dangling between her breasts. "What is this? The ring I gave you?"

She nodded, sucked in a breath when his fingers brushed against her chilled skin. "Y—yes."

His lids lifted, his searing sea blue gaze meeting hers. "Why would you tie it upon a ribbon? Why not just wear it on your finger?"

"I don't have the right to wear it yet, Your Grace," she said solemnly, her eyes never wavering from his. "Until I am truly your wife, I think it best I wear it around my neck."

"Mmm." He settled his hands upon her shoulders. "You're shivering."

A gasp escaped her when he drew her to him, their naked flesh pressed together for the first time. She closed her eyes as a myriad of pleasurable sensations swept through her, one after the other, overwhelming her and arousing her all at once. His hands upon her, her breasts pressed to his chest, her nipples, hard and aching, rubbing against his chest hair.

"And it's not cold in here," he continued as he dipped his head, dropping damp little kisses along her bare shoulder. "Do I make you nervous?"

"Yes," she whispered, whimpering when he cupped her right breast, his thumb skittering across her distended nipple.

"I don't understand why, seeing how bold you are, displaying yourself to me without batting an eyelash. Quite honestly, I've never seen anything like it." The words were murmured against her skin as he continued to blaze a path of heat with his mouth. Along her collarbone, lower, lower still, until he traced his tongue around her nipple, making her squeal softly.

"Did I disappoint you, Your Grace?" She clutched at his shoulders, bunched the fabric of his dressing gown beneath her palms. She wanted to tear it off and lick at his flesh much like he did hers. Nibble and bite and lick and suck until he was as undone as she.

"Not in the least." He moved away from her, grabbing her hand so he could lead her toward the grand bed that awaited them. "With every spectacularly bold move you make, my lady, I come to realize what a splendid wife you will make."

Pride suffused her, and she smiled. "Do you mean that? Truly?"

He hauled her to him, their gazes locking. "I have never been more serious in all my life. You, Lady Eleanor Fitzsimmons, will make the perfect duchess."

And with his firm statement, she knew she could never doubt him.

Chapter Ten

"I CANNOT BELIEVE you went through with it." Tristan shook his head morosely. "Shackling yourself with a new bride. Why, you hardly know her."

"I feel as if I've known her all my life." Ashton kept his gaze upon the new Duchess of Ashton, pleased with what he saw. She stood on the opposite side of the drawing room, her cheeks rosy, her eyes sparkling with happiness. She wore a dark green gown that brought out the pale creaminess of her skin, her flashing dark eyes and rich brown hair.

She was a vision, surrounded by her sisters and her mother. His mother stood nearby too, smiling and laughing, demanding everyone celebrate this most wondrous of nights.

For it was Christmas—and his wedding day.

"That you would bloody well marry her and on such a sacred day as this," Tristan scoffed. "It's rather unseemly."

"And now who's the stuffy old gent, hmm?" Ashton couldn't be bothered with his brother. Tristan was confused. Perhaps a trifle jealous. After all, Lady Olivia didn't seem to pay him any mind, not any longer. And the only lady who followed Tristan around adoringly was Lady Penelope. The very last lady he wanted to spend time with.

"I just think you've been rather—rash in your decision. If I'd done something like this, you'd say the same thing," Tristan explained when he saw Ashton prepare to interrupt.

Henry clamped his lips shut. His younger brother was right. But he couldn't worry about it. Yes, they'd married quickly, much to his mother's horrified shock and her mother's delight. He'd hoped for the earl's consent, but Eleanor had warned him no one knew where her father could be.

So he went ahead and made the decision to marry her now, before the year ended. He wanted to offer her protection. Guidance.

Love.

And by God, he wanted to bed her again and soon. Glancing at his pocket watch, he snapped it shut, glaring at everyone in the room. "When will this thing end anyhow?"

Tristan chortled. "Ah, who's anxious to take his wife to bed, hmm?"

"Don't embarrass her." He thrust his finger in Tristan's face. "She's had enough to deal with, what with her wastrel of her father. Tonight is her night. Let her revel in it."

Tristan looked shocked as he took a step back. "I wouldn't embarrass her. I like Eleanor. The only one I wish to embarrass is you."

Without another word, Ashton left his brother where he stood, ignoring Tristan's laughter as it trailed after him. He went to Eleanor, unable to stand it any longer. He needed to get her alone. In his bedchamber. In his bed.

"Ah, there you are." She beamed, so pretty she stole his very breath. "I was just explaining to Mother that we shall return to London after the Twelfth Day."

Ashton inclined his head toward Lady Cochrane. "Indeed, that is correct."

"But what of us? When shall we return? And what sort of conditions will you return us to?" His new mother-in-law's gaze was shrewd, as was her expression. The woman had no problem stating boldly what she wanted.

Sighing, he slipped his arm around Eleanor's waist, pulling her in close. God, how dependent he'd become on her for strength. "We shall move you to new quarters soon after I arrive in London. But until then, you'll have to stay in your house."

"And what of the creditors?"

"They will be taken care of properly." He'd already started the proper action in doing so. Cochrane's debts would be paid in full within the sennight, perhaps even sooner.

Lady Cochrane beamed. "Wonderful. I do say, sir. When you set your mind to something, you complete the task in a rather efficient manner, do you not?"

They escaped the cloying drawing room minutes later,

Ashton taking Eleanor's hand and leading her toward his bedchamber without hesitation His steps were eager, as were hers, and she couldn't seem to stop laughing.

"What's so funny?" he asked once he had her inside, his hands all over her.

Yet again.

"Don't you find it unbelievable, what has happened between us?" She kissed him, her lips sweet, her tongue hot as it licked inside his mouth. He set her away from him, hardly able to think, let alone conduct conversation with her.

"Unbelievable how?"

She slowly undid his cravat, tossing it over her shoulder so it landed on the floor. "Not so very long ago, I described you as my enemy. And now we are married."

"Many great marriages started out with husband and wife at odds with each other."

"Name five." She stood on her tiptoes and pressed her lush mouth to the side of his neck.

"Um . . ." He couldn't think of one, let alone five, which seemed to please her to no end. "You're distracting me," he murmured, slipping his hand into the back of her hair and ruining her coiffure with a few thrusts of his fingers.

"Is it working?" Her busy little fingers worked on the buttons of his waistcoat, tugged at the hem of his shirt, and pulled it from his trousers. A few secret nights together, and she'd become the wanton.

And wasn't he the lucky bastard?

"It is," he practically growled, picking her up so he could toss her onto the bed. She landed with a soft thump, her adorably angry expression making him chuckle. Striding toward the bed, he shed his clothes with quick ease, his gaze never leaving hers. She was still completely clothed, her breath coming so fast, he reveled in the rapid rise and fall of her breasts, how they strained against the fabric of her bodice.

Lord help him, she was the most delicious gift he could've ever been given.

"Are you going to ravish me now?" she asked hopefully.

"Is that what you wish for, my darling?" He settled his mouth upon hers, kissing her for long, delicious minutes. He'd known passion brimmed just beneath her surface. She was giving, curious, and so eager to please, he couldn't help but feel the same toward her.

He undressed her, nearly tearing the sleeve off her gown, shredding her thin, aged shift and not caring in the least. He would buy her a new wardrobe. The very best money could buy. He would outfit her with whatever she wanted and needed because, damn it, a duchess should dress like one, and years-old, hand-me-down rags were not the latest style.

She chastised him for destroying her clothing but only briefly. Soon he had her rapturous in his arms, his fingers between her legs, searching her wet folds, his lips sucking her pretty pink nipples deep. She writhed beneath him, reaching her conclusion quickly, beautifully.

Watching her climax in his arms shook him to his very core. He wondered if he would ever get over that.

He certainly hoped not.

"I want you inside me," she murmured as she slipped one hand down his chest before her fingers curled around the length of his cock.

A strangled groan escaped him. "What happened to my bashful wife?"

"She's been made insatiable by her husband." She stroked him, working him into a near frenzy within seconds, and he pinned her to the mattress, pushing inside her with all the finesse of an untried lad.

"You very nearly unman me, I'll have you know," he murmured as he withdrew almost completely before he thrust in deep.

She arched beneath him, a wicked smile curving her swollen mouth. "Can't have that, can we?"

He lost all control, pounding inside her with unrestrained passion. He wanted to take her, possess her, mark her as his. Sweat slicked their bodies, her nails scratched down his back, and the both of them came with trembling moans and exhausted shouts.

"I have never been happier," she murmured many, many minutes later, her head resting on his damp-with-sweat shoulder, her fingers threading through the hair that grew on his chest.

"Truly, darling?" He kissed her temple. "Even though I took you like some sort of feral beast?"

"I adore your beastly ways." She sighed contentedly, wrapping herself around him. "Do you think the *ton* will accept me?"

"Haven't they already? Besides, I really don't give a

damn if they accept you or not. I accept you. My family accepts you. That's all that matters."

Eleanor snuggled in closer, her tousled hair tickling his face, making his nose twitch. "I love how indignant you become for me. I've never had a champion before."

"A champion?" He frowned, an odd, achy feeling growing in his chest.

She nodded, strands of her hair sticking to the stubble that grew along his jaw. "I've always felt rather alone. And now that I have you . . ."

He released a shuddering sigh, dropped a kiss on her forehead. God's truth, he knew what that odd, achy feeling was. It was his heart, swelling with love for her. And he loved this woman.

More than anything or anyone in the world.

"Now that you have me, you will never be alone, Eleanor. Of that, I can assure you." Slipping his fingers beneath her chin, he tilted her face up, preparing her for his kiss. "I love you."

Her eyes grew wide and shiny with unshed tears. "You do?" She sniffed.

Nodding, he leaned down, kissing her thoroughly before he spoke once more. "I do."

"And I love you," she whispered, her expression shy. "So very much."

"We are in agreement then."

She nodded, her lips soft and swollen, her eyes glowing with love and affection. "You have made me the happiest woman on this earth."

"And you, my darling, have made me the happiest man." He slipped his hand beneath the covers and grabbed hers, entwining their fingers before he brought their linked hands out into the open air. Tracing his thumb along the thin gold band that Eleanor wore about her finger, it was a symbol of his love and fidelity, a representation of all the Duchesses of Ashton, past and present. "I love that you wear my ring. That you show everyone you belong to me."

"I do belong to you, Henry. I am yours in every way possible." She offered him a shaky smile.

"And I belong to you as well, Eleanor. More than you shall ever know." He smiled in return, reached out, and cupped her cheek to draw her to him.

And sealed his simple vow with a lingering kiss.

About Karen Erickson

Romance author KAREN ERICKSON writes what she loves to read—sexy contemporary romance and sensual historical romance. She's published over thirty novellas and novels since 2006. A native Californian, she lives in the foothills below Yosemite with her husband and three children. You can find her on the Web at: www.*karen erickson.com*, *twitter.com/@karenerickson* and *facebook.com /karenericksonwritesromance*.

War of the Magi

RENA GREGORY

Chapter One

Preston, South Dakota
1908

HE STOOD OUTSIDE her father's general-goods shop, not even ten feet away from her, separated by an inch of glass. Ginny squinted. Smudged, spotted glass.

She hurried to the window with a clean rag and peered over to see her father at the counter, haggling with Mrs. Clancy about the price of the bolts of fabric she wanted to purchase. If there was one thing John Overton despised, it was untidiness in all its forms. Ginny didn't mind the chore since it gave her an excuse to get closer to the object of her affection. She stared out again, her hand automatically making circles on the glass so that her father would know she was, in fact, working.

Phin Baldwin had only recently entered her life, and already Ginny knew more about him than he would have liked. On her part, she was fascinated. She'd never kept anyone's secret before, especially someone who hadn't personally confided in her. She wasn't particularly worried, as he was not someone with whom she had constant contact.

Ginny liked the way the crisp winter wind ruffled the sandy blond hair against his coat and how his dark eyes were so focused on what Mr. O'Brien was telling him. Phin laughed out loud, and the laugh lines at his eyes crinkled.

Ginny sighed.

"What are you doing, Eugenia?"

She had forgotten to keep up her charade of cleaning, and she swiveled to see her father's full mustache beetle up. Under his scrutiny, she diverted herself by counting the gray hairs that nestled within the mahogany brown that matched her own hair.

"I saw a smudge on the window."

He kept his gaze on her. "I assume you rectified the matter."

"Yes, Father."

"May I also assume you were on your way back to the counter but got weary, and so are now just taking a break until you can make the remaining few feet to your post?"

She saw the twinkle in his eye, and she arched an eyebrow. "Yes, sir." As she made her way back, she regarded him over her shoulder. "You have two more gray hairs than you did last time I counted."

She had the satisfaction of seeing his hand twitch, and she knew he'd caught himself before he could brush it over the offending gray hairs. He scowled at her. "Well, stop counting them!"

Ginny smiled and resumed her reading, deciding not

to look out at Phin Baldwin any longer. She could only coast in the clouds for so long before she realized she didn't have wings and came crashing down. She was careful to take Phin in small doses for fear she would become depressed by the knowledge that she'd never have him.

"Mrs. Clancy should run a bank," her father grumbled.

"You enjoy it when she berates you about the prices."

"I certainly do not."

Ginny looked over to her tall, neat father. He was always impeccably dressed, though modest, as he was a shopkeeper. His hair was parted right in the middle and slicked back with pomade. His gray eyes were intelligent and shrewd, and he rarely missed a beat. He was still an attractive man; it was a shame some woman didn't come along to catch his fancy. Her father would never admit to loneliness, but Ginny knew better. Her father missed her mother, and sometimes, Ginny was scared that he hadn't forgiven Marie Overton for dying. Ginny didn't like to think of her father carrying around that much pain, let alone grief and anger. It had, after all, been more than ten years. Ginny's older sister Eliza was married to a rancher out in California, and as for Ginny's brother . . . well, it was best not to speak of unpleasant things. So it was just the two of them. Yet another Christmas would come and go with father and daughter trying to keep up their spirits on Christmas Day.

The door opened, letting in another customer and once again, Ginny's head came up from her novel only to remain frozen on a face surrounded by the lovely golden hair she'd just recently been admiring.

"Good afternoon, Mr. Overton. Miss Overton," Phin Baldwin, love of Ginny's life, greeted jovially. He went up to her father and shook his hand.

"What can I do for you, Mr. Baldwin?"

"I was told by Mrs. Dixon that you have a catalog for women's garments. It's going to be Christmas soon, and I'm looking to acquire a lady's coat. I had a mind to take the stagecoach to Cheyenne or another city, but Mrs. Dixon assured me I could save myself the long trip."

As her father and Phin got down to business perusing the Sears and Roebuck catalog, Ginny's mind was scattered with questions. For starters, whom on Earth could he be buying a coat for? A man didn't buy a coat for a woman unless he was properly courting her, and one thing was certain: Phin Baldwin was not courting anybody. Since many of the mamas of women her age had their eyes and ears to the grindstone, his reputation as a single man was well-known. He had yet to show any indication that he was willing to get serious and settle down with someone. She, of course, knew better.

"Ginny."

She came out of her reverie in a flash as she realized that her father had been speaking to her.

"Come here, please."

She heard him making apologies for her and willed herself not to blush. "She gets wrapped up in her books sometimes; she's a daydreamer, my Ginny," he explained.

She maintained her composure and joined her father. "Yes?"

"Mr. Baldwin says he'd like a lady's opinion before making a final selection."

Phin smiled at her, and Ginny mentally chastised herself for feeling her knees buckle. Honestly, he was attractive, but she wasn't a fool. *Ground yourself in reality,* she reminded herself. For, even though her father said she was a dreamer, she considered herself more of a realist. Only a realist would have remained behind when Eliza had offered to take her to California, or opened the store every morning and closed it every night that first year after her mother died, when her father was inconsolable. And only a realist knew that dreaming about Phin was much safer than letting her well-guarded heart become too attached, knowing full well he wasn't for her.

"Miss Overton, you're looking lovely today." He flashed his crooked grin, and those laugh lines crinkled again.

"That's nice of you to say, Mr. Baldwin." Especially as she was wearing an old but serviceable blue calico dress, and her thick hair was already slipping from her pins. A long lock escaped, and she hastily tucked it behind her ear. "Which ones were you looking at?"

Another customer came into the shop, and Ginny's father excused himself to attend to him.

She felt Phin's gaze on her, felt him studying her as she studied the catalog. He had his eye on a flashy red coat, which made her wonder about the woman who would wear such a garment. Somebody confident, with a personality to match all that fiery color. Maybe tempestuous. Maybe even a disreputable woman.

His laugh made her look up, and when she met his gaze, she saw amusement there. "You're a serious little thing, aren't you?"

"I beg your pardon?"

"I've been in here for about ten minutes now, and you haven't once asked me if I'm attending the Christmas pageant."

"I wasn't aware I was supposed to."

"Sure. That's the way it goes. I go into a place with a young, unmarried woman—not so young, on occasion— and within five minutes, I get asked if I'm attending the pageant, if I'm doing all right on the newspaper, if I'm not lonely at Mrs. Dixon's boardinghouse. It's all very customary."

Ginny didn't know what to make of him and self-consciously worried the button on her wrist, wondering if he'd made the age comment about her. Twenty-three wasn't old, but around these parts, it wasn't young. Was he conceited or playing with her? She wasn't adept at flirting, so if that's what this was, they were both in for disappointment. She bit the inside of her lip. "What happens if I don't ask?"

She could see she'd surprised him, and his smile curved. "I don't know. It's never happened before. We can play this out and see, or you can ask."

She lowered her eyes to the catalog page to keep from arching a brow. He was definitely toying with her, and though she was attracted to him, she wasn't much in the market for being someone's plaything. Especially when that person had a few other playthings from which to

WAR OF THE MAGI 177

choose. "This red one is certainly going to turn any woman's head. It's finely made."

He was quiet for a few seconds. "It does make a statement, doesn't it?"

She nodded.

"Would you wear it?"

She chanced a quick glimpse at him. He was leaning over the counter, his forearms resting on the wood. His head was close to hers, and it struck her how funny it was to have him so close when only moments ago she'd exalted at the proximity a glass window afforded. He caught the touch of diversion. His voice colored with warmth. "Is that a no?"

She cocked her head and regarded the coat. It was pretty, but not her preferred style. "If I had a choice, no."

"Why not?" He straightened as he brought the page up for closer inspection. "Is there something wrong with it?"

"Not at all. It's beautiful, but I much prefer the blue one." When she saw that he was second-guessing his choice, she said, "Surely, you know this person's tastes better than I. We can place the order right now, and you still have a month before Christmas for it to arrive. She'll be very pleased with such a splendid gift."

He deliberated for a moment, sticking a hand in the pocket of his long leather duster. "You may be right. I like red," he shared, "but what do I know? She is more conservative. I'll take the blue one."

Ginny's father walked over, with the baker's wife and their daughter. "How's it going, Mr. Baldwin? Has Ginny helped you make a decision?"

"Yes, she has, and I'm very grateful. It's nice to get a woman's take sometimes, wouldn't you agree, Mrs. Jameson?"

The baker's wife agreed wholeheartedly. "Have you met my youngest, Mildred?"

The girl, only a couple of years younger than Ginny, colored prettily. "You buy a hot cross bun every morning on your way to the newspaper office."

"Nobody makes them like you," he said. Ginny bit the inside of her lip again to keep from scoffing. As if sensing her containment—he seemed to be able to read her movements—Phin turned to Ginny. "I admit, I'm in love with them. Where I'm from, you only get them at Easter time. Have you tried their hot cross buns, Miss Overton? They're amazing."

"Ginny's been in the bakery more times than I can count," Mrs. Jameson said. "She's like family to us. And before I forget, Ginny, will you be participating in the pageant this year? Pastor Morrow asked me if we could count on you to tend to the children like you did last year. It was such a big help."

She could already tell where this was going, and so did Phin Baldwin. He slanted a knowing grin her way before turning his attention back to the Jamesons. She ignored him and replied to Mrs. Jameson. "I'll go speak to him today. I'd be happy to help."

"Will you be attending our pageant, Mr. Baldwin,?" the younger Jameson woman asked.

Ginny stifled a groan.

As if a practiced team, the baker's wife chimed in.

"Oh, you simply must, Mr. Baldwin. You're new to our town, and so you haven't had the privilege of attending; the pageant is one of the biggest events in Preston, if not the biggest. We outdid ourselves last year, that's for sure. Don't you agree, Mr. Overton?"

"Oh sure."

"Mildred was Mary, the most beautiful Mary that ever played the part. Wouldn't you say, Mr. Overton?"

"Absolutely."

Ginny frowned at her father, who winked at her. She'd been Mary herself, a time or two.

"So you see, Mr. Baldwin, it simply wouldn't do for you to miss out. And besides, it's such a beautiful day, being Christmas and all. It brings out the best in people."

Clearly, Mr. Baldwin didn't know what to say under such a barrage of holiday cheer. Ginny busied herself making a note to place the order for the coat while she waited for the conversation to continue. When it stalled, Mildred repeated her question. "Will you be in attendance that day?"

Mr. Baldwin cleared his throat and patted his hat against his thigh. "I'll see if I can make it. Truth is, I might not be in town that week, but if I am, you can bet I'll be there."

He turned to Ginny. "Do you need me to sign anything or pay up front?"

"I'll send in the order today. I'll send over a bill once I know they can send it."

His coffee-colored eyes bored into hers with humor. "You're not going to ask me, are you?"

Ginny was well aware of Mrs. Jameson and Millie's interest in the conversation. She was also conscious of her father's presence. It wasn't exactly that she was doing anything wrong, but she wasn't in the habit of having personal conversations with eligible gentlemen. She looked him straight in the eye, and said, "No. Why ask the question when I've already learned the answer?"

He chuckled and donned his hat, tipping his finger against the brim in farewell. "Touché, Miss Overton."

He thanked her father for his help and, somehow, ended up leaving at the same time as the Jameson women. When the store was unoccupied once again, Ginny asked her father, "I thought I heard her say she needed canned beans? I didn't see anything in her basket."

"That's because Mrs. Jameson has a hankering for a big fish."

"Hmmph."

Her father's eyebrows rose at her tone, so she cleared her throat. "I think I'll go send a telegraph to the store in Rapid City to see if they have the coat." As she made for the back room where she stowed her coat and winter things, she heard her father muse out loud, "Mr. Baldwin's a nice man. Don't you think?"

She was glad she was out of his eyesight because the last thing she wanted to explain was the brightness of her cheeks. She was also glad of one more thing—she had spoken to Phin Baldwin. Now she knew to stay far away from him. He was a danger to her peace of mind.

PHIN WALKED THE baker's wife and daughter back to their shop across the street and politely refused their offer of a fresh roll and a cup of coffee. He could see the interest in the daughter's eye and the calculation in the mother's, and he considered himself too smart a man to succumb to such a simple trap.

He waited for riders to pass by before crossing the street and entering the newspaper office. He was greeted by Rick and Ed, the other reporters for the *Preston Gazette*. Their boss, T. D. Whitemore, was in Europe with his new wife. With as many newspapers and as much money as T. D. had, he had no qualms about leaving one measly paper in a small town to the care of three able men. At the moment, two of those able men were sitting on their bottoms, staring out the storefront window and flicking each other with the tip of their pencils every few seconds.

Ed leaned in quickly and rapped Rick on the knuckles before turning to Phin. "Saw you walking with Millie Jameson. Have you added her to your list of potential brides?"

Rick rubbed his sore knuckles. "Who was looking at Millie? I was looking at the cat-ate-the-canary smile her mama had. She looked like she was already planning the menu for the wedding banquet."

"I'll tell you what, son. I sure am glad you came into town when you did. If you hadn't, it'd be me Mrs. Jameson would be hauling off to the preacher. Everyone knows Millie's had her eyes on me since she was a girl."

Rick guffawed, and took the opportunity to fling

his pencil at Ed's midsection. "You keep telling yourself that."

Ed scowled, returned his gaze to the window. "Now that one, that one's a different story."

"Where?" Rick leaned in.

Phin joined them and peered out in the direction of Ed's finger.

Walking along the uneven sidewalk, in a world of her own, was Miss I Prefer The Blue Coat, herself. The wind was pulling at her hair, causing flyaways to dance across her face. She hastily tucked them back into place, only to have them fall out again. She wore a chocolate brown coat with the collar pushed up to cover her neck. She was of average height, and too slender to boot, as if she forgot to eat during the day.

Phin straightened and crossed his arms at his chest. "What's the story with her?"

"Ginny lives with her pa. They've lived here since before most of the families moved in. Her mama died when she was only thirteen, and she took care of her pa's shop when he went into a decline."

"When he became a drunk, you mean," Ed amended.

"She's had it rough."

"Why do you say that?"

"You weren't here a few years back. It was big news around these parts. Her elder brother Monty got himself into some trouble with the law. Both he and the old man turned a little screwy when Mrs. Overton died, only John pulled himself together again. Monty, on the other hand, took to riding with train robbers. He was killed in a shoot-out in a gambling hall in Deadwood."

"Why isn't she married?"

Ed reclined his head against the back of the seat and regarded Phin. "You interested?"

"No. Curious. A townful of lonely men, an eligible woman. She attended me at the general store; she seemed like a nice girl. No reason for her not to be married."

"Did she bat her lashes at you like the other lovelorn women?"

Phin went to his cluttered desk and took a seat. "Not at all, and Lord knows I gave her a chance."

Ed roared out a laugh. "Never met a woman you didn't give a chance to."

Phin looked up, grinned. "Can I help it if they like my smile?"

"She must have stunned you, then, not falling into a puddle at your feet."

"I'm not surprised. Ginny's not like that. Maybe it comes from not growing up with a woman around the house, but I can't see her using her wiles. Don't think she's flirted a day in her life," Rick ruminated.

Ed and Phin exchanged a glance. "How do you know so much about Ginny?" Ed asked.

"I've been friends with her family since we were both little. She's like a sister."

Ed shoved a pipe in his mouth and chewed at the bit without lighting it since smoking wasn't allowed near the printing press and its chemicals. "I'll tell you what, Rick. You ever come around my sister speaking like you do about Ginny, and I'll have to call you out, son."

"Your sister's married. Speaking of sisters, Phin. Did you buy Lisa's gift?"

"Yeah. Your lady friend helped me place the order."

Chapter Two

GINNY DIDN'T SEE Phin again until that Sunday. She entered the small church on her father's arm, and Mr. Overton took notice at the same time as Ginny.

"Mr. Baldwin sure is a popular man," her father said as he waited for her to take her seat in a pew. Ginny faced the front and refused to look over to Phin again; she already knew what she'd find. He was surrounded by doting mothers and fawning daughters. She could hear him being invited to Sunday dinners, and she had no doubt he'd accept one of them. He did have a purpose for being in Preston, after all.

"I can go over and ask him to supper, dear. What do you think?"

Her face must have shown her horror because her father laughed. "Would that be so terrible?"

"Father, the only reason those women are over there

is because they are trying to catch themselves a husband, something I have no intention of doing."

Thankfully, her father remained silent. She sighed, willing the service to begin.

"Maybe you should be over there, Eugenia. You should be thinking of getting married and starting a family, same as those girls."

Her mouth opened slightly as she turned to her father. She didn't know what to say. Did he want her out of the house? Had she worn out her welcome? It was true, most women her age were married and had children. She couldn't lie to herself, these were things she wanted as well. But she'd never been interested in a man enough to consider marrying him. There certainly wasn't anybody in her life for whom she would consider abandoning her father. Still, she hadn't considered that her father didn't need her anymore.

"Is that what you want me to do, Father? Get married?"

He took her hand into both of his, and squeezed it tight. "I would keep you to myself forever if I thought I could. But we got ourselves caught up in this little life, and I fear we might get stuck. I don't want you to get stuck, Ginny." She saw him swallow hard, and she felt the beginning of tears prick at the corners of her eyes. He wasn't a man who expressed himself easily or often, and that's how she knew this was important to him. So she listened as he continued.

"I want you to be happy, darlin'."

He didn't use the endearment often. She covered his hands with her free one. "I'm happy with you."

He shut his eyes and shook his head. "No you're not. Ginny, you're going to get old one day, and I'll be gone, and you'll be sitting alone in that shop thinking, "what if." It's not a good feeling. I don't want you to have any "what-ifs." I want you to have your own family and watch your children grow. If they're half as wonderful as you, you'll be blessed."

One hot tear rolled down her cheek. "Father . . ."

"Give it some thought, Ginny." He released his hands from her grasp, and patted them once before becoming the dignified, stoic man she knew.

She didn't listen to a word Pastor Morrow said, nor did she sing a hymn. She could only wonder what "what-ifs" her father was carrying around and if he was right in thinking she was starting to cultivate some of her own.

PHIN WAITED PATIENTLY with his landlady, Mrs. Dixon, and the others from the boardinghouse. Ed found him through the crowd and took a place beside him as they stood by the rectory.

"Looks like you're neck deep in alligators, friend," Ed commented, jutting his head to each side to illustrate his point.

Phin supposed it was a reflection of how quickly he'd become accustomed to the female attention that he didn't notice how they'd formed a circle around him. Mildred Jameson was to his left, and the hotel owner's youngest, who couldn't be older than fourteen, was to his right.

He felt an uncomfortable prickle race up the back of

his neck when the young girl's mother waved at him, then elbowed her daughter to do the same. By God, she was just a child.

Ed laughed at him and clapped a hand over his shoulder. "It's got to be the smile, right, Phin?"

"You're a jackass."

"I'll be a jackass to your stallion any day if it means I'm not the one being sought out morning, day, and night."

"I'll thank you not to curse in the Lord's house," Mrs. Dixon murmured through the thin line of her lips. She didn't even look at them when they offered their, "Yes'ms." They muted their voices as Pastor Morrow approached, holding something in his hands.

"What is that?" Phin asked.

Mrs. Dixon openly glared at him this time, and he apologized.

Pastor Morrow began. "Once again, folks, we are here for the annual gifting of the wise men. For those of you new to town, let me explain. This custom dates back twenty or so years when a man named James Peterson found himself lonely on a cold, wintry Christmas Eve. He'd left his family back in St. Louis to try to make a new life out here, but it didn't stop him from yearning for those he loved most. He wasn't doing too well at his venture, some of you here can attest to that."

A few murmurs from the crowd.

"Peterson was a fairly good hand at carving. That Christmas Eve, instead of going out to the pageant like everyone else, he stayed home and made his own company out of a hunk of oak. He created this little figurine, consisting of the three kings presenting the baby Jesus with three gifts. That's where you'll see these little empty boxes." He indicated them with the tip of his thumb. "He made the men's faces to reflect those of the men in his family whom he respected, thereby ensuring that he was, indeed, surrounded by family. And that night, he slipped a little paper with a wish on it into each empty groove. They were his wishes for the coming year, you see."

"I never tire of hearing this story," Phin heard someone behind him say.

"I hope I get it this year," a little red-haired imp whispered to his brother.

Phin's curiosity was definitely piqued; the preacher knew how to deliver a story.

"Now, we'll never know for sure what those three wishes were exactly, but something powerful took hold of Mr. Peterson. The next day, he felt rejuvenated, unlike anything he'd felt before. He told everyone he knew that his wishes had come true, and little more than a week after Christmas, Mr. Peterson found a vein of gold down by a stretch of land that had already been mined. He became wealthy enough that he returned home to his family, confident he could provide for them comfortably until he came upon a new enterprise. Not long after, he sent this very figurine to this church with a note, saying how he wanted others to be as blessed as he had been that lonely Christmas Eve. Ever since, it's become a tradition for us to have a lottery drawing to see who will have the chance at three Christmas miracles. For those of you with skeptical minds, ask anyone, and they'll tell you we've had our fair share of wishes come true in Preston. Who's to say it's not the work of the wise men? Now, gather round, put your names on the scraps, and give 'em to Mr. Overton if you'd like to participate in the drawing."

Phin watched as the people behind him dispersed to write their names on the slips of paper handed out by Ginny Overton. Her father held the tin canister where they were being placed. He turned his head to make a comment to Ed only to see his stalwart friend slipping his name into the canister. He crossed his arms at his chest and stared smugly at Ed as he made his way through a crowd. Ed shrugged. "I'm no one to say no to a miracle. If they're being handed out, don't see why I shouldn't get my fair share."

"Your choice."

"Put your name in, too." Ed grinned devilishly at him, and reached for the pipe in his right breast pocket. "Given your task at hand, you could do with a few wishes."

"All right, folks. Here we go." Pastor Morrow shoved his hand into the canister and withdrew a slip of paper.

Phin could feel the excitement of the people around him, almost as if it were Christmas morning itself. He had to admit he enjoyed the pleasure the people in Preston took in small things. He'd grown up in a family where only big events merited the type of delight on the faces of his current neighbors. He took out his leather-bound notebook and pencil to record the more salient details of the night's events to include as a personal interest story in the newspaper. It wouldn't be anything new since it was a town tradition, but Phin found that sometimes people preferred to read about familiar events in which they took part instead of the bigger, flashier stories.

He was busy jotting down the number in attendance when Ed tapped him on the shoulder.

Phin looked up and saw that everyone was beaming at him. "What happened?"

Mrs. Dixon took his notebook and pushed him up to the front. "You've been chosen as this year's recipient, Mr. Baldwin. Go on."

Phin couldn't find words, which was a sad state to be in, given his profession. He surveyed all the happy faces and settled on Ginny Overton's since she was the only one not smiling. She was regarding him with a serious expression on her face.

"I don't understand."

"It's you, Phin." Ed said, walking him up to receive the figurine.

Phin sat at a table surrounded by townsfolk, who were busy chatting away. He thumbed the rough-hewn faces of the wise men; the figurine itself was shaped into a circular ring with a diameter of about five inches, each wise man's shoulders pressing up against the next. The oak had been painted with earth colors, the three kings wearing robes of sienna, sage, and a gray-blue that reminded him of the South Dakota sky on a rainy day. The faces of the figures were distinguishable, and Phin could well picture the men who had inspired them. Noble men of strong moral character. Each wise man held a little box without a cover. Phin dipped his index finger in the warped wood

of the box of the sienna wise man and dug his nail into a
little nick created over time and wear.

"How does this work exactly?"

Mrs. Clancy, sitting beside him, spoke first. "It's really
quite simple. Tonight, when you go home, think about
three things you would like to happen. Wishes, you see.
You write each down on a separate sheet of paper, fold
them up, and put one wish in each of the boxes."

"Then what?"

She blinked. "I beg your pardon?"

Phin felt half a dozen pairs of eyes on him. He
scratched the back of his neck. "Well, ah, I just mean,
what happens after I do that?"

Mildred Jameson, Ginny Overton, and another young
lady joined his group. Millie giggled. "You don't do anything, Mr. Baldwin. You only have to wait until Christmas to see if your miracles were granted or not."

"Yes, and then?"

Mrs. Clancy spoke. "I guess it seems a bit silly to you,
coming from a big city, waiting on something magical
to happen. In our defense, though, we do seem to have a
lot of people who have admitted to having a dream come
true."

"You wouldn't admit otherwise, though, would you?"

"We don't tend to lie, if that's what you mean, Mr.
Baldwin."

"I wouldn't dare think so, Mrs. Clancy, and begging
your pardon if that's what you thought. What I mean
is, you'd want to believe something happened even if it
didn't. You'd convince yourself that you'd seen a change,

more so when the people in town are so invested in knowing the results. I can't blame you. The story is enchanting."

The gathering was quiet again, while the noise from the other sections of the room could be heard.

"It sounds like you don't believe in miracles, Mr. Baldwin."

The comment was made in a serious tone. Phin and the rest of the party looked over to Ginny Overton, whose face was inscrutable.

"I'm not saying I do or I don't. I take it you do?"

Her hair was well behaved tonight, every strand in place. "Yes."

"This is curious, indeed, Miss Overton. Please share your stories of wishes and miracles. I'm assuming you've had at least one little wish come true." He smiled at her, but she didn't smile back. He became conscious of the presence of tension that hadn't been there only moments before. Too late, he remembered her history. It wasn't exactly rife with glowing endorsements for the existence of miracles. Deceased mother and brother, absent sister. The dreary routine of a soon-to-be spinster in a small town.

"You don't intend to make your own wishes, then?"

He glanced at the ring in his hand, and shrugged. "I haven't decided. This might be the year the old fellows get a break from wish-granting."

"Oh, but you must follow the rules, Mr. Baldwin," Mrs. Clancy exclaimed. "It's tradition."

Phin saw a glimmer in Ginny's dark eyes that fascinated him. She was angry with him. Something he had said or done was provoking her ire, and he was mildly curious to know what it was, if only because he wasn't accustomed to having a woman upset at him.

He turned his attention to the matron. "I'm not sure, Mrs. Clancy, but don't fret. I'll display the figurine in the newspaper office and anyone who passes by can see it. They'll still be part of the Christmas season like they've been every year since the tradition started.

He looked up again to see that Ginny was gone.

Chapter Three

LET FATHER MOVE on past his grief.

Keep our family in good health.

Let me experience something truly extraordinary before the end of my days.

These were Ginny's three wishes. They had been her wishes since she could remember, and she was always hopeful that she'd get the opportunity to put her thoughts to paper and slip them into the wise men's boxes. Each year, she was disappointed, but she at least had the comforting thought that the recipient of the wise men would be a believer who wouldn't throw away the chance for something magical to happen.

Her wishes were simple. She wasn't asking for a pot of gold to fall in her lap or for the gift of flying. She only wanted to see her father happy, and not the facsimile he displayed for the world since her mother's death. She also worried for his health, and for Eliza's. Ginny's sister had miscarried two children and was delicate. Their father had had a terrible bout of influenza when Ginny was fifteen, and in those days of caring for him, she had really discovered what life would be like if he were gone. She'd have no one. Not only that, it wasn't fair that her father had only known happiness for such a short time, only to have it taken away. A person should have more to his life than that.

Her last wish was selfish, and it belonged to the young girl she'd been. She couldn't bring herself to change it. After all, its promise helped get her through many lonely days at the shop. She wasn't even sure what she wanted to see or do. Maybe she would travel by train to visit her sister, and the trip would be extraordinary. Or maybe she would witness something marvelous. The not knowing was part of the allure. This wish was one of the few dreams she allowed herself. And Christmastime was the perfect time to dust out the dream and hope all over again, for Christmas was full of magic.

Which is why she was so appalled, and truth be told, angry with Phin Baldwin. If ever there was a sign that he was not the love of her life after all, it was this. He came in with his big-city ways and his amusement at their expense, then, to top it all, he was chosen for something that everybody else considered an honor, and what did he do? He spurned it, that's what. Her cheeks burned just to remember his smug smile. He was a skeptic, and he was going to waste the opportunity that someone else would have cherished.

"You're very quiet," her father said.

She removed her gaze from her untouched supper. "Am I?"

She knew her father was curious about her, but he didn't ask; nor did she share.

Ginny's foot tapped a frenetic beat along with the wind outside, which was in full swing.

Her father had stared at her from across the store all morning, and she'd calmed herself enough to stop her foot's little jig. Only to start all over again a few minutes later.

Finally, he came out, and announced, "Ginny, if you've got something on your mind, I sure wish you'd come out and say it. You've got my nerves dancing to your ditty."

She tried smiling, only to have it come out flat. "Do you think we can visit Eliza this coming year?"

"That's what you're worried about?" he asked. She could read the skepticism in his furrowed brow.

"I'd like to see her. It's been years since she visited us. She has a new baby. I'm an aunt to a whole passel of children whose faces I've never seen."

Her father gazed at her directly, and she almost winced. He saw right through her, and even if he wasn't certain of the true reason for her distress, he knew it had nothing to do with Eliza. She started counting gray hairs again. She felt herself tense up as he walked around the counter and over to her section by the dry goods. He dug into his pocket and fished out a few pennies. "I think you need something to keep you busy for a bit. Go on over to Mrs. Jameson's and get us a few rolls."

The bakery. It only served as a reminder that Phin Baldwin liked the bakery's hot cross buns.

"When you return, we can talk about it."

Her eyes widened. "About what?"

"About what's really bothering you."

She bit her bottom lip. "I'm fine, Father."

He forced her to go, anyway.

I'm being ridiculous, she told herself as she walked over to the bakery. The wind was icy and sharp, cutting a path across her cheeks and neck that brought tears to her eyes. At least the dirt of the road was somewhat wet, so it didn't cast a cloud over her. She couldn't understand why she was being so sensitive about the figurine. She hadn't ever been called in the drawing, and she hadn't expected to be called this time, either. So it wasn't disappointment. It all had to do with Phin Baldwin, that's all. *That's it. You knew he wasn't for you, but you could still dream. But when he didn't take this one little custom seriously, you realized that he really isn't from this place or like its people. You're upset that this dream has died. That's all.* She felt her shoulders relax a little. She'd been silly, placing so much importance on a trifling matter, and now that she realized it, she could move on. She went into the warm, yeasty comfort of the bakery and sighed with relief. She went over to the counter and greeted Mr. Jameson.

"How's your pa, Ginny?"

"He's doing well, Mr. Jameson. It's been a spell since you've been over for a lunchtime card game. You should go over one of these days. He won't say it, but I know he gets tired of the all female company."

Mr. Jameson chuckled. "I know what he means." He worked the bakery with his wife and Millie, and they were teaching Millie's brother's wife the business as well while her husband worked in the bank.

Millie heard her father and came up to the front, her face rosy from the ovens.

"Don't mind him, Ginny."

"What he meant to say is he's blessed," Millie's mother said from the bakery kitchen.

"Might be I'll go visit him now." Mr. Jameson laughed. "Seeing as I've suddenly entered dangerous territory."

He made his way over to the door, and while he put on his coat, his wife called out, "If you should see some nice shiny buttons for sale over there and buy them, we might be convinced to let you back in."

"Buttons, she says. The woman wants buttons." He muttered a farewell to Ginny and left.

Millie burst out, "Oh goodness, I thought we'd never be alone. Have you been over to the newspaper office, Ginny? Mr. Baldwin didn't make any wishes."

Ginny felt all the tension she'd left outside pile back onto her shoulders. It wasn't unexpected, she reminded herself. He'd said as much last night, hadn't he?

Ginny shrugged. "He's allowed, after all, I suppose."

"Mother and I took a round by the office this morning just to see it. They look so lonely."

She got sidetracked by Ginny's hair. "Ginny, honestly, your hair is a mess," Millie said. She set out to tuck a few pieces back in, only to be disappointed. Ginny muttered an excuse, blaming the weather conditions.

"He might fill them in later." Mrs. Jameson came out,

flour on her forearms and a smudge on her nose. "He's getting used to it. He won't disappoint us, you'll see."

Millie shook her head. "Ed said he told them straight out that he's not going to. He called it nonsense that, though quaint, wasn't reasonable."

Ginny vaguely heard Millie's mother asking her when she'd spoken to Ed, but all Ginny could hear was the part about it being "nonsense," and her blood stirred all over again. She left the rolls forgotten and felt herself propelled outside and across the street. She couldn't even feel the cold flapping at her coat, or the icy mud clinging to the bottom of her skirt as she crossed over to the newspaper office. She quickly glanced over and saw that Millie was right. The three wise men looked bereft of their wishes. She swung open the news office door and went in.

Rick greeted her. "Hi Ginny. Can I help you?"

She didn't know what made her do it, but her body was acting without cluing her mind in. She reached for the ring of wise men, tucked it inside her coat, and left the way she'd come. If *he* wasn't going to honor it, then *he* didn't deserve it.

PHIN COULDN'T BELIEVE what he was hearing. Ginny Overton seemed like such a rational person. He absolutely could not reconcile the image of those serious eyes with the picture Rick was painting of a wild-haired harridan.

"She didn't even say 'hello'. Just walked on by, straight to the window, and plucked it right up. Left without uttering one word."

"Am I missing something about the figurine? Or about her, for that matter? Is she insane, and that's why she hasn't married yet." Otherwise, he couldn't explain it. Maybe she was mad—she was much too pretty to be single otherwise.

"She was mighty upset last night, Phin," Ed said. "Matter of fact, she wasn't the only one, but others are keeping their thoughts to themselves."

"If you give it back to Pastor Morrow, he can organize another drawing with folks who are really interested," Rick suggested.

Phin had been considering the very same idea, but not now. Not after little Ginny Overton took it into her own hands to steal from him. Steal, because that's what she'd done. He had a mind to go to the marshal right now and charge her for the theft. He'd keep the wise men just to amuse himself. But first he had to rescue them from the crazy woman. "I got it fair and square," he said, choosing to forget that Ed had put his name into the drawing. "I'll be back."

Rick called after him. "Phin? What are you going to do?"

"Have a friendly chat with our neighborhood shop-keeper's daughter." *And wring her neck.*

Ginny didn't have long to feel the exhilaration that had steamed through her. She wasn't sure what she was going to do with the figurine. This was, by far, the craziest thing she'd ever done, and the fact that she had done it against someone like Phin Baldwin filled her little rebel's heart with unholy glee. She'd take it back to the pastor, only he would ask her how she'd come into possession of it, then she'd have to explain what she'd done, and she doubted he'd agree with her righteous indignation. Oh, Lord, what had she done? She felt the hairs on her neck tingle as the bells chimed against the shop door.

"We're getting to see a whole lot of you, Mr. Baldwin."

Ginny felt her heart drop into her stomach as Phin zeroed in on her. "Mr. Overton," he ground out as sweet as pie, watching Ginny the whole time, "would you mind if I had a few words with your daughter?"

Ginny could see the confusion on her father's face, but there was something else there too. Something she couldn't quite pin down. *Say no, Father, say no*, she willed. But the traitor agreed affably.

"You can use my office in the back room. I trust everything is all right?"

Phin's long stride ate up the ground as he made his way to the back. "Of course. I just need Miss Overton's opinion on a matter."

"I can help you here," she was able to say.

"Ginny, don't be rude. Mr. Baldwin needs your help."

She had no other choice but to accompany Phin to the very room where she'd hastily hidden the wise men until she figured out her next step. She hadn't counted on having to figure it out so soon.

Chapter Four

PHIN SHUT THE door behind him though Ginny didn't think her father would like that.

Very slowly, he approached her, his arms at his back. His voice was deceptively smooth. "I keep asking myself, what on Earth would provoke a lamb like you to commit such a heinous crime?"

He bit back a laugh as her eyes flashed at him. "One, Mr. Baldwin," she emphasized his name, "please refrain from exaggeration as this was no such thing, and two, I am no lamb."

"Of course you are," he said, rounding on her. He had her pacing around the small room as she attempted to maintain distance from him. "I called it the other day. You're a serious little thing though one with a penchant for robbery, apparently." He ignored her offended gasp. "So tell me this. Why shouldn't I go to the marshal this minute?"

She stopped her pacing. He noticed that she swiped at her hair, which only caused it to come more undone. She really did have gorgeous hair, the color of dark sable, and it was thick. Right now, two curling locks framed her pale face, her eyes shooting bullets at him. "The marshal? Are you mad?"

"I will not argue the sanity of my actions, ma'am, when you're the one who went into my place of work and stole something outright from me."

She jammed both hands on her waist and tried to reclaim her sanity. She wouldn't admit it to him, but she was acting erratic. There was a simple solution to all of this. She would reason with him. "Mr. Baldwin—"

"Call me Phin."

That threw her a bit, but she continued. "I do apologize. It wasn't right of me to do so. However, I think we can both agree that you were not going to use the figurine in the spirit for which it is intended. I understand this is a rather trivial matter, when you come down to the facts; however, it does mean a lot to many of us here. It's obvious it doesn't mean a thing to you. Let me return the wise men to Pastor Morrow, and he can hold another drawing."

"No."

"Why not?"

"Because it was given to me this year, and I intend to keep it until Christmas, as is tradition."

He could see she was biting back a retort. "Mr. Baldwin—"

"Phin."

Her eyebrows jammed together. "Why are you being so difficult?"

"I've just realized there's a whole other aspect to this tradition that you opened up with your actions."

"And what would that be?"

He leaned in close, close enough to smell lavender on her. "You."

"Me?"

"Yes. You've made this infinitely more fun. I will keep the wise men because you don't want me to."

"Honestly, Mr. Baldwin, I . . ." She didn't know what to say, so she took a breath. "It is ridiculous that we are even speaking of this."

"I agree. Remember who started this, though. Now, please return what you took."

She eyed him with palpable disdain. Her hands rose to push up more strands of hair. "Are you going to submit your wishes?"

"I have not changed my mind in that regard."

"Why won't you reconsider?"

"Why does it mean so much to you?" And this, truly, was the crux of everything. He was beginning to think this was the first bout of irrationality this woman had ever exhibited in her life. Why over this, something so small? The answer, if she chose to share it with him, would prop open a little window into Ginny Overton's soul.

She wouldn't share, though. She stared at him with a steady gaze.

"I am waiting."

Her shoulders slumped slightly, and he almost felt

badly enough to tell her to keep the figurine. Almost. She dragged a footstool to the bookshelf by the window and stepped onto it.

"Careful," he said, heading over to her in case she fell.

She reached up to the top shelf and pulled the figurine from behind a ledger. She stepped down and faced him. The difference in their heights was most evident from his position directly in front of her. He suddenly had the wildest urge to run his fingers through her untamed hair and seek out every last hidden pin and throw it away. Hair like hers shouldn't be restrained when it could be free and flow over her shoulders.

She tore her gaze away from his and looked down at the wise men. "Did you know that Mrs. Clancy's husband was on his deathbed five years ago?"

Her voice had softened, and he was uncomfortable with how beguiled he was by it, and by the moment. It had started to snow outside, making everything beyond the room a white blur. He could hear Ginny's father speaking to a customer in the front. They were laughing. But in here, they might as well be the last two people on Earth.

His own voice came out low. "No."

She looked into his eyes. "The doctor said he wouldn't live past New Year's Day."

"Are you telling me the wise men healed him?"

A smile tugged at the corner of her lips, causing him to focus his attention on her mouth. "No. I'm saying Mr. Clancy's son Maxwell was gifted the wise men that year, and though I don't know what his exact wish was, I think he wished for his father's recovery."

"There are a lot of reasons for a man to heal from a serious illness."

She took his hand into hers and opened his palm. She placed the figurine there. "Yes, there are. There's also the chance that a wish came true."

He stared at her. She was beguiling him. He could feel it.

"You won't change your mind about giving somebody else a chance with it?"

He shook his head.

"Very well. Then be warned. There will be consequences."

"What are you talking about?"

"Good day, Mr. Baldwin." She left him in the office, staring down at the knowing expressions of the wise men. "What in the hell did she mean by that?"

GINNY LEFT IT alone for three days. Each one of those days, she walked by the newspaper office and gazed in at the wise men, always empty.

On the fourth day, she struck.

Phin walked into the bank and did a double take when he saw the object on the bank manager's desk. "Where did you get that?" he asked, pointing at the wise men he'd left at the shop, where it had been night and day for the last four days. He took note of the three strips of paper within the boxes.

"This? Oh, Ginny brought it over 'bout an hour ago. She says you're giving us turns with the magic fellas, here, and that it's to be returned to you by the close of the business day. It's awful nice of you to share with us this year. Don't know why we haven't thought of it before. I guess it's because it's special to have it to one's self, but this is nice, too. Can I help you with something?"

Ginny was going to hear an earful. He didn't know why he was fighting it so much now, given that it seemed like a good enough plan. But the fact that she had gone behind his back—and into his office—yet again, had him stewing inside. If truth be told, he'd become more than a little fond of sitting at his desk and looking out to the window where the three wooden men watched Preston's people come and go, three ancient sentinels. She'd robbed him of that peace. Again. He'd have to speak to her father. There was no other way because though he'd threatened to go to the marshal with the complaint, he wasn't willing to put in a formal charge against her. He also wasn't willing to let it go.

He went to the shop after the bank, only to find that she had gone over to spend the afternoon with the elderly mother of Mrs. Trinkett, a miner's wife who had her hands full with three young children and a newborn baby. Speaking to Mr. Overton—John, as he asked to be called—had been a dead end. He explained that Ginny had "willful moments, just like her mother," and that he could try to speak to her, but that was it.

When Phin walked back into the office that evening after having attended a town-council meeting, he saw that the ring of wise men had been placed in its spot.

"Did she bring it here herself?"

Neither Ed nor Rick had to ask to whom he was referring. "Came in wearing the brightest smile, too," Ed replied. His face contained bottled-up mirth as he pointed to Phin's desk. "She left you a gift."

In the center of his desk was a hot cross bun.

"She said she'd be back for it tomorrow morning," Rick said.

"Like hell she will," Phin ground out.

Chapter Five

REGARDLESS OF WHAT he did, Ginny always got to it. The morning after its stay at the bank, the wise men found their way to the bakery, where Mrs. Jameson displayed them next to her apple crumble muffins. Phin tried to ask for it back, but the woman talked him into a loop, and he left the bakery with two muffins, an invitation to Sunday supper, and a spinning head, but not his lottery prize. The figurine was returned each afternoon, sometimes by Ginny, but oftentimes by the person who'd been the day's beneficiary. The wise men visited the homes of several of the townspeople, the laundry business, the theater, and even one of the brothels, though he wasn't sure he wanted to know how that happened or about how many godly rules might have been violated by that act. It didn't matter if he hid the figurine in his personal room, or left it out—she always got to it. He accused Rick and Ed of aiding her in the madness, but he realized who her accomplice was when he saw the wise men at the dinner table of his boardinghouse.

"I take it it's your turn, Mrs. Dixon," he said dryly.

She raised her chin and smiled beatifically. "Yes, and thank heavens. I was despairing of my name's ever being called in the annual drawing. Now, my wishes will be heard along with everyone else's."

He shoved at the green beans on his plate. "You believe in it, too, then."

"Never turn your back on the chance for a miracle, dear."

"Are you helping her get into my room?"

She had the audacity to be indignant, but the flush on the bridge of her nose gave her away. "I will not dignify that with an answer."

Maybe once he got the wise men back from their daily captivity, he would make a wish himself. Maybe he could wish Ginny Overton to a different state.

GINNY HAD HER back to the door when Rick and Phin walked into the church, where the children were rehearsing for the Christmas pageant. She helped Millie and Millie's sister-in-law Beatrice fit the children in their outfits.

"My, we've got a hefty angel in this one," Beatrice muttered under her breath as she struggled to get a smaller-sized gown over the boy's chest. "I thought my Alfred was big, but I see now I was wrong."

Ginny and Millie exchanged looks and laughed.

Bea was about to say something else, only she saw the men speaking to Pastor Morrow.

"Ginny, there's your archenemy."

Millie couldn't contain her laughter as she saw the sour look cross Ginny's face.

"I don't know how you've done it, but you have managed to turn away the most eligible man in Preston. He can't stand the sight of you."

"That makes us even," Ginny said. She'd kept her distance from the former "love of her life," and it was working out perfectly for her. Honestly, she didn't know what she'd seen in him other than his obvious good looks.

"Why are they here?" Bea wanted to know.

"Mama says the newspaper is going to contribute a program pamphlet. They must be asking Pastor Morrow for specifications so that they'll have enough time to print."

"Is there anything your mother doesn't know about the goings-on in town?" Bea asked, a hand on her hip.

Millie had the grace to blush. "Everybody stops by the bakery, is all."

Both Bea and Ginny kept their comments to themselves. Everybody might stop at a bakery, but not every baker subjected her customers to an interrogation. Ginny figured if Mrs. Clancy was fit to run the bank, then Mrs. Jameson was more than qualified to be marshal.

Ginny risked a peek at Phin, only to see he was looking back at her though the pastor was speaking to him. She was aware of the moment he noticed the object on the pastor's podium, located a few feet away from her. His eyes found her again, and he nodded slightly. She averted her gaze.

Pastor Morrow called Ginny over, making the other two women laugh.

"And so they meet again. Round . . . what round is it now, Bea," Millie asked sweetly.

"It's got to be around nine, no, ten. Round 10."

"Speak loudly so we can hear," Millie said.

Ginny glared at her friend as she smoothed a hand over her dress. "Your mother would be proud of you."

Ginny tried not to fidget with her hair, or with the buttons on her shirtwaist. She'd been working with the children all afternoon, and she'd enjoyed every second. They were rambunctious, and definitely a handful. She understood a bit of what Beatrice must go through every day with two little ones. She must be tired every day. But part of that came with the reward of watching the children grow and knowing that they are yours. Ginny could understand a bit of what her father was saying when he said he didn't want her to be alone. At the end of each day when the merchandise had been sorted and stored, and the daily sales tallied, she was alone. She did not have a husband to cook dinner for, nor children to tend; somehow, cooking for father wasn't the same. She didn't know what it was like to hold a drowsy child in her arms and sing him or her to sleep. She imagined it must be wonderful.

The men greeted her politely.

"I see you have company this afternoon," Rick directed at her with an impish grin. She saw where he was looking, and a laugh escaped her. The scoundrel. The three wise men held court over the festivities on the pastor's pulpit.

"Oh yes, Mr. Baldwin. I'd like to thank you again for letting Ginny bring it over today. I confess, I'm the keeper of the wise men, but I've never participated in the drawing. It was nice of you to think of me."

Ginny bit back her smile as she saw Phin struggle with words. How was that, for a newspaperman, she thought with delight. On the one hand, he could ruin Ginny's plan by exposing her to a man whose counsel she most definitely would heed, and on the other, he would be exposing himself as not having been the person worthy of a holy man's praise.

He caught her watching him, and she read the annoyance in his frown. Rick was watching, too, and he shared in her fun.

"Phin's just a decent sort of man," Rick said solemnly.

"Well, again, I certainly appreciate the opportunity to join in the fun as one more of the crowd this year."

"Have you made your wishes, Pastor Morrow?"

The older man smiled. "I sure have."

"I wasn't aware a preacher would have any wishes," Phin managed.

Pastor Morrow chuckled, rubbed his beard. "Oh sure. I'm a regular person same as you all. If anything, my wishes are vast because I pray for all of you."

"Make sure you keep a wish open for yourself, Pastor. Indulge," Ginny said. She hadn't realized that the one person who was always excluded from a drawing was the organizer himself. He was too kind to take the chance away from somebody else. Despite the madness of the scheme, it had been a good thing to do. Already, so many had been given a chance to participate, and she could feel the excitement in them each time she took the wise men to somebody new.

"Ginny," the pastor said, "I would appreciate your help in the matter of the program. I know you're on the planning committee, and if you have time, I'd love it if you could help Mr. Baldwin and Mr. Jensen out with the schedule. Do you have time now to go over it with them?"

She couldn't say no, could she? Not when she was specifically being asked by a man whom she respected and admired? Pastor Morrow had been a great help and friend around the time of her brother's death. "It would be my pleasure." At least Rick would be present. She had always gotten on well with him, and felt as comfortable with him as she did with Millie and her family.

The pastor departed, and she was left with the men. Then Rick surprised her by excusing himself to go speak to the man in charge of music.

She bit her lip as she watched him walk away. She kept her back to Phin as long as she could. This would be the first time she'd seen him since they had spoken in her father's store. He cleared his throat, and she slowly turned. She took a deep breath. "Very well. Where should I start?"

He didn't waste any time. "Has anyone ever told you you are a pain?"

She raised an eyebrow. "That's not very gentlemanly of you."

"I find it hard to be polite to troublesome children."

"Although I had heard of your reputation as the most

gallant of men, I must admit to being disappointed. My father's horse has better manners."

"As does mine. Better manners than you, that is."

"Mr. Baldwin, we can continue this line of conversation, or we can get down to the business at hand. The sooner, the better, I think."

His eyes narrowed at the boredom in her voice. "You have more important things to do, I take it?"

"Oh, always."

"Yes, I can see it can be time-consuming to spend your time plotting against me. Between that, and working the shop, it is no wonder you do not have marriage prospects."

Her mouth widened at the unexpected blow. "Now, wait a minute. That was uncalled for."

"I suppose I would apologize if it were anybody else. As it is you . . ." His words trailed off.

They stood almost nose to nose, their dislike of one another hiding from them the fact that their interaction was being closely observed by the adults in the room, as well as a confused preacher.

She could have told him he could have avoided all of this if he'd returned the gift as she'd asked. She could have reminded him that the tradition meant more to others than it did to him. She also could have told him of the many people who had benefited and enjoyed having the wise men for a day, how their faces lit up when they saw her come in because they knew she was the envoy. Instead, she raised her chin. She began reciting the order of events for the pageant, thinking that she needed to be out of his presence immediately. "The pageant will begin at six in the evening. It will begin with–"

"Come with me to the office. If I'm going to have your input, I might as well have it in everything from the type to the graphics you would like to include."

She looked over to her friends and searched out Rick, only to find that he was no longer there. "Will we wait for Rick?"

"No. Like you said, the sooner we finish with this, the better."

SHE KEPT UP with him as they trekked down the main thoroughfare to the office. Phin tipped his hat to a few men in greeting, and Ginny kept her head down. She wasn't accustomed to walking beside a man who wasn't her father. She tended to run quick errands by herself, and those were usually at the neighboring shops. Otherwise, her father did not allow her to travel unescorted.

Phin gently took her elbow and steered her out of the way of an oncoming carriage and away from a cold mud puddle. She turned her head to look at his profile. "Thank you," she murmured in a quiet voice.

He merely nodded, barely taking notice of her gratitude. His hand left her arm.

He unlocked the office, as no one else was inside, and gestured for her to take a seat. She complied and waited for him to light a fire in the fireplace in the corner.

"Would you like some coffee," he asked brusquely.

She shook her head.

"I apologize for my comment. Before."

His back was to her as he leaned over his desk. She could see that his hands were still, which meant he wasn't searching for anything, and nothing kept him occupied. Surely, he didn't feel bad?

She'd behaved badly as well, and he was being more than tolerable. "Me too."

That caught his attention, and he turned around, reclining against his desk. Both his eyebrows rose at her statement. "For what?"

"I didn't make you say what you were sorry for," she accused.

"And now that's a lost opportunity. I, however, have asked."

The kind feelings created by his apology were starting to dissolve. She let out a hefty sigh and rolled her eyes. "Very well. I apologize for plotting against you."

"Well that wasn't hard," he said.

"But not," she said, leaning forward, "for taking the figurine away."

He let out an exasperated groan. "I don't want to have this discussion again."

Nor did she. "Take your pencil out, newspaperman. Let's begin."

And so they did, and they set aside their previous relationship of antipathy for one of interviewer and interviewee.

Phin had to admire her for temporarily calling a truce. She was the utmost professional as she enlightened him on the pageant. She was recounting the history of how the bells came to be part of the annual Christmas pageant, and he wrote it down, but he also studied her. He had been wrong to mention her marriage prospects, or lack thereof. She just got under his skin, and he became an irrational being. His mother would balk if she knew how badly he'd treated a woman. "Above it all, Phin, you must always be a gentlemen. You must be respectful and courtly toward every woman, whether she be part of your family or a complete stranger."

Ginny's face changed when she became animated, like now, as she smiled, recalling how Mr. Trinkett had been tasked to play Joseph in the play a few years ago and showed up inebriated. Only nobody knew about it until he started speaking words that were not in the script. She painted the story so well, he found himself laughing along with her. Ginny's cheeks had taken on the glow from the warmth of the fire, and she'd even removed her big coat. Phin couldn't help but study her tidy, female form. Her hair was left down today though she'd pulled some of it away from her face and fastened it with a pin at the back. Her brown eyes were the color of a good, mature whiskey, and they lit up, he noticed, when she was animated or incensed, and now he'd had a chance to see both sides of her. She wasn't the most beautiful woman he'd ever seen, but there was a wholesome appeal to her, a simple, clean way about her that was as elegant as the patrician women of his acquaintance back in Boston.

He had to control his eyes, though. She'd already caught him staring at her twice.

GINNY KNEW HOW she was going to have one of her wishes come true. She had not allowed herself to keep the wise men for a day, as it seemed like there was a conflict of interest involved, though she would have loved to place it in her father's hands. If only he'd be selfish, she thought. She had a list of who would get the wise men, leading up to Christmas, when she would let Phin keep it, as it was only fair for him to have them one day. Maybe the spirit would move him, and he would take advantage of his last chance.

Time was passing her by, and she was only a passive spectator. Although it had hurt to hear it, Phin was right. She was alone, with no prospects, and her conversation with her father had only served to make something very clear. She did not have the kind of life that she wanted. If she wanted to change that, she would have to make an aggressive move. Not for herself; she did not know what she was going to do about Father, or her life, for that matter. But she knew that she could make one dream come true. She would witness extraordinary things. Because she would make them happen.

She knew that many of the people in town had wishes and dreams that were out of reach, but they also had many more that could be accomplished. And why shouldn't they be? Her plan began as a wispy idea, growing into maturity as she regaled Phin with stories of her town and her people. People who were so very dear to her for the very fact that they were the family that she didn't have at home. They'd been by her side, helping as much as they could when she'd no longer had a mother or a sister to speak to. They'd been her father when he'd spiraled into despair. They'd been her brother when she needed a friend.

Mrs. Jameson and Mrs. Clancy, along with several of the other married women of Preston, had invited Ginny into their homes with flimsy pretexts, and they taught her how to sew, how to cook a ham, how to darn a sock. They'd fussed over her stitches because she didn't have someone to fuss over her at home. They'd harangued her over her dress choices and the state of her hair.

In the year following her mother's death, Mr. Trinkett and Mr. Jameson alternated days to pick her up from her home and walk her to the store to open up for the day. Those were the days before her father and she had relocated to the rooms above the shop, and the company of the men on those dusky mornings had always been welcome. Mr. Jameson's son had even offered to marry her once, before he'd met Bea. His proposal was a secret that they'd both keep to the end of their days, especially since Ginny was sure he'd only done it out of a misplaced sense of responsibility for her welfare. She was glad she had not accepted, as he and Bea were a perfect match. Rick had been her brother's friend, and then hers, providing a staunch shoulder to cry on when Monty was no longer there. These people had made her life so much easier, so much richer, and she wanted to repay their kindness.

She didn't know what had happened to her. Phin Baldwin wasn't wrong. She was a serious little thing. She had been, anyway. But this idea came from the purest place in her heart, and only a risk-taker could follow through. A serious little thing wouldn't attempt what she was going to try. But if she was to succeed, she was going to need help. She wouldn't be able to pull it off by herself. She was going to need an accomplice with resources and access to places that she didn't have.

Someone like Phin Baldwin. She caught Phin staring again, wondered about it. She was probably talking too much. How was she going to get him to go along with her plan, especially since, up until now, she had considered him her archenemy, as Bea called him, and he had called her a pain to her face?

Allies were made of the strangest people, she thought.

Chapter Six

"**WHAT?**"

"I need your help in a Christmas project of mine."

His eyes narrowed with suspicion. "What kind of project?"

She rested her chin in the palm of her hand. "Are you any good at granting wishes?"

Phin thought he had been as surprised by Ginny Overton as he was ever likely to be. She had already broken out of the box he'd set for her upon meeting her by stealing the wise men and passing them around to everyone in the community. In the following minutes, he realized she'd gone and done it again. Surprised the words right out of him.

"Let me see if I understand you correctly. You want us to look at everyone's wishes—everyone you gave the figurine—*my* figurine," he couldn't help but emphasize, "and somehow make it so that these things come true?"

"Yes, you've summed it up perfectly."

He was lost for words. She was out-of-her-mind daft. There was no other way to explain it. And what was worse, she was trying to turn him strange, too. "How exactly do you propose we do that?" Because she had started to smile, he clipped her hopes real quick. "And my asking does not mean I am in any way interested in helping you."

"I've been keeping their wishes." The look on her face was sheepish, as if she was embarrassed to admit it, and why shouldn't she be? Not only had she stolen from him, and made it a daily mockery, but now she'd even gone so far as to infringe on the privacy of everyone who had made a wish. He didn't even want to think about how he would feel if he found out someone had looked in on his uttermost desires. She must have seen the disapproval in his face because her brow furrowed, and she leaned in closer, saying in earnest, "I didn't take them to be a nosy Parker, I swear. I haven't looked at any of them."

She looked down at her hands. "I would never want to intrude on someone's personal things," she continued even though she must have heard his snort. "But each day before preparing to get the figurine back to you, I would collect the slips of paper and think, what a shame that their wishes didn't get a chance to take."

"I wasn't aware the wishes had to ripen," he said drolly. "Besides, how do you know they didn't take? I thought you believed in them. You're admitting to me and to yourself that this colored piece of wood has no more power in it than I have in my little finger."

She wouldn't engage in verbal sparring with him and simply raised her voice. "So, I collected the wishes, wrote down whom they belonged to, and tucked them into a page of my journal."

"You keep a journal?" Now this was interesting.

"All this time has passed, and I have journal pages filled with other people's wishes. Just talking to you right now, I thought, why not try and make some of them come true?"

"Because it's not your place. You have no business, and no right, as a matter of fact, to look at someone else's property." She didn't have a right to *take* other people's property either, but why beat a dead horse with a stick? What was done was done. It didn't mean he had to add to it by conspiring with this loon of a woman. "You know, Rick has only nice things to say about you. How you're a sensible girl, a responsible daughter. He goes on and on about what an exemplary person you are, and I have to admit, I'm stymied."

She was wary. "Why's that?"

"Because I wonder if he's a little slow, or suffers from a mental disorder. Maybe he's blind. In the time I have known you, I have seen none of these qualities. Clearly, I'm not seeing the person he sees."

She stood up, deciding she'd had enough. Her chin lifted as she regarded him. "I suppose you haven't considered the alternative?"

He knew he should rise, since she had. Good manners indicated he must. But he liked bucking courtesies when it came to Miss Ginny Overton. "Which is?"

"That *you* might be the one suffering from the mental disorder."

She left him alone in the office, grinning up to high heaven, despite having been insulted.

HE WOULDN'T HELP her, and that was fine. She didn't know what she'd been thinking anyway, asking someone like him for help. She'd offered him the adventure of helping one's fellow man, something she intended to do regardless of his refusal. She'd miscalculated by confiding in him, and though their dealings with each other were always civil, at best, she could only hope that he would not inform others of her intentions.

Her father was in his office, working on the week's accounts. Ginny took the opportunity to take out her journal and choose the first batch of wishes she'd be "granting." She was enthusiastic about the prospect of being part of something miraculous in someone else's life. Not just miraculous, she thought with a thrill in her heart. Extraordinary.

She took out the first three, the ones that belonged to the Jameson family.

The first one read, *Bless me with another daughter.*

Ginny suppressed a sigh. That was surely Bea's. Before having Alfred, Bea had miscarried a baby girl. She had been solemn for many months before becoming pregnant with Alfred, who would be her second son. *I can't exactly help with that one,* Ginny thought sadly.

The second one read, *Please keep our business boom-*

ing as it has been, so that maybe we can save enough to send Hank to school like he wants.

That one could have been made by Mr. or Mrs. Jameson, but since the one didn't do anything without the knowledge of the other, Ginny supposed the wish had been a joint venture. Millie's youngest brother was eleven, and the smartest child Ginny had ever met. He was always at the lending library, his puglike nose buried in a book. He could do sums in his head that dizzied his mother when he helped her in the bakery, and everyone knew if he ever had the chance, he could go far.

Ginny didn't know how she could possibly help with that. She hardly had enough savings to send a boy to college. Maybe if she saved up for several years and presented it to the family when Hank was of age. That would take too long, and she wasn't even sure it would be enough. Fancy schools cost fancy money.

A noise outside stirred her thoughts, and she checked to see that no one was watching. Outside the shop doors, business was happening as usual on the main street as people bustled here and there. Ginny returned her concentration to the wishes. This wish-granting business was not for the faint of heart. "Well, if it was so easy, people wouldn't have need of them," she muttered to herself. She retrieved the last scrap of paper on the page and prayed that she would find something she could work with.

The third wish was written in a child's writing. Ginny's lips curved. "Oh, Hank." She thought it was dear that the Jamesons had shared their opportunity to add something to the wish list. Given the nature of the first two, she doubted anyone but the wisher had been allowed to view the other papers. The paper read, "Help Millie find a husband, so she'll stop mooning around all the time. And if you can, I would like to see the world. But I understand if it's too much. Thank you."

Hank Jameson, you're the sweetest boy ever, Ginny thought. And this, she thought, is a wish I can work with. But she'd have to be quick since Christmas was less than two weeks away.

GINNY ORGANIZED THE first-ever Christmas "goods" auction within the church, the funds to be used to repair the roof over the school. Though Ginny was glad that her festivities would bring in much-needed aid to the school, her primary reason for organizing the event was much different. She needed a reason to throw a few people together.

Her father joined her at the table where she was organizing the home-goods section. Pastor Morrow was with him. He took her hand and squeezed. "Your father and I were just commenting on what a wonderful idea this was. I'm very grateful for your involvement in this event, Ginny."

She saw her father's pride by the way he stood with his hands on his suspenders, and felt the slightest twinge of guilt since her first impulse had not been completely selfless. Although, she reminded herself, her main goal wasn't selfish, so maybe she shouldn't feel guilty. It was all for a good cause, after all. Millie *and* the school repairs.

She was relieved when both men walked away to let her finish categorizing the items that would be up for auction. The Jamesons were going to auction off two items: a lesson in making apple pie as well as a two-week supply of free bread. The blacksmith offered his services for one full day; his wife included a home-cooked meal, which would go over well with the single miners, some of who were not lucky enough to live in boardinghouses or have homes of their own. The hotel was going to auction off a night's stay in the best room of the establishment, the banker a beautiful leather pouch for gold dust, and so on. Ginny once again marveled at the generosity of Preston and her people. Sillier gifts were being auctioned, like a dance with Cecilia Gilliam, the mayor's wife, but Ginny knew these would be auctioned off as well in the spirit of fun.

Ginny's main plan hinged on a specific item being auctioned. Ginny had coaxed Millie into providing a picnic basket filled with fried chicken, potatoes, and a chocolate cake she'd made herself. She'd managed to evade Millie's questions about why Ginny wanted her to do this by selling her on the romance. "Don't you want to see who's going to bid on it," she'd said. She'd seen the question in Millie's eyes and knew she'd won her over. Which was perfect, because her plan didn't work if Millie didn't provide something to the auction.

The pastor called for the bidders to take their seats so the festivities could begin, and Ginny looked through the crowd to find two very important people. She was quick in locating Phin Baldwin. She frowned because he was talking to her father. The coat he had ordered had already come in, and hopefully, he didn't have a complaint about it, but she didn't see any other reason for the two to look so chummy. His head swiveled directly to her, making her move back a step. He'd known exactly where in the room she was, and wasn't that a discomfiting thought? She bit down on her lip. That was one. Her eyes traveled over the bright, smiling faces of the people and finally hit upon the other person. Alfred Jameson, six years old, was at his mother's side. Ginny caught his eye and winked. He smiled wide, displaying a gap where one of his front teeth should be. She scowled at him to remind him this wasn't a game, and he sobered quickly, winking back.

"Dear God, help me," she prayed quickly. "If I'm using a child to help me in this endeavor, I must be out of my mind." This thought, however, did not cause her to relent. She was going to go through with her plan no matter what.

PHIN SAT BACK in his chair as item after item was auctioned off. He considered bidding on a few objects himself. There was a toy horse carved out of pine that his sister Lisa's son might like for Christmas, and as he had a mind to visit his family for the holidays, it was only right he come bearing gifts. He didn't raise his hand once, however. When he saw how Mr. Wheeler's son tugged on his father's coat when the toy was shown, Phin didn't have the heart. He couldn't drive the price up for something that would mean more to Mr. Wheeler's little boy than it would to Phin's nephew.

He jotted down a few notes about the event since it was the first of its kind in Preston. He found his eyes wandering every once in a while to the event's organizer. Ginny sat in the front with her father. She wore a kelly green shirtwaist with puffed-up sleeves over a long skirt made of brown linen. Phin knew from his sister's detailed letters that fashions in bigger cities were changing to a looser, vertical style of dress. The times hadn't caught up with little ol' Preston, it was obvious, since Ginny's cinched-in waist was evidence of the corset she still used. It suited her, as did the rich color of the blouse, and her dark hair, usually a rumpus, was combed back in a simple but elegant coiffure, accentuating the ear-bobs dangling at each ear. He frowned because he'd noticed her hair, noticed how her fair cheeks were suffused with warmth and how they curved up with her smile. Then he frowned some more because one wasn't supposed to find his personal pain in the ass attractive. And damn it, she was.

He caught Ed staring at him funny, and he scowled at him. The kid next to Phin stared at him, too.

The pastor brought out the next item, a picnic basket filled with homemade delights prepared by Mildred Jameson. Ed sat up a little straighter in his seat, making Phin snicker. This time, it was Ed's turn to scowl. Phin couldn't wait to see how much Ed was willing to bid on the dinner.

"Now folks, you're just going to have to take my word on it, but Miss Millie Jameson is among the finest cooks it's been my pleasure to meet. If you were standing where

I am now, holding this here basket, you might just faint of delight, it smells that good."

Pastor Morrow started the bidding low. Phin looked over at Millie and saw the flush of curiosity on her face. If ever there was a woman in search of a beau, it was Millie. The bidding war so far was between Ed, a miner named Steely Jack, Millie's brother, and Rick, and surely the last two were only bidding in order to heckle—Millie's brother wanted to embarrass Millie, and Rick wanted to do the same with Ed.

Phin felt a poke in the ribs, and looked over to the other side. The kid smiled up at him apologetically.

"Looks like we have a new bidder," Pastor Morrow said. "Phin Baldwin."

Phin's eyes widened. His hand had gone up when he'd been poked, but surely that couldn't be misconstrued as a bidding attempt?

The pastor asked for a counter to Phin's offer. He sighed in relief when Ed took it.

The kid tugged at a piece of his hair. Phin yelped and stared at the kid in befuddlement.

"I'm sorry, Ed, but it looks like Phin wants him some fried chicken. Do I have another offer?"

Phin waited to see if someone would get him out of the fix. He wouldn't be able to recant and say he hadn't intended to bid—twice—that would only serve to embarrass. Steely Jack helped him by upping the ante.

Out of the corner of his eye, Phin saw the kid preparing for another attack. He decided to take precautionary measures and ducked his head close enough for the kid to hear, but no one else. "I don't know if you think this is a game, boy, but I'm putting a stop to it."

The boy stared at him, blue eyes round and bright. Then he kicked Phin in the shin, and Phin barked out a grunt, and just like that, he was in the race again.

If he hadn't seen Ginny looking at him, biting her lips to keep from laughing, then turning away rapidly when she detected his scrutiny, he would have been none the wiser. But he was a smart man, and he put two and two together. He leaned down to the boy. "You're Millie's nephew, right? Sam and Bea's boy?"

The boy nodded silently.

"How about I tell your father what you've been up to? What do you think he'll say to that?"

The boy's face turned pale. "I'm sorry, mister. Please don't tell Pa. I apologize, really I do."

Phin shushed him quickly so that he wouldn't cause a scene. He leaned in once more, "All right. Listen to me. If you answer my next question honestly, I won't tell your father about this little incident, understood? But you have to be honest."

He saw the relief course through the boy.

"Who put you up to this?"

He saw the boy turn guilty, opening his mouth, then closing it. The boy didn't want to rat out his accomplice, which, Phin admitted, was admirable. He tried a different tack. "Let's do this. I'll say a name, and you nod if that's the person, all right?"

The boy nodded rapidly, this plan much more to his liking. Luckily, Phin only had one name on his list.

"Was it Ginny Overton?"

The boy nodded once more, confirming Phin's suspicions. When would the woman leave him alone?

"You're not going to tell Pa, right, Mr. Baldwin? A deal's a deal."

His grinned at the reminder. "You're right, son. A deal's a deal. Go on over to your family."

During his conversation with the boy, whom he belatedly remembered was named Alfred, the bidding had continued without him. Steely Jack had outbid the others, and Ed was grumbling beside him.

"Luck wasn't with you," Phin said to him.

Ed glared at Phin. "Nothing to do with luck. And just what in tarnation were you about bidding for Millie's basket? I thought you didn't like Millie."

Phin's eyebrows rose at the rankled tone in his friend's voice. "I like her fine, but not like that. I thought you felt the same way."

Ed's tongue tangled in his mouth, so that he somehow turned a muttered denial, a flippant joke, and a "hrmmph" into one syllable. The man stood up discreetly, as they'd taken seats in the back, and put on his coat. "Let's go. They're almost done anyway, and they're only going to have cookies and punch later before everyone goes home."

Phin couldn't go home. He still had one more task to do. "You go ahead. I'll see you tomorrow."

Given how that vixen had conspired against him, this next part was going to be delicious—and Phin had her father to thank.

GINNY WAS IN a stunned stupor as the remaining items were auctioned off. Her plan had been simple enough, but at some point, something had gone horribly wrong. She still couldn't believe it. Alfred had done his part, God bless him, and yet, Phin had stopped bidding so that someone else had gotten Millie's wares. Ginny knew Millie enough to know that she'd be hearing about *that* for the next few weeks to come. Millie wanted a husband, but not someone like Steely Jack, who was always three sheets to the wind and was missing several teeth, besides the fact that he was in his late forties. And then, as if her failure were not enough to contend with, she'd been thrown for a loop when, suddenly *she* was being included in the auction. Without her knowledge, she was entered to provide three sessions to paint a free portrait. When it was being announced, she turned to her father. He beamed at her. Ginny had dabbled with sketches and occasionally paints when she could get her hands on them, but she was nowhere near being accomplished enough to take someone's likeness and make it a portrait.

Her confusion became horror when none other than Phin Baldwin outbid everyone else for the sessions and portrait. The pastor brought the event to a close, giving her special thanks and a prayer for organizing the event. Then he gave people leave to go by the tables for refreshments before going home.

She swallowed audibly as she saw Phin walk toward her. She saw the devilish gleam in his eye and immediately knew that Alfred had sold her out. She couldn't blame the boy; he was no match for this sandy-haired heathen.

"You and I need to talk."

She looked to her father for help. The traitor only smiled and walked away to speak with acquaintances.

They both waited while a few citizens came over to praise Ginny for her involvement in the event and to gush about the prizes and who'd taken them home. When they were alone, Phin took her by the elbow and steered her to a secluded spot by the church's back door, used by the pastor to enter from his garden in the back.

Phin would have taken Ginny somewhere where they could be completely alone if it were not improper to do so. He was upset and, quite frankly, confused by her, but he couldn't do that to her, or to himself.

He expected her to be ashamed. Therefore, his confusion was compounded by surprise when she lashed out at him the moment they obtained a degree of privacy. She yanked her arm out of his grasp, and hissed, "What were you thinking, bidding for me?"

He stared at her for a good five seconds before he found his tongue. He had to play this just right, though, because when he was around her, he suddenly forgot his cool, not to mention his manners.

"Miss Overton, Ginny if I may?"

"You may not."

"As I was saying, Ginny, first, I did not bid on *you* per se. Secondly, if I bid on your auction item, it was at the behest of your father."

It was Ginny's turn to remain silent as she contemplated his words. "What do you mean?" But she had a feeling she knew, and it all started with her father's friendly chat earlier that evening with the man before her.

"Your father says you are too modest about your artwork to have entered on your own, and he wanted to make sure someone bid on your work, lest you be disappointed."

She would have words with her father tonight. She could feel the flush of embarrassment reaching her hairline. Her hands found their way to her waist, and she leaned in. "This may all be as you say, but the question remains, what on Earth would you want with a portrait? Done by me? You've made no secret about your feelings for me."

That was true. Staring at her huffing and puffing, he felt the beginnings of a smile coming on. She was the most royal of pains, he'd decided tonight, but, it had to be said, she was certainly fun.

"I can't think of anything that I need less than a portrait of myself. However, like I said, I was simply doing your father a favor." He could see that she wanted to continue, but it was past time he took the upper hand. "Since you have started us off nicely with recriminations, I'll make a few of my own. Why did you turn Alfred loose on me?"

He could see that he'd painted her into a corner because her hands left her hips, and her mouth clamped shut.

"Whatever do you mean?"

"Let's not play the game where we both pretend I don't

know what you're up to. I see through you so much, it's beginning to scare me. Are you going to deny that you are trying to match me up with your friend?"

She took a breath and lifted her chin so that her eyes directly met his. She practically looked as if she was about to challenge him.

"Well, now that you know, there's no use in denying it. And perhaps it's better this way."

"How so?"

Her eyes sharpened, and he felt, rather than knew, that he wasn't going to like the answer.

"Because you are looking for a wife, yourself. Isn't that why you're here in Preston? Because your family tasked you with finding an 'appropriate' wife? Are you going to deny the truth behind my words . . . Mr. Whitemore?"

Damn, she'd gone and surprised him again.

Chapter Seven

PHIN HADN'T COUNTED on anyone but his immediate circle of friends, which included only Rick and Ed, knowing his true identity. He couldn't begin to fathom how she'd discovered the truth.

Still, he attempted a bluff. "I don't know what you're talking about."

She threw his own words back in his face. "Let's not play the game where we both pretend I don't know what you're up to."

His eyes narrowed.

"Yes, I know all about you, Mr. Whitemore. I know you belong to the ever-mighty Whitemores of Boston, who own our town newspaper as well as several other properties across the country. I know you're here at the behest of your father and grandfather, whose desire it is that you find a wife among the 'average' people. Why, I do not know, nor do I care. And lastly, I know that you don't want anyone to know who you really are because it will make your task much harder to complete."

He wasn't going to be able to have this discussion with her in the open, where everyone could see. Already, Millie was walking over to them, and he could see she had flirtation on her mind. He had to act quickly.

Millie approached them, with a side glance at Ginny. Phin risked a look at her and saw that she had that look in her eyes that said she was about to do something stupid. She probably viewed this as another opportunity to throw Millie and Phin together.

"Mr. Baldwin, I didn't know you had a taste for fried chicken. I'm sorry you didn't get the prize, but I'd be happy to whip you up a meal anytime you want. You just have to ask."

"You know, Millie, Mr. Baldwin was just saying how upset he was that he wouldn't be able to try it for himself. Perhaps you–"

He cut her off. "Thank you for your generosity, Miss Jameson. I'll be sure to keep that in mind. If you'll excuse Miss Overton and me, I have to take her over to her father and discuss something with him. Good evening, Miss Jameson."

He herded Ginny over to her father and quickly obtained permission to walk her home. Thankfully, her father didn't offer an objection, and soon, he was helping her don her coat and scarf before leading her out.

He considered offering her his arm as they walked down the silent thoroughfare, then thought better of it.

"You realize you've given the people something to gossip about."

He was aware of the looks he'd been given. First, he'd bid for her prize in the auction, then he was accompanying her home, unescorted by her father. Luckily, only she and he knew the true reason for this nighttime stroll.

"How did you learn of my intentions, of my name?"

Ginny stopped at the door of the Overton store. He looked up. "You live here?"

She turned the key, letting herself in. She looked out at him. "We live on the upstairs level. We used to live out by the hill, but Father decided to sell the house several years ago."

"We're not done speaking."

He could see her weighing her next words. "You can come in for a little bit. I can put on some coffee to warm us up."

He entered the darkness of the store and soaked in the smells of the spices, the leather goods, and the oranges brought in special for the season.

She turned her back to him as she prepared the coffee. "I found out unintentionally. You see, your brother wrote my father a detailed letter setting up an account for you with the store and asking my father to help you with anything that you needed. By the look on your face, I can see you are surprised. Your brother, Theodore . . ."

"T. D." He should have known it was T. D.

"He visited our establishment on his first visit to Preston five years ago, when he became responsible for the *Preston Gazette*. He and my father formed a quick friendship, and every once in a while, my father receives correspondence from him."

T. D. would be idiotic enough to share the secret with someone in town, thinking he knew best. Worse, Phin couldn't hate him for it because he knew that his older brother meant well. He just wished he hadn't involved anybody else in the scheme. Naturally, the one person in T. D.'s confidence would also be the person with the daughter that wanted to make Phin's life difficult. Phin listened as Ginny shared the story of how she'd mistaken T. D.'s letter for a letter from a creditor, and read it. She was ashamed, he could see, when she admitted to continuing her reading after discovering what the letter actually was. She'd known about him before he'd ever set foot in town.

"Please don't tell my father. He doesn't know that I'm aware of your identity. He'd be mortified."

Phin considered that and nodded. He didn't want his relationship with the older Overton to change, either. It was in both their best interest if John continued to think he'd kept T. D.'s secret.

"You're probably curious about why my father sent me here to find someone to marry."

"I admit, it does seem more than a little odd. I would imagine your family would want you wed to one of your acquaintances."

Phin's mother certainly had. She'd been infuriated with her husband's plan, but she had failed in getting him to retract. "My brother is recently married."

"Yes, we know. He announced it in the paper."

"My sister is also married." He could see she didn't understand him, and it pained him to have to continue because doing so would mar the image of his family in her eyes. Not in a scandalous way, but it would demonstrate that the "average" person was not wrong in thinking the wealthy had skewed priorities in life. "My siblings have married people who come from our station in life. Wealthy, educated, cultured."

"How nice for them." He heard the edge in her voice, and it made him want to laugh.

"Yes, you would think so. However, these people can feel very entitled. My sister's husband lives each day on money his family made. He has not contributed to their wealth and doesn't appear to want to change that. My brother's new wife is the same way. My father and grandfather are of the opinion that if my brother were not from a family such as ours . . ."

"Rich."

"She would not have married T. D. As men who worked very hard for the things they have, they are more than a little disappointed." He took a breath. "As the last of my father's children to be unmarried, it came to me to rectify the matter."

"You came here to choose someone to marry solely because your father asked you to?"

She was incredulous.

"That, and they have agreed to give me control over the family's company. As the youngest, that is something I would not have had without this opportunity."

GINNY WAS UNCOMFORTABLE about what she'd just heard. He always seemed so composed, a natural-born charmer, and yet, right now, he was showing himself in a poor light. He was calculating, indeed, if he had agreed to go along with this senseless plan as a means of obtaining power in his family's business. She felt a little sick to her stomach, which was odd because it shouldn't matter to her one way or the other if he was not quite the paragon she'd thought when she'd first seen him.

She noticed him searching her, but he continued when he saw she wouldn't comment. "They want me to marry a sensible woman from an 'average' family—their words, not mine—because they believe doing so would prevent me from going down the incorrect path of my siblings. They want someone who will be a true companion to me, and one who will not bleed the coffers dry with frivolous spending. They chose Preston because my brother really liked it, and it reminds Grandfather of the town where he was born."

She still didn't speak, and Phin felt his face a touch warm despite the cold.

"It's a compliment," he explained.

She cleared her throat. "I suppose they think it is. Maybe it is. I don't know."

"Are you offended?" he asked, disconcerted by the severity of her expression.

Her gaze rose to meet his. "I have no reason to be. But now that you know that I am aware of your real reason for being here, you must admit I can be helpful. Millie would be a perfect match for you. She is ready for marriage, and you need a wife. It's kismet."

Phin didn't want to explain to her that he had imposed his own conditions on his family's scheme when he accepted it. It was agreed there would be no time limit as to when he must marry. Also, his would be a love match, as his brother and sister had made. He wouldn't jump into marriage simply to fulfill terms set out by his father and grandfather. But these were private, personal feelings, and they had no place in this store with Ginny Overton. So, instead, he shook his head. "I can't marry Millie."

He saw her bristle. "Why not? Is she too average?"

"I told you, that was their word. No, Millie is a lovely girl. But, at best, I feel brotherly affection toward her."

"That could change."

"It won't," he said firmly. "A man knows his feelings."

She rolled her eyes. "A likely thing for you to say. It seems to me like you're sabotaging yourself. If you want control of the company, I wouldn't think you'd be so picky."

Except it wasn't only about the company, Phin wanted to say. Whomever he chose, he'd be with for the rest of their lives. One didn't go into marriage lightly.

"There's a stronger reason for me to stay away from Millie."

She waited, her arms crossed at her chest.

"Ed's in love with her."

Her mouth dropped open slowly. "Ed? Has he told you that?"

"Of course not. Ed doesn't even want to admit it to himself. I've discovered that Ed has an issue committing to the idea of monogamy. But you only have to observe him when Millie is around. I couldn't marry Millie even if she'd have me."

Ginny smirked, sneaking a look at him. "Oh, she'd have you." She thought about Ed's bidding for Millie, and she thought back to several other instances. It was true. Ed's demeanor changed whenever he was in Millie's presence. Why hadn't she seen it before? Her plan didn't have to be ruined after all just because Phin wasn't going to willingly participate. Still . . . he could be wrong.

"You don't know that for sure," she said.

He threw up his hands. "I can see you're not convinced, and your head is probably concocting more silly schemes."

"They're not silly," she said. "In fact, I almost had you today. A little fine-tuning on my part, and my plans will go ahead just as planned."

"Which is what I'm scared of," he said. Before she could offer an argument, which was inevitable, he continued, "Ginny, I'm going to offer you a solution in return for your silence."

"Oh, good." She let out a sigh. "That saves me from having to blackmail you."

That threw him. "Was that ever a possibility?"

She bit her lip, causing him to look at her plump lower lip. "It was my backup plan."

Well that was alarming. "It's a good thing I got to you before you put that in motion. Now I see that it is necessary that I offer this alternative."

Chapter Eight

GINNY KEPT LOOKING at the timepiece by the front door of the store. Phin said he would be in for his first portrait session by three o'clock, and he was twelve minutes late. Her father kept looking over at her, asking her if everything was well with her. She'd smiled so many times at him, she felt like her cheeks might freeze and keep the expression for the rest of her life.

She wasn't worried about not starting on her portrait; in fact, that was the furthest thing from her mind. She was, however, apprehensive about the pact that she'd made with Phin the night she'd invited him in for coffee. He was her archenemy, after all, and nemeses were notorious for being untrustworthy.

Phin had decided to help her with her undercover wish-granting campaign if she would fulfill certain conditions. "If anything," he'd teased, "it will get you to stop soliciting help from the schoolroom." His first condition was that she was forbidden from pairing him up with Millie or with anyone else. "You are not allowed to interfere in my personal life even if you think you are being helpful." She'd argued, of course. She had several friends from good, honest families who might make a good match with Phin. He'd quickly let her know that the condition was nonnegotiable. She could also not tell anyone about his true last name, or his family, at which point she'd reminded him that she could have told anyone at any point and had chosen not to. "I understand that," he'd said, "But you've clearly had a winning card up your sleeve, one you could use at the slightest provocation. You'll have to promise not to even if you get upset with me."

"How will you know I haven't," she'd countered.

"I'll have to trust you." That had made her smile because he'd looked so unhappy about it.

She had to admit, having Phin as an ally was already proving beneficial. With a speed and resourcefulness he would not divulge to her, he'd procured a stereoscope for Hank Jameson. When she'd first seen it, she'd turned to him in confusion. He'd placed the wooden Holmes stereoscope in her hands and raised both to her eyes. While she held it in place, he'd swept one stereo card after the other until it dawned on her. Each card was a print of a different place in the world. The collection included several from the United States—Boston, Sitka, Alaska, and Oregon. The rest of them quite literally took her breath away as she pulled back and stared down at the double images in her hands. Algeria, Austria, England, France,

Germany, Holland, India, Italy, Mexico, Spain, Tangier, Morocco and Turkey.

"It's the world," she'd told him in wonderment. It wasn't the literal world, no. It wasn't a ticket on a boat to sail through the seas to every spot, nor a train ticket to cross the land from west to east. But it was a start. She'd almost choked up in front of Phin because it was quite literally the best gift. She'd managed to tamp down the emotion enough to express that she was impressed with his ingenuity. "Hank is going to adore this gift." And begrudgingly, "Thank you."

Being the miscreant that he was, he'd taken every opportunity to throw those two words back in her face. "I think that should be the only thing you should say to me from here on out," he'd said. To which she replied, "That smug look on your face might be the reason you haven't found the future Mrs. Whitemore."

Phin rushed into the store with a gust of wind at his back. He greeted her father and walked over to Ginny's section.

"I'm here for my portrait session," he said, loud enough for her father's benefit.

Ginny tried not to groan at his theatricality. He was too cheerful an actor.

"Who has my three pals today," Phin asked.

Ginny's father chortled. "Mr. Smith."

"I hope he wishes for a good barber," Phin muttered under his breath. Only Ginny heard his comment, and she couldn't stop herself from laughing. Mr. Smith had the longest, most unflattering mustache and beard, and no one had the heart to tell him how unattractive it was. "If only he'd trim it," Millie had said once, "he might turn out to be the man of my dreams."

"Ginny, you go ahead with Phin to the office, so you can have some privacy while you sketch."

So it was Phin now, was it? Ginny had spoken to her father about his unexpected contribution to the auction, and about her embarrassment at having Phin prevailed upon to bid for her artwork. Her father had genuinely looked perplexed and told her he thought she would be pleased. She'd tried to explain how what he had done was not pleasing but stopped herself shortly when he seemed not to comprehend her reasons for distress.

"Phin, we're having a round of roast that Ginny put into the oven earlier. It's a simple meal, but we'd love you to join us for supper if you don't already have plans."

Ginny wanted to stomp her foot with frustration. Her father was utterly clueless! She had agreed to be partners with Phin, and in public, he was only seeing her to collect his auction prize, but that was the extent of their relationship. She didn't want to sit in their cramped dining room above stairs and share a meal with him. She glared daggers at her father away from Phin's view, but her father never once turned her way. She could only hope Phin would refuse since he wasn't too fond of her company, either.

"I would love to, John. Thank you for the invitation."

Ginny goggled at him, quite openly. He extended his arm out toward the back office. "Shall we get started?"

She huffed out of the room, her mind set on murder.

WAR OF THE MAGI   251

The question was: should she go for her father first, or Phin?

SHE SKETCHED IN silence. Phin figured that was because she was too busy scowling at him. He liked having her wary around him. She was too unpredictable when she was sure of herself, and it put him on edge. He was waiting for the day when he'd step out of the newspaper office to see her, the preacher, and a woman Ginny had decided would be the perfect mate for him. The woman was trouble, and the longer he had her guessing, the safer he'd be.

She stared at him from over the top of her sketchbook. "Is Phin your real name?"

She startled a laugh out of him. "Yes."

"What's your full name?"

"Phineas Franklin Whitemore. And yours?"

"Eugenia Leonie Overton."

"Leonie?"

"My mother was French."

Phin nodded slowly, careful not to move too much since she was drawing his face. "Do you remember anything about your mother?"

At first, she seemed reluctant to speak about the deceased matriarch of her family. With a few subtle questions, he got her to open up about the woman who had departed and left a lasting void. Ginny spoke in spurts, starting off slowly, as if speaking about her mother was not something she did often. She probably avoided the topic so as not to injure her father. That had to be hard since John was not the only one to have loved and lost her.

It wasn't until her father called her out that Ginny realized they hadn't once spoken about the next person on the wish list. She turned to Phin. He read her mind. "I'm working on it. I've asked Ed to pick up breakfast at the bakery to get him in constant contact with Millie. I've called a friend in Cheyenne to help obtain the piano for Mr. and Mrs. Wilder, and I'm working on ideas for Mrs. Clancy's wish. Go ahead. We'll talk later."

She stopped at the door. "A piano? That sounds expensive. I don't want you spending your personal money on this. We're only going after wishes that are feasible."

"It's a small price to pay to keep you from blackmailing me with the truth."

She placed a hand on her hip. "I'm not actually blackmailing you."

He shrugged.

She decided to leave it at that and turned to leave.

"See you tonight, Ginny," he called out.

She felt her shoulders tense. She didn't have to see him to know that his eyes were twinkling with the delight of knowing she'd rather swallow splinters than see him across the table.

In the days that followed, Ginny saw as much of Phin as she did her own father. Her father had taken to inviting him over for meals, and surprisingly, Phin had taken him up on the offers. They saw each other regularly with the pretext of portrait sessions, and used the time to plan and execute their list of wishes. They'd decided not to actually give out the gifts until Christmas Day, since the last thing they needed was to raise suspicions. Phin told her she would have to carry out that last part on her own since he would be in Boston with his family.

"Don't you want to see the look on everyone's face?"

"I would love to, but I already promised my father I would go. I haven't seen my siblings or my mother in some time."

Ginny only wished it were as easy for her to travel to California to see her own sister. It made no difference, she reminded herself. She had an extended family here, family whose wishes she'd worked very hard to fulfill. Already, they'd been able to grant at least one wish for everybody who had had possession of the wise men, and that made her happy.

FIVE DAYS BEFORE Christmas, Ginny snuck into Mrs. Dixon's parlor and hurried up the stairs to the room on the right to return the wise men to Phin so that he would have it at least one day before he left for Boston. Mrs. Dixon told her she would have the hour between five and six to return the ring since Phin had accompanied Ed for supper at the Jamesons. Hopefully, Ed would soon come to terms with the fact that he was interested in Millie as more than the daughter of his baker. Ginny was happy to think that Millie had caught on to Ed's pronounced interest, given their daily morning run-ins at the bakery. Phin had been right about that match though it was a twist Ginny hadn't expected.

Another little startling twist had been how much

she'd enjoyed Phin's company. They argued a lot, too much, in fact, but she had come to regard it as normal. Arguing with Phin was like talking with Millie. She was always careful not to allow herself to reveal too much, or to prolong their time together after their "wish" business was finished each session. Now that they were aware of each other's secrets, the last thing she wanted to do was drop her guard. He was funny and charming, and creative, it turned out, but she couldn't let herself forget that he was doing this for a reason. He was going to get married to somebody so that his family's company would be his. She couldn't let herself fall in love with a person as calculating as he. The only frightening thing was getting herself to stop from falling all the way because, unfortunately, all the time they'd spent together had pushed her along that route.

Ginny's plan had been to immediately enter Phin's room, place the ring on his nightstand, and leave before being found out. Once she was in his room, however, her plans evaporated. She'd never been in a man's personal space before, excluding her father's. Her brother Monty had left home after their mother died, and before that, they'd shared a room.

She was careful not to move anything and to tread lightly as she perused Phin's little kingdom. The room was sparse, with only a bed, two nightstands, a mirror, and a wooden chair to recommend it. Phin's shaving kit as well as pieces of paper (presumably notes for stories), littered one nightstand, while a comb and bay rum—he must have splashed some on before departing since Ginny could smell the spicy notes of the cologne—cluttered the other.

Ginny was amused to learn he was a messy tenant. His clothes were strewn about the small room, with trousers slung over the back of the wooden chair in the corner. Scribbled notes dotted each surface of the room, showing a diligence to his work that belied his pampered upbringing. She sat down on his unmade bed, wondering what his room was like in his mansion back home, for surely he'd been raised in a mansion. His quarters were probably the size of the store.

That was how Phin found her. She scrambled up as soon as she heard the door scrape open, but it was too late. There was nowhere to hide, and so she could only stand up to face his inevitable ire.

He didn't disappoint.

"What are you doing here?" He was quick to peer out into the hallway to see if anybody had seen her before closing and locking the door behind him.

She winced and held up the wise men. "Surprise," she said meekly.

His eyes flashed their dismay. He was not amused, and Ginny knew he had a right to be angry. She'd be furious if anybody had entered her room without her permission. Of course, the likelihood of that happening was slim, but—

Phin couldn't believe she was choosing this moment to clam up. He took a step toward her and got a mean thrill from watching her eyes widen. He took another step, which caused her to fall back. Luckily (or unluckily), the bed cushioned her fall.

"I apologize, Phin." She shoved the wise men into his hands and tried to make a break for the door. He arched a brow and held her firm, becoming the barrier between Ginny and the door. He capitalized on her uncharacteristic silence by twirling her so that her back was to the door, and he pinned her there. He relished her gasp and felt his anger dissipate. What a night for happy coincidences. The headache that had spurred his early departure from the Jamesons' was now but a memory.

Ginny wriggled around him, trying to free her hands from his clasp. "I said I was sorry. You may let go of me now."

He bit the inside of his lip to keep from laughing outright. Only she would give so imperious an order while in her submissive position. "You don't have permission to speak. I have some questions for you."

She sputtered with indignation. "Permission? Of all the—"

He leaned in an infinitesimal bit to close the gap between their faces. "Are you ever quiet, woman?"

She couldn't answer for several beats of her overwrought heart. She had to close her eyes to regain a bit of sanity. She'd never had a man so close to her before; she could even smell where on his skin he'd applied the bay rum she'd noticed. Her eyes still closed, she spoke quietly. "I'll answer your questions if you'll let me go."

She opened them again to see Phin gazing at her in a peculiar way.

"Phin?"

He seemed to become aware that she was speaking,

and he took a deep breath and removed his hands from her wrists. "Excuse me, Ginny. I didn't mean to . . . I'm sorry."

He cleared the clothes from the chair and gestured for her to take a seat.

Sensing a change in his demeanor, Ginny thought to push her advantage. "I shouldn't be in here. We can speak tomorrow before you leave."

"Nice try, but if you didn't care about propriety before looking through my things, I don't see what difference a few more minutes will make."

She sighed deeply and folded her hands in her lap. "Very well. But if Mrs. Dixon sees me, she's going to go tell my father, and you'll have to deal with him."

He raised his hands in the air as if in surrender. "Consider me forewarned." He took a seat at the edge of his bed and picked up the ring of wise men she'd brought. "Do I finally get full custody of them?"

Her lips curved into a smile, and he smiled back. "It's only right. Since you won't be here for the holidays, I thought you might like to have them one last time."

He rubbed the back of his neck, knowing why he'd kept her here but not sure where to begin. She'd explained to him what she was doing upon his arrival, and therefore, he didn't need to ask her any further questions. But he was feeling uneasy about leaving, and a lot of that had to do with the woman sitting across from him. He didn't know when he'd become so comfortable with her, or when her presence had been something he sought, but it had happened. He looked forward to their "portrait sessions," which really served as their organizational meetings for the wishes they were going to fulfill. He liked watching her hair tumble down from its pins, first slowly, a few wisps at a time, then more quickly, until her bun would end up at the back of her neck when it had started at her crown. He enjoyed how she flushed over it, as if embarrassed that she couldn't manage to keep her hair in place.

He respected her; not everybody would have been so invested in a project that benefited others rather than oneself. She made him laugh—though not always on purpose—at the colorful solutions to completing a wish.

And, as he'd discovered when he accidentally caught the tail end of a conversation she had with her father, she moved him. John and Ginny had been in the back office, where John had been telling her not to worry about him, reminding her that everybody got sick at some point. Phin heard Ginny and John bicker until Ginny had enough and let her father know that she wouldn't lose another parent. Phin could tell by the ensuing silence that Ginny hadn't meant to divulge so much. The conversation that followed demonstrated the high regard and the love Ginny had for her father, and vice versa. Phin knew he shouldn't be present for such a private moment, and yet, nothing in the world could have made him leave. Afterward, he'd walked straight home, not being able to concentrate on anything else that day. He'd skipped dinner and spent the night staring up at the ceiling as the frigid wind howled against his window. Plain and simple, she moved him. It was unnerving.

Sensing his discomfort, Ginny said, "You must be looking forward to going home."

His gaze met hers, and there was a piercing quality to the way he looked at her that made Ginny's stomach start hopping to the rhythm of her overactive heart.

He cleared his throat. "I am. It will be nice to be surrounded by family for Christmas, and to visit friends and acquaintances."

She nodded, more because she thought she ought to than because she had reason. "And you won't have to worry about your wife-hunt. Although I suppose your father will want to know how you're doing on that count."

This was what he'd been waiting for, an opportunity to see her reaction when she heard his news. Would she care? Knowing her, she'd probably be happy for him, clueless to how his feelings had changed. To keep his hands busy, he traced the circumference of the wise-men figurine. "Actually, my grandfather's business associate has a granddaughter he'd like me to meet. My father has met her and agrees she'd be a good match for me. My mother agrees." He gave a little laugh. "And you'll have to trust me, it's not easy to get both my parents to agree on something."

He watched her face closely to see how she would receive the news.

Her mouth opened, as if she might speak, but she didn't. She stared down at her hands, then smiled up at him. "That's good news, then. But . . . that is, I thought your family wanted you to marry someone 'average.'"

"You refuse to let go of that word, don't you? Well,

yes, that was the original plan, but they seem to all like Abigail, and—"

"Abigail."

Phin waited for Ginny to say more, only she didn't seem to have words tonight. He went to her, kneeled in front of her. He covered her hands with his. "Of course, if I had someone else, I suppose there would be no need for me to meet Abigail."

She was refusing to meet his eyes. Hers were on their joined hands. He continued, thinking this might likely be his only chance. "Ginny." He waited for her to look at him. "Can you think of any reason why I shouldn't court Abigail?"

Ginny felt like she could no longer breathe. She couldn't reconcile the picture of Phin kneeling in front of her with the one of the man who had flirted with her at her father's store, the one who had bought a coat for another woman. How long had he known about this other woman? Was he only playing with her feelings now?

She looked down at his shiny golden hair, the ends of which she wanted to rub between her fingertips. His gaze was earnest, searching for the truth from within her. No, it wasn't fair to think ill of him. She didn't know whom the coat belonged to, but she couldn't believe he had bad intentions toward her. In the past month, she liked to think she'd come to know him as a person, and he was a good man. He had started out in her wish-quest to keep her from meddling in his life—or so he said—but since then, he'd gone out of his way to see that as many wishes as possible were granted. He liked to tease her, and, as it was a new experience for her, Ginny enjoyed it. She liked having a secret with him and mourned the fact that when Christmas was over, their time together was likely to end. Given this talk of a woman both his parents approved of, he might even leave Preston for good. She couldn't begrudge him that. He'd been a good friend to her, going so far as to listen to her when she spoke of her mother, of Eliza, and even of Monty (that had been a painful conversation, but she'd felt lightness after speaking of it with him). A part of her still felt betrayed by him since she couldn't truly forget his reason for being in town. He had his eye on full ownership of his family's business, or else he probably would look elsewhere for an acceptable bride. But this, too, was nonsense. Ginny simply had to remind herself the good in him far outweighed the bad.

She was acutely aware of the warmth of his palm and the roughness of his fingers, a surprising detail since he wasn't a man accustomed to hard labor. Nothing had changed. He was not a dream for her to have. He belonged to a different world, where a person like this Abigail would fit completely and make him happy. She would undoubtedly be exactly the sort of woman Phin would have chosen for himself if not for this ridiculous deal with the patriarchs of his family. Ginny took a cleansing breath and remembered that Phin was her friend. She had to think as his friend and do what was right for him. Was there any reason he shouldn't be with Abigail, he'd asked.

She shook her head. "No." She felt her heart breaking even as the words left her mouth.

She saw the anger in him, felt it in the tightening of his fingers on her hand.

His words rang with bitterness. "Nothing at all?"

She disengaged her hands from his and quickly rose. She had to leave this room now, or she might do something utterly absurd, like cry in front of him, something she hadn't done in a long time. She was beginning to wish he'd never come into the store that day. No, that wasn't true. She wouldn't have passed up the chance to have the wonderful times they'd shared. She'd just be careful next time she fancied a man.

She lifted her chin to say good-bye, but in a blink, Phin pushed his body against hers, and he was strong, lean, and hard . . . and upset. Very upset. His eyes held her like his body did, and the only movement in her was the tremble that started at her neck and went down to her arms and legs.

"Phin?"

His eyes were concentrating on her lips. A furrow line creased his forehead. "Stop talking," he said, each word punctuated with frustration. "You talk too much."

"What do you want me to—"

He covered her mouth with his lips, thus, giving Ginny her first kiss. She felt herself start to sag against the wall. She needn't have worried about wilting to the floor, for Phin's arm snaked around her back, pulling her in closer at the waist so that she could feel every inch of him. She was wrapped up in his heat.

He deepened the kiss, bringing his thumb and forefinger to cradle the back of her neck. She moaned so softly, Phin felt as if it left her mouth and entered his. He felt the tremulous way in which her mouth moved against his, at first in tentative strokes, causing a tender wave to course through him. He angled his head so as to allow for better access, and he worked diligently until she opened her mouth to him. He growled with satisfaction and tasted the sweetness of her, holding her so close he could smell the starch in her collar and the lavender against her skin.

Ginny had lost herself to the new sensations of being devoured mind, body, and spirit by Phin, but as his hand roamed over her back and settled on her backside, she felt herself tense up. She jerked away from him so fast he didn't have time to keep her in the confinement against the wall.

His eyes were glazed over with . . . desire? She could almost smile right now at the knowledge that she'd put that look there. In this moment, he desired her. He ran a hand through his hair and took a step toward her.

The kiss didn't mean anything, of course. Ginny knew that men could feel lust for a woman without caring for her the way a man should before giving her such attentions. They'd been spending so much time together that Phin might think she had been after him all along, and, nice man that he was, he was probably only settling her curiosity. She fought the urge to run her fingers over her bruised lips. She knew better than to let herself hope that he'd really feel the same inexplicable draw that she felt for him, the desire to see him every day, to hear his voice. She delighted in his laughter. She . . . she stopped herself. Had she finally done it, then? Had she forgotten that she was not supposed to fall in love with him and done it anyway?

"Ginny."

She swallowed hard and made her way to the door, her knuckles blanching on the doorknob. "We'd both do well to forget this happened. I hope you have a nice time in Boston, and . . ." She let her voice trail off. She'd been about to wish him well with Abigail, but she could only lie to herself and to him so much.

"Ginny, wait!"

She ran out of his room before he could convince her that she really wanted to stay and find out where those kisses led. She didn't care if anybody saw her leave his room; and thankfully, nobody did.

Chapter Nine

THE DAYS LEADING up to the Christmas pageant resembled each other in every way. Ginny woke up at the same time, prepared breakfast for herself and her father (though she didn't eat). She opened the store and went about her daily business. The one stark difference in this week from the last was that Phin wasn't a part of this routine. She'd become too dependent on watching him saunter in with that teasing smile, and too accustomed to the fun she had when he was around. He'd left, and she was sad to say, a part of her she'd come to like had disappeared as well.

She tried to smile as often as possible to avoid any more concerned looks from her father, and though she doubted she fooled him, he'd respected her enough not to come out and ask her what was going on. He'd managed, "Just tell me this, are you all right?" and when she'd nodded, he'd seemed satisfied, proving that fathers couldn't compete with mothers in some respects, and unfortunately, Ginny didn't have someone she could speak to about Phin. Not when it was something so personal and so intimate. If only his kiss weren't seared in her memory, she might be able to sleep at night.

A part of her knew she'd pushed him away. If he wasn't here, it was her fault. Then the other half of her reminded her that she'd done what was best, for surely if he'd had stronger feelings for her, he would have stayed. She had these mental bouts all day, neither side winning over the other. It hardly mattered now because he was, in fact, gone, and should he return, things would be different. That was the good thing about time, she supposed. She could hide her feelings and thoughts in time and try to forget.

GINNY TRUDGED INTO the bakery on Christmas Eve alongside her father. She was quick to blow into her gloved hands to warm them from the cold outside. Her father nodded a greeting to Mrs. Jameson, then went to the back to collect Mr. Jameson, as he did every year. It was tradition for the two families to walk to church together for the pageant, then have supper together at the Jameson table.

Ginny focused on trying not to freeze to death when Millie came bounding through to the front and hugged Ginny with all her might.

Ginny couldn't help laughing as her friend pulled away, keeping her hands on Ginny's shoulders.

"I'm getting married!"

Ginny's amusement turned to shock. "What? To whom?"

Millie laughed and hugged her again. "To whom? To Ed, of course."

"You'd have to be blind not to have noticed his pursuit of Millie," Mrs. Jameson said.

Millie turned to her mother and giggled. "Oh, don't listen to her." She returned her attention to her friend. "He came over this morning and asked Pa for my hand. And then he asked me. Of course, I said yes."

"Naturally," Ginny murmured. She couldn't believe the plan had worked, and so soon. Phin had been right. All Ed had needed was a little nudge to make him aware of his feelings. She let herself be embraced again.

"I'm so happy for you, Millie."

"Not as happy as Hank," Mrs. Jameson said dryly.

Millie laughed. "Oh, I know! Ginny, it's the funniest thing you've ever seen. He's going around the house with the biggest smile, as if he were the one who was going to get married."

Ginny felt a genuine laugh bubble up inside of her because she knew exactly what it was Hank Jameson was celebrating.

"Come on, you cheerful lot," Mr. Jameson called, tugging on a hat and gloves as he made his way to the front. "You'll have months yet to gab and gossip about Millie's wedding. We don't want to be late. I've got baby Jesus," he said, patting the bundle tucked under his arm.

Ginny listened to Millie's excited whispers about the

proposal as they walked arm in arm to the church, feeling relief at being able to focus on something other than Phin. For once, Millie's mother was not part of the conversation, as she was too busy scolding her husband for carrying the porcelain Jesus as if he were a pile of dirty laundry, to which Mr. Jameson responded, "I'm just keeping the little fella warm."

Ginny felt her own excitement welling up; it wouldn't be long before people would have the gifts they'd wished for. Instead of getting creative to somehow secretly distribute the gifts all at once, as she and Phin had originally planned, Ginny realized that it would be easier for her to do so in two waves. She'd been stealthy as she delivered the first gifts, whose recipients would receive them once they reached home after the pageant. Thankfully, Phin had dealt with the bigger projects prior to leaving. The piano for the Wilders would be delivered sometime after Christmas, and the stained-glass window for the church was on a train traveling to Preston that very moment. She would sneak out later tonight to leave the rest of the gifts on doorsteps, and the thought made her giddy. Who would have guessed she'd be playing Santa Claus this year?

The church looked lovely, with boughs of pine and holly pinned to the pews and another larger garland decorating the pulpit in front, with several white taper candles adding a nice, homey glow. The small stage was already set up to look like a barn, with an empty manger in the middle, where Mr. and Mrs. Schmidt's baby would be placed later in the program. Ginny always felt most moved by the spirit of Christmas when she was in this building during the pageant. Despite the hardships or weather, or whatever trials a person was dealing with, it was all put to the side on this day to celebrate with friends. Her heart might be sad, but she had plenty in front of her to lift her spirits. She turned to Millie and smiled at her, at the flush of happiness that had her eyes glowing. She glanced to her other side to see if Bea and her family had arrived and felt her smile slip. Phin was by the front entrance of the church, and he was looking directly at her.

Ginny's father came to her side and bent to whisper in her ear. "Darlin', Phin would like a word with you outside."

She couldn't take her eyes off him even as her father waited for a response. She drank in every detail of his appearance. His expression was serious in the extreme. His nose and cheeks were red from the cold, and his hair was shorter than the last time she'd seen him. She realized he'd only been gone four days. It had felt like a year. Ten years.

Her father repeated himself, and she locked gazes with him. He gave her a peck on the cheek, which was alarming, and cupped her chin. "Go on."

HER LEGS WEREN'T steady as she walked over to him, and they threatened to buckle when he guided her back outside into the empty path.

They didn't say anything to each other for several minutes. She could only stare at him and remember the last time they'd seen each other. She couldn't take it any longer, and she cleared her throat. "You came back."

He dusted a few snowflakes from her coat lapel. "I never left."

"What do you mean?"

"Well, I left, but I didn't go all the way to Boston. I meant to"— he took a breath—"until I realized I forgot to do something."

It was hard for her to breathe. She swallowed to wet the dryness that had lodged in her throat. She wanted to ask him what he'd forgotten to do, so badly, in fact, that she was twisting her fingers in pain, but she couldn't bring herself to ask.

He'd been so good at reading her that he did so again now. He reached down and took one of her hands in his own, then maneuvered it so that her palm faced up. He reached into his coat, and what he took from there made her gasp. He rested the ring of wise men on her outstretched palm.

His voice was as soft as the snow falling to the ground. "You never got your turn to make a wish."

Ginny felt the tears begin to well up at the corners of her eyes. She looked at him rather than at the wise men. She wet her lips. "Is that all?"

He laughed quietly. "No, Eugenia Leonie Overton, that's not all." He looked deeply into her eyes. "I was angry at you when I got on the train, and I was committed to meeting this other woman and courting her, leaving Preston for good. I was mad at you because you hadn't told me what I wanted to hear, and it hurt because . . ." He closed his eyes.

"What? Because what," she prompted.

His eyes opened, and he searched her own. "Because I had come to feel so much for you. But you never said anything."

Ginny tried to speak, but he shook his head so that she wouldn't interrupt. "Then, sometime before I reached Chicago, I realized something important. I was guilty of the same thing I was angry with you for. I'd never once confessed my feelings to you. You're the most unpredictable person I know," he said with a slightly crooked smile, "but I know you would never say the words before I did. You couldn't take that chance." He bridged the gap between them. "So then I had to worry. I thought, maybe she doesn't feel the same way, and wouldn't I look the fool if I bared my soul to her?"

"Phin—"

He wasn't done yet and silenced her with a brief peck on the mouth. "But then I thought, I should at least give you the chance to reject or accept me in person. There, I'm done. What do you have to say?"

She was warm all over now, snow forgotten. There was a sensation within that felt as if her heart were being pumped up in size, so that soon it wouldn't fit in her chest. She could see the hope in Phin's face and the fear that matched her own. She couldn't help but smile. "You still haven't said it."

"What?"

"You keep speaking of these things you're going to share, but you have yet to actually share them."

His jaw clenched, and his eyes flashed, whether with nervousness or anger, she didn't know. With two of his fingers, he pushed her palm up to eye level. "Look inside and say that again."

Ginny looked at the wise-men figurine that had started their feud, then jolted in surprise, for there in one of the boxes shone a gold ring. In the other two boxes were slips of paper. She glanced at him before taking the slips and opening them. One of them read, "I love you," and the other, "Will you marry me?"

She could now understand Millie's earlier joy when recounting her proposal from Ed, but she wasn't ready to celebrate yet. Despite the fluttering fury of her heartbeat, she was steady as she said, "Is this because you need to fulfill certain conditions to win your enterprise?"

Phin wasn't angry she asked. He knew she had to know for herself. "Damn the conditions, Ginny. Marry me."

He scooped the ring out of the box and held it in front of her. "What do you say? Do you think you could stand to be married to me?"

Ginny's smile was wide now as she shot him an arch look. She took the ring and slid it onto her finger. "I don't know that I can stand it," she said coyly. She laughed at his expression, then surprised him with a kiss. "But I know that I wouldn't be happy without you."

"Ginny," he sounded exasperated. "Are you going to say it?"

"Very well . . . are you going to the Christmas pageant?"

Phin barked out a laugh at the reminder of the first time they met, when he'd teased her about not asking the customary question. He pulled her in close, resting his hands at the small of her back.

She made a big show of sighing. "Oh, all right. I will marry you." She looked into the face of her former arch-enemy, former and current love of her life, and felt the magic of Christmas envelop her. "I love you, Phin."

"I love you more, Ginny."

They stayed in a warm embrace, each picturing a future of wonderful moments, until the chimes sounded inside the church, signaling the commencement of the program.

"We can make the announcement after the show."

"Oh no, Phin," she said hastily. "Millie's just gotten engaged as well. I don't want to ruin her moment. Let's wait until tomorrow."

Phin didn't see how it would be ruining it, but he let her have her way. They couldn't, however, keep the good news from Ginny's father, and so they shared it with him during the intermission. Phin promised he would finish the last bit of the wish-project, and join her father and her for breakfast the next morning. For the rest of the show, Ginny kept her ring hand tucked away so that others might not see her ring, but Phin was content in the knowledge that soon everyone would know his happy news, and as soon as he could, he would be making Ginny his forever and always. And he couldn't have done it without the help of a few wise men.

JOHN EXCUSED HIMSELF from the breakfast table for a moment, leaving Phin and Ginny talking about the miraculous Christmas gifts that many in town had received. Already, Mrs. Clancy and Millie and her nephew had been to visit, exclaiming over the wondrous surprise.

"I've never seen anything like it," Millie had said.

"I can see you were also the beneficiary of a gift," Mrs. Clancy had said slyly, upon hearing the news of Phin and Ginny's engagement.

"Do you see, Mr. Baldwin," Millie began. "Do you see how lucky you were to have the wise men this year? And I can't even imagine how everyone's wishes came true. But I'm so happy they have." John saw Phin and Ginny exchange looks. He supposed they were thinking that now wasn't the time to reveal Phin's true identity. They'd have more than enough time to explain.

John sat at the edge of his bed, reaching below until his fingers found purchase on his box of treasures. He pulled it out and placed it on his lap, opening the lid to look down at the objects within. This was where he kept his memories—a daguerreotype of his parents, a curl of hair from each of his children upon their first birthday, a gold nugget Monty had sent him from California, a small portrait of a horse Ginny had painted him when she was younger, a few of his late wife's trinkets. He reached for the most important one, a photographic portrait of his Marie. He took in a hitched breath as he looked into the face of the woman he'd adored. There was a time when he'd kept this photograph on his person, but he'd had to break himself of the habit in order to cope. Now, he only looked upon that lovely face when he felt like speaking to his wife.

"Marie, my love," he started, feeling the knot in his throat, "We did it. We made the miracle happen. You know, I've been praying for some time that she'd find somebody worthy of her, someone who will love her as I loved you. And you made it happen, darlin'. The people in town may have their wise men, but I have a wise woman in my corner, and you finally made it happen. Merry Christmas, love, and thank you for the gift."

He took a few more minutes before putting his treasures away and returning to the joy of his family.

About Rena Gregory

RENA GREGORY, a former middle-school teacher, has been writing stories—romantic and otherwise—since she could hold a pencil. She enjoys stories that make her laugh and think, and tries to establish a little of both in her work. She received an MFA in Creative Writing and lives in Southern Arizona. "War of the Magi" is her first published short novella.

Her Christmas Knight

SANDRA JONES

Chapter One

Pembroke, Wales
Christmastide 1272

THE FOREST TOLD Lady Nia de Brionne something was amiss long before her escort gestured for their horses to stop. The birds stopped singing, the clouds rolled ominously above, and she felt the eyes of an audience somewhere in the frost-laden trees.

"We're being followed." Her breath made a puff of mist in the frigid morning air. She twisted in her saddle, her gaze following the flight of a startled chough. Its loud *chee-ow* sent more of the birds into the woods. She clutched the hilt of the sword at her side. "Someone is east of us."

"More guests of the castle, likely," the fair-haired knight, Sir Maddoc, a guest himself, grumbled. "Do not worry, my lady." He edged his mount close enough to hers that his knee brushed her kirtle.

Maddoc's interest in her was clouding her judgment.

Most of the recipients of her father's invitations were entrenched in the castle these past few days, vying for the hands of her and her sister in marriage. Nia had only wanted to get some relief from the cloying men by taking fresh air. She knew that the well-traveled road leaving her father's estate was safe, but that was no reason to take risks. Outlaws were always a possibility in the forest.

Nevertheless, she had eagerly accepted Sir Maddoc's invitation to spend the morning hunting outside the curtain wall even though it came at the price of more unwanted attention. Despite the lamentable flirtation from the eager suitors, she hoped she hadn't led her companions into danger.

There were three knights and herself in her riding party, but against how many?

Ignoring her suitor's assurance of safety, she motioned for the men to be quiet. In the utter stillness of December gloom, she could sense every breath, every stir of the dead leaves.

In the distance, a twig snapped, and her ear twitched toward the sound. In a flash, she unsheathed her sword, and Maddoc and his men followed suit.

"Look out!" one of the knights cried behind her.

As Nia turned her horse's head, an arrow whispered over her shoulder before striking an oak tree. Hurriedly, her gaze tracked the arrow's path to its source, and she saw a pair of brigands on foot darting between the pines. Maddoc called her entourage to form a protective circle with their mounts, but before they could rally, another arrow flew overhead in their defense, striking one of the attackers in the shin. The outlaw's cry was drowned under the distant sound of horses. Two groups of them. One just beyond the brigands, and a group approaching opposite.

"Heads down!" An authoritative tone issued from the trees.

Nia obeyed with a ripple of new fear, reining her skittish horse with one hand while covering her head with her sword in the other. Suddenly, a volley of arrows pelted the woods in the direction of the first attackers. Another brigand yelped as the tip struck, just as his companions reached him on horseback. The bandits wheeled in the opposite direction and thundered away into the gloom, taking their injured with them.

Sir Maddoc, face gone crimson from the assault, whirled his horse toward the archers who'd come to their aid. "Show yourselves!"

Later, she would take time to think on her escort's curtness, but for now, all she could focus on were the archers. The deep voice of the leader commanded his men to lower their bows. Her insides tugged with a sense of familiarity. Did she know that voice from somewhere? She could scarcely tell the beat of her heart from the sound of the approaching riders as she lowered her weapon.

A half dozen men on horseback emerged from the tree line to join them on the road. Dressed in mail and helmets, she couldn't identify the riders, but two of the party bore blue-and-gold tunics emblazoned with the crest of the Baron of Rhiwdinas.

The fallow, untamed land of Rhiwdinas bordered theirs, but they seldom laid eyes on the overlord himself. Rumors of his demise had been common for years though they'd always been deemed false.

"Do I know you?" She felt their piercing stares as sure and sharp as any arrow.

The newcomers exchanged a glance. The larger of the two rode forward. He removed his helmet and revealed a tumble of brown hair. His dark eyes were steady and fierce, demanding her acknowledgment though he refused to answer.

His skin was the almond shade of the tenants who worked her father's fields, but the regal tilt of his shaven chin told her he hadn't earned his color by laboring on some fief. As a child, she'd once seen her father wearing a similar hue of brown on his flesh when he'd returned from Jerusalem.

Crusaders.

Knights. Oddly, this knowledge failed to reassure her. At her side, Maddoc sucked in a breath but said nothing.

Nia nudged her horse closer to study the man's striking face. She'd known only a handful of men, youths mostly, gone abroad with Prince Edward through the years. Their neighbor, the Baron of Rhiwdinas, was one, but he'd returned around the same time as her father; and then, of course, there were his sons. The boys were born only two years apart but were worlds different in height and personality.

A rush of warmth tickled her cheeks, and she smiled politely. "You would be Padrig then or"—she faltered, stumbling upon the name of the older brother she'd struck from her thoughts—"Caerwyn."

When he'd left with the prince, he'd been a spindle-limbed boy of eight-and-ten years, nothing at all like the warrior sitting astride his destrier with legs like tree trunks and a man's face that seemed more stone than flesh.

But his eyes were similar, deep walnut and intelligent . . .

Her pulse exploded to life in her neck, thumping so wildly she thought he might notice. She rubbed the spot with her suddenly clammy hand. *Caerwyn*. She should've been prepared to see him again. Should've known he, of all those youths who'd squired under their roof, would survive the war to return someday.

He made a faint bow. "My lady." His lowered gaze traveled over her possessively, likely assessing the changes in her appearance. Her blood boiled at the boldness of the man even though she conceded she'd surely done the same to him. He'd grown so long, so broad of the shoulders, so powerful.

"Nia." Her name rumbled off his lips with a hint of humor in his dark eyes and a trace of malice.

After all the men her father had paraded before her and her sister, demanding that she must choose one in the next twelve days, here was the one example of what Nia wanted in a match.

Brave Caerwyn. Self-reliant. Loyal. A champion.

He'd been her first love. Her first *kiss*.

And then she'd betrayed him.

CAERWYN DRAGGED A hand over his face, trying to adjust his vision as his younger brother Padrig rode forward and greeted the woman. *Nia de Brionne.* Three years had changed her in vast ways. Womanly ways.

No longer was she the forlorn child he remembered, always in her older sister's shadow. He had never forgotten Nia's face, for it had gone with him into every battle, graced the head of every opponent. Nia, his greatest enemy. Thief of his young heart.

"You came at a fortunate time. We owe you." She addressed them as a group, the tightness in her voice matching her expression as she swept a loose tendril of her hair with the back of her hand. The sun crowned her cinnamon-colored hair with gold, but such lovely gilding surely belonged on an angel, faithful and pure, not on one of such little devotion as Nia. "Pray tell, did any of you recognize the attackers?"

Snapping back into his senses, Caerwyn shifted the helmet under his arm. "Nay. I was going to ask you the same."

Nia's lips parted. He sensed he'd startled her, made her uncomfortable somehow.

He smiled.

Her hands tightened on her reins, and she stiffened. "We were merely hunting. There was no reason for those men to attack. I ensure that our tenants are peaceful and well fed. We haven't had any outlaws for a long time, so they could not have been from our woods. I ride with the guards each day myself, patrolling the roads and maintaining the castle curtain. Walwyn is secure."

One of her entourage, a knight hovering close behind Nia's horse, cleared his throat. Caerwyn studied him for the first time since he'd fallen under Nia's spell. Time had altered the faces of many of his acquaintances since they'd been out of England, but something told Caerwyn he should remember this one, nearly the same age as Padrig and Nia. However, whiskers obscured the knight's face. His hair, so blond it was nearly silver, was unlike any of the families Caerwyn knew in Pembroke.

Ah, realization sank in with an icy chill to his bones and instant dislike, this stranger was another guest of Walwyn Castle. A suitor for the ladies.

Nia made a brisk introduction. Caerwyn hardly heard their names as she spoke. Maddoc so-and-so, son of someone-he-didn't-give-a-damn-about. The knight's eyes were pure blue flame with hate for him. Caerwyn told himself he didn't care. He wasn't competing for Nia. Nor for her promiscuous, older sibling, Lady Serena. The sooner he was done with this visit, the better. He was here for two reasons. For one, because his ailing father decreed it, and more importantly, to bring his brother home unscathed by female claws.

God save them both from scheming wenches.

"Welcome back to Walwyn. I hadn't heard you'd returned." Nia leaned forward and ran her slender hand down her horse's glossy mane. She watched him from the corner of her eye. "Did my father's . . . invitation reach you?"

Caerwyn noted the subtle difference in her coloring, how her face flushed with pink, matching the fire of her hair as she addressed him. He risked another perusal of her figure. Wrapped in a pale green kirtle, seated sideways atop her horse with authority, her effortless sensuality captivated him, but her eyes held a surprising amount of shyness.

"Indeed. Padrig and I are both here for Christmastide."

"Well"—she laughed softly, ducking her head—"this is a surprise, to see you both returned. I . . . Serena and I will be pleased to have you join us."

He nodded politely. *Not likely.*

She turned her horse toward Walwyn. "Milords, I no longer feel like hunting. Shall we?" Without waiting for her fellow hunters' responses, she set off in a gallop toward the castle.

Maddoc's mouth turned down at the corners. Padrig joined them while Caerwyn replaced his helmet. The three knights rode alongside each other.

Padrig, seemingly unaware of the tension between them, spoke around Caerwyn to Sir Maddoc. "We'd only just arrived when we received the missive from de Brionne. I suppose the baron's call is wide, and there are many competing?" His smile was self-deprecating.

Maddoc sniffed, his gaze fixed possessively on Nia's back. "Aye. We're battling in a tournament as well as competing for the ladies. Wait until you see the hoard of presents under the ivy in the great hall. Gold, silver, gems—"

"Ah. There, you see?" His brother leaned to Caerwyn's ear with worry in his tone. "I told you, you're expected to bring a gift. For Twelfth Night, if not for the ladies. You'll insult the baron."

Caerwyn touched his chest, feeling the length of chain hidden beneath his hauberk until he found the ring. Resting over his heart, nearly forgotten, the tiny treasure could've easily been lost in the fray. Relieved, he sighed and dropped his hand away. Tempting fate was foolish. He should never have risked bringing their mother's ring. He'd only done so because his father expected it of him.

"In truth, you may be right. I fear the ladies will find my suit lacking in comparison to yours and the others'. I do pray your reputation is not sullied by our shared blood."

Padrig passed him a withering glance. His brother had no idea what it felt like to be favored by a woman, then be tossed aside for another.

Maddoc chuckled and smiled brightly. "I could not help overhearing your dilemma. To show my thanks for your aid against the brigands—and to prove my good sportsmanship—I will share some advice. You could have some trinkets made for the women by the craftsmen in the market. They wouldn't be anything grand, but 'twould save you from insulting Guy de Brionne, likely."

Padrig laughed. "Aye. An excellent gesture. Brother, you should take his advice."

Caerwyn grunted his agreement, but he scowled underneath the helmet. Now there would be no excuse for his empty-handedness.

How awkward it would be if, by some cruel happenstance, either of the ladies or the baron picked him out of the lot to be a bridegroom?

At least if he chose his gifts, he could pick something foul. For certes, he would make sure he would be the very *last* man under de Brionne's roof anyone would want as a husband.

Chapter Two

As THE FIRST shadows of dusk obscured the alleys of the bustling Christmas market, Nia walked unrecognized by the villagers. She dropped the hood of her cloak and breathed in the scents of spiced nuts, burning firewood, and beeswax drifting from the vendors' tents.

After the scare with the brigands, she couldn't bring herself to ask another of her guests to escort her outside the castle wall, but she couldn't remain inside, either. Since the first suitor had arrived, she'd felt cornered, caged. How could she stay trapped with those fools, accepting her fate to marry one of them when she knew she was the second-place prize and not the trophy?

Besides, Caerwyn hadn't stayed inside either. He was out here somewhere.

Nia slipped between two tents to block the chill of the breeze and brought her hands to her mouth to warm them with her breath. No one could see her, but her skin tingled as if someone was watching. She chafed her arms, suddenly anxious. Mayhap she should've brought her maid Gwynneth or one of the castle guards.

Waiting another moment, the feeling subsided. The brigands' attack had her imagining things. She shook her head at her foolishness and reemerged into the market's thoroughfare.

If Caerwyn were here, she would find him. She surmised the knight hadn't come to Walwyn prepared to woo either her or Serena because she'd overheard him telling his brother he was going to the market to purchase a gift. Even Padrig, also just returned from war, had managed to bring a wedding offering. That Caerwyn came empty-handed proved he wasn't trying to barter his way into matrimony. And if he had no interest in marriage, he would make Nia a *perfect* husband.

Her father was determined to see her betrothed, so let it be Caerwyn, she decided—a good, noble man who would not bring her shame nor try to twist her to his will. But *could* she win him?

She'd never had a chance to explain her actions, and his heated glares proved he remembered her erroneous treatment of him in the past. Compelled by Serena, she'd set a scene meant to make him jealous, making him think she'd bedded another man, a rival for her hand. If only she'd listened to her heart instead of Serena's scheming plan that day, Caerwyn might still be hers.

Daylight faded, and the craftsmen were taking in their wares to close their stalls. She had to admit, the man was nowhere to be found. Disappointed and cold, Nia pulled her cloak tighter around her shoulders and rounded the final row of merchants.

Ka-thing, ka-thing, ka-thing.

The clang of iron and the light of the forge from the metalsmith's tent gave her hope, but her stomach sank as she approached, finding the stall had no customers, only three workers. *Ka-thing.* Henri, the talented craftsman, pounded a hammer against a metal plate, while a young boy, perhaps an apprentice, watched his progress. Recognizing her, Henri nodded and smiled as she strode by. Nia liked the nice young man, who made Serena the delicate silver circlets she preferred in her hair. Courteous and thoughtful, he had once delivered his ornaments in a storm when the weather prevented the sisters from leaving the castle.

She nodded in return and glanced at the third worker. Then she did a double take.

Caerwyn?

Nia froze in bemused shock. Why was he working in a metalsmith's shop?

Scrape, scrape, scrape. He kept his head bowed under the low ceiling, but it was definitely Caerwyn, wearing a leather apron as he filed something in his hands. Nia's gaze roamed past his dark forearms, moving slowly up the smooth muscles of sleeveless shoulders to his face, glistening in the firelight of the forge. He glanced up at the same moment and lowered the tool. Surprise flashed across his face, and he returned her curious stare with one of his own. His dark eyes returned such heat that they might've radiated sparks to rival those showering from Henri's anvil.

A nervous laugh broke from her throat. "What are you doing?"

"Filing, as you can see. I should ask the same of you." He returned to his grinding movements, working with a vengeance. His hair, so brown it was nearly black, fell loose against his jaw as he worked. He'd worn it cropped very short as a squire, and she'd once enjoyed running her fingertips through its soft spikes. Now her hands curled at her sides as she wondered how it might feel today.

"I've come to inquire about a circlet."

"Another circlet? Aye, milady." Henri set his hammer on the anvil and scuttled to the back of his tent with his apprentice to rummage through his chests.

Caerwyn snorted. "A circlet? Is that all you can think of, with so many men traveling from far away to see you? After this morning's ambush, I would think you'd send someone else to do your shopping."

His sarcasm stung. Verily, she supposed she must seem vain for making such a trivial quest. "The circlet is for Serena. She says she cannot attend tonight's feast without it." Nia cringed at the memory of her sister's whiny voice, demanding to be allowed to leave the castle to fetch the hair ornament herself. Serena had behaved even more irrationally when Nia had volunteered to run the errand. "I wouldn't endanger anyone else," Nia added.

"Is Lady Serena well?" the metalsmith called from the back.

"Oh, aye. Thank you, Henri. She's just preoccupied with the festivities at home."

He nodded and silently went back to his search.

Their father, interrupted from his reunion with Sir Padrig, another of his former squires, had told Serena she mustn't leave the castle and all her attentive swains. The selfish girl's blubbering made the perfect excuse for Nia, and the baron granted her permission to come to the metalsmith's. She doubted she'd be missed much anyway.

The knights' lack of interest was nothing new to rankle her. Nia had accepted her place as the "plain" little sister long ago. But with her father's open invitation for bridegrooms, she'd had plenty of unwanted attention the past two days.

Caerwyn scraped the tiny metal object in his fingers with gusto.

Nia looked down at the state of her garment. Her dress was simple, smudged with dirt from sliding along the castle curtain to avoid the eye of the persistent, groping Sir Maddoc, who would've followed her whether she'd wanted him to or not. Her hair lay on her shoulder in a wild plait she'd assembled herself instead of one of her maid's artful creations. 'Twas no wonder Caerwyn paid her so little heed.

"What are you making?" Nia braced her hands on the metalsmith's table between them for a closer look, careful not to disturb the glittering assortment of cuffs, chains, buckles, and knives on display.

Caerwyn's jaw tightened, but he didn't raise his face to answer. "You'll see soon enough."

Of course, Caerwyn, of all people, would want to make his own gifts. As a youth, he'd helped Henri's father at the forge, making his own sword and spurs. He'd insisted on caring for his horse, fletching his own arrows. For his industriousness alone, Nia had kindled a childhood crush on the boy, two years older than she.

Her cheeks warmed at the sudden memory of those long-ago feelings now flooding back to her. Childhood fantasies. How certain she'd been that Caerwyn would be the only boy she could ever marry.

"Here." Caerwyn set the file aside and moved closer. When his hand brushed hers on the table, she jerked away, but quick as a snakebite, he caught her wrist, keeping her near.

"My lord?" Her heart pounded, locked in his rough grip. It had been years since he'd touched her. *And yet once you knew his touch so well.* She leaned closer, rather than away, hoping for a reprisal of those days. He smelled of metal, leaves, leather, and man—the erotic mixture aroused her curiosity. A few more inches, and they could kiss. Now at twenty-and-one and no longer an awkward boy, Caerwyn's mouth would claim hers as a man's. Her lips would part without reluctance, their tongues exploring, making up for the time they'd been apart . . .

"Tell me what you think." He turned her wrist over, sliding his thumb across the heel of her palm, until she opened her fingers reflexively.

He placed a silver ring in her open hand, and her pulse thundered.

Childish, she berated herself. Rough, dull, and plain,

the jagged circle appeared cruder than any jewelry Nia had ever beheld. "I . . . it's not quite . . ."

"Good. That's the response I was looking for." Still holding her wrist, Caerwyn's grip loosened, and he smiled. The expression was one born not of humor, exactly, or pleasure, but of satisfaction and more than a hint of anger. "Not impressive enough for your sister either, you think? Or your father?"

Nia studied the ring in her fingers, still feeling the warmth from his hands in the metal. Was he serious? Did he really hope to impress Serena, who wouldn't leave her antechamber for breakfast without wearing a treasure of gems around her neck, with such a rushed piece?

"I am very sorry to say you'll likely draw my father's ire with this present before you will his approval. And as for Serena, well—"

"Perfect." Caerwyn's lips drew in a real smile, devilish and dangerous. He cupped her hand in both of his with the ring wrapped in her fist. Warmth poured through her to be held by him and to be the apparent source of his pleasure. "I've made one for you both."

"I knew it!" She smiled, though sadness swept her. "You're here to plead your suit to my father like the others, but you don't *want* to marry either of us."

Releasing Nia, Caerwyn slid the ring from her hand and tucked it somewhere inside his clothes. His expression turned suddenly somber, and he regarded her through hard eyes again. "Why should I? Marrying either of you would offer naught but a lifetime of misery."

She deserved that, but sudden tears stung her eyes.

She glanced sharply over her shoulder, collecting her emotions. When she trusted herself not to crumble, she said, "I think you'll find I'm not the same girl you knew."

"Neither am I the same boy." Caerwyn reached to unfasten his apron. Tossing a coin and a nod to Henri, he strode around the table. "I'll see you back safely, my lady."

Walking the darkened alleyway side by side, Nia watched Caerwyn from the corner of her eye as he pulled his blue tunic on over his sleeveless garment.

It was true; she didn't know him anymore. He'd grown at least a foot and had hardened into a colder, more serious man. Nothing like the cheerful youth he'd been.

"Nia," he said in a more gentle voice, "I do not mean to wound you. I am sure you will make someone a good wife. But I am not for you. Nor am I for"—he paused to hiss with distaste—"*Serena*. When I'm ready to take a wife, she will be a woman of the highest character. Responsible. Trustworthy. Loyal."

"But I am all those things." She shook her head, fighting her frustration. He didn't know her. He'd been gone, missing how she'd taken charge of Walwyn. How she tended to the needs of the castle villeins, the guards, and the servants. She chose the crops and oversaw their rotation. She'd predicted the early winter, the early harvest, and a pestilence that would've starved them all had she not ordered precautions. She'd learned to ride, to hunt, and shoot whilst all the men were battling the Saracens in the east. And she, not her father, kept Serena from trouble. "I know I took a risk going riding this morning, but the woods have been safe for years. And I would not knowingly harm anyone for my whims. I am *not* my sister."

Caerwyn rubbed his temple with his thumb, and spoke quietly. "Then someone will be very pleased to wed you, indeed."

Her face heated. Mortified at her display of emotion, she jerked her hood up and cast him an angry glare. "If you're not here to get a wife, then why *did* you come?"

He drew a ragged breath, turning his face to the darkening sky as if he'd wondered the same thing. "For certes, our fathers have been in correspondence. Your sire issued the invitation when he heard Padrig and I had returned—mayhap because our land borders his or because he didn't want to slight us. But," he paused, kicking at a stob of weeds in the road, and continued, "I didn't come for your sire. I wanted to accompany Padrig, and . . . it was my father's final wish. Our father is dead."

"I'm sorry." Nia hung her head, stung to hear the sadness in his voice and unable to offer him any consolation. She felt shamed beyond all redemption by her actions in the past.

The deception she'd undertaken with Serena's help had been a snare to try to win Caerwyn, but it had only succeeded in casting him away from her forever.

CAERWYN CONSIDERED NIA'S words as he lingered over his trencher of uneaten meat. Her claim that she'd changed echoed in his mind. She sat at the far end of the baron's table in the shadows. She'd been the last to sit after making sure her sister was safely ensconced between the baron and Padrig, away from the advances of other suitors. Knowing flirtatious Serena, she'd have the nearest knight betwixt her legs as soon as the meal was over. 'Twas her way. Nia's too, or so he'd thought.

Unless he'd been deceived, she was even less interested in choosing a match than he was. Caerwyn sat at one of the long tables below the family dais, along with Maddoc de Guildo, and watched Nia's every movement. Maddoc had attempted to catch Nia's eye as she'd passed, but the girl would have none of him. Caerwyn recalled where he'd met the knight before—at a tourney in Walwyn days before he'd left Wales.

He pushed his food away.

"You don't like the baron's food?" Michael de Chaucy, a knight and companion of Maddoc's, leaned close enough to Caerwyn he could smell the wine on his breath, then grabbed a piece of greasy meat from Caerwyn's trencher.

" 'Tis not that. I am not hungry." Caerwyn dropped a hand over the pouch on the table and slid it into his lap. The sack held the two silver rings along with his mother's for safekeeping while he'd bathed, and he'd not risk his drunken neighbor snatching the jewelry, as well, while he wasn't looking.

Maddoc, having overheard, chuckled and flexed his back. "A man wanting to marry one of the baron's daughters would take better care not to insult his kitchen. I see your brother is in no danger of that."

Caerwyn's gaze snapped to Padrig. His little brother's cheeks bulged as he chewed, smiling, and he took a bite of a roasted drumstick held in Serena's hand. The mischievous blonde had him enthralled as she pressed her bosom against his arm. At his age, Padrig wouldn't be prepared for a woman of her experience and caprice.

Caerwyn shoved away from the bench and stood.

The other men at his table laughed harder, but as he rounded the corner, headed in the direction of the dais with his sack of gifts in hand, he noted with smug satisfaction that Maddoc had stopped laughing.

The baron glanced up as Caerwyn's shadow fell over him. Serena, too. A small frown creased her pretty brow beneath an elaborate golden circlet in her hair. She wore the fine kirtle Padrig had brought, rich red trimmed with gold, while Nia wore an emerald one. Though his brother wasn't much of a man for making conversation, Caerwyn had always been envious of his thoughtfulness. He gripped the bag of rings behind his back.

"Ah, you've finally decided to grace us with your presence, milord." Lady Serena eased away from Padrig and directed an inviting smile at Caerwyn.

Guy de Brionne, a trained Marcher lord with a warlike disposition and a cunning mind, acknowledged him with a slight nod of his grizzled head. "Very good of you to come, Sir Caerwyn. How do you fare this evening? I've not heard much from your table."

"My mind is still in Acre. It has been a long time since Padrig and I have been entertained with good food and company. As I'm sure you'd understand, my recent stories and conversation would cause discomfort in others."

"Aye. The Crusades are not a topic I trust myself to

speak of in front of my daughters. Would you care to join us at our table on the dais?"

"Please do, Sir Caerwyn. Padrig won't mind moving down for his brother, surely." Serena turned her head, scowling down the length of the table at her sister. "Nia should have seated you here. You are our neighbor, after all."

Caerwyn waved a hand, declining Lady Serena's suggestion, and smiled. "You're both too kind. Nay, Lady Nia chose our seating arrangement satisfactorily. Besides, how else was I to survey my competition?"

Caerwyn indulged himself with a glance at Nia. She held her bottom lip between her teeth, her bright eyes suddenly anxious. He longed to watch her more but couldn't afford to be distracted.

"I trust you'll be the envy of every nobleman at court when you don the suit of armor our talented metalsmith is creating for the winner." Serena's gaze inched over Caerwyn as if imaging him in a very different suit. She purred, "His work is unparalleled. Of course, you must stay with us as long as it takes for the armor to be completed. For the measurements, the fittings. Henri will not mind more trips to Walwyn."

"There are several equally capable opponents, my lady. I would not presume—"

"I do hope you and your brother will accept my apologies," the baron broke in, saving Caerwyn from further humiliation, "for sending the invitation and hosting this gathering at what must be the gravest of times for you and everyone of Rhiwdinas."

"Aye, but our father always spoke highly of you, my

lord. On his deathbed, he expressed his wish for us to continue our friendship with Walwyn." Behind his back, Caerwyn drew the string on the bag and reached inside to handle the contents—two rough bands and the other, more elegant piece. He cleared his throat. "I fear I am the last knight to offer presents to the ladies this Christmastide."

Guy made a wave of dismissal. "Gifts are not required at such a time. The eleven knights before you have plied my daughters with more than enough."

"Nevertheless, I have a gift for each of them."

Caerwyn presented the first silver band to Serena with a sweeping bow. "My lady."

Her dazzling smile crumbled as she studied the silver circle cradled in her hand. When she tore her eyes from the object, she looked up at Caerwyn with an unsteady gaze. "Well. A ring. Thank you."

He couldn't help thinking that his coarse handiwork matched its new owner's morals: rushed and crude.

Caerwyn's boots thumped along the wooden dais as he walked to Nia. He felt the stares of the other knights and guests as he stopped in front of her. Perhaps they remembered the last time he'd visited and his hasty departure at finding her with another lover.

As he stood over her, her fingers played around the edge of her goblet, and he thought she even trembled. Then she surprised him with a smile so darling and playful, he felt all the air leave his lungs.

The shadows had kept her loveliness hidden from him most of the night, but seeing her now, so close, he cursed himself for not taking a seat beside her. Amazingly, she'd grown more desirable than he remembered. Though not the painted beauty Serena was, Nia had natural charm. Her eyes flashed with wit, and her fair skin betrayed her every emotion. Caerwyn was certain he could bring her flesh to a brilliant rose with the lightest touch of his hand in the right spot.

"Do you have something for me, my lord?" She blinked up at him, knocking him out of his fantasy.

Her chin wobbled, no doubt trying to keep from laughing. She was prepared for the ugly ring he'd made. She expected it, accepting that she wouldn't have to marry him. Caerwyn reached in the sack and fumbled past his mother's ring for the band.

Eleven other knights. One of them Padrig, one the hotheaded Maddoc, and another mayhap the drunken oaf from his table. What of the others? Were they equally as unappealing? Guy de Brionne would force the girls to choose. Which man would Nia want?

What do you care? Whoever married Nia would have to worry about her tumbling into another man's bed. Not you.

But a person could change. He'd seen proof of that in the men who went to Jerusalem. In himself. Mayhap Nia was right.

He pulled out the ring, handed it to her, and stalked away, determined not to wait for her reaction, which would tell him if he'd made the right choice.

Or the wrong one.

Chapter Three

THE DOOR TO the stables was open when Nia arrived. Yellow firelight flickered within, and her stomach twitched with excitement. She paused, gathering her thoughts, imagining what she ought to say first. A half hour earlier she'd been pacing the floor of her bedchamber, unable to sleep for wanting to talk to Caerwyn, then a knock at the door had ended her torture. One of the local boys with a familiar face and name she couldn't recall had come from the barracks with a message that Caerwyn wanted to meet. The stables were an odd place to talk, but he knew she had loved to ride as a child. Mayhap he wanted to take a quick trip in the moonlight. Besides, where else could they be alone at night? And she had so many questions to ask.

He'd given her a ring of value—a lovely, true treasure. Could he have changed his mind about her?

She knocked on the door. "Caerwyn?"

No answer. She went inside and noted that the sconces set beside the entrance were unlit. She followed the source of the light to find a small fire coming from one of the horse stalls. Her own horse's, Merlin's!

The stall was open a crack, smoke spilling out from inside. She pushed the door back.

"Merlin?"

The black gelding had backed into the corner. The fire was near the door, flames licking at the wall and spreading through the rushes.

"Hold on, dear," she murmured low, trying to calm him despite the panic gripping her. Smoke burned in her throat, and she coughed into her fist. Shielding the heat from her face with only her hands, she surged forward to avoid the flames, but they were too high. She stumbled backward, away from the thick smoke. Without her father's groomsmen, she had no idea where to find a bucket, but she would have to try. The horse had been hers for years. And if the fire wasn't put out immediately, the roof would cave in, the entire building would be destroyed in minutes, and all the animals killed.

Nia hurried to the wall where hooks held bridles, spurs, and harnesses. Against another wall stood a storage trunk. She threw the lid open, searching for a water vessel, and found a stack of blankets. She snatched one and whirled around.

"Lady Nia." Maddoc appeared in the doorway, his eyes round in the firelight. "I received a missive you were looking for me. What—"

"Merlin's stall is on fire!" she called as she ran, unfolding the blanket.

Back in the stall, she hurled the fabric over the flames, smothering the majority of the fire in the rushes. Maddoc ran inside after her, cursing at the sight, and together they began stomping out the tiny glowing straws. Maddened with fear, Merlin whinnied and reared over Nia. Too late, she realized she'd gotten too close to the frantic horse.

Maddoc grabbed her and pulled her out of the way as Merlin's hooves came flying down.

Cupping Nia's face in his hands, he said, "Come outside. I know where to get water. Just stay away from the animal."

Nia nodded reluctantly and followed him outside. There were still flames climbing the wall of Merlin's stall. Still time for more damage.

Maddoc left the building and came back in a flash, carrying a bucket brimming with water. Nia followed him to the source and found another bucket. After two more trips, they had the fire out and led Merlin safely to another stall.

Finding the stables unbearable with the stench of smoke, she led Maddoc to the hay barn to rest. They sat side by side on a pile of clean hay, waiting while Maddoc's tunic dried. Had he not been helping her, she would've believed he'd taken his garment off on purpose for a chance to flex his muscles. But that thought was unkind. He'd done naught wrong. If she should think ill of anyone, let it be Caerwyn, who'd promised to meet at the stables but failed to appear.

Sitting in an entirely unladylike manner, Nia leaned on her knees and played with the pretty gold ring on her finger. The piece took her breath away from the first moment she'd laid eyes on it.

Could it be that he'd given it to her by accident?

Oh, God, if he had! The idea sickened her. Returning it would break her heart. She'd never beheld a gift more dear.

The gold formed a rose shape with a brilliant emerald in the center. It fit perfectly, but after the fire and the heat from her panic, her finger had swollen. The ring wouldn't budge.

"Would you like me to help you take it off?"

Maddoc caressed her arm, and kindness shone in his blue eyes.

"Nay. But thank you for the offer. It will come off when I bathe."

He grinned and leaned so close his shaggy gold hair brushed her arm. "I could help you bathe, too."

Nia frowned at him. "Nay."

The only man she wanted seeing her naked was Caerwyn. And they nearly had been naked that day they'd shared their first kiss—the first of many, lying beneath the orchard trees. Their hands roving over each other's young bodies, sweet touches and loving whispers.

"What do you think happened, Nia?"

She glanced at the knight, having nearly forgotten him as she was lost in memories of Caerwyn's tender caresses. She found her voice, "It seems almost as if some-one is trying to harm me. But it doesn't make sense. First the brigands, who were probably robbers travel-ing through our woods from afar. Then earlier today, I thought someone was following me in the market. Now Merlin's stall—"

"Bastards. Mayhap you, or your sire, have an enemy. You know, if you were betrothed to me, no one would dare attempt to harm you."

She caressed the stone of her ring. How sad that anyone would want to harm a horse—or her, for that matter. If someone asked her for money, she would gladly give it.

Maddoc captured her ringed fingers and brought them to his lips. "Your finger will turn blue if you don't allow me to remove the ring. Here, I know a trick."

Nia shook her head, smiling, and braced herself for a tugging contest between the knight and her fingers. Instead, he brought her hand to his lips and opened his mouth to draw her ring finger inside. Nia heard herself gasp as his hot wet mouth closed around the ring. His tongue swirled around her finger, sending her into a panic to rival Merlin's. If only he was Caerwyn, but he wasn't!

She shoved at his shoulder. "Stop that! Get off!"

He suckled her finger, making a mewling noise that made her stomach roll.

"Maddoc, STOP!" Even if he severed her finger with his teeth, it would be worth getting him off the digit.

His mouth slid away from her, and he covered his lips

with his hand. Eyes wide with affront, he cursed. "Nia, I only wanted to help."

She scrambled to her feet and cradled her offended hand. "When I need your help, I'll ask."

He chuckled, rose on his knees, and encircled her legs with steely arms. "Come back down here with me. I've no wish to fight, only to prove my worth as your lover."

"My l—" Nia tried to walk out of his arms, but his hold held firm. She bent over him to push against his shoulders. "We are not betrothed. I've no wish to lie with any man but my future husband."

Maddoc released her legs and snatched her shoulders with lightning speed, dragging her toward his lips before she knew his intentions. His mouth was hard and hot against hers, his beard grating against her face. She strained against him as anger poured through her. Unable to bear it, she closed her eyes to survive his assault on her mouth. This felt nothing like Caerwyn's kisses, but her mind returned to the day in the orchard again.

Caerwyn's youthful face, still untouched by the harsh desert sun, loomed over her. His cheeks were tinged red from tickling her as they lay beneath the apple trees, and he leaned down, beaming with delight between kisses.

"You're a thief." He tweaked her chin with his thumb.

"'Twas one apple, and it is my orchard, after all." Lying on her back, she could see the tiny black whiskers underneath his chin, and her toes curled in her slippers to see such proof of his masculinity.

"Nay." He shook his head and lowered his face to hers. "'Twas my heart."

"Your heart?"

"You stole it, and I trow you will never return it to me."
He pressed his mouth to hers softly, slowly, lingering as if to
make the moment last forever.

Pressure from Maddoc's hands brought her toward him and the hay, and the imminent danger of what would happen if she allowed him to continue. The image of Caerwyn vanished. Tumbling down with her captor, she dropped her knee at the juncture of his thighs.

"You whore!" he bellowed, releasing her shoulders.

Nia gave her knee an extra grind as she pushed off his prone body, eliciting a high-pitched cry from the man. "You think I owe you my body for helping put out the fire?" She dragged the back of her hand across her burning lips.

He cupped his sex and winced. "Nay. I know you to be a de Brionne, a whore just like your sister, but you're worse. You're a cock-tease—a damned, lying harlot."

Nia scrambled toward freedom.

Pausing at the door, she turned, seething. "And you are a bastard and a brute, Maddoc de Guildo! You can be certain my father will rescind his invitation to Walwyn for you forever."

Fury propelled Nia through the darkness and across the bailey until she reached the sanctity of her bedchamber. Sore and frustrated at her naivety, she shirked off her kirtle and splashed cold water on her face. She still smelled of smoke, and worse, hay, keeping Maddoc's actions fresh on her thoughts. Taking a damp cloth, she scoured at her face and bare arms while practicing her explanation of the night's events that she would share with her father.

Then she noticed her hands for the first time since the tussle with Maddoc.

Caerwyn's gold ring was missing.

PADRIG SLEPT ON his side, snoring peacefully, oblivious to the other men in Walwyn's barracks doing the same. The cramped accommodations were far from the worst Caerwyn and his brother had ever experienced, and with bellies full of food and ale, no one complained. Still, Caerwyn found that sleep eluded him.

The sentry sat outside the barracks door keeping watch, and Caerwyn gave him a nod as he walked past on his way to tend the fire in the hearth. Most Christmastides, the lord would've given his servants the fortnight as a holiday from their duties, but after the attack in the woods, he took better care to guard his guests. Something about the brigands bothered Caerwyn, along with the conversation he'd had with Nia as they'd walked back from the metalsmith. She'd said she thought she'd seen someone following her in the market.

He picked up an iron and poked at the embers of the hearth as he mulled over the danger.

While he didn't wish the baron any harm—he respected him perhaps even more than he'd respected his late father—his greatest worry was keeping Nia safe. Although she seemed to be a woman who could take care of herself.

On the forest road, she'd held her own amongst the men, arming herself and keeping her head. And what a pretty head it was.

The flames licking at the Yule log reminded him of Nia's hair as she'd worn it earlier at the feast, unbound, with the long, cinnamon-gold tendrils curling just below her breasts. Aye, he'd made the right decision, giving her his mother's ring, and he'd seen from where he'd sat at his table, she'd placed the ring on her finger. Her cheeks bloomed with red that even her shadowy corner could not hide.

The ring had been his father's gift to his mother. A symbol of faith and trust. Whilst gone on the Seventh Crusade, his wife, the boys' mother, had taken a lover. Her deceit had broken his father in many ways, but in time, he forgave her. She wore the ring until the day she died, returning it to him only on her deathbed. Though his father had said nothing ill about the daughters of de Brionne, Caerwyn wanted to take care in making his choice of wives.

Nia had sworn she was everything he sought in a match, and in truth, her behavior had been the exact opposite of her scandalous sister's during the feast. He'd followed his instincts to give her his mother's ring, and his instincts hadn't misled him in years.

Tomorrow, he would seek Nia out, ask for her vow of faithfulness, and if it sufficed, he would ask her father for her hand in marriage. Again.

The last time he'd asked had been after they'd shared an afternoon in each other's arms, coming so very near to a precipice from which there would've been no return.

Blossom petals fell from the trees like a gentle shower, dusting the grassy bed around Nia. Her gray eyes danced as she watched the orchard's show above her, laughing as if she'd been tickled. Stretching out beside her, Caerwyn found the notion of tickling his darling girl more than he could resist. While the petals distracted her, he reached across her stomach and gave her ribs a fast stroke.

"Ack!" She jerked like a fish. "Stop!" Her cheeks dimpled with her grin.

"You don't like it?" He swept his hand along her side, making her writhe in a breathless tide of giggles.

"Serena says I shouldn't laugh too much. She says you'll not like me anymore if I do."

He groaned. "Nay. You pay your sister too much heed. Nothing she says is ever sound, Nia." Leaning over her, he brushed a petal off her forehead and delighted in the excuse to stroke her smooth brow.

Her nose wrinkled, seemingly opposed to his viewpoint, though she still smiled. "She's had scads more wooers than I."

He stopped his motion, freezing with the thought her words conjured. "Do you want more wooers?"

Her turn to pause, she grew serious, and her throat moved as she swallowed. "Nay."

Warmth spread through him, and he leaned closer to her face. He whispered, "My lady, your laughter fells me more surely than any opponent in any tournament. It's like listening to the sweetest music." He lowered his mouth to her shoulder for a kiss.

Her skin felt warm and pulsed with life beneath his lips. Her hands wrapped around his arms, not pushing him away for his boldness but actually holding him—nay, drawing him closer, keeping him there.

His heart surged with gladness . . . and hunger for more.

Caerwyn bent closer to Nia, stretching long over her while taking care not to crush her. He wasn't much bigger than she was, but he was a boy in training to be a warrior, built of harder muscle and sharp bones. His hip rested against hers, and he braced a knee beside her thigh while he made a trail of kisses along her throat.

"Nia, you are mine always," he murmured, prayerfully.

"Aye." She ran her hand up the back of his neck into his hair the way she often did when they played together. Now, the familiar action teased him in a different way than it had before, stoking a fire within.

He lifted his head to look in her eyes, to see if he'd see the same heat reflected there.

Her chest heaved, slightly winded, as she stared up at him. So innocent, she looked up at him with worry, as if she'd done something wrong. That look was his undoing.

"My lady, I must kiss you." Must? Nay. He shook his head to clear the fog of his brain. Then he tried again, "What I-I mean to say is 'may I kiss you?'"

"Aye." Her small hand curled against the back of his head, and he heard himself moan before he lowered his lips to hers.

Voices brought Caerwyn back to the present. The sentry spoke to someone. He pushed himself away from the stone mantel of the hearth and went to see who would be about at this late hour. His hand reached for the sword that wasn't there. He'd forgotten he'd removed his belt and scabbard before lying down earlier. His hands closed in fists, his only weapons as he approached the men.

The sentry laughed and touched the shadowy figure's shoulder. Not an enemy, then. Caerwyn relaxed as the moonlight from outside fell on Sir Maddoc's face at the doorway.

"Isn't it late for you to be walking the bailey?" Caerwyn said, as the knight stepped inside the barracks.

The sentry stepped back outside to his post, leaving the men in the darkened entry.

Maddoc wore no mail, only breeches, and carried some garment, probably his missing tunic, over his shoulder. The white of his teeth flashed in a grimace. "Would that I hadn't left my bed this night!"

The man smelled of ashes. A dart of alarm went through Caerwyn. "What happened to you?"

Maddoc sniffed, dragging the back of his fist under his nose. "That female. The whore! She nearly maimed me."

He immediately pictured Lady Serena taking the lusty de Guildo to her bed, where she'd be more than even he could handle. Still, anger stuck in Caerwyn's craw for the knight's lack of respect for a woman, no matter her sexual proclivities.

He jabbed a finger in Maddoc's chest. "If you spoke to Lady Serena like that, you likely deserved it—or worse."

"Ha!" He raked a hand through his gold locks, casting off a cloud of dust and bits of straw that then vanished into the shadows. "Lady Serena, *Lady Serena*. As lief I *had* been with her! Unfortunately, I spent the evening with Lady Nia, for what good it did. I saved her life. Pulled her from what would've been her death in the stables. And this is how she thanks me." He shook his head and shuffled off, limping toward the rows of sleeping men and his empty pallet.

An invisible dagger ran through Caerwyn's heart. *Nay, he must be lying!* Surely Nia hadn't met Maddoc in secret.

Caerwyn thrust out an arm, stopping the man. "Is what you say true? You and Lady Nia—"

Maddoc gave him a half smile. "Aye." He winked.

Caerwyn dug his fingers into Maddoc's arm, feeling the pinch and twist of the man's muscles yielding to his superior strength.

"Damn it, Caerwyn! Would you see me wounded twice in the same night?" He grimaced painfully though his smile grew.

"What did you do to her to *make* her maim you?" Caerwyn spoke through his gritted teeth, rage pressing hard inside his skull. He shook the man so hard, his head popped back.

Alarm crept into the knight's expression, wiping the smugness from his countenance. "Nothing. Nothing to warrant her spite or yours. A betrothal is still available to the best man, still worth winning, I suppose. But know you this, Caerwyn, I *will* win her. When we wed, and I come to her bed as a husband, I trow she'll be more biddable."

Caerwyn released a breath but kept his firm hold on

Maddoc. "If she tells me you hurt her, I will tear you apart, piece by piece—"

"I swear, she is unharmed and alive thanks to me."

Maddoc pulled loose from Caerwyn's clutch and rubbed the white lines where Caerwyn's hands had gripped him.

"God's blood, you must control yourself, *Crusader*. Besides, after I beat you in the tourney, she's as good as mine." He lifted his hand, scratching at his beard, and the moonlight reflected on something metal on his little finger.

A foul grin spread on Maddoc's lips, knowing and wicked, and Caerwyn stood transfixed by the deliberate action, watching as light winked off his mother's gold ring.

Chapter Four

SERENA POKED AT the straw on the floor with her toe while Nia crawled on the ground. Her sister's arms were crossed over her chest, anchoring the heavy gold chain around her neck to keep it from swaying across her breasts like a pendulum. Looking as ridiculous as ever, by Nia's estimation, she'd gilded herself with gifts from suitors whom she would later scorn.

Out of the corner of her eye, Nia caught the flash of the morning sun on something in the hay. She scrambled for it, being careful not to look away.

"Did you find it?" Serena stilled.

Nia reached in the straw and retrieved a polished buckle. Drained, she sighed, and tossed the piece to her sister. "Only that. Keep it for the groomsman. It may be Christmastide, and Father is feeling more generous, but you know he isn't easily forgiving of waste."

Serena rolled her eyes and went back to poking with

her feet. "Why the barn? You could've brought the man to your bed. By my troth, Nia—"

"I didn't want him. He's a brute." Her hands and knees ached as she sifted through wads of hay. "Unlike you, I'm still innocent. I didn't bring him in here for anything sordid. We were merely collecting ourselves after the fire."

Serena tossed her shiny blond hair off her shoulder. "There is only one reason I would've come to *this* place with a man." She flung a hand at the rustic barn walls. "Maddoc is a suitor, and a very handsome one, at that. You came here with him alone, after he helped you. It's what he expected—what *any* of your suitors would have expected. No doubt our sire thought so, too."

Bitterness surged in Nia. She slung a handful of hay at the wall. Her father had ignored her complaints. He'd refused to throw de Guildo out of their keep. The very idea that her father would continue to welcome that savage made her chest tighten with anger.

Her sister's attitude sickened her further. "A true, chivalrous knight would not expect payment in flesh. Your way of thinking is erroneous and simply wrong."

"Look, sister dear, you've been at this for an hour. 'Tis time to stop. You'll not find the ring. And mayhap that odious Maddoc kept it. You don't even know for certain it's here. I could always ask Henri to fashion another when I go to the market again."

"That would take many days, a sennight or more. The tournament will be over before then. Besides, I wouldn't dream of engaging in such deception." Nia sat back and rested her hands on her lap. The hay barn was enormous, the straw spread from wall to wall, pile to pile, and the men had beaten her to the place that morning to fetch fresh hay for her horse's new stall. *Poor, Merlin. Such a scare for him.* "I guess I should check on Merlin and see how he's faring. I can come back and search more later."

Serena lifted her face skyward. "Thank the heavens."

She floated outside, leaving Nia to struggle to her feet. Her legs had fallen asleep from crawling so long on the ground. She bent, rubbing them awake

"May I be of assistance, my lady?" Caerwyn filled the doorway in a casual stance.

How long had he been watching? A dark tremor passed through Nia. She straightened and instinctively held her hands behind her back. "Nay. I . . . lost something in the hay."

He glanced at the floor for a flicker of a moment, then approached. His hair fell across his forehead, but Nia noted his half-hidden frown. "I heard about the fire last night. They said you were in the stables at the time?"

She nodded and arched a brow at him. "But you knew that. I received your message. I went to meet you, and you weren't there. Merlin's stall was already on fire when I arrived."

"What message? I didn't send a message." He folded his arms, causing the tunic to pull down across his muscular chest. With his legs planted wide and a haughty slant of his head, he seemed to doubt her.

"The page." Nia rubbed her temple, trying to conjure the face of the familiar-looking boy who'd spoken with her. Where had she seen him before? And Maddoc had mentioned receiving a missive as well. "I'll ask the steward to find him. He must have gotten you confused with someone else, but I cannot imagine who would've asked to speak with me there."

"Can you not?" Caerwyn scoffed, staring at the floor. Then his gaze returned to her face with new intensity, and he drew closer. "But you're all right? At daybreak, I went to look for you in your chamber. Your maid told me you were here."

His question held a note of concern, which caused a jangle of delight, as well as guilt, to run through her. "I am fine. I put out the fire . . . with Maddoc de Guildo's help." She added the last grudgingly.

"So I've heard." Caerwyn let out a long breath, but the tension of his expression remained. He circled her slowly, his gaze raking her kirtle, which was once yellow and now brown from her fruitless exploits on the barn floor. "De Guildo has been bragging in the barracks." His lip curled as he spoke.

Her stomach dived. This was exactly why Maddoc needed to be sent away. "What did he say?"

Caerwyn touched her arm. His hand glided up to her shoulder. "I try not to give him my ear. His words and voice set my teeth on edge."

Nia tried to smile, but her lips trembled. Though Caerwyn's touch was tender, something about the way he stared sent sparks shimmering through her. Mayhap it was only her guilty conscience, but his lips twitched as if he took pleasure in her fidgeting movements.

"Mine too," she admitted.

He rubbed her delicate collarbone under his thumb. "Nia, you have changed so much. I've often wondered if you would still remember me when we met again."

Nia's fortitude, or what there was left of it, melted.

"Caerwyn." She touched his lips with her fingertips, stopping him. His words were crushing her heart, remorse making every beat a punishing blow. "I must tell you the truth. I've done something horrible, but it wasn't my fault entirely. I meant nothing wrong, even though it would seem . . . I hadn't intended—"

"Don't explain." He shook his head. The corner of his mouth quirked, but there was no humor in his eyes. He put his other hand behind her neck, keeping her close as he moved near. Nia felt his thighs touching her through their clothes, and her body responded with a rush of heat to her feminine valley. The brown of his irises disappeared in the blackness of his eyes, hooded now as he stared at her mouth like a predator hungering for its meal. "I've grown weary of the past. The things you say remind me of how things were between us when I trusted you. But the way you act belies every word. You mock the past—and us. You mock me."

His fingers tangled in her hair possessively as he studied her reaction.

Wariness had Nia bracing inwardly. This was a side of Caerwyn she'd never witnessed before. He'd never seemed capable of violence off the tournament field. Then again, she had no idea what his hands had done in Jerusalem or whether his enemies had deserved his wrath.

She slid her own hands between them, only to discover more frightening evidence of his conflicted emotions—the solid pounding of his heart. Her knees threatened to buckle. "I'm not mocking you. I would ne'er do that."

"I may never have my boyhood dreams, but I *will* have my grown fantasies," he growled. His thumb left her collarbone and swept her bottom lip. Nia's mouth opened in surprise, and he caught her chin, tipping her head back.

His brow furrowed as he leaned forward, capturing her mouth. Excitement unfurled within her, elation and trepidation clashing in one overwhelming moment. Caerwyn's tongue stroked across her lip, chasing the sensation his thumb had left with a peculiar brand, then invaded her mouth, seeking her tongue. Nia met his stroke, matching it with hers, lifting on her toes to ease his access.

For so long, she'd wanted to feel this with him again.

For so long, she'd wanted the chance to show him he was the only one she'd ever wanted to kiss. The only one she wanted to feel naked beneath her hands. She'd always hoped he would recognize the truth when they were in each other's arms once more. Then he'd realize what he'd thought he'd seen before years ago was naught but a lie, trickery by her and her sister. No man or boy had ever been before him.

Presently, she felt his hand loosen in her hair as if he'd become aware that she offered no resistance. He traced her neck and shoulder with his gentle hand as he deepened his kiss, exploring her with every touch, every point of contact between their bodies. Nia longed to do the same, to burrow under his clothes and bring him closer in her embrace. His mouth loved hers, kissing her furiously, then tenderly, with his tongue brushing hers in a rhythm she soon followed instinctively with her hips. Emboldened by passion, she smoothed her palms down his chest over the solid ripples of his flat torso and felt the hard pressure of his need against her stomach.

Caerwyn broke the kiss and caught her hands in his, halting them at his waist. Regarding her through narrowed eyes, he asked, hoarse, "Have you forgotten what I gave you?" His jaw tightened, and his thumb grazed the vacant spot on her finger where the ring had been.

Nia's face flared with heat. She swallowed against the lump in her throat. "The ring. I—"

"The ring I gave you as a present was my mother's, the only thing of hers my father and I kept. I gave it to you, just as I gave you my h—" He broke off, swallowing. "You've chosen not to wear it?"

Nia winced. It meant more to him than she'd imagined. When she opened her eyes again, her soul felt exposed. Heat continued to pulse in her lips from their passion. She longed to hide her face yet wanted to reach for him and drag him back into her arms.

Mouth suddenly dry, she croaked, "Not by choice. You see, Maddoc took—"

"And I'm to believe you're innocent? With your past transgressions? You and de Guildo were in here—*the barn*—talking?" He tilted his head, frowning dubiously.

Nia nodded. "'Tis true. I have only my word to give you. I don't trust Maddoc to speak with honesty."

"Nay. On that point I believe you. But for the rest . . .

how can I pledge my vows to you, to take you as my wife, if I cannot know if you speak true? If I cannot trust you will be faithful to me, Nia? We've been through this before."

"On my life, Caerwyn, I thought I was meeting *you*. If I could get the ring back from Maddoc, then find the person who sent me the message and bring him to you, would you trust me then?"

He shook his head, slipping away from her. When he spoke, his voice was broken and defeated, "I've been imprudent to trust you again . . . to want you again. I'm a fool, and I've only myself to blame. But hear me, Nia, if what you say isn't a lie about this page, do not, *do not* go looking for this person. Let it alone. If he . . . if he's even real, he could be dangerous."

Nia hugged herself, wounded by his mistrust. Yet his concern for her safety provided the tiniest hope . . .

He paused at the door and held her gaze with a sudden vulnerable expression that sent her back once more to that glorious day in the orchard.

He said, "You *have* forgotten what I gave you."

Of course. She should've known the right answer.

His heart.

A FORTNIGHT AGO, Guy de Brionne had offered a full set of valuable armor to the winner of the tournament on Twelfth Day, but Nia knew everyone expected the true prizes would be her and her sister. Before sending his invitation for the festivities, her father had called the women to his solar, sitting them down to explain his intentions. Wanting to sort the weeds from the garden, so to speak, he'd said he hoped to eliminate the noblemen who weren't up to the challenge of protecting his daughters.

Well, Nia mused now, scanning the weapons stretching from one end of the table to other, why should men have all the fun?

Each morning since the competition began nine days ago, the bailey transformed into a practice field. Knights and squires parried, chopped, thrust. Arms and weapons flew, bodies fell. Metal clanged incessantly. In fact, Serena claimed the noise from the yard gave her such headaches, she took refuge in her bedchamber, far from her adoring suitors.

Her sister's caprice boggled Nia's mind. On some days, Serena flirted outrageously, throwing herself at everyone, including even poor Henri when she thought no one was looking. On other days, she moped, inconsolable, like today, wanting nothing to do with men in general.

The present clamor didn't thwart Nia from visiting the field, though. She skirted past two aggressive opponents, locked in each other's arms in Greco-Roman combat, struggling for ground. For the past few days, she'd had more solitude and quiet than she could stand. Being alone with her thoughts, she'd ruminated on Caerwyn and their last exchange of words and kisses until she could neither eat nor sleep. His grudge against her was unfounded, and she would prove it once and for all.

"Lady Nia? You shouldn't be here." Padrig stopped her, running across the field to greet her. Coming directly from practice, he carried a mace, its weight pulling him sideways where he stood. Sweat rolled down his face despite the chilly winter day.

"I'm getting tired of everyone's telling me where I should or shouldn't be." She rested her hands on her hips, wrapping her fingers around the hilt of the sword strapped at her side. "Before you came here, I practiced on this field every day myself."

If her father had his way, she'd be in the solar stitching tapestries, flirting with every passing swain like her sister.

It wasn't fair. She eyed the crowd, knowing she could compete successfully in some of the events herself.

Her friend ducked his head, paling with chagrin. "My apologies. I didn't know." Dark eyelashes fanned above his cheeks, which still held a trace of their boyish roundness. He reminded her of his brother in that moment; however, the older knight would never have shown blatant remorse. With his head down, Padrig explained, "Some of the men aren't as skilled as others, and I feared you might get hurt."

"Thank you, but I'm fine." She patted his arm, and her hand met the startlingly thick padding of mail. "Oh my."

He glanced up with a lopsided grin. "My gambeson is the one I wore in Jerusalem. It conceals the mail of my hauberk inside its padding. 'Tis patched, heavy, and uglier than most, I trow, but it's never let me down."

Nia nodded. "It is good armor. I wish you luck. Who is your next opponent?"

"There are six of us left. Bruce of St. Penmore, Brecon,

Maddoc de Guildo, Denbigh, Caerwyn, and myself. We compete tomorrow." Suddenly serious, he swallowed.

Fear? Surely not. He'd fought beside Caerwyn and Prince Edward.

She tucked her hair behind her ear and pulled Padrig close to speak where no one would overhear. "My father is choosing the opponents, is he not? If you're afraid you'll be asked to face your brother, I could—"

"Nay. I have no qualms about facing an opponent." He planted the heavy, spiked end of the mace in the earth beside him and leaned on its handle. "It's the running of the rings, my worst event, so I'll probably be eliminated." He shrugged a shoulder. "My eyesight has never been good enough for small targets."

Nia bit her lip. There was nothing to help poor eyesight, and sadly, Padrig's weakness would soon be exposed. A series of quintains would be erected with small metal rings suspended in the air for each knight to spear with his lance while riding at top speed. Difficult, even for those with good eyesight.

"It's all right, my lady. I've enjoyed my days here, and at least I know your father won't turn me out of his keep for the defeat."

Nay. God knew what it would take for Father to send any of these suitors away!

She glanced around the field, spotting Caerwyn sparring with his squire, a redheaded man, far too tall to be mistaken as the page who'd sent her into harm's way. Reminded of her mission, she gestured for Padrig's ear again.

"I'm trying to locate a boy. He's about six-and-ten years of age, black-haired, nearly your height. He brought me a message."

Padrig shook his head, frowning. "I'm sorry. He doesn't sound familiar."

Nia twined a strand of hair around her finger as more disappointment settled within. The castle steward hadn't recognized her description of the lad, either. She stole another glance at Caerwyn and found him watching her across the bailey. Beneath the smooth metal dome of his helmet, he scowled and slung his shield to the ground.

Flooded by the confusing emotions of anger, regret, and the desire he invoked, she backed away from Padrig, blurting, "Don't tell your brother I asked. If you see anyone fitting those details, would you please find out whom he serves and fetch me at once?"

"Of course, milady." He bowed and hefted the mace onto his shoulder.

No longer spoiling for a fight—at least not with Caerwyn—Nia picked up her skirt and hurdled over one felled warrior as she hastened for the nearest exit from the practice field. Finding a door to the keep open, she slipped inside, watching from afar as Caerwyn caught up with Padrig.

God's blood, that didn't go well. She cursed, then bit her lip for using one of the expressions she'd picked up from her father's men.

It just wasn't fair. She might never find that page again. Many of the guests didn't mingle with the family of the castle, and she couldn't even be sure he still resided in Walwyn. The only way to find him would be to mix amongst the knights, and she couldn't do that with Caerwyn's eyes following her.

Unless she became one of them.

Chapter Five

OUTSIDE THE DOOR, the footsteps of the crowd passing the armory sent a shiver of excitement through Nia. She crammed Padrig's helmet on her head, hiding the tight braids she'd made of her hair. His heavy mail and gambeson made movement difficult, and in no more than a few moments under the weight, her arm muscles ached. When she'd dreamt up the idea of taking his place at the running of the rings, she hadn't planned how her movements on the horse would appear—let alone how she would walk on her own two feet.

Too late to change her mind now, she forced her concerns to the back of her mind. Dressed in the armor, she hoped she could be Padrig's twin, and none would be the wiser. "Well? How does it look?" She tugged at the hauberk and turned in a circle for her friend to see.

"Wretched." He wrinkled his nose, and his scrutiny followed the line of her legs encased in the thick, padded chausses. It had taken much convincing to get Caerwyn's cautious little brother to warm to the idea of the switch. He covered his eyes with a hand and stumbled toward the door. "I would rather not look a'tall. It's an abomination."

Nia laughed and shoved him away from the door. "You must stay here until the contest is over. But pray, you would warn me if you didn't think it was convincing, would you not?" If the knights got word of her scheme, they'd banish her from the place before her search for the messenger boy ever began. She had to be allowed to enter chambers where their young grooms and squires followed.

He sighed. "Aye, you look like a man. With the helmet on, you've hidden the last trace of your identity. Are you sure you want to do this? I do not have to win."

"I know. But you're too good to be eliminated over such a silly event. Don't consider this as wrong, Padrig. We're merely making the competition even." The helmet was too tight, causing her braids to pull and sting her scalp. She reached to adjust them, but her gloved fingers were too thick to help.

Padrig chuckled and thumped her helmet, making the metal rattle in her ears. "You're a good friend. And don't worry if you lose. I wasn't expecting to win. I could never beat Maddoc or Caerwyn, at any rate."

Nia sucked in a breath. "Really? Have faith. Even if we don't win, I doubt you'll come in last."

Walwyn's outer yard had been turned into a small tournament field. The larger area outside the castle walls that the baron usually reserved for such events was being prepared for the final joust. Sir Padrig's squire brought his horse around and helped Nia mount. She sighed with relief as the fellow led her to the field, where the other contestants were waiting. If Padrig's own man didn't notice, no one else would either.

Nia was the fifth combatant to take the field. Reining Padrig's mount, she waited her turn in line, feeling jittery with anticipation. Very soon, she hoped to find the missing page.

Caerwyn appeared last, sitting tall astride his Arabian horse. Nia had seen the animal in action, and its grace and agility in Caerwyn's skillful hands made it seem an extension of its rider. Together, they were one fluid machine as they approached Nia and sidled in beside her. She watched Caerwyn through the slit of her helmet, suddenly glad of its smothering fit over her face. She heard her heated breath in her own ears, coming faster, deeper, within the metal dome, as she felt her beloved's powerful presence.

Caerwyn nodded to her in greeting, sending fear through her like the crack of a whip, and the horse, sensing Nia's state of alarm, pawed an impatient hoof. *Oh, by the rood, Nia. He's nodding at Padrig, not you!* She blew out a calming breath and gave the horse's shoulder a gentle rub with her gloved hand. If Caerwyn noticed anything different about his brother, he didn't show it, gazing out at the small gathering of guests and onlookers lining the wall of the keep. His helmet obscured his brow from her, but from his side, she observed the lines of concentration bracketing his mouth. Serious and stern amidst the Christmastide revelry of the tournament, Caerwyn was a man who needed pleasure in his life. Too long he'd experienced war and pain, only to come home to watch his father die. Nia recalled hearing that his mother had been unfaithful. By the time she'd learned about his family's history and the sordid affair, it was too late; she'd pulled her stunt to try to make Caerwyn jealous. If she'd known, she wouldn't have acted with such disregard for his feelings.

She would have to remember to caution Padrig not to tell Caerwyn about their new deception. Her beloved distrusted her as it was. Another perfidy on her part might be the last straw, ending any feelings he had for her.

Caerwyn, though the last to arrive, was called first to compete. He took a lance from his squire and charged toward the rings with steadiness and accuracy. The lance struck the objects one by one. At the end of the row of quintains, he held up his weapon, displaying three rings caught out of five.

Each knight followed in turn, running through the course, snagging rings. Padrig's name was the last one called, and Nia, watching Caerwyn at the far end of the field, almost didn't hear her friend's name. The crowd went silent, watching her, and her stomach dropped as she realized her mistake.

She shook off her anxiety, grabbed the lance, and hefted it against her hip to ride out to the quintains.

Her horse bolted beneath her spurs, zooming toward the first target. Her lance clinked as it struck the first ring dead center. *One*. Keeping her aim true, she held her course. *Two.* The lance felt as if were a part of her. *Three.* Faces whizzed in her peripheral vision. *Four.* The horse's gait a steady rhythm beneath her. *Five.*

At the end of the row she grinned and turned, showing her father and the crowd her lance decked with five metal rings. A perfect event. The audience cheered, chanting Padrig's name. Her heart soared, knowing her friend would now be able to continue to compete with the rest of the men.

The squires and grooms came out directly to help the knights dismount and remove the horses to the stables. This was her chance. Hidden under the helmet, Nia parted with her horse to walk in the crowd and scanned the faces of men and boys, searching for the one who'd come to her the night of the fire. She swiveled, struggling to see through the helmet's orifices, but there were so many people, all moving too quickly. After several exhausting minutes of circling the area, going in and out of the equipment rooms, she watched the men trickle away from the stabled animals. The crowd thinned, and her page was nowhere in sight. She sighed, resolved to another disappointment. Then from behind, a gloved hand fell on her shoulder.

Startled, Nia gasped and turned around, her sword hand reaching for the weapon she'd forgotten to wear over the armor. Her gaze lifted to find the scowling face of Caerwyn bearing down at her.

"God's blood, 'tis you!" he murmured.

CAERWYN BLINKED, BUT his eyes weren't playing tricks on him. Verily, Nia was staring back at him through Padrig's helmet. Her gray eyes were wide with fear.

Good. Let her be afraid.

It wouldn't do to scold her in front of the men. It would only bring shame on Padrig, and he didn't want that though the stupid fellow deserved it for his part in the perfidy.

He clamped onto her arm and hauled her against his chest. "Come with me, *brother*. I think Lady Nia would like to have a word with you."

She blinked and nodded.

Caerwyn marched her across the bailey and into the keep. In the chaos of preparing for the evening's feast, none of the servants stopped them or took notice, and they reached Nia's bedchamber unobstructed. Once inside her closed door, Caerwyn took hold of Nia's helmet and threw it off.

Nia yelped, hands reaching for her braided head. "St. Anthony! That hurt, Caerwyn." Tears filled her pretty eyes when she looked up at him.

He bit the inside of his cheek. *Damn.* He hadn't meant to hurt her. He touched her face softly in apology, only to see his rough glove against her alabaster skin.

He swore and stripped the gloves off. The woman bedeviled him, for certes.

"Are you mad?" she asked, tugging off her own gloves. She dropped the pair on the floor beside his. "I didn't beat you at the rings on purpose."

Fear for his brother's and Nia's safety gave him a wild

rush of hostility, making him want to lash out, to yell, or break something. Caerwyn kicked at one of the gloves.

However, the sight of their discarded articles strewn side by side caused something primal in him to raise its head. His mind strayed to darker, pleasurable places, to thoughts of more discarded clothing, to uncovering Nia's lovely body beneath the bulky gambeson. And then his gaze focused on the bed behind her—large, soft, and beckoning.

Nay!

He dragged in a calming breath and squeezed his hands into fists in an effort to keep from reaching for her. "I don't care that you beat me. I care that you deceived everyone by pretending to be Padrig. You two are cheats, frauds. 'Tis despicable."

"He couldn't do the rings. The competition was unfair. Besides, that was only a small part of my reason for dressing like him." She pulled at the knotted stay under her chin, loosening it with trembling hands. Her braids fell around her face as she worked.

Caerwyn groaned. It usually took a second person to help Padrig remove his battered armor. There was no avoiding it, he had to help. Taking pity on her, he grabbed the second ratty ribbon and worked at the knot although his hands weren't steady, either. "I knew you weren't Padrig. He could ne'er have captured so many rings. He can't see anything until it's less than two-and-thirty paces away. What madness made him allow you to compete in his place?"

She tilted her head, and the room's firelight glowed

on her expression of triumph. Trying to read her clever mind, his gaze traced the elegant line of her smooth cheekbone to her lips. She pursed them thoughtfully, and murmured, "I was trying to locate the messenger from the night of the fire before you came along and brought me here. Does it surprise you Padrig's trust in me is greater than yours?"

Her answer splashed over him like a tub of ice water. "He's younger and more foolish." He stepped away, leaving her still half-swallowed in the unfastened chain mail. God, but she still stirred him, even dressed in pounds of armor. The shapeless form forced his eye to her beautiful face and made him long for the rest of her body hidden beneath. "Aye, you've become an excellent rider, skilled with a lance. But underneath all Padrig's trappings, you're still female."

"I practice at the quintain more days than not, and I'm a good horsewoman. There was no combat in the event, so I was never in any danger. You must admit I convinced you." Her face brightened, and she stood straighter. "I'm sure you would say it was Serena's influence again. Just like three years ago, the last night in our keep, before you left. You and I were to meet. When you arrived, I wasn't alone . . ."

His chest tightened. He'd kept the memory at bay for too long to let her remind him. He barked, "Now you want to tease me! Aye, you deceived me today, and you betrayed me then. What point are you trying to make?" Mayhap she enjoyed pushing the knife deeper into his heart.

"Caerwyn, you've never believed me, but I'll say it again. *I've never been with another man.* Look." She turned her back to him, gathering her braids in one hand and twisting them up to hold on top of her head. "Do I look like a woman from behind now?"

"You know you do not."

"I practice in mail often. My father disapproves, of course. Serena's worn it only once. In armor, she would look like a man from behind, don't you think?" She moved closer to the bed, took hold of the thick banister. When she glanced over her shoulder at him, the sight of her posture, so sensual, so seductive, yet so unpracticed, his manhood strained against his chausses. Sweat glistened on his brow.

"Aye. I suppose . . ."

"And if I leaned over the bed, and you saw me then, in my gown, of course, lying underneath her?" She bent over the bed, bracing her knee on the mattress while she reached out as if to touch an imaginary lover.

Caerwyn remembered. Nia had sent a page to ask him to come to her chamber. He had planned to ask to marry her, having already received her father's permission. How his cheeks had ached from smiling so much that day! But when he opened her door, he found Nia with another young man in her arms . . . leaning over her *bed.* The whole sickening scene replayed in his mind, how he'd left the chamber and heard Nia's voice calling after him as he'd thundered down the stairs and slammed out the door of the keep, never to return. Until now.

Now, standing in front of him in the armor, Nia moved

with the fluid grace of a lover, or a young knight, bending to caress the soft form of a girl . . . Caerwyn's girl. Just like before, he felt the room around him turn on its axis in that moment, a blur before his eyes. His first clear thought that night after the black veil of rage had lifted, and his eyes had finally dried, was how slight in size his rival had been. Nia's same height. More capon than boy.

Over the years, his pride had convinced him Nia's lover had been less of a man than he—after all, he was soon to become a Crusader—when in fact, mayhap his memory had been accurate. Verily, the fellow had been quite petite after all . . .

His feet led him a step closer. "'Twas Serena in your chamber! Why?"

Her eyes held a glimmer of tears. She blinked, turning her face from him. "Serena said if you were truly mine, you wouldn't leave on Crusade. And she said the only way to make you mine was to get you to fear you would lose me to another."

Caerwyn closed the space between them and pulled Nia around to face him. "The two of you conspired together?" Was he a puppet on a string, forever manipulated by this girl . . . *nay*, this woman before him? He'd fought powerful, trained enemies and stood his ground against their blades and arrows. Yet he found himself condemned to defeat when it came to Nia. Incredulous, he held her shoulder and turned her chin on his fingers to search her eyes. Confronted by the honesty he found, he asked, "Why would you believe I wasn't yours? I know I never treated you falsely."

"Serena told me you acted like you liked her, too. Everyone I've ever known prefers her, so I didn't think you would be any different. She said if you feared I had another, you would ask to marry me and . . . stay."

CAERWYN RELEASED HER without warning.

Nia crumbled inside. She'd never seen him so angry. He left her swaying unsteadily by the bed as he paced the room. His movements were jerky, his breathing heavy— like an angry bull in a pen.

"You two must've thought I was ridiculous," he chortled, dragging a hand through his hair as he paused mid-stride before her. "I didn't even stay to challenge your supposed lover, running off to seek solace in the war, like some yelping pup who'd gotten his tail stepped on."

She'd attempted to follow him on Crusade, and would have, had Serena not wagged her tongue to her father, who put an end to her plan. In the weeks that followed Caerwyn's departure, she'd lain awake in her bedchamber, imaging the horrors he faced in battle, knowing he surely hated her. She'd hated herself. "Caerwyn, my regret runs deeper than you'll ever know." Her eyes swam with unshed tears. At any moment, she would melt into a sobbing mess. He couldn't see her like that. He would feel sorry for her, pity her. She shielded her face from him, acting distracted as she shrugged off the outer layer of Padrig's clothes. Bracing one hand on the bed, she kicked off the chausses and was left in a thin linen undergarment. Cool air connected with her skin, making her shiver. When she'd begun undressing, she hadn't considered how bare her last clothing layer was, only that she needed to be free of the armor's restricting weight. Now cold, sniffling, exposed, and miserable, she wished she'd stayed dressed.

She sank on the bed.

Holding her head down, she didn't notice that Caerwyn had drawn near until she felt his heat. She stared at his boots, waiting for him to berate her. Looking up at him from beneath her wet lashes, she caught the movement of his hands unfastening the buckle on his sword belt. Not even in her worst nightmare could she picture Caerwyn hurting her—unlike Maddoc. Curious, she lifted her gaze.

"You have been the death of me. I trow I'm not a fit prize for your games anymore." He dropped the belt and grabbed the edge of his tunic and mail.

Nia swallowed, and her tongue felt thick. She wondered at his intentions.

He revealed the side of his torso for her scrutiny. At first glance, she spied the warm, smooth, tan skin of a life lived in the desert sun. Then as he twisted in the firelight, the wide white stripe of an old scar came into view just above the bone of his hip. She heard the breath whoosh from her lips, and her fingers shot out to trace the puckered edge.

Her gaze flicked up to catch him watching her with extreme interest. "The wound came from a Saracen when I charged him. I was clearly outmatched, but I didn't care if I died. I begged my opponent to put an end to my suffering, and he would have if Padrig hadn't cut him down from behind."

Nia cupped his warm skin beneath her hand, imagining Caerwyn on the battlefield with life ebbing from the spot.

"There are more. Have I shocked you beyond recovery?"

Unable to speak for fear of her voice's breaking, she shook her head.

"Help me with this."

Nia stood and aided him, removing his armor and raiments until he stood before her in his breeches alone. His chest was riddled with scars of different lengths and widths, some faded and pale, some more recent. He took her hand and slid it to a four-inch-long gash that began just above his nipple and ended midway across his ribs. He flattened her now-trembling hand over the mark, and she braced her other hand on his shoulder to keep steady.

"It's from another enemy I charged. It was dark, and I was too drunk to hold my own weapon."

She'd never seen him drink when they were young. For him to abandon his common sense, he must've been a different person entirely.

"How can you still be alive?" Pain clogged her throat. A tear dripped on Nia's cheek, but she left it, unwilling to remove her hands from Caerwyn. She wanted to hold him close, to swallow him up and be his shield, to keep him safe for the all the times he'd been in danger.

"Padrig again." His eyes gave a hint of a smile. "He sliced the warrior's hand off. My brother always has the advantage when his opponent's vision is similarly obscured. He's honed his other senses. He can hear the sound of an arrow cutting through the air and somehow senses its direction well before others can even see it. Still, after that night, I quit seeking death for fear Padrig would be the one to suffer, not I."

Nia put her hand against his cheek and traced the smooth plane of his skin under her thumb. "Your suffering was worse than I'd imagined. You must hate me beyond measure for what I did . . . to do that to yourself."

She licked her dry lips and tasted the salt of her tears. Her vision blurred as she waited for him to confirm her darkest fear: he hated her still.

His hands came up to frame her face. "Aye." He pressed his lips to her damp cheek. "I hate you. I even welcomed death when I could not have you." He kissed the trail of her tears, following it to her mouth. He whispered above her lips, "You see how I hate you."

Nia wrapped her arms around his neck, and his eyes widened with surprise. He murmured low and pressed his mouth to hers. His tongue swept beyond her parted lips, and Nia felt the weight of his arm against the small of her back, bringing her forward against him. She pressed her length along his, longing to touch the magnificent body he readily despised. Although he claimed to hate her, his response told her otherwise. His thick sex rubbed the apex of her thighs through the paltry membrane of their clothing. Heat and urgency at her core made Nia push against him, adjusting her position to allow him more contact.

Caerwyn groaned and lifted his mouth.

His face hovered over hers, their breath mingling. He took her hands from his neck and flattened them against his chest. "My body, my wounds—are you not revolted by the sight of me and"—he dropped his gaze, swallowing—"my cowardice?"

Entrapped, Nia couldn't move to show her true feelings, so she willed everything she had into her words. "Never. Your scars remind me how precious you are, how I nearly lost you. Caerwyn, you could never be a coward. You're the bravest man I know."

His dark eyes held her gaze steadily, then he closed them. He pressed his mouth against hers in a kiss so deep and encompassing, she felt her very essence lifting skyward.

Locked in his passionate kiss, in fact, she didn't realize he'd actually picked her up until she felt the bed beneath her backside. Caerwyn stretched out beside her as he hungrily kissed her mouth, and Nia tunneled her fingers in his hair, keeping him close. She sensed the shimmy of the bed as he struggled to keep his weight off her while loosening the final ribbons of her clothing. Losing herself in these new sensations, she became aware of her nakedness when she felt the gentle brush of his coarse fingers across her skin and heard the concentration in his breathing as he tenderly caressed her nipple.

"Nia," he breathed, and pressed his mouth against her neck. "Fairest, most beloved."

Her body melted beneath his caresses and kisses, and her bare feet dug into the sheets. He pressed tiny kisses against her neck and along her hairline, then she felt the delightful relief of her scalp beneath his soft touch as he took down her braids.

Once his fingertips unbound the last plait, he returned to kiss her again, lowering his body against hers. Nia spread her legs, feeling him move between her thighs. His hand parted the tie of her pants and opened the fabric to expose her feminine core. He bent over her breast and took one of her nipples into the wet heat of his mouth. Lovingly, he tasted her breast, swirling his tongue around her tightening bud. His hand swept across her belly and cupped the gentle swell between her thighs. Nia lurched, surprised, when his fingers moved between her lips to find the sensitive petals of her sex. Her face flushed and heat spread from her womb to the rest of her body. His mouth found her other nipple and repeated the ritual, swirling, sucking, nibbling, until Nia squirmed with delight and need. Her fingers gripped his sides and swept inside the barrier of his breeches, smoothing over the hard muscle of his buttocks and forward, seeking his aroused flesh.

"Caerwyn, please," she murmured, not even sure what she wanted to convey.

He lifted his head, tickling her with his soft shaggy hair in the motion. He regarded her through serious dark eyes, his chest moving as if slightly winded. "You have ne'er had another lover. If we continue, you ne'er will, for I won't share you with another."

"I understand." *I love you. Why would I want another?*

"It will hurt at first." His brow creased, watching her.

"Not as much as I've hurt without you." Nia pushed up on her elbows and put her hand on the back of his neck, guiding him to return to her.

Caerwyn muttered an oath, and his lips brushed over her exposed skin. With every sweep of his mouth, she lost a piece of herself, thoughts scattering. Her flesh sizzled with heat and longing, like sandy desert lands starved for rain. His hand passed down her bare thigh, removing her clothing before traveling back up her long leg. Freed from all restriction, Nia bent her knees under the exploring pass of his palm, allowing him greater access to the place where she needed him the most.

He pressed his lips against her neck, kissing and tasting, murmuring words of his love, and his sex nudged against her. Feeling the weight of his organ, need intensified within Nia until she was frantic to join him at last. She lifted beneath his thrust, impaling herself on his sex. Their gasps rang out together—her pain and his surprise.

Caerwyn went still. His arms encircled her, cradling her as he pressed soothing kisses against her cheek, his breath ragged in her ear. The pain, which had originally been a sharp pang, ebbed away as her flesh relaxed around him, accommodating his size. His heart thudded against her breasts, fast and strong, a driving rhythm that her body responded to instinctually. She fanned her hands over his back, exploring his wonderful body, and the action elicited his groan of need.

"Rest, Nia. I can wait until you're ready."

Caerwyn withdrew, pulling away, but she wrapped a quick leg around his hip, ensnaring him.

"Nay." She brought him back. "No more waiting."

He exhaled, his eyes dark slits as he moved deep inside her, slowly, tentatively. But Nia could not be contained. She lifted against him, taking his thrust. He growled and cupped her buttocks, lifting her as he drove into her.

Again and again, her lover pounded deep inside, and dark desires, primal desires, took control of her body, possessing her. Kissing, grinding, tasting, they gave in to their urges, which had been forbidden and buried far too long. With the rocking of their bodies, pressure crescendoed in Nia until her mind and bones melted. She heard herself stutter his name, and she exploded.

Caerwyn followed soon after, surging, until spent and shaking, he collapsed beside her. He smiled and drew her against his chest. Nia smiled, too. Both their eyes were damp, lashes spiky with tears.

"Am I dreaming?" she murmured. His face rested a breath away from hers.

His fingertips brushed her face and lips as if in disbelief, too, and he grinned. "I trow this is real. We cannot have the same dream, surely."

She smoothed her index finger along the swath of jagged white skin beneath his heart and swallowed, suddenly fearful. "Was it . . . worth waiting for . . . for you?"

He kissed her forehead and looked into her eyes until she floated in the warmth of his brown gaze. "Listen to me, Nia." His hand cupped her cheek. "Nothing compares to this. To you. It was . . . worth . . . the . . . wait. Even better."

She grinned, meeting his lips with hers in a series of kisses, punctuating his words.

"Well," she rolled over him to sit atop his narrow hips, "shall we try this from a different angle? Or is there only the one way?"

He brought his fist to his mouth, playfully gnawing his knuckles. He groaned. "My lady, I am yours any way you wish to have me."

She smiled and leaned to kiss him, feeling him stiffen beneath her once more.

They played for hours, loving each other until they lay breathless and spent on the bed, a tangle of bodies and linens.

Caerwyn caressed her arm, draped across his chest as her head rested on his shoulder. "Nia, you know I would ne'er ask you to stop running the quintains because you enjoy it. But next time, please tell me 'tis you under the armor. I'm not always proud, but I'm still a man."

"I will." She gave his hand a reassuring pat, admiring the faint color on his cheekbones. "But that was the point of my attire. Aside from helping Padrig, I wanted to see if I could find and recognize the boy who summoned me to the stables before the fire."

His touch halted on her arm. "Aye. I would like to find him, too. I've a feeling 'tis de Guildo. He's sought to be part of your family since before I left."

She tried to be surprised but wasn't. After Maddoc's advances in the barn, she'd imagined he might've put her in danger's path just so he could save her and reap her father's rewards.

Caerwyn ran his thumb along his brow, frowning.

She sat up, leaning over him. "You have an idea. What is it?"

He shook his head. "I won't endanger you."

"I will be endangered every moment the fiend walks amongst us, and you know it." She moved over him and gazed into his eyes. "Tell me your plan, Caerwyn."

NIA AND PADRIG padded through the woods, following the road home from the market. The bramble grew thick, obscuring her faithful guardian hidden just a short distance out of sight. She felt Caerwyn's presence, though, and smiled to herself at the thought of his watch on her. She'd announced during last night's feast that she was going to market the next day to see the metalsmith, and Padrig had volunteered to escort her. If anyone wanted to attempt another assault, there would be no better opportunity. The trip to market had been uneventful, and the return home equally so. Once again, they reached the narrow stream where they'd been certain the fiend would've ambushed them. But he hadn't.

Although the attacker had failed to show, she was satisfied with the prize she'd commissioned from Henri, the blacksmith—a silver gauntlet. On Twelfth Night, she would award the piece of armor to the winner of the tourney. Henri had seemed surprised to see her and eager to accept the commission. The lucky winning knight could wear the cuff on his arm for all to see, along with the right to brag and a seat at the table beside her father.

Presently, the water of the stream made a black slash through the woods but was no obstacle for Nia on the back of sure-footed Merlin. Padrig usually forded first to give her a hand, but riding her dear Merlin again—the first time since the fire—emboldened her. And Merlin, too. She knew the gelding anticipated the clearing just beyond the copse, where she often allowed the horse to run at will.

Once across the water, Merlin snorted, sides trembling with excitement. She cooed, "Go ahead, then."

Water crashed behind her, far louder than the sound of a lone knight. She glanced over her shoulder to tease Padrig, but found him facedown in the stream.

"Oh!" Nia unsheathed her sword and turned Merlin about.

A hooded stranger carrying a bow rushed from the woods for Padrig, and Nia saw the arrow in her escort's shoulder. She slid from her horse to thwart the attacker, but his rough hand caught her sword arm first and sent her whirling around.

"Henri?" she gasped. Panting and grimacing, the metalsmith twisted her arm, attempting to force her to drop her weapon. "What are you doing? Let go!"

She glanced around, looking for Caerwyn, who should be close enough to aid her. She heard him shout nearby but was unable to locate him for the dense forest. Henri wrestled her forearm. She jabbed his thigh with her free elbow, and he cursed. His eyes widened with disbelief, but his hold tightened. Pain shot up her limb, and she feared it would snap in two. Her fingers opened automatically, letting the sword fall free to the ground. From the corner of her eye, she saw Padrig rise slowly from the water.

Caerwyn's horse crashed through the bramble. "Release her!"

Henri spun her around, using Nia as a shield. His fingers dug into her throat, lifting her in a way that would've reminded her of a Christmas duck if her heart weren't bashing against her ribs.

"You?" Caerwyn yelled as he drew near. He extended his sword menacingly toward Henri in a steady hand covered in fresh scratches. "What are you doing? The lady has done naught to you!"

The metalsmith spoke, his whiskers scouring Nia's cheek with each syllable. "Not her. 'Tis the baron's fault. I-I meant her no harm."

"Good Lord, release her then!" Caerwyn's gaze held hers, and a vein stood out against his powerful neck. "Your lookout, the one you left upstream, is trussed and bound to a tree."

"And Rhys, my young apprentice? What did you do to him?"

"Let Nia go, and I'll tell you."

Nia felt her captor's grip loosen ever so slightly. She surveyed Caerwyn again and noted the bloody smear on his clothing.

Padrig hacked, bending over as he spat out leaves from the stream.

"I'm sorry. So sorry." Henri shuddered behind her and dropped his head to her shoulder with a whimper. Silent sobs racked him as he released his hold on her throat.

"The apprentice is fine. I sent the boy home." Caerwyn released a long breath.

Nia turned around and pushed Henri's chin up. He regarded her through wet eyes.

"What did my father do to you?" she cried. "You've been Walwyn's armorer for years!"

Caerwyn moved to Nia's side and placed his hand on the small of her back. "My love, are you all right?"

She spun into Caerwyn's ready arms and held him tight, pressing her face against his neck. His warmth and strength steadied her trembling body.

Whatever the cause, they were safe.

Chapter Six

"YET ANOTHER OF your conquests, Serena." Guy de Brionne rubbed a hand over his spiky gray hair and slumped against the arm of his great chair. "Now you've cost me the best armorer in the Marchlands."

The windows of the solar had been adorned with tallow candles and wreaths of holly, and afternoon sunlight filtered through the glass, casting a glittering geometrical prism across the stone floor of the sitting area. Serena sat quieter than usual, her pale face pressed against the cushioned back of her chair, lost in thought. Nia and Caerwyn sat side by side, facing her father. Caerwyn traced his fingers across the back of Nia's hand.

The baron had been all smiles and joyful pleasantries about her union with Caerwyn until he'd learned about the metalsmith's plot. Now his salt-and-pepper brows crushed together over his stormy eyes.

"Father," Nia began, drawing his attention away from

her aloof sister. "I know Henri endangered me, and I know the damage he and his friends caused, but for you to turn him over to the sheriff would be to send him to his death."

The baron's eyebrows lifted. "Verily, he deserves a severe punishment. It doesn't matter if he thought himself in love with Serena. You wouldn't ask me to offer him reprieve if he had killed Padrig or Merlin or Caerwyn, would you?"

"Of course not."

According to Henri, he'd fallen in love with Serena, hence the many circlets he'd fashioned for her hair. Knowing the baron would never allow a mere craftsman to marry his daughter—and fearing Maddoc or another knight would steal his place in her bed—Henri lashed out at those he blamed. He'd ambushed them in the woods twice and set the fire in the stables, hoping to scare the baron by luring Nia and Maddoc into the dangerous traps he'd set. In his twisted mind, he needed them all to suffer as he'd suffered for not being able to be with Serena.

"I still cannot believe he thought Maddoc was your first pick for Serena's husband." She winced, sickened by another memory of Maddoc's unwanted advances. Her thumb rubbed the vacant spot on her ring finger.

"But he was. He still is." The baron lifted his glass in the air, gesturing for the cupbearer.

"Father!" Nia scolded, and Serena's voice chimed in, as well.

"What? He has made his interest in this family known

for years. He's been very patient, loyal, and now he's here, pledging to protect—"

"He is a liar and a thief." Nia leaned forward.

Caerwyn took her hand in his and warmth traveled up her arm. "Now you know my interests, my lord."

The baron inclined his head, and his features softened. "Aye, you and Nia have my blessing. 'Tis not an easy thing, guarding these two girls, but I trow you're up to the task, Sir Caerwyn. And if you love her, as I believe you do, you'll treat her fairly."

Serena unfolded herself and looked on their father with keen interest. "If love is important to you, then reconsider Henri's fate, again. I beseech you. He . . . I might . . . well, some blame should rest on my shoulders."

The air of the room went so quiet, even the fire on the Yule log seemed to cease its crackling.

The baron's mouth fell open.

Serena scowled, wringing her hands in her lap. "I complained to Henri bitterly about Sir Maddoc and the others. I flirted; I flaunted them under his nose. The whole time, I knew how Henri felt. I was horrid!"

Her father recovered, stammering, "Serena, do you *care* for this man? The *metalsmith*?"

She blinked, eyes brightening. Her head bobbed. "I always have. Why do you think I fought the idea of marrying for so long?"

Nia covered her mouth. Her sister's tiny voice made the hair on her arms rise. *Of course!* Then her gut turned— she should've known her own, poor sister's heart.

"Oh, dear me," the baron mumbled, turning his head, and downed the rest of his wine.

ON THE EVE of Twelfth Night, Nia waited in the orchard. The gray, wintering trees reminded her of stark weathered bone, reaching up from the frozen ground in a tidy graveyard row. But on any day, hot or cold, damp or dry, there was nowhere on earth she'd rather be. The orchard was where Caerwyn and she had first kissed, the place where he'd given her his heart forever, and now their secret meeting place. This time, when a page had approached her requesting that she meet Caerwyn in the orchard after the tourney, she knew she could be assured it was for real.

If only she didn't freeze to death waiting for him!

Pacing, she rubbed her arms and smiled to herself. In another fortnight, they would need no more interludes, no more worrying who watched because they would be betrothed.

She stopped and tilted her head to the evening sky, smiling again. A falling star replaced the falling blossoms of that blissful spring day years ago. Now, instead of leaves, the only bit of greenery left on the apple trees was a small sprig of mistletoe, which had somehow managed to escape the hands of the castle's servants, who'd covered Walwyn in the festive evergreen.

"Ah, I see the lady has found my secret." Caerwyn walked up behind her and wrapped his arms around her waist.

She rested against him, snuggling into the warm space beneath his chin. "You've very naughty, milord. You intended to catch me beneath the mistletoe, didn't you?" She rested her hands on his forearms and felt the icy metal cuff of the gauntlet he'd earned for winning the joust against Maddoc. "I still can't believe Henri was able to finish this in time."

He kissed her temple. "And he hopes to have the suit of armor I won ready by spring. But he had better incentive than money to keep his forge hot. Your father was more than generous with the man."

"Aye." Nia turned around and wrapped her arms around his neck. At least Padrig was content with his own mail and gambeson, preferring it, however battered it might be. She suspected Padrig had allowed Maddoc to beat him at swords so he wouldn't have to face Caerwyn in the joust. Neither brother wanted to admit defeat to the other. For certes, she and Serena wouldn't, either. She loved her sister no matter her faults. "Would you and Padrig encourage Father to let Serena marry Henri?"

"Nia." He rested his head against hers and held her hand between them. "Please give the matter some time. I nearly lost you, thanks to his schemes. 'Twill be a long while before this grudge can be forgotten."

"Of course. You're right." She nodded. His mention of grudges made her glance at her bare hand. Caerwyn had forgiven her for losing his mother's precious ring, and she was grateful. However, she hadn't forgiven herself.

"Enough of this." Caerwyn sighed and dropped her hand.

Nia glanced at him askance as he dug inside his tunic. A moment later he withdrew his hand and held the beautiful gold ring in his fingers.

She gasped. "Where did you find it?"

He made a lopsided grin and pushed the band onto her shaky finger. "I've had it since the night de Guildo took it from you."

"You . . . wait. You knew I was looking for it!" She snatched her hand to her chest and cradled it protectively. She tried to scowl at him beneath her lashes, but relief poured through her, making anger impossible.

He rubbed her shoulders. "At first I wasn't sure you took the ring as seriously as I did, but when I saw you searching the barn floor, I knew for certes. You seemed genuinely distraught. And then I wanted to wait until after this business with Henri and Serena." He tilted his head, studying her face with love in his eyes. "Do you think I deserve a woman as amazing as you? Am I worthy enough to be your husband?"

Tears pricked Nia's eyes. "Of course you are. Always, Caerwyn."

He kissed her urgently, drawing her against him. Their tongues twined, and her heart raced.

When he lifted his mouth from hers after a length, he grinned and gave her playful squeeze. "Now that Twelfth Night is finally here, how long before your father tells those other fools to leave?"

Nia laughed. "Soon. I think he's found his winner."

About Sandra Jones

SANDRA JONES is the author of historical romances. She's worked as a bookseller and a librarian, where she indulged in her love of old books.

When not researching or writing, she enjoys being with family, reading, and watching British TV. A self-proclaimed history geek, she currently lives in a 1905 Greek Revival home in the Mississippi Delta. Sandra loves to hear from her readers. Please visit her Web site at www.sandrajonesromance.com.

Tempting
Mr. Weatherstone

VIVIENNE LORRET

Chapter One

*London
1822*

PENELOPE RUTLEDGE WAVED to her sister as the carriage disappeared from view. After a month of parties, shopping, and utter chaos, their father's London town house was now quiet. Perhaps even too quiet.

"I imagine Eugenia will be glad to return to her own home," her father murmured from the winged chair facing the desk, his head bent over this morning's paper.

Even though he couldn't see her, she nodded. "The children will be glad to have more room to scamper about, I'm sure."

She moved away from the window and closer to the hearth, her fingers toying with the fringes of her shawl. While the fire was well tended, it still did not warm her. For the past week—or perhaps a bit longer—she couldn't seem to escape this ever-present chill. Today, it was worse than before.

"I daresay, Marcus will be delighted by their return,"

her father said with a smile in his voice. "Not to mention the happy news."

Penelope stared into the fire. Yes. The news. Eugenia—her younger sister by two years—was expecting her third child.

Of course, Eugenia had married Marcus at the end of her first season, when she was not yet nineteen. Penelope, on the other hand, had had four seasons and two marriage proposals by the time she was two-and-twenty, but no husband.

It was her own fault, she knew. She'd found too many flaws in her suitors. If they weren't handsome enough, then they were too handsome. If they weren't simpletons then they bored her with their intellect. Too awkward, too graceful, too drab, too smartly dressed, too verbose, too quiet. The list was endless. All she'd wanted was someone who wasn't too . . . anything.

Her shoulders sagged on a deep sigh. Out of the corner of her eye, she peeked over at her father. He merely turned the page, apparently unconcerned.

Hmph. It wasn't the least bit contrived, and still her father did not inquire about the cause of such a *meaningful* sigh.

"Perhaps I should have accepted my sister's invitation after all," she grumbled. What good was having a father if he didn't become alarmed by such a sigh?

"What was that, dear?" he murmured, still not bothering to look up.

"I was just thinking how lonely you would be if both your daughters were married."

At last, he looked up, wiry eyebrows lifted in question. Wry amusement curved his mouth. "Have your sights set on a fellow, do you?"

Crossing her arms, she turned to face her father, not bothering to hide her irritation. "I am five-and-twenty, Father. It has been three years since my last season. By all accounts, I am well into spinsterhood."

Unconcerned, he went back to his paper. "I've told you before that you could have as many seasons as you like. Fetch yourself a husband if you are so inclined."

Fetch herself a husband? He made it sound as if he didn't care in the least. Even when she had announced that she planned never to marry, he'd merely accepted her decision, stating his belief in the fact that she must know her own mind better than anyone else.

Which she did, of course. There was no arguing that. However, it still irked her that he didn't care one way or the other. "There are fathers aplenty who force their daughters into marriage."

He murmured his agreement without looking up.

"Some even make their dowries shamefully tempting."

"Your dowry is handsome enough to tempt the right sort of man."

Her fingers plucked at the fringes of her shawl, pulling on the threads to make them even before twisting them into knots. "Honestly, I don't care about any of that. Truly. I don't even want to marry. There isn't anyone of interest to me. Not like the way it was with Eugenia and Marcus, anyway."

She still remembered the night of her sister's debut.

Marcus had been the first to sign her dance card. "You could tell right away they were meant for each other. They had a spark from the very beginning," she mumbled more to herself than to her father. "Some people do, I suppose, while others . . . don't." A fact that had taken her years to discover.

She sighed again, troubled by the turn of her thoughts. She didn't want to marry, so what was she going on about?

Perhaps it was the aftereffects of her sister's visit. Yes. That must be it. She'd been so busy lately that she hadn't had a spare moment to breathe. All she needed was a bit of fresh air and to settle herself, once again, into the life she had chosen.

"I'm going for a walk," she announced, knowing it didn't matter one way or the other.

As if to prove it, her father merely murmured.

Outside, the bracing early-December wind caused her to rethink her walk. The streets were damp and muddy from rain, and the sky was a gloomy gray that matched her mood. The persistent chill that had plagued her for days now turned icy. She felt cold to the marrow of her bones.

A blanket over her lap and a steaming pot of tea on a side table beckoned her. Yet the vision was far too depressing. If she went back inside at this moment, she could easily imagine herself remaining there. Not simply for today, but for a lifetime.

A horrible specter of herself, sitting in a chair by the fire with her needlework in her lap, loomed before her. She would grow old there. Perhaps not in that chair, but in *a* chair by *some* fire, her hands slowly wrinkling and curling from age.

That could easily become her life from this point forward if she returned to 7 Danbury Lane.

In fact, the thought of returning to the quiet house and the murmured acknowledgments of her father terrified her.

The wind picked up, blowing hard against her back. At this time of year, few of their circle remained in town, so this street was practically deserted. Only one other family remained on this side of the lane. Her gaze settled on a door nearly as familiar as her own. Number 3.

The notion of disturbing Ethan Weatherstone's morning solitude banished the horrible specter, at least for the moment. In fact, the idea sparked a bit of warmth in her. Besides, she had one of her latest needlework creations in her pocket, and his mother would be glad to have it.

Mind made up, she walked briskly down the street, up the stairs, and just before she could rap on the door, it swung open.

Hinkley, with his usual severe, unmovable expression, stood aside for her to enter. "He's in the library, Miss Rutledge."

"Thank you, Hinkley. Your soothsaying abilities never cease to astound me," she said with a smile as she handed over her cloak. One of these days, she'd manage to surprise him.

Unruffled, he bowed. "Happy to be of service, miss."

As Hinkley predicted, Ethan was in the library. His morning routine never faltered. There he sat, quill in hand, ledger of accounts open while writing figures in a column. The top of his desk was neat and orderly, nothing out of place. His chair never sat at an angle, but four legs on the floor, in precisely the same direction as the legs of his desk. As usual, his cravat was tied into a perfect knot. The line of his coat, equally perfect. His posture . . . perfect.

In anyone else, these particularities would make her feel entirely inadequate, what with her many flaws—freckles and fidgeting at the very top of the list—but with Ethan, she managed to overlook them. Perhaps it was because his hair was the color of walnut shells and had an unruly wave through it. She knew he hated it, and for that reason alone she found it oddly endearing. His eyes were that way, too. He'd referred to them as muddy. But she thought they looked more like the dregs of tea, sort of a clear, paler brown, with flecks of darker brown strewn about.

In profile, his nose was straight and true. Yet, from the front, there was a slight bend from when he'd fallen as a child. His teeth weren't perfect either, white but not straight. In fact, she would say he had a rather wolfish smile, his canine teeth slightly too long and too pointed.

"Has lurking in doorways become your new interest, Pen?" he asked, his deep voice edged with amusement, as if they were sharing a long-standing joke between them.

Even though the fire in the hearth did not appear overly grand, when she breezed in, she instantly felt warmer. "Perhaps I was waiting for a proper invitation."

"Waiting for an invitation? You?" He didn't look up from the ledger but shook his head and chuckled.

"Oh, all right," she said with a hint of drama, so he wouldn't take her seriously. "I was staring at you."

"Cataloging my flaws, no doubt."

"You know me so well." At least that part was true. After fifteen years—not to mention the fact that they were neighbors, both here and at their country estates— they knew each other well. Sometimes, she thought, *too* well.

Like now, for instance. She knew he was hungry. Most likely, it had been hours since he'd breakfasted. Like Penelope, he was an early riser, as they had often spoken of their mutual enjoyment of those quiet hours. However, the true reason she knew he was hungry was by the set of his mouth. He pursed his lips ever so slightly and swallowed, his Adam's apple moving up, then down above his cravat. Then the tip of his tongue gave a leisurely swipe over his bottom lip, before his teeth raked it dry.

She found herself mimicking the action and shifted uncomfortably. Glancing again at the small fire, she was amazed at the heat it put out. She stepped away from it and moved toward the door. "Hinkley?"

The butler appeared before she finished calling his name.

"Would you please see if the cook would prepare a pot of tea for Mr. Weatherstone? Oh, and if she has any scones, those would be nice, as well. No cream, but orange marmalade instead. Thank you."

"Very good, miss," he said. Was there a hint of a smile on Hinkley's face?

No, she told herself. It couldn't have been. The streets

of London would be overrun by toads before Hinkley's mouth would ever break into a smile.

"Did your sister steal away your cook this morning?" Ethan asked as he printed figures in a tidy script at the bottom of the page before he moved on to the next.

"No. I simply know you're hungry." She ignored his scoff of disbelief and fished the sachet out of her pocket. Pulling at the corners, she examined her needlework and found it lacking. Lacking *what* precisely, she didn't know. The chrysanthemums were blooming bright red and vivid green, just as they should be. The leaves were pointed and plentiful, just as they should be. And yet, *something* was lacking.

Nevertheless, she knew his mother would appreciate the gesture. "It's my guess that your mother is only now breakfasting in her rooms, and so it will be hours before she invites you to luncheon."

He shook his head as if negating her ability to know this for certain. "And from our many years of acquaintance, you've deduced that, like you, I am an early riser, and it's been hours since I've breakfasted. Not to mention, the clock says it's nearly noon."

"Yes, there's that," she allowed. "And the fact that you always lick your lips when you're hungry."

He moved his quill away from the ledger and looked up at her, a curious expression clouding his tea-colored irises. "And the marmalade?"

"You always eat marmalade on your scones." She shrugged and pulled again at the corners of the sachet.

"Well, you always slather yours with cream," he announced rather smugly.

"Are we competing now?" She wanted to laugh, but instead felt rather perturbed. How dare he know her so well and still be so . . . so . . . *obtuse* about everything else.

Turning back to his ledger, he smirked at her. "If we were, I assure you, I would win."

"Oh really? Then you already know precisely what I came here to tell you this morning." She smirked back at him and waited.

"Pen, I know better than to fall into one of your traps. If I tell you and get it right, you will hate me."

She waited for him to finish with another scenario, but when he didn't continue, she prompted him. "Or?"

"I should amend that," he said, turning the page of his ledger. "I meant to say, *when* I tell you and get it right, you will hate me."

She wanted to throw the sachet in his face. Or better yet, pour ink all over his precious ledger.

Instead, she felt her lips curl into a rueful smile, delighting in the fact that she would shock him to no end in the next moment as she confessed her idea. After all, there was no way he could have heard her conversation with Eugenia last night at her sister's farewell dinner. He'd been all the way across the room at the time.

Of course, she hadn't been serious. Not entirely. However, now she was overcome by a sudden urge to make it true. "I am going to hire a coach to take me as far away from here as possible. And, quite possibly, I may never return. I might find myself on the Continent, or on some sailing vessel to an island where native people teach me to make jewelry from seashells."

"I seem to recall a similar plot a few years ago," he added in a bored tone, never looking up at her.

He was positively unnerving! How dare he bring that up to her face. How long had that been . . . four—no, five years ago? It had been right around the time when Eugenia and Marcus had left for their honeymoon trip. Nevertheless, she hadn't even been serious then. Not truly. At the time, she simply wanted . . . oh, she couldn't even remember.

That was not the point.

"I fully intend to go through with it this time." She raised her voice to cement her conviction.

"Is it as bad as all that?"

"Yes, it is—Are you even listening?" This time she was serious.

Years ago, she'd resigned herself to a certain life, and she'd been content with her decision. For a time. Yet now, an uncomfortable restlessness settled over her, prickling her skin from beneath the surface, making her fidget all the more in an effort to shake it loose.

Being near Ethan made it worse, and that knowledge only served to irritate her. She needed some distance to discover if the source of her disquiet was what she feared. Distance to resign herself to this life once again.

Because if she didn't get away, then she feared she would never truly live.

ETHAN MOVED THE quill off to the side, hovering over the blotter so the ink wouldn't spot the ledger. He regarded Pen with a speculative lift of his brow. Had there ever been a time when she allowed him to ignore her?

As if unaware of this simple fact, she stared back at him, waiting for a response. He obliged her, repeating her ridiculous statement back to her, verbatim—all accept for the bit about the natives. "You are going to hire a coach to take you as far away from here as possible. Quite possibly, you will never return. You might find yourself on the Continent or on some sailing vessel—Though I might add that *finding yourself* in another place suggests a shock of some sort. In other words, a complete *lack* of planning."

She let out a huff and crossed her slender arms, the action causing her woolen shawl to bunch over her breasts. "Oh, why do I even bother?"

"Haven't the faintest."

This time, Penelope glared at him, her nose wrinkling in a way that drew his attention to her freckles. He liked her freckles. They were balanced and orderly—four on the left and four on the right.

It was ironic that eight such sensible freckles could be on someone so lacking in sensibility.

A quiet knock sounded at the door before Glenna brought in the tea tray. Apparently sensing Penelope's dark mood and wanting to stay clear of it, she set the tray on the corner of the desk and bobbed quickly before she left.

Ethan wished he could do the same. Instead, he was trapped by an angry blond goddess. Or was her hair brown? He could never quite tell. There were so many shades that it appeared each strand was unlike any other. Some of them pale like butter, others glistening like corn silk, some earthy brown, a chestnut here and there . . . It would take a lifetime to catalog every color.

He situated the tray the way he liked it, lining it up corner to corner with his desk. He noted the two cups and the addition of cream as well as marmalade, most likely from Hinkley's assumption that Penelope would join him.

But Ethan knew her better than that.

She was still fuming at him, her cornflower blue eyes darkening to midnight. Her lips were pursed in disapproval, making her mouth appear smaller and less generous than it normally was.

"Would you like some tea?" he asked, already knowing her answer.

She uncrossed her arms and pressed her hands to the edge of the desk, leaning forward in a way that caused the fringes of her shawl to brush against the tip of his quill. A strange jolt rushed through him.

"Believe me when I say, you do not want to know what I would like at this precise moment," she hissed. And before he could summon the will to blink, let alone breathe, she took a spoon from the tray, scooped up a dollop of cream, and proceeded to stir it into his dish of marmalade. "Enjoy. Your. Tea. Sir."

Chapter Two

EARLIER TODAY, PENELOPE had managed to surprise him after all.

Now, Ethan wasn't certain that she would keep their standing family dinner engagement.

He didn't like not knowing. He didn't like wondering if a message would arrive any moment, stating that Mr. Rutledge and his daughter were not coming. Of course, in all these years, no such message had arrived. The Rutledges had always come for dinner, unless they invited Ethan and his mother to dine with them.

Such was the way of things between their families. In this regard, they were unlike any other families in their circle. They had been closely knit from the very beginning, sharing a bond of profound loss in the same year.

Fifteen years ago, after his father had died at the family's seaside estate, his mother moved his elder brother, Edmund, and him to a country house in Surrey. The very day, they were introduced to their new neighbors, the Rutledges, and summarily invited to dinner.

That night at dinner, he'd learned that Pen's mother had died of a fever a few short weeks before his father's accident. With a whisper between them, they'd offered condolences. He still remembered the look in her eyes. On the surface, they were sure and strong, but in their blue depths, he saw the despair she carefully concealed for the sake of her family. She must have seen the same concealment in his gaze, too, because a look of commiseration had passed between them, forging their friendship.

From that point on, their dinners together had become a monthly event. Soon, once a month had become twice a month. Then, during that first summer before he and Edmund had returned to school, twice a month became once a week.

Years drew on, and the closeness remained. His mother and Rutledge formed a kindred friendship, often likening each other to siblings. The Rutledge girls had their seasons. Edmund grew into their father's viscountcy, while Ethan learned he was rather good at numbers and investments.

Three years ago, Ethan had purchased a town house just doors from the Rutledges'. It seemed the thing to do since their families were still close and would likely remain that way. Around that same time, Penelope had made her announcement of never marrying. Shortly thereafter, their dinners had become as frequent as four nights a week.

Now, after all these years of expecting the same dinner to go on in the same manner . . . this time, he wasn't entirely certain.

Apparently, uncertainty made him sloppy. He'd gone through three cravats—*three*—before the knot was right.

As he entered the study and saw that his mother was the only one in the room, he felt downright surly. "Good evening, Mother," he said with a slight bow, then went directly to the sideboard to pour a brandy. He murmured a perfunctory, "To your health," before tipping it back in one swallow.

She sipped her claret and smiled over the rim. "And what has you in such a fine temper?"

He poured another finger of brandy and didn't answer. By her amused expression and the way she always had her ear tuned to the servants' gossip, he knew she already *had* the answer.

"From what I gather, you won't be the only one in a foul temper at dinner this evening."

"Not by my choosing," he grumbled into his glass.

His mother chuckled, tsking as she shook her head. "I'm not certain Penelope feels that way, or else she would *not* have put cream all over your scones."

The servants had a tendency to embellish facts. "She merely mixed the cream into my marmalade. The scones were still edible." He finished his brandy, wishing his mood had improved after the second glass. Yet, as the clock struck the hour, he remained ever conscious of the fact that he and his mother were still the only two people in the study. "As for her temper, if she *chooses* to be angry because I laughed at her foolishness, then so be it."

His mother lowered her glass, and down with it went her amusement. "You didn't."

"I did," he said, trying not to sound like he was defending himself. "I would react the same way if she came to me tomorrow with her idea of hiring a coach to take her as far as she could go. *The very idea.* For her to do that would be the same thing as arranging for her own kidnapping. Angry or not, if nothing else, I've helped to save her from herself. "

"Oh dear." His mother sighed. "I wondered when this would happen."

This was not the reaction he expected. Where was her alarm? Where was her outrage?

"You wondered when Penelope would concoct a scheme to set about her own ruin, did you? Well, you might have warned me." He scoffed and thought again of another brandy.

"Ethan, you must remember that Penelope is a lot like you."

Like him? Hardly.

He was about to correct her when she held up her hand. Not wanting another woman to storm out of the room, he politely bit his tongue.

"She finds comfort in the things that remain the same day after day," she continued, staring at him pointedly. "Yet she has also watched her younger sister discover love and happiness in a new life of her own making. Eugenia was young when she leapt into the unknown. She didn't know what she risked leaving behind if her leap fell short. However, Penelope knows."

He was still waiting to see a shred of surprise, but instead all she did was make excuses for Pen's lunacy.

His mother drew in a deep breath. "Above all, she fears risk. She catalogs all that could possibly go wrong and whom she could hurt in the process. She also fears abandoning her father, not wanting him to feel as they all felt when her mother died so many years ago."

"Then there is no question," Ethan said, releasing the breath he didn't realize he'd been holding. "The way she felt when her mother died—that fear of loss—is still very much a part of her."

Their mutual loss was what had drawn him to Penelope when they were younger. Somehow, she helped fill the void. He was only thirteen when he discovered he could talk to a ten-year-old girl about the most painful experience of his life. That pain wasn't anything he would have ever wished on her, but it was an undeniable part of both their lives. And, as much as he hated to admit it, this was the first time he ever thought something good might come of it. Because if she feared leaving, then she would abandon her foolish idea.

He hated to admit it, but this time, he was afraid she meant to go through with it.

He looked down into his glass and willed the brandy to help restore his mood. Then he willed the knot in his stomach to unwind.

"You may be right," his mother said, all too cryptically.

He didn't like the inevitable "but" that was sure to follow. The knot tightened further.

"*However,* there comes a time in everyone's life when you have to make a choice." She held her hands aloft like balancing scales. "You can choose a life of the sameness you hold dear, or you can charge blindly into the unknown, never knowing what may come of it but all the while hoping to find true happiness."

True happiness. Penelope was happy, wasn't she? Essentially, she was free to do what she pleased. She went shopping and to parties. People thought highly of her, even cared for her. She didn't have to worry about her father's being alone in his house. Her sister was well provided for and, by all accounts, happy in her marriage.

In addition, if Penelope were ever struck by a female inclination to nurture a baby, she could always visit Eugenia. While Ethan had never been struck with the desire to have his cravat crumpled or puked on, he knew that if he ever was, Edmund had children aplenty to see to the task. Truly, what else could she want?

AT A QUARTER past the hour, James Rutledge and his daughter arrived for dinner. Rutledge graciously blamed their tardiness on his old bones, and Ethan kept his doubts to himself. Shortly thereafter, the usual dinner went off without a hitch. Well, almost.

Apparently, his mother had forgotten Penelope's aversion to asparagus. So before they entered the dining room, Ethan spoke secretly with Hinkley and asked if a

TEMPTING MR. WEATHERSTONE 383

hasty addition could be made. Perhaps a bowl of cook's special pickled beets? He knew they were her particular favorite.

After that, dinner proceeded smoothly. Penelope sat in her usual place to his left, fidgeting with the napkin across her lap. The soup course came and went with the usual compliments to their cook. And when the beets were brought to Pen, her lips curved in her usual smile of delight.

The knot in his stomach was a mere memory now.

"Superb wine, Rutledge," he commented with a salute of his glass to the opposite end of the table. "If I didn't know any better, I'd almost believe the lamb fed from this very vintage, with how well they complement each other. Wouldn't you agree, Pen?"

"I would," she offered graciously though lacking his enthusiasm. Her attention seemed engaged on her plate, where she cut her potato in imprecise cubes.

He felt his brow furrow as he watched her and wondered if she was brooding over their earlier argument. She was quieter than usual, or at least it seemed she was. Then again, perhaps he was looking too closely, the memory of his mother's words lingering like smoke after an explosion. But why should it bother him if Pen chose to stew over his reactions?

The more he thought about it, the more he wondered if all he could expect from her were these two words, or if he should draw her out further. Wondered if the return of his good humor was premature.

"While my fondness for Minerva's pickled beets is unparalleled," she continued, oblivious to his momentary angst as she laid down her knife with care, "I must admit that her parsley potatoes are running a close second in my esteem."

Ethan felt his brow unfurrow, and the corner of his mouth hitched upward. Pen was back to her usual self after all.

"I couldn't agree more," his mother added, dabbing her napkin to her lips, all evidence of potatoes gone from her plate. "They came from our garden in Surrey—Oh, how I look forward to returning. The country is so lovely this time of year."

Rutledge offered an easy grin that went well with his nature. "In three more days, you will have your wish. I daresay, there isn't parcel of land in all of England as lovely as the rolling hills and thicket of trees that our neighboring properties share."

Ethan was looking forward to the trip, too, though he kept the sentiment to himself. He enjoyed the quiet of the country, particularly in the mornings, when he and Pen inevitably found themselves walking together.

Dinner conversation went on as if nothing had happened between them earlier. And if she wasn't going to bring up their earlier argument, then neither was he.

When dinner ended, they retired to the music room for dessert and listened to his mother play the fortepiano.

It seemed everything was as it should be once again.

"You play so beautifully, Abigail," James Rutledge commented from one of two winged chairs that banked the hearth. He gave his glass of brandy an absent swirl in the firelight. "Each time you play one of those trilling little notes, I can imagine a pair of dancers floating along with the music."

"I was just thinking the same thing," Penelope said, her mouth curving in a dreamy smile as she closed her eyes briefly. "When you play, I feel transported."

His mother blushed at the compliments. "Transported? Why that is high praise, my dear. And where did you go on your journey?"

Ethan tried to remain relaxed, with one arm draped over the carved back of the settee, but the instant he discovered that Penelope was imagining herself somewhere else, all his earlier tension returned.

"A ballroom at first, with candles glowing all around. Then a lush meadow alive with butterflies. And at the very end, I was on a mountaintop, with the first flakes of snow falling," she said, her smile remaining. When she opened her eyes, it was as if they were strewn with stars, glittering with a light from within.

He shifted, suddenly uncomfortable in his skin. All this talk about being transported, and journeys, and hiring coaches was positively maddening. Why was she so determined to vex him?

"It has been ages since I've played for people dancing. It always brought me such pleasure," his mother said, her face glowing with a newly formed plot, no doubt. In fact, he was sure she was about to ask him to dance with Penelope in her next breath.

He was trying to come up with an excuse when she interrupted his thoughts—

"James, would you indulge me this once and take your daughter for a turn?"

Ethan jerked his gaze toward his mother, to see if this was also part of her plot. But for all the world, it looked as if she hadn't even considered him as a viable partner for Pen.

Rutledge gave an apologetic shake of his head. "I haven't danced in so long I'd surely end up crippling one, if not both, of us."

A small laugh escaped Penelope as she looked over at her father with affection. Ethan's mother resumed playing as if the matter were settled.

Still, no one regarded him.

He was trying not to be offended. Clearing his throat, he stood. "I'd be happy to indulge you, Mother."

His mother's face fell, and the notes ended with a sharp discord. "Oh, Ethan, please do not suppose I did this to corner you. We are all aware of how much you dislike dancing." From her expression, he could now tell that she truly hadn't been trying to manipulate him.

Now, he actually was offended. "I don't dislike dancing."

Speculative eyebrows rose from everyone in the room, but it was his mother who spoke. "And yet you managed to avoid dancing with Penelope during each of her seasons."

"That's simple," he stated with a shrug, fixing a mocking grin to his lips as he crossed to one of the winged chairs. "The reason for that was because I had no desire to repeat that first dance."

Penelope scoffed and ignored the hand he offered her. "Afraid that you'll tread all over my feet again, Pen?"

The stars left her eyes in a flash when she glared at him, leaving nothing behind but midnight blue. Taking his challenge, she stiffly slipped her hand into his and stood.

He grinned at the small victory. Tucking her arm in the crook of his, he strode across the room to the open area in front of the wide doors that led to the garden.

"I was only fifteen at the time, as you well know," Pen grumbled when they stood facing each other.

"A very awkward age, if I remember correctly." He grinned when she glared at him, the moonlight behind him casting a glow over her freckles. "What type of dance would you like, Mother?"

"A waltz of course," she replied, adding a delicate trill of the keys. "I want to see all those swirling butterflies and snowflakes for myself."

Pen straightened her spine and elongated her neck until she looked as proud as a queen before she deigned to rest her hand on his shoulder. "I don't recall you were any more graceful at eighteen."

He drew her a half step closer with the slightest pressure on her waist. "Dancing takes two, Pen." His hand curled over her waist, his fingertips settling into the small of her back.

Strange, he didn't remember her being so slender at fifteen. Or perhaps it was that he didn't notice the subtle flair of her hips before now. Through the soft silk of her blue gown, he could feel the heat radiating from her body.

It was in that exact moment when Ethan realized he'd made a grave error in believing everything was still the same.

This—*whatever this was*—was not the same. Not at all.

She slipped her hand into his, and he was suddenly very aware of the softness of her fingers and how delicate and cool they were against the warmth of his palm.

Anger receded from her gaze, replaced by what he would call uncertainty, as if the same vague sense of grave error had fallen upon her as well. "Aside from my dancing master, you were my first partner. I thought between the two of us, at least you would know what to do."

The music began.

It was too late to turn the clock back to a few minutes ago. Too late to undo the challenge he had issued her by asking her to dance. Far, far too late.

As if by rote, he stepped forward, moving with meticulous precision. He held her fluidly, yet firmly, just as the dance demanded. Her carriage was equally exact, her steps just as precise. She felt sublime in his arms, supple and graceful. They moved together as one, in perfect harmony. And yet . . .

All at once, he wasn't sure of himself, either as a competent dancer or as Ethan Holbrook Weatherstone. His entire world shifted in the space of single moment.

You were my first partner.

Those words were his undoing, shooting through him like a cataclysmic event, destroying everything inside of him that he knew to be true.

This was Pen. By all accounts, she was his best friend,

a fixed structure in his life. She was the one he teased just so she would her wrinkle her nose at him. She was the one whose laugh he could pinpoint in a crowd. She was the one person he knew better than he knew himself. He counted on the stability of *knowing*.

Yet now, he wasn't sure of anything.

The music picked up, and so did their steps. He swept her across the floor, swirling in circles. Every breath he took was filled with her familiar scent. Roses and orange blossoms, all fresh and clean like springtime . . . and *Pen*.

His body trembled with the effort to move with the dance, when all he wanted was to stop this madness. He wanted to pull her into his arms and crush her against him. He wanted to kiss those lips that were parted in wonder as she gazed up at him right now—

The music ended.

Ethan huffed from exertion and relief as they stopped. A sheen of perspiration cooled the back of his neck.

Penelope was out of breath as well, her cheeks flushed, her lips parted. "That was . . ."

"Yes. Quite." He wished he hadn't noticed her lips. Now, he was unable to look away, even as they curved into a smile.

"It seems you've worked up an appetite," she said with a small laugh. Her eyes were filled with light again, like stars on a blanket of midnight. When he questioned her with a lift of his brow, she supplied, "You're licking your lips again."

He took a step back, struck again with the certainty that nothing would ever be the same from this point on.

Chapter Three

THE NEXT MORNING at her needlework, Penelope was determined to branch out and try something new. Her stitched flower arrangements seemed stifled, suffocated even, to the point where she didn't think she ever wanted to stitch another flower again.

Now, in the draper's shop, she stared at a collection of colored thread, hoping a new color would inspire her. However, disappointment washed over as, yet again, her hope for something different failed. She'd already used every color here.

Last night after dinner, she'd hoped for something different, too. And for a while, it had happened. She'd danced with Ethan for the first time in ten years.

Their first time, she'd been horribly awkward and uncharacteristically shy. In fact, she was surprised her clumsiness hadn't maimed him. Back then, she couldn't understand it. She'd danced well enough with the dancing master. But with Ethan . . . it was as if she'd noticed her limbs for the first time, and she wasn't quite sure how they were all supposed to work together. Months of instruction flew from her head like dandelion fluff on a summer breeze. Unfortunately, her feet were not quite as light. Fluff might have left her brain, but fieldstones seemed to have filled her shoes.

Thankfully, no permanent damage had been done during the dance; instead, Ethan merely used her tromping all over his feet as a basis for teasing her.

He teased her until she was eighteen and began her first season. Then, at their family dinners, he'd teased her more, asking if she'd managed to stay on her feet or her partner's. He continued to tease her even when she'd turned two-and-twenty and had ended her fourth and final season with the declaration that she would never marry.

Now, three years later, he was still teasing her.

Normally, she didn't mind the teasing, but lately . . . he irked her to no end. And it wasn't just the teasing that irritated her. His propensity to want everything to remain the same was about to drive her mad.

Didn't he ever long for something new and exciting?

For a moment last night, she thought she'd recognized a kindred spirit in the way his eyes blazed with light. There was something positively molten in them. His dark pupils expanded, pushing the pale tea color to a rim along the outer edge, where it seemed to glow from within. She'd had a wondrous notion that something monumental was about to happen.

But she'd been wrong. In the very next moment, he'd taken a step back. The heat in his gaze diminished in a blink, making her realize it had only been a trick of the moonlight. Everything was the same as it had always been.

It was maddening.

Once, just once, she'd like to see him ruffled. Or at the very least, unsettled. Because that's how he made her feel. And after so many years, Penelope Alexia Rutledge was tired of it.

The truth was—a truth she never admitted aloud—he was the reason she hadn't accepted the proposals she'd received. Of course, she hadn't known it at the time. Not entirely.

She'd had her first inkling after she'd danced with Ethan's brother at her debut. She feared that her clumsy, gangly limbs would return. Yet, for some reason, dancing with Edmund was simple. It was nearly like dancing with her instructor. Or like dancing with a brother. Since their families were so closely knit, it had always been easy to imagine Edmund as an older brother.

For years, she'd tried to think of Ethan as a brother, too. She'd tried . . . and she'd failed.

Especially last night.

For a moment, she'd thought for sure he felt it too, but she was wrong. Now, she couldn't help but wonder if, all this time, Ethan thought of her merely as a sister.

She sighed, trying not to dwell on it. Instead, she focused on her reason for being here.

"I think I'll take the deep green, the peacock blue, and

the black," she told the clerk before she turned toward a selection of ribbons.

"I thought I'd find you here," said a familiar voice.

Standing beside the display was none other than the source of all her angst and frustration. As usual, Ethan looked perfectly groomed, his cravat perfectly pleated, his shoulders perfectly straight. His unruly curls were tamed into submission. His pale camel coat made his features appear darker and accentuated the color of his eyes. This morning, she noted how they were an interesting mix of tea and firelit copper.

However, she was sure it was simply another trick of the light coming through the shop's window. "Good morning, Ethan."

"Good morning, Pen." He grinned, flashing his pointed teeth as if laughing at his own private joke.

She didn't know what to make of that grin and didn't particularly like the way it made her aware of how her heart fluttered. "Surely, you haven't run out of handkerchiefs and are here for a fresh supply."

His grin remained. "Surely not. I have an entire drawer dedicated to the handkerchiefs you've given me over the years."

Ah yes. He *would* like that she'd given him the same gift each year. If she didn't already know his middle name was Holbrook, she'd almost believe it was Same. Ethan Same Weatherstone. "Then why are you here?"

He blinked at her terseness. "As I said, I knew you would be here."

She saw her own sameness as a mark of failure. When

was *she* going to branch out? When was she going to alter *her* routine?

Soon, she promised. Very soon. "Yes, of course."

As a matter of fact, she was one step closer. After hailing a hansom cab for this morning's excursion, she proceeded to ask the driver a few important questions. She soon discovered that her idea of a private coach would be far too costly. However, the helpful driver made a quick suggestion of traveling by mail coach and offered to take her to the nearest posting station. Now, she had a new plan and the list of stops along the mail coach's route tucked inside her reticule.

"I knew you would want plenty of supplies for your needlework before we left for Surrey the day after tomorrow," he supplied, as if this somehow made her predictability more acceptable. One of her regrets would be missing their combined families' Christmas and the winter months in the country. When it snowed, their neighboring estates shared an expanse of land that resembled what she imagined heaven would look like if it drifted down to the earth.

"I'm out running errands as well," he continued.

This was her cue to ask even though she already knew. His mother had spoken of the jewelry last night at dinner. "Oh?"

"Mother is giving Edmund's wife a portion of my grandmother's jewelry for Christmas. She's asked that I take it to the jewelers to have it cleaned and polished. I thought you would accompany me." He gave her a look of uncertainty, as if this was the first time he thought of her not agreeing. "Unless you have another engagement."

If only. "No, of course not. I'd be happy to accompany you."

Ethan approached the clerk at the counter, asking to settle her full account. He knew her father would have seen to it, yet each year he paid for her needlework supplies. There was no use trying to talk him out of it. She'd tried before without any success.

She would almost say he was generous to a fault, but she could find no fault in this particularity of his. Years ago, he'd explained that this was his gift to her. That, because she enjoyed her needlework so much, he could think of nothing better to give her.

Her heart had tripped at the time, or perhaps even still.

Foolish, foolish heart.

Most likely, he did it because it was easier than shopping for her. Their families always celebrated Christmas together, and they exchanged small trifles. By doing this, Ethan didn't have to worry about wrapping anything for her. Each year, he merely held her gaze for a moment and gave her a nod before he proceeded to unwrap his embroidered handkerchiefs.

For him, it was probably simpler this way.

Yet for her *and* her foolish heart, it made her think of him each time she held her needle and thread. With each stitch, she knew she was holding his gift in her hands. His thoughtfulness. His generosity. Perhaps even his regard for her, little though it might be.

They left the shop and strolled together down the

damp walk. The air was misty and cold, but not so much that it would force them to take his carriage. He told his driver to go on ahead and wait for them at the jeweler's a few doors down.

Outside the shop ahead of them, stood a mother with her two children, and another woman a step apart, who Penelope surmised was the nurse. The two little boys in their caps and coats beamed up at their mother with cherubic grins as they each twisted a peppermint stick in their mouths.

"A treat, indeed," Ethan murmured quietly, bending his head so that his comment was only heard by her. "No wonder they're behaving."

She looked up at him from under the brim of her hat, a smile tugging at her lips. "Is that all it took for you when you were young?"

"Sometimes, but not as often as mother would have liked, I'm sure." He chuckled and touched her elbow, guiding her steps around a puddle. "Unfortunately, Edmund and I were very good at discovering trouble. I'd even go so far as to say we were scholars of mischief."

As much as she liked the thought of his younger self, she laughed and shook her head. "You? Abandoning yourself to chaos? I can hardly believe that."

His grin faded, and his eyes were suddenly cast in a far-off look. "Yes, well, those were the follies of youth."

He said it in such a resolved way that it caused her to understand immediately. He'd been a hellion, but only before his father had died. After that, and since she'd known him, he'd left behind his *scholarly* endeavors.

Penelope had gone through a similar transformation, choosing to leave behind her childhood rather abruptly when her mother had died. This was why she understood Ethan. She knew he liked order and structure because he could count on it. He liked the control it gave him.

Until recently, she'd looked to Ethan for *her* structure. He was so regimented that it was comforting for her to know that she could count on him always staying the same.

Only now . . . *she'd* changed.

It wasn't his fault. It was hers. She didn't want *same* any longer. She wanted more.

"We are fortunate in that regard," he said, breaking into her thoughts. After a curious glance from her, he continued with an absent gesture to the children as they passed. "We don't have to worry about mischievous children, tears, or sticky hands. We can spoil our nieces and nephews with peppermint sticks to curb errant behavior, then hand them over to their parents."

She nodded thoughtfully, realizing that a few years ago she would have agreed with him without question. However, since her sister's last visit, she wasn't entirely sure.

In fact, she believed that her uncertainty was one of the reasons behind her restlessness and her need to get away. She was sure that if she had a moment to look at these feelings, from a distance, she could begin to under-stand and overcome this terrible disquiet.

"Yes, in a few years, when my sister's children are older, I may offer them a sweet to earn a plump-cheeked grin," she said, as they neared the jeweler's shop window. "However, I can tell you this with certainty, when my nephew scraped his knee last week and ran crying into the room, it wasn't into my arms but into his mother's. There is a profound difference in that, I'm afraid."

Ethan opened the door for her but stared at her quizzically as if her response was something he'd never considered. In a sense, she'd just spooned cream into his marmalade again.

However, their conversation ended abruptly as they entered the jeweler's. Wearing an apron over his waistcoat and shirtsleeves, the bearded shopkeeper greeted them. Ethan went straight to the business at hand, asking if his grandmother's jewelry could be cleaned tomorrow since they were leaving for the country at the week's end.

The shopkeeper looked at Ethan, then pointedly down to his wares beneath the glass, a gesture that even Penelope recognized as a request for a favor in turn.

"We are so fortunate to find such a lovely selection and so close to Christmas," she said, coming forward and placing her gloved hands on the glass, her face crafted in a mask of delight. "I daresay, Mr. Weatherstone, your mother would love a pair of these emerald earbobs."

Ethan caught her eye and nodded in understanding, transforming his brusque business manner into one of cordiality. "I do believe emeralds are her favorite. Might I see the pair?"

"Yes, of course," the shopkeeper said with grin, and chafed his hands together. "These are very special. Not another pair like it. All my jewelry is one of a kind."

She'd heard those words before at other jeweler's shops, each one vying to appeal to a woman's vanity and desire to stand out from the crowd. However, it would hardly serve Ethan's cause to point out that she'd seen similar pieces on her friends. "These are lovely, as well." She pointed to a pair of pink coral clusters suspended from an inverted silver urn.

"One of my particularly favorite pairs. They would complement your coloring—"

"Miss Rutledge doesn't have pierced ears," Ethan interrupted.

She never knew he'd noticed. Self-consciously, she reached up to touch one bare lobe and realized he was watching her. "Do you think I should?"

His wolfish grin came out to play again, as if he was enjoying his own private joke. Surely, there must be something different with the light this morning to cause his eyes to smolder like copper over a fire?

Leisurely, his gaze seemed to take in every detail of her face, sweeping over her lashes, down the bridge of her nose—slowly as if cataloging every freckle—and then to her mouth. Here, she could almost feel his gaze on her flesh, like a phantom kiss. A kiss they'd never shared.

Finally, he looked from one bare lobe to the other. He pursed his lips slightly as he swallowed. "No," was the only answer he gave, but something in the way he said it made her feel quite warm.

She averted her face to hide her blush.

"Perhaps she would prefer a beautiful brooch?" The shopkeeper eagerly reached into the next case and produced a jade tortoise accented with cabochon garnets. "This came from the farthest reaches of the Orient."

"No doubt," Ethan said convincingly, as if equally certain. Yet she knew him better than that and wondered what game he was playing. "And perhaps all manner of reptiles make for fashionable jewelry in the farthest reaches of the Orient, as well. What say you, Miss Rutledge," he asked without turning away from the shopkeeper. "Do you prefer one reptile over another? Snakes, perhaps?"

She pressed her lips together in an effort to hide her smile. "I cannot say I'm overly fond of any type of reptile, Mr. Weatherstone."

"Miss Rutledge does not care for tortoises," Ethan said, matter-of-fact, causing the shopkeeper to snatch away the brooch.

"Yes, of course," he stammered apologetically, as he found yet another brooch, this one even larger than the tortoise. "Perhaps a young woman of her refined taste would prefer something more like this bird of paradise."

The bird was truly hideous. Nearly the size of her hand, the brooch was a garish conglomeration of multicolored gemstones, so bright it nearly hurt her eyes to look at it. In an effort to save her vision, she looked up to study Ethan's profile.

"One of a kind?" he asked.

"Yes, of course," the shopkeeper stated proudly. "It comes from the farthest reaches of Africa."

He tapped his index finger against his lip as if truly considering it. She was about to balk, but then noticed the faintest smile curve the corner of his mouth. "Do you have anything that doesn't reach quite so far?"

A laugh escaped her, the sound coming out like a strangled hiccup. She pressed her fingertips to her mouth to stifle any more sudden bursts of joviality. Neither of the gentlemen regarded her, but she was certain that Ethan was also fighting to control his amusement in the way he scrubbed his hand over his mouth as if smoothing his nonexistent mustachios.

The shopkeeper put the enormous bird brooch back in the case. "Perhaps if I knew her favorite gemstone, I might be of greater assistance."

"Miss Rutledge prefers sapphires."

Her gaze turned sharply to his. "I do?"

Smug as ever, he grinned, practically daring her to deny it. Of course, the smile was most likely left over from a moment ago. After all, how could he know such a thing? She was sure they'd never spoken of gemstones before.

"I have just the thing," the shopkeeper announced with excitement, as if this were a scavenger hunt, and he was determined to win the parlor game. "Wait a moment. I keep my most prized possessions in the safe."

In the next instant, he disappeared behind a curtained doorway.

Penelope studied Ethan. She was used to his teasing, but this . . . this was something different. Truthfully, she didn't know what to make of it. "I do believe that all you had to do to get your mother's jewelry cleaned was to buy the emerald earbobs."

"I know." He chuckled and reached his hand up as if to

touch her face but then lowered it instead and shrugged. "I wanted to give you an adventure. You are having fun, are you not?"

She blinked in wide-eyed awe. "This diversion is for me?"

He looked away as if embarrassed by the admission. "A small morning adventure."

It was probably the sweetest thing he'd ever done. If she hadn't always loved him, she would definitely have fallen in love with him in this moment.

Oh, how she hated him for surprising her and making her love him all over again. It made being close to him all the more confusing.

"Ethan, I—" She was about to tell him that this didn't change anything, that especially now she needed to put some distance between them, but at that precise moment the shopkeeper came back in, holding a small, blue velvet box.

"Now this is truly unique. Very special," he announced with a flourish as he set the box down and opened the lid.

This time he did not exaggerate. The ring was like nothing she'd ever seen. She gasped, because that was what one did when confronted with such brilliance and beauty. The ring was a masterpiece of artistry with a single center diamond surrounded by six dark blue sapphires the color of midnight.

"See how they catch the light?"

She nodded. It was impossible that stones so dark could give off such radiance, but they did.

"And the filigree work in gold. See how the artist filled the swirls with blue enamel?"

Penelope couldn't speak. She could only stare. It was the most beautiful piece of jewelry she'd ever seen.

"Surely, it was crafted for royalty." Even Ethan sounded awestruck.

"You have a discerning eye, sir." He carefully adjusted his glove before he picked the ring from the box, enticing them by turning it in the light. "Yes, indeed, it was a betrothal present for an Egyptian princess. Her young man commissioned this ring to be made for their wedding, but when word reached him that her father was not going to approve the match, the young man took matters into his own hands. He stole away with the princess in the middle of the night. Fearing capture if they returned, the ring stayed at the jeweler's for decades until finally it ended up here."

Ethan had the strength to look away, apparently not as captivated by the ring and its history as she. "With a story like that, you'll be sure to sell this ring in no time. And to think, the earbobs took no story at all for the sale."

The shopkeeper smiled pleasantly, taking the news without argument. He set the ring back inside the box and closed the lid without warning. She watched the velvet box disappear behind the counter as Ethan drew the pouch of his mother's jewelry from his inner coat pocket.

The men completed their transaction with few words, and, before she knew it, she and Ethan were climbing into his carriage.

Ethan settled himself across from her, eyeing her with curiosity as the driver returned them to Danbury Lane.

Since he'd tried so hard to give her an adventure, even a small one of silliness, she didn't want him to think her silence was because she was displeased. "I feel sad for the ring."

He chuckled. "Whatever for?"

"Because it was left behind," she said simply. "It's been sitting in a box all this time, just waiting for something monumental to happen."

In an instant, Ethan's gaze turned from amusement to disapproval. "You're still talking about adventures, I see."

Hurt that his mood could alter so quickly, she frowned. For one moment, Penelope thought he understood, but now she realized that his *small morning adventure* was only a diversion to placate her. "I suppose so," she said, her defenses up.

"And what did your father say when you asked him for the money to hire a coach and traveling companion to take you to the Continent?"

"I have money of my own." Her father would not approve, she knew. One of the reasons she'd yet to commit herself fully to this new adventure was because she knew leaving him, even for a short time, would hurt him. If Ethan knew her better, he would realize this was not an easy decision for her.

He glared at her, his thick brows casting dark shadows over his eyes so that she could no longer see their color, only their hardness. "Surely, you're not thinking of going alone, without his consent?"

She drew in a breath to calm her rising temper. "I am five-and-twenty, not fifteen. Surely, a woman of my age can enjoy a few freedoms. Even if you don't understand, I'm thankful my father does." *Or will,* she hoped.

Ethan was quiet, studying her as if he'd never seen her before. As if she'd sprouted from the ground, and he was the first to discover this strange creature.

Then, after a moment, his features settled into a look of calm understanding. He offered her a friendly smile that didn't quite remove the hardness from his eyes. "You're obviously restless and needing something to occupy your ever-fidgeting hands. We leave for the country by week's end. You'll have plenty to do once you are home, I'm sure, running your father's house, planning menus, writing letters—"

"Don't forget my needlework," she added, not bothering to keep the bitterness from her tone. "And if I'm still restless and want to occupy my time with other things, I'm sure I can take my sister up on her offer to become governess to *her* children."

He blinked. "You would go to live with Eugenia?"

Until this moment, her answer would have been a resolute "No." But now, she didn't know if she could continue like this any longer. For years, she thought it was better to resign herself to a life of eternal friendship simply to be near him. Now, she knew she couldn't bear it. "I feel that if I don't break free of the sameness of each day, I will go mad," she admitted quietly. "I need this, Ethan. Can't you see how important it is to me?"

They stared at each other like two strangers seeing

each other for the first time, neither of them entirely happy with the introduction. Gradually, the carriage slowed to a stop, signaling their arrival.

"Can't you see how I'm required to save you from yourself? To save you from ruin . . . or worse?"

Penelope felt tears sting the corners of her eyes. He didn't understand. She'd hoped that, of all people, Ethan could. But he was only one more obstacle. "Then allow me to release you from any imagined obligation you might have."

Chapter Four

ETHAN REACHED FOR Penelope. He had to make her see reason.

Yet he stopped, his hand hovering in the space between them. At this precise moment, he knew he could say nothing to convince her. Their tempers were too close to the surface, and he was likely to say something he would later regret. Instead, he watched as she left the carriage. Watched as she didn't require his assistance. Watched as she made it safely to the ground, without any help from him.

She wanted to leave. No, she was *determined* to leave. And for what, an adventure?

Why did she do this to him? He felt as if his blood were boiling, not in anger but in desperation so keen he didn't know the source of it. All he knew was that he had to make her see reason.

He growled as the carriage moved a few doors to

Number 3. But he could not go inside in the temper he was in.

Instead, he instructed his driver to take him to the fencing salon. Perhaps an hour or two, or three or four, would help him clear his head before dinner this evening.

As ETHAN AND his mother walked through the door of Number 7, he was reminded again that this was to be the last dinner before they set off on their journey in two days' time. Knowing Penelope the way he did, he knew this might very well be the last chance he had to make her see reason.

At least, with the dinner at her father's home, he hadn't been plagued with the notion she would not be here. Because of that, the first knot of his cravat looked precisely as it should this evening. Also, he chose to wear his charcoal coat and silver-embroidered waistcoat she'd remarked on with favor on three separate occasions.

Handing off his overcoat and hat with thanks to Vernon, their head butler, Ethan prepared to escort his mother into the parlor, where James Rutledge stood preparing drinks at the sideboard. However, out of the corner of his eye, he caught a glimpse of Penelope descending the stairs.

Ethan hesitated, allowing his mother to precede him while he waited for Pen. He turned to the stairway and looked up, expecting to gauge her mood.

Instead, the sight before him arrested all thought. Pen was a vision of exquisite loveliness in a shimmering champagne gown. His gaze traveled up from the ruffled hem to the long skirt that seemed to accentuate the length of her legs. Not only that, but it was fashioned in a way that drew his keen notice to the curve of her hips and the slenderness of her waist. His palm tingled with the memory of holding that waist.

He tried to blink, to turn away, but all he could do was watch her slowly descend into his field of vision. But no—she *was* his field of vision. He saw nothing except for her and how the bodice fit her to perfection. The champagne color of the gown made the enticing swells of her flesh look like sweet cream, or perhaps it wasn't the color at all but the fact that she was usually covered with a fichu.

Ethan swallowed, wondering how he was going to get through the night without making a complete fool of himself. He couldn't think. He knew he should utter a word of greeting, but he was sure he'd trip over his tongue.

By the time her face was level with his, he was angry at her for being so damned beautiful. "Pen," he managed.

She smiled up at him coyly, like a woman who knew the direction of his thoughts. Thankfully for him, he knew her better than that.

"Did you skip luncheon again?" she asked, her gaze drifting down to his mouth. When he didn't answer, she continued. "You look very fine in your eveningwear, Mr. Weatherstone."

He inclined his head and offered the expected response. "As do you, Miss Rutledge."

She beamed up at him. "I wanted to try something *n*—special for this evening."

He caught her slip and knew she was about to say that she wanted to try something *new*. However, in the end, she decided not to go down that road with him again, and he was grateful for it.

"Minnie tried something different with my hair, as well. Do you like it?"

When she turned, affording him a glance of the back, he caught a hint of her fragrance and nearly groaned. Her usual elaborate configuration of braids was gone in favor of a simpler twist, gathered by a pearl-encrusted comb. In the light of the sconces on the wall, her hair looked like rich, spun gold. And her shoulders were enticingly bare. Far too much of a distraction.

"While I should love nothing more than to flatter you until you swoon with delight, I would much rather know why this night, of all nights, is such a special occasion."

She tucked her slender arm into the crook of his, her long white evening glove a brilliant white against his dark coat as she gave him a pat. "This is our last dinner . . . in town . . . together. I simply wanted to make it memorable."

He gazed down at her, not liking the deception he saw in her eyes. He knew her too well to believe her this time. But he did not call her on it. Instead, he answered her softly. "Then you have already succeeded."

Without another word, they walked into the parlor together, joining his mother and her father in an aperitif. Soon after Pen soaked up more compliments from his mother, they went into the dining room and sat in their usual places. However, the Rutledge dining room was grand, indeed. With the two pairs of them sitting at opposite ends of the long, polished, walnut table, it made for difficult conversation with the entire party unless one chose to raise one's voice.

Strange, he'd never noticed the intimacy of their arrangement before now.

Ethan glanced over at Pen, his gaze again arrested by her beauty. He forced himself to turn away and did his best to clear his head. Thankfully, he had food to distract him.

The soup course was a velvety mushroom, a particular favorite of his. He wondered if Pen knew this, or if it was a coincidence.

He regarded her, noting her sly smile at his nearly empty bowl. *Ah*, then he had his answer. Perhaps this was a peace offering, and their conversation from earlier today was at last forgotten. Perhaps she was ready to leave this silliness behind, as she'd done before. "This is a pleasant dinner. Wouldn't you agree?"

She dabbed her napkin to the corner of her mouth, her smile fading. "Our dinners are always pleasant."

Or perhaps it was just wishful thinking on his part. "*Pleasant* . . . hmm."

"It is the same adjective you used."

His mood darkened, and her statement from earlier came back to haunt him. She'd made a point of mentioning that this was their *last* dinner. "Yes, but I sense it has a mundane meaning for you now."

"Please, let us not start this again." She sighed and reached for her glass. After a sip of white wine, a tentative smile curved her lips. "You already know how highly I regard these dinners . . . and the company."

"Do I?" *This is our last dinner . . . together,* that was what her eyes were telling him.

The slightest blush colored her cheeks. "After all these years, how can you not have a full understanding of my high regard for"—she broke off, searching his gaze—"these dinners?"

He held his breath for a moment. "Then I do not understand why you want to leave . . . these dinners."

"I don't want to leave these dinners behind. I simply want—No, not *simply*, for it is anything but simple." She shook her head as if to clear it. "I want to alter the menu. I want my plate to be filled with . . ."

"Adventure," he supplied.

"Your contempt for that particular word is palpable. Tell me, Ethan, after years and years of soup first, haven't you ever wanted to start with dessert?"

Start with dessert? His mouth went dry at the thought.

Had he thought of it? Had he thought of abandoning his carefully crafted order? Had he thought of risking their friendship, which gave him the greatest happiness of his life? Had he imagined every possible scenario of what could happen if he lost control and gave in to his craving for one taste of her lips?

Only a million times.

He could prove it easily enough. The impulses were

always directly beneath the surface, threatening to break through. Lately, more often than not.

She vexed him to no end. She drove him mad with each of her smiles. She tempted him beyond the limits of his sanity, where he could easily forget how acting on his impulses could risk everything he held dear.

Start with dessert? The words suggested that he would be able to stop once he started. But he knew there would be no going back if he did. There would be no way to regain what might be lost in the process. It was far too much of a risk to take.

"No, of course not," he lied. "Dessert first is too far out of the realm of possibility."

Chapter Five

AFTER DISMISSING MINNIE for the night, Penelope packed her satchel, all the while wishing she didn't have to leave. But she couldn't remain this way any longer. The same dinners. The same conversations. The same disapproving gazes from Ethan.

She felt foolish for ever having dreamed it would be different. And even more foolish for having been in love with Ethan for most of her life. She'd turned down two marriage proposals from perfectly respectable gentlemen in the hopes that someday Ethan would see her as more than a fixture in his life, more than a plate that sat to his left at dinner. Yet, he'd summed up her worst fears with one succinct sentence: *Out of the realm of possibility.*

The sense of resignation she'd acquired over the years refused to comfort her now. She knew that if she had any hope of forgetting him, of starting a new dream, of finding a shred of happiness, she needed to be far away from wherever he was. Because whenever he was near, she began to dream of things that were out of his realm of possibility.

After a few useless tears, she wrote two letters, one to her father and one to Ethan. They both asked for understanding, they both offered a surface explanation of her wanting to see more of the world, they both begged for forgiveness. But only Ethan's letter mentioned how futile her love had been all these years and how she needed to escape immediately before sorrow crushed what was left of her heart.

Once he read the letter, the words would seal her fate forever. She could never see him again.

DRESSED IN HER conservative burgundy traveling costume, she set out in the wee hours of morning on her new adventure, determined to leave futility and routine behind.

Portsmouth was as good a place as any, she thought as she looked down to the mail coach's schedule in her hand. She had an aunt there. Flora was her mother's younger sister, who had invited Penelope to stay with her on numerous occasions. Now, she would finally accept. The only problem was, this would be a surprise visit. Since her aunt was a carefree sort, given to whims of her own, Penelope knew she wouldn't mind.

The faint gray light of dawn was starting to creep over the horizon. A few other travelers milled in the area while the horses were being changed. There were eight travelers altogether, which made for a very cramped journey, especially considering only four would be seated inside the coach. She looked around, noting that she was one of three women. Surely, the gentlemen would defer their own comfort and politely offer the inside? However, skepticism warred with reason as she watched not one but two gentlemen hover near the coach's door.

Yet, in the next instant her choice of seat was forgotten as a carriage came thundering down the street as if the hounds of hell were directly behind it. The older woman beside her gasped when it came to an abrupt halt behind the mail coach.

Penelope blinked in disbelief. She knew that carriage.

With a glance up at the driver, she felt a horrible sense of dread in her stomach. She inclined her head in greeting to Tom, the Weatherstones' driver, and he returned the gesture. The tiger, young Arthur, hopped down and lowered the platform stairs. He, too, acknowledged her with tilt of his cap and a grin that spoke volumes on the reason they were all here.

She stared at the carriage door, waiting for Ethan to burst out and rail at her about being foolish and insensible. He would try to drag her home, ranting about her potential ruin. He'd probably expect her to thank him for it, too.

Thank him for driving pell-mell and making a scene in front of complete strangers, who were all looking at her with interest now, as if she were some runaway child who needed to be taken home for safekeeping.

She was five-and-twenty! She could make her own decisions, and if something horrible were to happen, then she would be the one to suffer the consequences.

The more she stared at the door, the more her ire sparked. He couldn't have received her letter yet because she'd left it in the care of her father, and her father wouldn't open his letter until he went into his study after breakfast. So then, the only way he would know she was here was if he'd been spying on her. Of all the interfering—

The passengers started filing into the coach until any hope for an inside seat was gone. She glared at Ethan's door. He was going to ruin this for her. She'd finally found the courage to get on with her life, the courage to escape the haunting specter of her future self, and *he* was going to ruin her chance.

She looked to the mail coach. All the passengers were on. All but one. If she squeezed, she could manage to sit in between the driver and a rather rotund male passenger. And, of course, it was starting to drizzle, the air not quite cold enough to make it freeze, but close. Very close.

The angrier she got, the more she could see her breath turn to cloudy vapor. Ethan Weatherstone was due for a piece of her mind. It was about time he understood that he had no right to interfere with her life.

Mind made up, she took one last look at the mail coach and shook her head. She reached down for her satchel and stormed over to Ethan's carriage.

Penelope threw open the door and climbed inside, seething as she sat across from him. He didn't even have the courtesy to look at her. Instead, he sat back against the squabs, his head turned to the window. The only reason she knew he was aware of her presence was from the way he clenched his jaw, a muscle twitching just beneath the surface of his skin.

"Were you waiting to humiliate me? Waiting until I was already seated before you dragged me away from the mail coach? Or perhaps you planned to follow me all the way to Portsmouth?"

He refused to respond or even so much as look at her. If she hadn't been angry before she entered the carriage, then she certainly was fuming now.

"Truly, Ethan, for someone who cannot live outside the lines of your carefully crafted order, your sameness that covers you like a shroud, this is quite surprising behavior," she hissed, baiting him. "I only wish your concern for my happiness were as great as your concern for my reputation."

At that, he glared at her sharply. Ah, so she'd struck a chord.

Good. Yet still, he did not say anything.

There he sat, perfectly groomed, his cravat perfectly pleated, his temper perfectly managed. She wished just once he'd lose some of that control. Because here she sat, with her eyes, most likely puffy and red from having cried most of the night instead of sleeping. She was certainly not perfectly groomed since she could feel a soggy tendril of hair plastered to her cheek. Her cloak was damp from rain. Her nose was cold and likely red as well.

"How can you be so . . . so *unaffected* all the time?" Her voice rose with her accusation. "Haven't you ever dreamed for something outside the realm of possibility? Or are you content with each day so long as your cravat is perfectly pleated?"

She glared at the offending garment, struck by a ridiculous notion to crumple it. No sooner had the idea formed that she gave in to the impulse and moved forward on her seat, her arm reaching forward.

Ethan stopped her, taking hold of her wrist. His eyes flared. Before she could react, he yanked, propelling her forward to land clumsily on his lap.

"How dare—"

His mouth covered hers, silencing her outrage. Her head spun, reeling from the sudden scorching heat of his kiss.

This was a kiss, wasn't it? Yet, it was nothing like her dreams, where his rehearsed request was followed by carefully controlled actions. No, this was no gentle dream. This was hard and demanding. His tongue didn't request entrance but swept in and plundered.

His arms were not gentle either. In fact, he held her so tightly she couldn't move, and grasped her wrist so she couldn't touch him or push him away.

But she'd never push him away.

Instead, she wanted to cling to him. Her anger evaporated in a rush of steam. Her mind cried out for more of this glorious punishment. She wanted his kiss to burn her, through and through. This was the first time she'd been warm in months.

A mew of frustration tore from her throat when his firm hold would not budge. She wriggled and pulled. Finally, she managed to free her hand, but at the cost of the buttons at her wrist as her glove was stripped away. Yet, she didn't care.

Now, she was free to touch him. Her bare hand found its way to his hair, threading through the thick, heavy waves. The smooth locks wound around her fingers in a caress. How long had she wondered at the texture or longed for this freedom? Forever, at least.

She returned his kiss with the fervor she'd kept locked away for years. Her tongue mingled with his. A tentative stroke at first. Then a few slow swipes until she knew the intimate interior of his mouth as well as he knew hers. She touched the sharp ridges of his teeth and felt compelled to rake hers across his tongue. He groaned in response, his arms tightening around her.

She squirmed against him, feeling very much like a cat in need of affection. He seemed to know this, because in the next instant he unclasped her fur-trimmed cloak and let it fall to the carriage floor. His hands were on her, caressing the length of her back. From her nape to the swells of her derriere, his fingertips traced every vertebra of her spine, leaving none unexplored.

Never once did he break the kiss. Never once did he ease the pressure. The kiss remained a force to be reckoned with, too long denied. With her eyes closed, she felt the pull of his lips more keenly and was mesmerized into answering with the same urgency.

Ethan...

Those same hands, which were meticulous with writing figures in a ledger, were just as meticulous with the row of tiny buttons at the front of her half jacket.

Penelope did not know how to describe what happened next. Until now, she could have only dreamed of such a passionate kiss. Let alone ever imagined how wondrous it would feel to have his hands on her body.

The heat of those hands seared through the thin fabric of her dress and her chemise as her jacket parted. Her flesh grew taut, responding to his touch. A sharp spear of sensation stabbed her with the most exquisite pain, which tightened low in her belly. She arched against his hand, wanting more of this sublime torture.

He obliged her, chafing the fabric over her nipple with the pad of his thumb. She squirmed against him again, feeling hot and liquid and never wanting this to end. She was infinitely glad she did not get on the mail coach. This was a far better way to travel.

Ethan deepened the kiss, stripping away her ability to think. Every glorious pull of his lips, every sublime stroke of his tongue exposed more of the yearning she'd locked away. She could not get enough. He dragged down the front of her dress, exposing her breast to the chilly winter air, her nipple contracting in the cold. Yet his warm hand covered her instantly, pressing and kneading her flesh until she ached for more.

Her body was a mass of tingles. The quivering low in her belly intensified unbearably. She pressed herself against the hardness of his thigh to quell the throbbing ache between hers. A sweet sob escaped her at the contact.

He tore his mouth away, his eyes hooded and fiery. When he looked down at her flesh in his hands, an expression of blatant ownership swept over his features. It was as if he said she was his, and there was no denying it.

Yes, something desperate inside her cried. *Yes, I am yours. Make me yours!*

In answer to her unspoken plea, he bent his head and closed his mouth over her taut flesh. The sensation was like nothing she'd ever felt. Hot and wet, he drew her deeply into his mouth. It was like being stung, but the pain was sweeter, sharper. Relentless, his tongue flicked over her, abrading her, making her squirm more against him. His skilled fingers plucked her other nipple, intensifying the feeling until the sharp stings and the throbbing ache below were in rhythm with each other.

Her whole body tightened. She rocked her hips again. Suddenly, her body convulsed, her hips moving without her consent, her breasts tightening to the point of shattering. He groaned again, his teeth gently raking over her flesh.

And then she did shatter on a wordless moan, clutching him fiercely as wave after wave of pleasure washed through the shattered pieces of her.

All at once, she was so exhausted she couldn't open her eyes. She sagged in Ethan's arms, barely holding on to him as he settled back onto the seat with her.

THE NEXT THING she was aware of was Ethan's carrying her into her father's study and laying her down on the settee. It was still early yet; the sweet aroma of freshly baked breakfast pastries filled the house.

He paused to tuck a strand of hair behind her ear. "We will talk about this later."

She blushed and nodded. Now that they were no longer in the confines of the carriage, knowing what had just occurred made her feel shy. Strange, she didn't feel shy at all *while* it was happening.

He must have been feeling a little shy as well because he looked guiltily away. Then, as if he'd known her plot by heart, he made his way to her father's desk. On top, sat two folded letters. Ethan picked them both up and likely noted that one was addressed to him. She swallowed nervously, wondering if he would read it now. How could she bear to look at him after what she'd written, after admonishing him for being the cause of her needing to leave?

Yet, in the next moment, he moved to the hearth. Without asking for her consent, he threw the unopened letters into the fire.

He glanced over at her again, his unruly hair delightfully disheveled. "When Vernon let me in, I merely told him you suffered a fall on your morning walk. So, perhaps you could limp around a bit to make it convincing."

"Oh. All right." She blushed again, realizing only now that her clothes were back in order.

Looking up, she hoped to find reassurance in his gaze. She received a small smile instead and a nod before he left.

Chapter Six

THE WEATHERSTONES AND the Rutledges set out late the next morning and traveled all day. Once they reached the halfway point of their journey, they stopped at an inn for the night. Being so late in the year and with the threat of snow hanging in the dark-lined clouds overhead, there weren't many travelers, and the owner and his wife doted on those who were there. In fact, they were so well tended to that Penelope didn't have a single moment to speak with Ethan.

Of course, she wasn't expecting a declaration of love over a bowl of turnips, especially with their parents so close by. However, she did expect more than their usual conversation, which consisted of remarks on the delicious pork pie, the fine crust on the jam tart, the robust flavor of the mulled wine . . .

Yet, when she mentioned how the country air must have given him quite the appetite, he averted his gaze.

For her, something monumental had occurred between them. Something that changed her entire outlook. Something that made her hope for the first time in . . . forever. Surely, their relationship wasn't destined to remain the same. The specter of her future was far away. In place of the old woman at her needlework was a life filled with dark, passionate kisses and a love that was its own adventure.

Yes, she would be very happy to have many more adventures like the one she had with Ethan yesterday morning. She wouldn't even mind if kisses were somehow worked into their daily routine.

She smiled on a sip of wine and glanced down to her plate, situated, as usual, to the left of his. "The roasted parsnips are particularly fine. Wouldn't you agree, Mr. Weatherstone?"

For the first time since they stopped here in their separate carriages, he regarded her. A look of relief washed over him as he nodded. "Very fine, Miss Rutledge. And how did you find the beets?"

"Fair. But not nearly as fine as your Minerva's beets." She wasn't entirely sure she liked that look of relief. It certainly didn't bode well for where her thoughts were at this precise moment. Because she was still wondering how to approach the topic of scheduled kisses. Perhaps once they were settled, she would join him for a morning walk in the country and discuss it.

She could picture their debate clearly in her mind. He would suggest Tuesdays and Thursdays before dinner, and she would state that Wednesdays and Fridays after dessert would be better, simply for the sake of being contrary.

"I see your ankle has recovered from yesterday morning," Abigail Weatherstone commented from across the table, startling her from her musings. "You were so fortunate to have Ethan so close at hand."

She did her best to hide her blush behind her wineglass. Abigail had a way of being too direct at times, and her gaze now told Penelope that she suspected something other than a morning walk had gone on between them.

"Yes, very," she said quickly. "As you suggested, I do believe resting in the carriage was the best thing for it. I used the time to work on the most beautiful butterfly. I'd love to show you after dinner."

"I would like that," she said with a smile, but her direct gaze remained. "I've always been fascinated with butterflies. For so long, they go about seemingly unnoticed, then one day they are transformed, and the world suddenly changes. For the better, I think. Wouldn't you agree?"

Penelope nodded, knowing that an understanding *had* passed between them. An uncontrollable smile curved her mouth. "Yes, very much so."

Abigail lifted her glass. "To butterflies, my dear?"

She reached forward and touched Abigail's glass with a clink.

"What say you, Ethan?" her father asked with a chuckle from the opposite end of the table. "Shall we toast to a more manly insect? Perhaps a centipede?"

However, the joke appeared to have been lost on

Ethan, for he did not smile. In fact, he seemed in another world, lost to his own thoughts. Once he realized he was being studied by the group, he cleared his throat. "Yes, of course," he said, and absently lifted his glass to mimic the rest of them.

PENELOPE AND ABIGAIL were to share a room, just as Ethan and her father would. However, when she returned to her room, she discovered that her needlework was not with her things. Knowing that her satchel had probably been put in her father's room, she stepped across the hall, prepared to knock on the door.

Yet, before she could, she encountered Ethan pacing the narrow hall. His cravat was askew and, by the way the wavy locks drooped over his forehead, his hair looked as if he'd run his hands through it repeatedly. Noticing her, he stopped suddenly. The dark worry in his gaze caused her own worry to rise.

"Are you unwell?" Truly, she'd never seen him like this.

"No," he said after a moment, then appeared to think on it, and again replied, "No."

Without thinking, she went to him, lifting a hand to touch his face to see if he felt overly warm. But like before, he seized her wrist. "No," he said again, sterner this time.

She pulled back as if he'd slapped her. "Am I not allowed to display my concern?"

He lowered his head on an exhale and raked his hand through his hair. "Of course. And you have. I know you care for me, Pen."

A feeling of dread washed over her. Suddenly, she understood, but she didn't want to. She didn't want the terrible understanding to fully form because she feared her heart could not take it. Butterflies were fragile creatures.

"Care for you?" She loved him. She'd always loved him. It had simply taken most of her life to realize how much her happiness depended on him. "Surely, since you know practically everything about me, you would know my feelings better by now."

He looked nervous, his eyes darting to the closed doors on either side of them. With a jerk of his head, he gestured for her to follow him to the end of the hall near the window that overlooked the stables.

"First of all," he began quietly, his troubled expression turning to resolve, "I don't know what I would have done if I hadn't found you yesterday morning. I was in a panic and overwrought."

"No, you were angry," she corrected. "You thought I was simply being foolish."

"Yes, well . . . there's that." He locked his grave gaze with hers. "You put yourself in danger, and I didn't know how to react. If I hadn't been up all night . . . Hadn't chanced to look out the window to see you leave on your foolish—" He stopped and drew in an unsteady breath. "When I finally saw you, I wanted to shake you. Try to shake some sense into you."

She blanched, hating where this conversation was going, but she had to ask. "What stopped you?"

"I couldn't hurt you, Pen. And yet, I was so . . . overwrought that I simply reacted." He raked a hand through his hair again and paced in the small space in front of her. "In the light of things now, I realize my actions were unconscionable, on an equal footing with my first impulse."

The kiss. The perfect, magical, passionate kiss that transformed her life had happened solely because he couldn't rationalize shaking her?

Penelope's head spun, her world tilting. She wanted to step back and lean against the wall for support, but her feet were rooted to the floor. She wanted to close her eyes with the hope that if she didn't look at him, his words wouldn't hurt as much, but her gaze remained fixed on him.

He stopped in front of her, his expression full of contrition, his arms locked at his sides. "It was a most unfortunate incident, and I do hope you'll forgive me. I think you know, my life would never be the same without you," he added, almost inaudibly.

She swallowed against a sob that was building in the back of her throat. "The same?"

"Our family dinners. Our chats in my study. Surely, you must also regard those moments with fondness." He attempted a smile, but it did not reach his apologetic eyes. "We keep each other sane, you and I."

Sane? She was feeling anything but sane at the moment. She wanted to crawl out of her skin and be anywhere else.

"I would hate for my lapse in decorum to risk that."

"Lapse in—" Her heart sank, but she refused to allow him to notice. "No, of course you would not. Everything must remain the same."

Ethan must not have heard the censure in her statement because he nodded. "Then, if you'll excuse me, I bid you good night."

Without waiting for her response, he turned sharply on his heel and walked down the hall, disappearing into the shadow of the stairway.

She stared at the vacancy he left long after the echoes of his footsteps died away. For knowing Ethan as well as she did, she should have known better than to believe the whispers of her foolish heart.

Chapter Seven

WHEN PENELOPE MISSED the first of their dinners once they'd arrived in the country, it was completely understandable. After all, her father had said she was still weary from their travels.

However, then she missed another. And then two more.

Ethan, too, had been plagued by an ailment. In fact, he couldn't seem to shake free of it. Every day for a week, he'd felt listless, unable to focus on his accounts or clear his head. His appetite disappeared. Even the cook's scones and orange marmalade held no appeal.

Still, he waited for a visit from Pen. Of course, it was colder now. The walk between their country houses was longer than the distance between number 7 and number 3. Still, a carriage would make the journey shorter. He'd make it himself, if only he knew she would receive him . . .

Damn. He wished she would walk in right now, letting him know that everything would be the same again. Letting him know that he hadn't irrevocably harmed everything they had by losing control.

Surely, the heavens would not punish him for one time. Surely, *they* knew how many times he'd denied the impulse to hold Pen in his arms, to taste her lips, to feel her body against his . . .

He doubled over as a deep, welling emptiness tore through his heart, an ache so profound he did not think he would survive it.

"*Ethan!*" his mother exclaimed, rushing into the study to his side. "What is it, dear?"

He held up a hand in reassurance. "It is nothing." Clutching the side of the desk with his other hand, he gradually stood and drew in a breath. He faced her and offered a smile of reassurance. "Breakfast did not appeal to me, and so I have not eaten today."

"Nor did you eat last night," she chided, hovering next to him as he made his way to the chair. "Even James commented on it, wondering if both you and Penelope were suffering the same ailment."

"Surely not." He knew the true reason Pen had avoided the dinners. She couldn't forgive him for losing control. She must hate him. She must . . .

"She's leaving, you know."

"What?" He shot up, feeling his head spin and all the blood drain out of his body.

His mother nodded gravely. "She's going to live with her sister. Eventually, she'll be governess to Eugenia's children."

No. No. No, his mind railed. This could not be happening. Surely, in time, she could find a way to forgive him. Surely, in time, the kiss would become a mere memory and everything would go on in the same manner as it always had.

His life depended upon it.

"How can she do this?"

His mother turned away with a shrug. "It really is the best thing for Penelope. After all, what does she have to look forward to by staying with her father? All she has is her needlework."

"She has more than that. She has—" He stopped abruptly, not wanting to reveal the depth of his heartache. Not even wanting to admit it to himself.

"You?" his mother asked, finishing his unspoken admission. As if she could see into his heart, she dared him to deny it with the sly lift of her brow.

He refused to respond, turning to stare out the window. He wasn't going to have this conversation with his mother. He didn't even want to think about it.

"But she doesn't really have you. All she has are dinners a few nights a week. All she has are conversations in your study. All she has are the morning walks when you find yourselves running into each other as if by chance."

She has more than that, he argued. She had his high regard. She had his undivided attention. She had his . . . heart.

All of it. She possessed every single beat and even the space in between.

"She's spent so long being content with what you two

had, that I believe it quite surprised her to discover that her life was passing by. I think it took seeing her sister so happily settled with a husband and family for her to realize that she wanted more."

More? A desperate need awakened inside of him. He wanted more, too. But there was too much he risked losing in the process. Already he'd altered one thing between them, and look at how that turned out. She was leaving.

His mother sighed. "I know you fear that a single action or alteration on your part will put everything you have with Penelope at risk. What you don't see is that by doing nothing, you risk even more," she said simply, then lifted her palms, weighing her words with one, then the other. "All you have to do is decide if what you have now is worth risking for the chance at greater happiness."

"I could lose her," he said before he could stop the words from tumbling out.

His mother blinked up at him, surprised by his admission, but pleased. She gave him a watery smile. "Or you could gain so much more."

Chapter Eight

CHRISTMAS EVE WITH the Weatherstones had been a standing tradition for the past fifteen years. For Penelope, it was to be her last.

After next week, she would be living with her sister and celebrating next Christmas with Eugenia's family. Of course, her father would most likely travel to Plymouth for the season, as well. So this could very well be the last year for any of them.

She did her best not to think about it when she arrived and saw the country house decorated with fragrant pine wreaths and red and silver bows. She tried not to think about it at dinner when Ethan mentioned they were having the last of Minerva's pickled beets—which, according to Abigail, he'd made a special trip to London in order to bring them back for this occasion. And she tried not to think about it now, as they sat in the living room, listening to Abigail play joyful carols on the fortepiano.

Penelope felt anything but joyful. Weren't there hymns or carols that expressed one's melancholy on this holiday? She sighed, thankful the sound was disguised by the final trilling notes of "Here We Come A Wassailing."

In fine spirits, her father clapped and stood up from the settee beside her. "Marvelous playing, Abigail. I could listen to these happy tunes for hours," he said as he made his way to the tree and plucked a ribboned scroll from one of the branches. "Which reminds me of a special gift I thought of just for you."

Having drunk far too much Christmas punch, he presented the scroll to her with a flourish. Smiling, Abigail eagerly took the scroll, slipping the ribbon off with haste like a girl unwrapping her first doll.

"James Rutledge, you spoil me," she tittered in delight. "Why it's the perfect piece of music for this day. However did you know?"

Hooking his thumbs beneath the fabric of his lapels, he rocked back on his feet and grinned. "I've had my suspicions for a while now. It is Bach's most celebrated work."

Abigail took his hand, thanked him, then stood to retrieve a small package wrapped in brown paper, handing it to him. "For you."

Her father made a show of shaking it by his ear and wiggling his eyebrows as if he'd guessed some great secret before he unwrapped it. "My favorite pipe tobacco. How thoughtful, Abigail." He lifted her hand to his lips and kissed her knuckles. "Thank you."

Penelope watched them with a bittersweet joy. They

were all such good friends, close as any two families could be. She would miss this. She would miss this very, very much.

Ethan jumped up from his chair, which was unusual for him. This evening, he'd had a sort of nervous energy about him. He never fidgeted, but she'd noticed him toying with his napkin at dinner, then, just a moment ago, pulling on the fringes of a pillow.

It was almost comical in a way because she was *not* fidgeting. Instead, she was unusually reserved, sitting on the settee with her hands sedately clasped in her lap.

"I believe I saw a familiar-looking package in the tree for me, Pen," Ethan said, as he fished through the boughs to the small, square package. This year, she'd chosen to wrap his gift in a scrap of linen she'd purposely stained with tea in an effort to match the color of his eyes.

He resumed his place on the armchair, poised at the very edge as he unwrapped the package, as if he didn't already know what was inside. When he saw the handkerchiefs, a smile broke over his face. "Pen, you have no idea how much I look forward to these each year, to admire your fine stitching and the designs you loop off the letters. I see the tiniest of gray moths on the tail of the *E*. Yes, I do believe these are the finest yet."

Every year it was usually the same thing. First the handkerchiefs, then the nod of acknowledgment. However, this year, of all years, he chose to flatter her needlework. This year, of all years . . . and when she needed the sameness in order to keep herself sane.

His pretty words were too much. Her emotions, already like a cup full of Christmas punch, were threatening at each moment to spill out. She didn't want his compliment. She'd wanted to take one last nod from him with her. One final nod to bury in her wounded heart.

"I—" she stopped, her voice cracking. She had every intention of telling him how glad she was that he liked them. But when she tried again, nothing came out. Instead, a sudden rush of tears flowed from her eyes. All she could think of was how this was going to be the very last Christmas with him.

Unable to bear it any longer, she fled the room, rushing to the safety of the dark study.

Standing beside his desk, she wiped away the tears with her fingertips, and when those became too damp, she used the heels of her hands. She tried to compose herself. After all, she only had to wait a short while longer, and she could thoroughly give in to her misery, and no one would be the wiser.

"You left without your present, Pen," Ethan said from behind her, his voice low.

She sniffed and discreetly wiped her wet hands over her knitted shawl. "Present? But you already gave me your present." He'd settled her account for needlework supplies. *For the very last time.* The thought caused her next breath to come in ragged.

"Yes, but this year, I have one more gift for you." He remained behind her, and something in the controlled manner of his tone made her realize that stepping away from the routine must be very difficult for him.

She blinked her eyes, keeping her face averted as she

tried to make it appear she hadn't been crying. "You didn't have to. I enjoy our standing tradition."

He was quiet for a moment. So quiet, she wasn't sure if she'd offended him. But just as she was about to apologize, he spoke. "When I saw it, I knew it was made solely for you, no matter what story the jeweler told."

The jeweler? And then suddenly she understood. He'd gotten her a gift—no, more of a memento—from their small morning adventure. She turned, expecting to see the odd jade tortoise in his hand or even the hideous bird, a joke shared between them.

However, when she saw what he was actually holding, the carefully crafted smile she wore died on her lips. Tears threatened again. In fact, they were probably spilling down her cheeks, only she was too shocked to notice.

It was the ring.

Even in the dimness of the room, the dark sapphires glinted with a fascinating light that held her stare.

"I love you, Pen," Ethan said simply, as if he'd said it a million times, and she'd heard him utter the words for years upon years.

She blinked, staring at him, wondering if she'd gone mad and was imagining all of this.

It wasn't possible. In their world of routine and sameness, nothing like this was possible.

"Everything is chaos without you. You, who can never be still for a single moment. You, who constantly challenges my sanity. You, with your wry wit and the way that you know me better than I know myself. You"— he took a breath and stepped forward, using one of his handkerchiefs to wipe the tears from her face—"are the only way I can find peace in my own life."

She shook her head in disbelief.

He grinned, contradicting her by nodding. "I need you, Pen. I need you more than I need a straight cravat or a smudgeless accounting ledger or even orange marmalade. I need you more than I need air to breathe." He stepped closer, slipping his arms around her waist, and pressed a kiss to her forehead. "Because you are my air. I can only breathe when you are near. And if you will not be mine, if you will not consent to be my wife, then I may never breathe again."

She looked up at him and saw that his expression was no longer teasing but serious. "Wife?" She couldn't have heard him correctly. This was very . . . *not* sameness.

He nudged her nose with his, gazing intently at her. "Yes."

"You want to marry me?" She felt she had to clarify, just in case.

He chuckled and kissed her all-too-briefly on the lips. "That is the general idea. I don't know of another way to go about trying to have you as my wife, so yes, I believe I'm asking you to marry me."

She smiled at his teasing. This, she knew, would always be the same. "You can't blame me for needing clarification. It is rather unlike you, after all. I would have expected a paper marked with notes on how to proceed."

Again, he laughed, squeezing her tightly to him. "You know me so well. I *had* planned to get down on bended knee in the music room, in front of our parents, and very poetically ask you to be my wife." He kissed the corner of her mouth. "My plan was much simpler than what turned out, I'm afraid."

She closed her eyes as he trailed kisses along her jaw. "I like this way much better."

"You do?" He smiled against the spot just below her ear, nipping her bare lobe gently.

Mmm . . . She made a sound of agreement. "Do you really need me more than you need a smudgeless ledger?"

Ethan lifted his head and regarded her. "You doubt it?"

She lifted her brows and gave him a teasing grin as she shrugged, challenging him to prove it.

Without releasing her, he moved to his chair and sat down, pulling her down with him. He opened the top drawer to his left, and there, he drew out his ledger. She recognized it as the one from town by the volume number stamped into the cover. Opening it, he showed her. With a look of triumph, he pointed to a large smudge of ink near the center that completely obscured the figures beneath it. "That was the day I realized how much I love you."

She looked up at the date, her heart warming at the sight, and now understanding why she'd seen such a peculiar light in his eyes the day he took her to the jewelers.

"Oh, Ethan, it took you that long to know?" She released a dramatic sigh, one of her best, she was sure. "I've known for years."

Epilogue—Christmas

PENELOPE AWOKE THE next morning, happier than she'd ever been in her life. She skipped down the stairs before any of the servants were awake. She couldn't wait to start planning the rest of her life with Ethan.

Stepping into her father's study, she noted the tufted armchair by the fire. While it was similar to the one in his London study, she was no longer haunted by the specter of her future self. Instead, the happy vision of children and laughter filled her mind. She sighed with contentment and spun around.

"Good morning," Ethan said, surprising her by standing in the doorway.

She went to him, rushing into his arms for no better reason than because she could. "Good morning." She lifted her mouth to his and received a very nice kiss. A perfect kiss. "What brings you here so early?"

He grinned at her, his eyes alight with molten copper. "A morning adventure."

"Oh?" Hmm . . . Perhaps he was here for more than a perfect kiss. The idea warmed her to her toes.

He chuckled as if he knew the direction of her thoughts. "I'm here to kidnap my would-be bride and take her to Gretna Green."

She drew in a startled breath, her mouth curving in a wide grin. "But what about our parents? Surely, they will be heartbroken." However, at the moment, it was difficult to quash her excitement and summon the proper degree of concern.

"Don't worry, I left a note on your father's desk," he said, anticipation glowing brightly in his eyes. "And I left a note for my mother as well."

"You know, for not having much practice in spontaneity, you are very good at it," she said, as they walked together out into the hall. There, she saw her traveling cloak and her satchel waiting on the table.

She eyed him speculatively and shook her head, feigning disappointment. "You planned this?"

He shrugged, looking mildly chagrined. "I asked your maid to pack for you last night."

Once again, Penelope threw her arms around Ethan and kissed him, simply because she could. "Mr. Weatherstone, I love you dearly. You are, by far, the best adventure of all."

About Vivienne Lorret

VIVIENNE LORRET loves romance novels, her pink laptop, her husband, and her two teenage sons (not necessarily in that order . . . but there *are* days). When she isn't writing, you might find her in line at Starbucks, eager to refuel with a chai latte and randomly handing out crocheted cup-cozies with a *way-too-much-caffeine* smile on her face. For more on her upcoming novels, visit her at *www.vivlorret.net*.

NIGHTS OF STEEL
The Ether Chronicles
By Nico Rosso

ALICE'S WONDERLAND
By Allison Dobell

ONE FINE FIREMAN
A Bachelor Firemen Novella
By Jennifer Bernard

THERE'S SOMETHING ABOUT LADY MARY

A Summersby Tale

By Sophie Barnes

THE SECRET LIFE OF LADY LUCINDA

A Summersby Tale

By Sophie Barnes

An Excerpt from

NIGHTS OF STEEL

THE ETHER CHRONICLES

by Nico Rosso

Return to The Ether Chronicles, where rival bounty hunters Anna Blue and Jack Hawkins join forces to find a mysterious fugitive, only to get so much more than they bargained for. The skies above the American West are about to get wilder than ever …

Take his hand? Or walk down the broken stairs to chase a cold trail. Anna's body was still buffeted by waves of sensation. The meal was an adventure she shared with Jack. Nearly falling from the stairs, only to be brought close to his body, had been a rush. The hissing of the lodge was the last bit of danger, but it had passed.

The wet heat of that simple room was inviting. Her joints

and bones ached for comfort. Deeper down, she yearned for Jack. They'd been circling each other for years. The closer she got—hearing his voice, touching his skin, learning his history—the more the hunger increased. She didn't know where it would lead her, but she had to find out. All she had to do was take his hand.

Anna slid her palm against his. Curled her fingers around him. He held her hand, staring into her eyes. She'd thought she knew the man behind the legend and the metal and the guns, yet now she understood there were miles of territory within him she had yet to discover.

Their grips tightened. They drew closer. He leaned down to her. She pressed against his chest. In the sunlight, they kissed. Neither hid their hunger. She understood his need. His lips on hers were strong, devouring. And she understood her yearning. Probing forward with her tongue, she led him into her.

And it wasn't enough. Their first kiss could've taken them too far and she'd had to stop. Now, with Jack pressed against her, his arm wrapped around her shoulders and his lips against hers, too far seemed like the perfect place to go.

They pulled apart and, each still gripping the other's hand, walked back into the lodge room. Sheets of steam curled up the walls and filled the space, bringing out the scent of the redwood paneling. The room seemed alive, breathing with her.

Jack cracked a small smile. "This guy, Song, I like his style. Lot of inventors are drunk on tetrol. Half-baked ideas that don't work right." He held up his half-mechanical hand. "People wind up getting hurt."

"Song knows his business," she agreed. "So why the bounty?"

He leveled his gaze at her. It seemed the steam came from him, his intensity. "You want a cold trail or a hot bath?"

She took off her hat, holding his look and not backing down. "Hot. Bath."

Burbling invitingly like a secluded brook, the tub waited in the corner. The steam softened its edges and obscured the walls around it. As if the room went on forever.

With the toe of his boot, Jack swung the front door closed. Only the small lights in the ceiling glowed. Warm night clouds now surrounded her. A gentle storm. And Jack was the lightning. Still gripping her hand, he walked her toward the tub, chuckling a little to himself.

"My last bath was at a lonely little stage stop hotel in Camarillo."

The buckle on her gun belt was hot from the steam. "I'm overdue." She undid it and held the rig in her hand.

"I'm guessing you picked up Malone's trail sometime after the Sierras, so it's been a few hundred miles for you, too."

It took her a second to track her path backward. "Beatty, Nevada."

"Rough town." He let go of her hand so he could undo the straps and belts that held his own weapons.

She hung her gun belt on a wooden peg on the wall next to the tub. Easy to reach if she had to. "A little less rough after I left."

His pistols and quad shotgun took their place next to her weapons. He was unarmed. But still deadly. Broad shoulders, muscled arms and legs. Dark, blazing eyes. And the smallest smile.

They came together again, this time without the clang of gunmetal. The heat of the room had soaked through her clothes, bringing a light sweat across her skin. She felt every fold of fabric, and every ridge of his muscles. Her hands ran over the cords of his neck, pulling him to her mouth for another kiss.

Nerves yearned for sensation. Dust storms had chafed her flesh. Ice-cold rivers had woken her up, and she'd slept in the rain while waiting out a fugitive. She needed pleasure. And Jack was the only man strong enough to bring it to her.

An Excerpt from

ALICE'S WONDERLAND
by Allison Dobell

When journalist and notorious womanizer
Flynn O'Grady publicly mocks Alice Mitchell's
erotic luxury goods website, the game is on. They
soon find themselves locked in a sensual battle
where Alice must step up the spice night after
night as, one by one, Flynn's defenses crumble.

AN AVON RED NOVELLA

Flynn O'Grady had gone too far this time. It was bad enough
that Sydney Daily's resident male blogger continued to push
his low opinions about women into the community (he
seemed to have an ongoing problem with shoes and shopping), but this time he'd mentioned her business by name.

How dare he suggest she was a charlatan, promising the

world and delivering nothing! The women who came to Alice's Wonderland were discerning, educated, and thoroughly in charge of their sexuality. They loved to play and knew the value in paying for quality. They knew the difference between her beautiful artisan-made, hand-carved, silver-handled spanking paddle (of which she'd moved over 500 units this past financial year, she might add) and a $79.95 mass-produced Taiwanese purple plastic dildo from hihosilver.com.

Still, while Alice didn't agree with the raunch culture that prevailed at hihosilver, she'd defend (with one of their cheap dildos raised high) the right of any woman to take on a Tickler, Rabbit, or Climax Gem in the privacy of her own home. Where was it written that men had cornered the market for liking sex? O'Grady had clearly been under a rock for at least three decades.

Alice reached for the old-fashioned cream-and-gold telephone on her glass-topped desk and dialed. She knew what she needed to do to make a man like Flynn O'Grady understand where she was coming from. As the phone rang, she re-read the blog entry for the third time. Anger rose within her, but she pushed it down. She'd need her wits about her for this conversation.

"O'Grady."

Alice took a deep breath before she began. "Mr. O'Grady, we haven't met, but you seem to know all about me."

A brief silence on the other end.

"I see," came the answer. "Would you care to elaborate?" His voice was deep and husky around the edges. He should have been in radio, rather than in print.

"Alice Mitchell here. Purveyor of broken promises."

Another pause.

"Ms. Mitchell, how . . . delightful." His tone made it clear that it was anything but.

"I'm sure," said Alice, raising one eyebrow slightly, allowing her smile to warm her words. "You've had quite a lot to say about my business today. I was wondering if we could meet. I think I deserve the right of reply."

"I'm not sure what good that would do, Ms. Mitchell," he replied, smoothly. "You're more than welcome to respond via the comments section on my blog."

She'd had the feeling he'd try that.

"I think this is more . . . personal than that," Alice purred down the line. "I'd like to try to convince you of my . . . position." She stifled a laugh, enjoying every second of this. She could easily imagine him squirming in his chair right now.

The silence that followed inched toward uncomfortable.

"Er, right. Well, I don't have any time today, but I could see you on Wednesday," he said.

It was Monday. Give him all day Tuesday to plan his defenses? Not likely.

"It would be great if you could make it today," she said, a hint of steel entering her tone. "I'd hate to have to take this to your boss. I suspect there may be grounds for a defamation complaint, but I'm sure the two of us can work it out . . ." She left the idea dangling. The media was no place for job insecurity in the current climate, and she knew he was too smart not to know that. He needed to keep his boss happy.

"I could fit you in tonight, but it would need to be after 7.30," he said, his voice carefully controlled.

"Perfect," she said, "I'll come to your office."

She put down the phone, allowing him no time to answer, then sat back in her chair. Now all she needed to do was select an item or two that would help her to convince Flynn he should change his mind.

Standing quickly, she prowled over to the open glass shelving that took up one wall of her domain. Although it might be of use in getting her point across, it was probably too soon for the geisha gag. She didn't know him well enough to bring out the tooled leather slave-style handcuffs. Wait a minute! She almost spanked herself with the paddle that Flynn O'Grady had derided for overlooking the obvious.

Moving to a small glass cabinet in the corner, she opened the top drawer and inspected the silken blindfolds. She picked up a scarlet one and held it, delicate and cool to the touch, in her hand.

Perfect.

An Excerpt from

ONE FINE FIREMAN
A BACHELOR FIREMEN NOVELLA
by Jennifer Bernard

What happens when you mix together an
absolutely gorgeous fireman, a beautiful but
shy woman, her precocious kid, and a very
mischievous little dog? Find out in Jennifer
Bernard's sizzling hot *One Fine Fireman*.

The door opened, and three firemen walked in. Maribel
nearly dropped the Lazy Morning Specials in table six's lap.
Goodness, they were like hand grenades of testosterone rolling in the door, sucking all the air out of the room. They wore
dark blue t-shirts tucked into their yellow firemen's pants, thick
suspenders holding up the trousers. They walked with rolling
strides, probably because of their big boots. Individually they
were handsome, but collectively they were devastating.

Maribel knew most of the San Gabriel firemen by name. The brown-haired one with eyes the color of a summer day was Ryan Blake. The big, bulky guy with the intimidating muscles was called Vader. She had no idea what his real name was, but apparently the nickname came from the way he loved to make spooky voices with his breathing apparatus. The third one trailed behind the others, and she couldn't make out his identity. Then Ryan took a step forward, revealing the man behind him. She sucked in a breath.

Kirk was back. For months she'd been wondering where he was and been too shy to ask. She'd worried that he'd transferred to another town, or decided to chuck it all and sail around the world. She'd been half afraid she'd never see him again. But here he was, in the flesh, just as mouthwatering as ever. Her face heated as she darted glance after glance at him, like a starving person just presented with prime rib. It was wrong, so wrong; she was engaged. But she couldn't help it. She had to see if everything about him was as she remembered.

His silvery gray-green eyes, the exact color of the sagebrush that grew in the hills around San Gabriel, hadn't changed, though he looked more tired than she remembered. His blond hair, which he'd cut drastically since she'd last seen him, picked up glints of sunshine through the plate glass window. His face looked thinner, maybe older, a little pale. But his mouth still had that secret humorous quirk. The rest of his face usually held a serious expression, but his mouth told a different story. It was as if he hid behind a quiet mask, but his mouth had chosen to rebel. Not especially tall, he had a powerful, quiet presence and a spectacular physique under his firefighter gear. She noticed that, unlike the others, he wore a long-sleeved shirt.

His fellow firefighters called him Thor. She could certainly see why. He looked like her idea of a Viking god, though she would imagine the God of Thunder would be more of a loudmouth. Kirk was not a big talker. He didn't say much, but when he spoke, people seemed to listen.

She certainly did, even though all he'd said to her was, "Black, no sugar," and "How much are those little Christmas ornaments?" referring to the beaded angels she made for sale during the holidays. It was embarrassing how much she relived those little moments afterward.

Tossing friendly smiles to the other customers, the three men strolled to the counter where she took the orders. They gathered around the menu board, though why they bothered, she didn't know. They always ordered the same thing. Firemen seemed to be creatures of habit. Or at least her firemen were.

An Excerpt from

THERE'S SOMETHING ABOUT LADY MARY
A SUMMERSBY TALE

by Sophie Barnes

When Mary Croyden inherits a title and a large sum of money, she must rely on the help of one man—Ryan Summersby. But Mary's hobbies are not exactly proper, and Ryan is starting to realize that this simple miss is not at all what he expected . . . in the second Summersby Tale from Sophie Barnes.

Mary stepped back. Had she really forgotten to introduce herself? Was it possible that Ryan Summersby didn't know who she really was? She suddenly dreaded having to tell him. She'd enjoyed spending time with him, had even considered the possibility of seeing him again, but once he knew her true identity, he'd probably treat her no differently than all the other gentlemen had done—like a grand pile of treasure with which to pay off his debts and house his mistresses.

Squaring her shoulders and straightening her spine, she mustered all her courage and turned a serious gaze upon him. "My name is Mary Croyden, and I am the Marchioness of Steepleton."

Ryan's response was instantaneous. His mouth dropped open while his eyes widened in complete and utter disbelief. He stared at the slender woman who stood before him, doing her best to play the part of a peeress. Was it really possible that she was the very marchioness he'd been looking for when he'd stepped outside for some fresh air only half an hour earlier? The very same one that Percy had asked him to protect? She seemed much too young for such a title, too unpolished. It wasn't that he found her unattractive in any way, though he had thought her plain at first glance.

"What?" she asked, as she crossed her arms and cocked an eyebrow. "Not what you expected the infamous Marchioness of Steepleton to look like?"

"Not exactly, no," he admitted. "You are just not—"

"Not what? Not pretty enough? Not sophisticated enough? Or is it perhaps that the way in which I speak fails to equate with your ill-conceived notion of what a marchioness ought to sound like?" He had no chance to reply before she said, "Well, you do not exactly strike me as a stereotypical medical student either."

"And just what exactly would you know about that?" he asked, a little put out by her sudden verbal attack.

"Enough," she remarked in a rather clipped tone. "My

father was a skilled physician. I know the sort of man it takes to fill such a position, and you, my lord, do not fit the bill."

For the first time in his life, Ryan Summersby found himself at a complete loss for words. Not only could he not comprehend that this slip of a woman before him, appearing to be barely out of the schoolroom, was a peeress in her own right—not to mention a woman of extreme wealth. But that she was actually standing there, fearlessly scolding him . . . he knew that a sane person would be quite offended, and yet he couldn't help but be enthralled.

In addition, he'd also managed to glimpse a side of her that he very much doubted many people had ever seen. "You do not think too highly of yourself, do you?" He suddenly asked.

That brought her up short. "I have no idea what you could possibly mean by that," she told him defensively.

"Well, you assume that I do not believe you to be who you say you are. You think the reasoning behind my not believing you might have something to do with the way you look. Finally, you feel the need to assert yourself by finding fault with me—for which I must commend you, since I do not have very many faults at all."

"You arrogant . . ." The marchioness wisely clamped her mouth shut before uttering something that she would be bound to regret. Instead, she turned away and walked toward the French doors that led toward the ballroom. "Thank you for the dance, Mr. Summersby. I hope you enjoy the rest of your evening," she called over her shoulder in an obvious attempt at sounding dignified.

"May I call on you sometime?" he asked, ignoring her

abrupt dismissal of him as he thought of the task that Percy had given him. It really wouldn't do for him to muck things up so early in the game. And besides, he wasn't sure he'd ever met a woman who interested him more than Lady Steepleton did at that very moment. He had to admit that the woman had character.

She paused in the middle of her exit, turned slightly, and looked him dead in the eye. "You most certainly may not, Mr. Summersby." And before Ryan had a chance to dispute the matter, she had vanished back inside, the white cotton of her gown twirling about her feet.

An Excerpt from

THE SECRET LIFE OF LADY LUCINDA

A SUMMERSBY TALE

by Sophie Barnes

Lucy Blackwell throws caution to the wind
when she tricks Lord William Summersby
into a marriage of convenience. But she
never counted on falling in love . . .

"Do you love her?" Miss Blackwell suddenly asked, her head tilted upward at a slight angle.

Lord, even her voice was delightful to listen to. And those imploring eyes of hers . . . No, he'd be damned if he'd allow her to ensnare him with her womanly charms. She'd practically made fools of both his sister and his father—she'd get no sympathy from him. Not now, not ever. "You and I are hardly well enough acquainted with one another for you to take such liberties in your questions, Miss Blackwell. My relationship to Lady Annabelle is of a personal nature, and certainly not one that I am about to discuss with you."

Miss Blackwell blinked. "Then you do not love her," she said simply.

"I hold her in the highest regard," he said.

Miss Blackwell stared back at him with an increased measure of doubt in her eyes. "More reason for me to believe that you do not love her."

"Miss Blackwell, if I did not know any better, I should say that you are either mad or deaf—perhaps even both. At no point have I told you that I do not love her, yet you are quite insistent upon the matter."

"That is because, my lord, it is in everything you are saying and everything that you are not. If you truly loved her, you would not have had a moment's hesitation in professing it. It is therefore my belief that you do not love her but are marrying her simply out of obligation."

Why the blazes he was having this harebrained conversation with a woman he barely even knew, much less liked, was beyond him. But the beginnings of a smile that now played upon her lips did nothing short of make him catch his breath. With a sigh of resignation, he slowly nodded his head. "Well done, Miss Blackwell. You have indeed found me out."

Her smile broadened. "Then it really doesn't matter whom you marry, as long as you marry. Is that not so?"

He frowned, immediately on guard at her sudden enthusiasm. "Not exactly, no. The woman I marry must be one of breeding, of a gentle nature and graceful bearing. Lady Annabelle fits all of those criteria rather nicely, and, in time, I am more than confident that we shall become quite fond of one another."

The impossible woman had the audacity to roll her eyes. "All I really wanted to know was whether or not anyone's heart might be jeopardized if you were persuaded to marry somebody else. That is all."

"Miss Blackwell, I can assure you that I have no intention of marrying anyone other than Lady Annabelle. She and I have a mutual agreement. We are both honorable people. Neither one of us would ever consider going back on his word."

"I didn't think as much," she mused, and before William had any time to consider what she might be about to do, she'd thrown her arms around his neck, pulled him toward her, and placed her lips against his.